PRAISE FOR J.A. PITTS

Black Blade Blues

"A hip, urban take on dragons and dwarves, and add to that a sexy black-smith in Doc Martens. It's about time we had a fantasy heroine like Sarah Beauhall!"

—Kay Kenyon, author of *City Without End*

"Dark urban fantasy with some clever touches that should appeal to urban fantasy fans."

—*Kirkus Reviews*

"Pitts is an exciting new voice on the fantasy scene. Black Blade Blues takes the reader on a rollicking adventure full of pathos and humor."

—Brenda Cooper, award-winning author of *Silver Ship and the Sea*

"A rousing beginning to this sword-swinging urban fantasy series."

—The Cleveland Plain Dealer on *Black Blade Blues*

Forged in Fire

RAINBOW BRIDGADE

A Sarah Beauhall Novel

J. A. PITTS

WFP
WordFire Press

EBook ISBN: 978-1-68057-042-7
Trade Paperback ISBN: 978-1-68057-041-0
Cover design by Janet McDonald
Cover artwork images by Jeff Sturgeon
Kevin J. Anderson, Art Director
Published by
WordFire Press, LLC
PO Box 1840
Monument CO 80132

Kevin J. Anderson & Rebecca Moesta, Publishers

WordFire Press eBook Edition 2020
WordFire Press Trade Paperback Edition 2020
WordFire Press Hardcover Edition 2020
Printed in the USA

Join our WordFire Press Readers Group for
sneak previews, updates, new projects, and giveaways.
Sign up at wordfirepress.com

❀ Created with Vellum

CHAPTER ONE

When you're a dragon slayer, it's rare to think that your life could ever be normal. And this isn't some LARP where I run around the woods with friends playing pretend; this is the real deal and I have the scars to prove it. There are far too many graves in my wake for me to ever think I'd find a little house with a picket fence and live a life of quiet contemplation.

But in this moment, I was experiencing the closest thing to normal that I've seen in a couple of years. It was glorious, and something I would give my right arm to keep. At the moment, Jai Li and Katie were both happy and hale. Well, Jai Li was healthy. Katie was in a sort of remission. Whatever was attacking her body had taken a hiatus and that's the best I could hope for. I was content.

So, when Katie asked me to go with her to a birthday party in Bellingham for Ginny Prine, one of her old college cronies, how could I refuse?

To be honest I didn't even try, but on the drive up I came up with several spectacular ideas. By the time Katie and I were in the fancy-schmancy restaurant and the hosts were handing out wacky party hats and noisemakers, I was ready to give a couple of them a whirl.

I didn't exactly hate Katie's friends. Not all of them, anyway. There was this one couple: Melanie, an ER doc, and her squeeze Dena, who was an EMT. They were cool enough. Katie and Melanie had been friends since high school and sometimes lovers in college. Nothing there but friendship these days.

I could take her.

And I really dug all the Black Briar folks. We'd gotten into enough fights together, protecting each other's backs, standing toe-to-toe against cultists and giants, dragons, and all manner of creepies, that I trusted these people with my life.

But her old college friends? That was a whole 'nother world. I didn't know any of these people when I went to Western Washington University, even though they were only a few years behind me, and I didn't care to know them now.

Right or wrong, I pegged them as pretentious and judgmental. I could feel them staring at me, talking behind their hands. Okay, maybe I was being paranoid. These were mostly faculty, grad students or lawyers, doctors and teachers. You know, professionals. I was the only one with her head half shaved and calluses on her hands from hammering steel and wrangling horses. I was being the good partner, sitting in clothes that made me want to vomit while Katie beamed at anyone who looked our way.

She'd tried to get me into a dress, but I think she was kidding. Gods, I hope she was kidding. Either way, I had T-shirt, jeans, and boots in the truck. The second this soiree was over, I was ditching the gawd-awful pant suit and getting back into my shit-kicking gear. Even if I had to strip down right there in the parking lot.

The things we do for love.

The party was at Madrigals, one of those posh restaurants perched on a cliff overlooking the Bellingham Bay. It was famous for its seafood and breathtaking views. No way I'd ever afford a place like this. Good thing the party was a buffet. I managed to eat two plates of lobster ravioli without an ounce of buyer's remorse.

All the time I watched them, watched Ginny with her new girlfriend, I wondered if that was how other people saw me and Katie. I don't think we were quite as effusive about our love, nor as over-the-top with the public display of affection. Hard to see yourself with others' eyes.

I'm pretty sure Ginny had crushed on both Katie and Melanie back in the day—maybe at the same time. Either way, they hadn't dated. I think there were a few drunken make-out sessions and maybe some underwear dancing, but it never led to sex. At least not with each other.

I glanced out over the bay. The restaurant had the best damn view. I marveled at the bright blue of the sky, and how it fell to meet the deeper colors of the bay beyond. This exclusive balcony was probably worth every penny it cost to eat here. You could see all the way down to the rocks if you leaned out. It was a little disconcerting, but the day was beautiful, and the company was good. Katie looked hot in her long dress. I was imagining how she would look with that dress on the floor of our hotel room. Fat chance with her being as sick as she was, but it was a nice thought.

I took Katie's hand and gave it a squeeze. I needed her to be better. We'd survived the battle with the blood cult out in Chumstick at the winter solstice, but the jury was still out on whether or not we'd really emerged unscathed. Something had happened to Katie, and the fact we didn't know what continued to haunt me.

There was a commotion and I looked around to find Ginny standing, gathering all our attention.

"The last five years have been glorious," she sang out, throwing her arms wide.

The crowd cheered. I raised my beer to her and cast a glance at Katie, who laughed as she slipped her hand out of mine and clapped with abandon. Ginny was a total attention whore. She was dressed in a flowing evening gown that I'd have expected to see at a prom. Or maybe on a drag queen. It was a bit much for brunch.

"Louder," someone called from the back. Ginny laughed, waved at the crowd and climbed up onto a chair to get above all the people on their feet.

Her partner, Samantha, stood next to her, one hand on Ginny's hip. They were cute together. Ginny was a tall redhead, thin with a long face and big hands—boyish. Samantha was shorter, about Katie's height, with short cropped black hair and a round pleasant face.

"Careful, hon," Samantha said.

Ginny just laughed and waved at her. "I'm fine." She put her hands up to shade her eyes and looked over the crowd. The air was warm and golden, as you'd expect for an August in the Pacific Northwest: low seventies with a few clouds scudding across the sky. Beautiful day for an outdoor event. They couldn't have wished for better.

"I don't know half of you half as well as I should like; and I like less than half of you half as well as you deserve."

People looked around, confused. Only Katie laughed. She leaned in and kissed me on the ear. "She's quoting Bilbo's birthday speech."

"Bilbo? Like the hobbit?"

I missed most of the rest of the speech as I turned to kiss Katie. By the time I turned back Ginny was standing on the table, holding her glass of wine aloft. Someone in the crowd whistled and Ginny curtsied. People were milling about, raising their glasses of white wine in salute.

"As I said, five years is much too short a time to spend among you."

She drained her glass of wine in one long pull and someone cheered.

She wiped her mouth on her hand and grinned. She was quite lovely in that moment. "So, I have an announcement."

Don't ask me why. One second I was thinking maybe I could

see the charm of Ginny, and the next, alarms were going off in my head. I remembered how that speech ended, and her table was too damn close to the edge of the balcony.

Katie whispered, "Oh, no," and I was on my feet.

"This is the END. I am going. I am leaving NOW. Goodbye." Ginny's voice echoed across the patio, washing over the confused crowd.

I tried to stop her, honest I did.

Ginny gave a silly little wave as she hopped backward off the table and over the edge of the balcony.

I lunged over their table, made a grab for her without going over the balcony myself.

Someone in the back screamed as I grabbed empty air.

I leaned over the edge, holding my hands out to her, too late.

She fell backward, her arms out wide, as if expecting the embrace of a lover. The look on her face was rapturous.

She smashed into the rocks far below, a broken and bloodied ragdoll.

People were screaming. I just stood there, the railing pressed against my chest, arms outstretched. She was a broken doll on the rocks below and I couldn't stop reaching for her.

Katie pulled me back, grabbed me by the shoulders and wrestled me into a seat.

"She jumped," I said. My brain refused to put the pieces together. This was insane.

Katie was crying. Nearly everyone was hysterical. One of the guys, Jake something, was screaming for everyone to just calm down.

Samantha had passed out, striking the table on the way down. There was blood.

Someone was talking into a cell phone nearby. Calling 911.

All I could see in my mind was how freaking happy Ginny looked on the way down. No terror, no fear. Just pure bliss.

What the hell?

CHAPTER TWO

Days later, I stood looking over the Bellingham Bay from the student union at Western. We'd come up for the memorial service the university put on for Ginny. They had several counselors set up in the student union to answer questions. Most of the students just passed through, not really paying attention to all the fuss. I remember being that self-absorbed.

A couple dozen kids stood clumped in groups, crying or talking. Ginny had been a well-liked teaching assistant in the theater department—explained a bit about her flamboyant personality.

Katie was out in the lobby chatting with one of her old professors while Jai Li and I finished our lunch in the commons. I'd polished off my burger, but the remains of Jai Li's lunch had congealed into a mass of cold fries and ketchup. She claimed she wasn't hungry. I figured she was worried about Katie and contemplating all the death she'd been witness to in her short life.

"You okay, hon?" I asked her. Jai Li was tiny for six. She looked like a doll with fine facial features and long black hair. She'd decided to grow it out after Christmas. I thought it looked good on her. Nidhogg, the dragon who'd owned Jai Li before I came along, had insisted her servants keep their hair short.

We changed most of the rules when she came to live with Katie and me at Christmas. All our lives had grown to be more amazing than any of us could have imagined. I can tell you Jai Li was full of typical little kid attitude most of the time. The fact she'd had her tongue cut out at birth gave her a bit of a disconnect with normal folks, not that she let it stop her. One thing about our foster kid, she was tenacious.

"Are you going to finish your lunch?" I asked, stroking her hair.

She looked up at me and shrugged.

"It's okay. I understand." I wrapped my arm around her and pulled her close. She snuggled into my arm, a little sigh escaping her.

Mei Hau, Jai Li's twin sister, had been killed just over a year ago. They had been thralls of the most ancient of dragons—Nidhogg, She Who Must Be Obeyed. Nidhogg ruled Seattle and all of Washington. Think steel fist in a velvet glove.

It was a year ago, around the same time that Mei Hau had been killed, that we had all found out that dragons really exist. Jai Li had known her whole life, of course. The rest of us had been more sheltered.

As it was, the minute I remade the sword Gram, Nidhogg went into a rage, setting all our lives on a roller coaster of battle, pain, and unexpected joy.

I held one of those joys in my lap as we sat and looked out over the bay, letting the clear day hold our attention while our minds whirled off into secret directions.

Katie had wanted to come up to the memorial service. We'd both gotten off work, as it was Friday. The funeral wasn't until Saturday afternoon, so we decided to visit Rolph and Juanita as well. Juanita was staying with her sister here in Bellingham, since she'd just had the baby and all.

Juanita was a human, like most of us, but her hubby, Rolph, was a dwarf. Not the Disney type of comical dwarf—all waggling beards and bulbous noses. Rolph was a Nordic dwarf. He stood over six feet, with a shock of black hair and a great bushy black beard, more of a cross between Albert Einstein and Santa Claus hair-wise. His job kept him over the Canadian border in Surrey most days. I wasn't sure exactly what his job was—he didn't talk about it and I didn't ask. He'd had a rough life. I'm sure he was doing what he had to to get by. It would be good to see them.

If we could only get out of here.

Unlike Mei Hau, Ginny had chosen to check out. Not something that jived with my worldview. She'd been happy, a good student, well-liked. She'd written and produced several plays and had been up for a national award for one of the musicals she'd created.

No one was sure what had triggered the jump. Samantha had needed a few stitches from where she'd hit the table when she passed out. She was a real mess. We'd expressed our condolences to her when we arrived at the memorial, but she was too far out of it. Shock, I think.

I spoke with one of the counselors before the memorial had gotten started, and she told me that it was not uncommon for people with depression to commit suicide when they were at their most successful. They'd achieved their dreams and knew it could only go downhill from there. Funny thing was, no one ever thought Ginny was depressed. If she was, she hid it really well.

Samantha didn't think Ginny had been depressed, and she'd know. You can't wake up with someone every day and not begin to get a pretty clear picture of their moods and issues.

The funeral Saturday would be small. Not sure why we were having a service anyway, not with the memorial. Ginny had no family. She'd told everyone she was an orphan when she first showed up at Western. Katie took her under her wing that first year, made sure she was surrounded by people. It hadn't lasted. They each had their own wants and desires. Katie had Melanie at first, and Ginny experimented with a whole rainbow of choices. Katie said Ginny had seen the world as an array of flavors, and she was in a hurry to try them all.

You had to admire her lust for life—and undergrads. Until we got the call for the birthday party, Katie hadn't heard from Ginny in a couple of years, other than the occasional social media update. They were all so busy. That's just how life got to be. But the suicide brought important things back into focus. Like the little girl who counted on us to keep her safe.

Katie was still in deep conversation, so Jai Li and I headed out to the balcony along the back. The view was just as breathtaking as it had been when Ginny took the plunge. We stood at the railing and looked out over the bay toward the open ocean. I couldn't get Ginny out of my head. The way she fell like that, peaceful and content. Made me wonder what she knew that I didn't.

We walked around to the front of the student union, and I pointed out the various buildings. Jai Li drank it all in. Until Christmas, she'd lived the majority of her life inside Nidhogg's mansion. The outside world fascinated her.

That was one of the wonderful things about having a kid. They made you pause and look at the world through new eyes. Made you think about things you'd long forgotten. Not all of them were pleasant, mind you. There were plenty of things in my past I'd have liked to never think of again.

Like this campus, for instance. Jai Li saw it as wondrous and full of secrets to discover. Me, not so much.

It was haunting, being back here after going on seven years. I'd started at seventeen, excited to be away from home and scared out of my mind. I'd felt like such an outsider here, no matter how hard some of the people around me tried. I'd lived up on The Ridge for four years, never daring to go out and get my own place. It was too terrifying. Da couldn't afford for me to get my own place, and I barely got by on the cafeteria food and student housing.

There had been this one kid, though, who had been worse off than me. She had to be a girl since she lived in my dorm, though you wouldn't know it by looking at her. Not sure she was sure who she was. She lived down the hall from me. Kept her hair over her face and her body buried in layers of bulky clothes. I tried talking to her a few times, but she only grunted. She disappeared partway through my sophomore year. I heard she got a place in one of the local boarding houses. I'm not sure if she ever finished the year, but people I know said she didn't come back junior year.

I always wanted to talk to that girl, see what her deal was. I felt that if I'd reached out to her, maybe I could've been a friend, you know. Instead I kept my own shields up around me. Safer that way.

Katie finally finished with Doctor Weepy-McCries-a-lot. They hugged and I tried not to gag. I remembered that professor. I didn't take her classes, but I knew people who did. *Brilliant*, they assured me. Only thing was she always reminded me of that Trelawny character in Harry Potter.

Katie loved her, though. Go figure.

"You ready to get out of here?" Katie asked me, giving the good professor a little wave as she walked out to meet us.

I shrugged and let her fall into my arms. At least Katie had stopped crying.

"Death sucks," she said.

Had to agree with her there. I know she was thinking of Jimmy. I didn't blame her, losing him while she was in a coma, not getting a chance to say goodbye. Never resolving their outstanding issues. It was the same with her parents. Just gone one day with no recourse.

And don't get me started on funerals in general. I couldn't take all the thrashing and moaning. Maybe I'd seen too many die over the last year. Maybe I was a cold-hearted bitch. Likely both.

"Why don't we stop at Mallard Ice Cream before we head over to Juanita's?" I asked.

Jai Li's head snapped around at the words "ice cream." Girl had a sweet tooth.

Katie rolled her eyes at me. "Of course. Can't come to

Bellingham without getting ice cream at Mallard's. I think that's where the freshman fifteen was invented."

I hadn't been able to afford Mallard's when I went to Western. I never gained the freshman fifteen, either. But she knew both. She was just busting my chops.

Katie was looking worn, thin. I was putting together a theory about her ailment. She seemed to be better, stronger when she was eating huge amounts of calories. Ice cream would definitely fit the bill.

"Juanita just had the baby, of course she wants ice cream," Katie assured me. "We should get something with dark chocolate. Really helps with the post-delivery hormone crash."

Whatever, as long as Katie had a supersized portion.

Jai Li was practically vibrating by the time we were all buckled into the pickup. She loved ice cream and babies. Today would end up full of wins for her. Now if my stomach would unclench and Katie would stop looking so haunted ...

CHAPTER THREE

Juanita and her sister Evelyn spoke in rapid Spanish. I could understand bits and pieces, but not enough to make heads or tail of the conversation.

I'd met Evelyn once before, when Juanita had gone into hiding at her place. She was short and plump, like Juanita. Older by about six years. They'd come to the States when they were little. At first, Evelyn wasn't too sure about me. She was protective of Juanita.

With the necromancer, Justin, killing people around me back before Christmas, Evelyn had viewed me as a threat. The fact we killed Justin and his psycho cronies didn't totally clear me in her books. I courted trouble, had some seriously bad mojo in her world. Rolph vouched for me, explained about how I'd reforged the Norse sword Gram and all, but she wasn't convinced. I had no beef with her. I'd probably be the same way in her shoes.

When Katie and I showed up with Jai Li and chocolate ice cream this time, her attitude softened somewhat. Raising a kid apparently meant I wasn't a complete lunatic.

Our elf friend Skella had been ferrying Rolph back and forth from his job in Surrey for the last few weeks. She traveled by mirrors—step into one, step out another. A damn handy skill to have.

Juanita had the baby in late June and, by the pictures Rolph had shown me from those first days, it looked like a cross between a naked mole rat and that chest monster thing from *Alien*.

It was a huge deal that I was willing to hold young Jacob Rolphsson after those pictures. Parents shouldn't show children until they started to look human. Even the troll twins were better looking than poor Jacob just after birth. I questioned the sanity in how the naming passed from the father's first name. Rolphsson was awkward.

I sat in a rocking chair and Juanita placed little Jacob in my lap. He was asleep, with the most amazing look on his face. Here this child was, sleeping in my arms, and I had the strangest urge to lean in and sniff his hair. I have no idea what brought that on, but it was heavenly. Pure bliss. There was like thirty seconds or so there where I thought I might slip into walkabout—just let my spirit leave my body for the pure joy of it—the sensation was that powerful.

Jai Li was very reverent of the baby. She approached him with care, only dipped her head in long enough to sniff his hair, then scampered away. She wasn't upset though. Just seemed afraid to touch the little squaller.

Her caution was justified. Almost immediately he woke crying and filled his diaper. It was precious and disgusting. Rolph laughed and took the amazing fluid translator away from me before something started to leak. Katie thought I was being a big baby; Jai Li actually laughed.

I dreaded touching the little guy ever again. At least he hadn't puked on me.

After the sun went down, Rolph and I went out onto the back porch to talk.

Things were getting more stable in Vancouver. The longer the self-proclaimed King of Vancouver held sway, the more settled things had gotten. The gang warfare that occurred right after I'd killed Vancouver's tin-pot dictator dragon had died off. Rolph said the king had been fairly ruthless in the beginning, reconciling the old factions that had once worked for Jean-Paul. Some retribution had been bloody, but now things were calm. Vice was still as rampant. Plenty of drugs and prostitution, gambling and such. But there were fewer deaths, fewer predators on the streets. Bad for business, the king claimed.

"The King sends his condolences and his congratulations on defeating the necromancer and his cultists. He has asked once again that you visit him. He considers you a hero of the realm."

I laughed. "I'll pass. Last thing I need in my life is to get mixed up with another spooky underworld type. Dealing with Nidhogg and Qindra is more than enough for me, thanks."

"How fares the witch since you rescued her?" Rolph asked.

"Nidhogg has kept her pretty close to home. It's been strange. You remember Stuart?"

"One of your Black Briar compatriots, correct?"

"Yeah, anyway. He's been hanging out with Qindra. He's gotten pretty protective of her. It's cute. First Gunther takes up with Anezka and now Stuart is with Qindra."

"It is fitting. Finding a mate helps one find themselves."

I glanced over at the big guy. He was delirious with Juanita, and now Jacob. He'd been alone for a long time. But I didn't think you needed someone else to complete you. Don't get me wrong. I love Katie. But if I relied on her for me to be a whole human, what would I be if something happened to her or to us?

"What's the king like?" I asked, changing the subject.

Rolph shrugged. "I have not met this king in person," he said. "Always an emissary between he and I. Not that it matters in the grand scheme."

I wanted to know what Rolph did for a living these days but was afraid of the answer. He had been willing to get his hands dirty in service of the sword Gram. I just didn't know fully where his limits were beyond that. My instincts told me he was a good man—cared for his family. That was good enough for me.

"Something Evelyn said recently has piqued my curiosity," he said after we'd let silence fall between us. "She said there was a *bruja* in town."

"Witch?" I asked, thinking back to college Spanish. "Like Qindra?"

"Doubtful," he said. "But not something we should overlook. She was at the grocery the other day, met this woman in the produce section. Evelyn did not like the way she selected her avocados."

I laughed. "Seriously?"

He grinned at me and shrugged. "Maybe it's nothing." He grew silent again. "Still, I'd hate to risk my loved ones just because it seems silly."

"Good point." Hell, we'd found worse with less clues. "I'll be here all weekend. How about I poke around tomorrow?" Could it be Madame Gottschalk? She lived down in Kirkland. Why would she be messing around up here? Or maybe her sister had come over from Minsk. Didn't feel right either. Something I'd have to look into.

Rolph smiled and nodded. "That would be much appreciated. Do you have the blade with you?"

Here it came. I never knew if he was being generally interested, or if the old crazy cult of the sword stuff was gonna rear its ugly head with him again. He'd searched for that blade for a couple a hundred years after he'd lost track of it. Kinda obsessed.

"Yeah," I said. "I have it here in town—"

He turned quickly, started to speak, but I cut him off.

"—and it's in a safe place, no worries. You concentrate on your family."

He let a sigh escape him and leaned against the railing once more.

"It is as you say. My priorities are with my family now. I have surrendered my responsibilities for the blade to you." He turned his head slowly and looked at me. The dark of the night and the thick shaggy hair made him look even more sinister than normal. "Do not forget," he said quietly. "Never let down your guard."

I nodded and clapped him on the shoulder. "It's under control, bud. Don't you worry your pretty little head about it." I gave him my best grin and he smiled finally.

"You are insolent and brash," he said, but his voice had lightened. "I question the wisdom of Odin to have marked you in his service. You are capricious. More Loki's temperament."

I stepped back, shocked. Loki? The betrayer? Seriously?

He looked back at me and recoiled. "My apologies," he said, holding up his hands. "I meant no disrespect. I just meant that you are unpredictable, headstrong. No enemy could discern your next action, as you yourself don't seem to know what it will be."

I rolled my shoulders and let the muscles loosen up. I'd gone into serious fighter mode at those words. Loki indeed. The Norse gods were a crazy bunch, the whole lot of them. But Loki had betrayed them to the dragons. Who cares that he fell to them in the same assault? Bastard. Fire pulsed through my veins as the runes on my scalp and left calf burned with the call to action.

"Evelyn is on edge," he said. "The day of the suicide, she collapsed. Juanita found her on the kitchen floor. She said she had felt something powerful. Something she said dealt with death and obligation." He looked at me. "She has the sight. I have seen this. But this makes no sense."

Something niggled the back of my mind. Hadn't Gletts said something about a portal somewhere in Bellingham? Maybe there was more woo-woo activity here than I'd given credit.

"Did this have anything to do with the witch who was picking avocados?"

Rolph grinned sheepishly. "She said that was the biggest reason the woman stood out. She said her aura was painted with the same sweep of energy as when young Katie's friend killed herself."

Strange coincidences, I'm sure. But I'd promised to look into things for him. I'd call Qindra; maybe she felt something.

After Rolph went back into the house, I stayed on the porch, rolling my head from side to side, trying to loosen the knots. I needed to go for a run. I had way too much pent-up energy. Sleeping tonight was going to be tough.

After a quarter of an hour or so, Skella came out onto the porch and leaned against the railing to my right.

"Hey," she said.

She was still dressing like a Goth—all black loose-fitting clothes and black makeup. It was a lot neater, more put together than when I first met her. I guess she was doing okay with the income Black Briar was paying her as an emergency transportation consultant.

"Things have been pretty slow since we busted up Chumstick," she said. Her voice was full of longing and woe. "I'm bored. At least when I was helping Black Briar keep an eye on that haunted house, it was something. Taking people through the mirrors isn't exactly high adventure, but it beats sitting around the sick room waiting for Gletts to get better. And don't get me started about Gran."

I laughed. Her grandmother Unun led a clan of fairly xenophobic elves. The fact she tolerated me and Katie was close enough to a miracle. "How is the old lady?"

She sighed again. "Gran is getting worse, honestly. Gletts is just pissing me off." I could see the frustration in her. I was pretty sure she was a few decades older than me, but she acted like she was fourteen most of the time. "He's stable, the jerk. Personally, I think he's sandbagging, you know? Perfectly good body and he refuses to step up and carry his load. Just moans about how weak he is. Selfish, that's what it is."

She loved Gletts. I knew it. It's the way she worried about him and protected him. In those first days after he'd been wounded, she was on edge all the time, afraid he'd die. Now he was just being churlish.

"And Gran is just making it worse. She hovers over me all the time, like I'm in danger or something. It's creepy."

"She loves you," I offered. "Cut her some slack."

Skella sighed and leaned against the railing, like all the wind had been knocked out of her. "I just wish there was something to do."

"You could get a job, right? I'm sure Rolph could help you get the right papers and all. I don't suppose you have a birth certificate or driver's license or anything?"

I knew the answer by the look on her face. Elves don't usually register with the government. "Strictly underground work for me," she said. "And that's getting harder to come by. I don't want to become a stripper or deal drugs or anything."

The wind was picking up a little and the temperature was dropping under fifty. I wished I'd brought my jacket.

"What if," Skella said quietly, as if she said it too loud it would go away, "I was thinking maybe you could get me a job out at Flight Test. I know you're working on a new movie. I could be an extra or something. Or maybe be a runner. I'm good at getting supplies and such."

Now that was an idea. My night gig as a props manager was an exercise in managing chaos. Flight Test was in the early stages of filming *Cheerleaders of the Apocalypse*, and our director, Carl, was always looking for unpaid interns.

"I think we can work something out," I said. "I'll discuss it with Carl and Jennifer, but I don't see why not. Extras aren't paid very well."

"Honest?" she asked standing up straight and clapping, totally blowing her Goth mystique.

I looked at her, quirking my eyebrows up.

She quit clapping and grew solemn once again. "Yeah, right. That's cool."

Kids. I promised I'd call her and let her know. She was beaming by the time we'd all said our goodbyes and headed to the hotel.

As we drove away, Rolph stood on the porch with little Jacob in his arms and waved to us. I wanted to talk with Katie about what Rolph had told me, but I didn't want to do it in front of Jai Li. Katie would be concerned, maybe even upset. Jai Li was likely to just be scared, and I didn't want that.

Family definitely made things different. Having Jai Li in our lives was a curse and a blessing. I loved her. It's just that the logistics of having a six-year-old hadn't occurred to either Katie or me at the time. This would be the first time we'd checked into a hotel since we got her. No grown-up time this trip.

I'm not sure I knew how to behave in a hotel room if I had to keep my clothes on all the time. No wonder parents were so crazy. Kids really put a crimp into things. But they're totally worth it.

CHAPTER FOUR

I got up early on Saturday to find Jai Li already awake. I tucked her in with a bottle of orange juice and a new coloring book, then changed into my running outfit and tied on my trainers. Katie was still asleep. I was looking forward to unwinding a bit—lots of tension in the last few days. Katie had snuggled right up against me and did a few things that would have led to noise-making. I wasn't comfortable with that while Jai Li was on a roll-away four feet away, so we settled in for a little smooching and a night of anxiety dreams.

Once I pushed through the doors out into the damp and foggy air, I started to feel a little better. I double-checked my fanny pack, making sure I had my phone, water and my wallet. Then I put on my ear buds and cranked up a long play list containing all my favorite thrash metal. By the time I was off the property, "Dragula" by Rob Zombie was pounding in my skull.

The music and the first mile of road added to my energy levels. I loved the way the ground felt beneath my feet, jarring my body with each long stride. Nothing too drastic, but enough to build a good solid rhythm. By the time the sun was burning off the wispy fog, the music had evolved to a section of retro-metal, led off by Judas Priest from like way back in the eighties.

I found my way to familiar streets. The second mile came and went before my shoulders began to loosen up. Mile three fell away in my wake, and I picked up speed listening to the Graceland Five and their punk version of Elvis's "Suspicious Minds." I was flying. The last hundred yards or so I was head-into-the-wind sprinting—sprinting directly into the Blank.

I slowed, letting my heart rate settle down, and looked around. The Blank was what the college kids called the part of town that had been practically abandoned. There were burned-out buildings, vacant and broken-down storefronts, and empty foundations where older buildings had once stood. Something about it sang to me.

This place was totally perfect for the movie we were working on. I spent twenty minutes shooting pictures on my cell phone and emailing them to Jennifer and Carl over at Flight Test. I told them we should totally do location shooting here for *Cheerleaders of the Apocalypse*. It would give the movie a level of authenticity we'd been lacking by only doing set shots. I was really excited. The morning was great. The afternoon, however—that was not looking to be a real fun-fest.

We got to the funeral later than I would have preferred. We were all dressed in our best outfits. Jai Li looked uncomfortable in the dress Katie had gotten her into—better her than me. Katie was dressed like a work day, so I followed suit. I had on my best jeans, concert shirt, and Docs. I'm not sure if Katie knew I had Gram and my hammers tucked behind the bench seat in my truck. After the last year, I wasn't taking any chances. At least I didn't make us all wear armor. It would suck if Ginny got all zombified and tried to eat the mourners. Not likely, but I was prepared, just in case. I kept replaying the conversation with Rolph. If there was something hinky about Ginny's death, I didn't want to be caught unaware.

We walked in a few minutes before the services were supposed to start, and I was surprised to see Skella was there. She waved us over and did some preliminary introductions. She was buried in a pack of local Bellingham folks—Hamsters, they called themselves—kids in college, or just out. Not that much younger than me, about five years or so, but worlds apart. Seemed Skella had met them at one of the local bars doing karaoke. Who'd a thunk it---Our angsty Goth friend singing in front of a drunk crowd. I wonder if you could get Siouxsie and the Banshees via karaoke. After the funeral, they were going to commence an early night of drinking and singing to send Ginny on her long journey into the dark lands.

The service was short and sweet. Katie cried a little, but Jai Li surprised us both by really getting broken up over the whole deal. I don't think anyone thought to say words like that when her sister Mei Hau had died. No closure, no group mourning. And the thing with Jimmy, that had been different—as much a party as a funeral. She'd been with her friends and there'd been music and dancing to go along with the grief. Here she just had the quiet and her own thoughts.

Jai Li huddled in my lap for a long time in that hard pew, long after the officials trundled out with the show casket. Ginny was going to be cremated. Katie sat snuggled up against us, talking to Jai Li in soft tones and stroking her hair while I rocked her. Her crying tapered off after a little bit and she hugged me tight before moving to Katie and holding her by the neck for a very long time.

When she pulled back, she took my hand and placed it in Katie's lap and motioned for us to kiss. Katie smiled and leaned in, kissing me gently on the lips. This seemed to make Jai Li happy, and she wiped the tears from her face.

We were the last to leave the funeral home. I was surprised to find a car parked across three places in front of my truck and a second car parked in the drive behind my truck. It was Skella and the Hamsters.

"Oh dear," Katie said, eyeing the crowd.

"We're thinking you don't understand the local customs," one of the guys said, stepping toward us. "There's a local pub, serves food, totally kid-friendly."

I glanced at Katie and Jai Li, who both shrugged.

The guy held out his hand and I took it. "Sprocket," he said.

Sprocket? Nice. He was small, you might say petite, with several obvious piercings. His hair was blond streaked with bright green swathes, with matching eyeshadow.

He pointed back at the crowd and called everyone out by name.

"Skella you know," he said, pointing to where she hung in the back, holding a small tow-headed boy about a year old and talking with a rocking soccer mom type. "She's holding Thing Two, who belongs to Scarlett there." He pointed to the smoking-hot mom. "And the lucky guy beside her is Brian, holding Thing One." That was a girl, a couple of years older than Thing Two.

"They have real names," Sprocket said, conspiratorially, "but it bugs the crap out of Scarlett, so we have to call them that to help offset the imbalance she's caused in the universe by being so freaking gorgeous."

Brian laughed, but Scarlett frowned toward us.

"The guy in the driving gloves and goggles is Dante."

Dante was about five-four and built like a football player, all muscle.

"On the other side of the car is Bianca," he said, pointing to a pretty girl with shoulder length brown hair and a shy smile. She had a hat pulled down to her eyebrows like she was hiding from the world.

Then he turned and motioned with his head toward a tall brunette with waist length hair who looked like she was ready to whip this whole crew into shape. She had a bearing I liked, very subtle command. "And that's Lilith."

I nodded at each of them, and Katie said hello. We spent a few minutes shaking hands and introducing ourselves.

"So this pub lets in kids?" I asked, seeking confirmation from Scarlett, as she looked like the most responsible of the lot.

She smiled, taking Thing Two from Skella. "Brian has a band," she said. "We go to Lucky's all the time. They have good food and love when we bring in the kids. Is that your daughter?"

I looked over at Jai Li who was watching me intently. "Oh, yeah," I said. "Totally. Funeral was hard on her." I lowered my voice. "She lost her sister not that long ago."

"Poor kid," Scarlett said. "Death is hard at any age."

We milled around and chatted for twenty more minutes before Brian said they had to get the kids some food soon or there'd be a national emergency. We got directions from Lilith and piled into the truck. Soon we were all walking into a really cool Irish pub with plank tables and a stage in the main room.

There were already a few folks in the place. The Hamsters grabbed a couple of tables near the stage and a few other folks came over to join us. Katie, Jai Li, and I sat on one end of the long picnic-style tables, and Scarlett sat beside us. Jai Li pulled out a couple of coloring books and crayons which she shared with Thing One, whose real name turned out to be Anastasia. Thing Two was really called Bard, after the archer in the Hobbit who killed the dragon, Smaug. Katie loved that one. I watched the kid, curious if he would live up to his name. Never hurts to know another dragon slayer.

Food appeared along with pitchers of water, iced tea, and beer. Dinner was family style, with lots of things like macaroni and cheese, lamb stew, soda bread, green beans, roasted potatoes, and stewed apples.

Once everyone had tucked in for a bit, the karaoke began. There were six or seven full tables by this point, mostly college kids. The songs started out just as you'd expect. Popular ballads and rock operas. We heard Rush, Styx, the Rolling Stones, the Beatles, Judas Priest, which I cheered for, and several other songs I didn't know. Katie seemed to know all of them and sang along.

Most of the folks were decent enough, but it wasn't until this old drag queen got up on the stage that things shifted gears. The crowd cheered and whistled, and the lights dimmed a bit.

Scarlett rolled her eyes at me and leaned in. "Mimi," she said. "One of the local divas."

She wasn't joking. The first note out of Mimi's mouth was pure smoke. Before I had time to set my beer down, fire rained down on the audience. Katie sat up straighter and paid attention. Mimi started out with a little Etta James, slipped into Patsy Cline and ended a four-song set with a heart-palpitating version of "Suspicious Minds" that the King himself would have approved.

The coincidence jarred me.

I'd been listening to a version of that this morning. And it wasn't just the fact she chose that song. It was the way she looked over at our table when she sang it. The Hamsters were apoplectic, stamping and cheering as she wound through the last chords, but I swear she was staring right at me.

The energy in the room was nuts. I looked over at Katie who was looking at me, a very perplexed expression on her face.

"I think she was singing to you," she said in a hoarse whisper. "And did you feel the way the music flowed over the room? There was something there. Something powerful—like magic powerful."

I glanced up to see Sprocket watching us and grinning. I leaned in and spoke in Katie's ear. "We should meet this Mimi. There is definitely something spooky about her."

Katie nodded.

Back in the fall, when I'd first held the vial of blood mead Qindra had showed me, there had been a tingle like a low current of electricity. Fafnir's ring had a similar buzz that only seemed to affect women. Gram was a different level of magic, more aligned to me, or my kind of sympathetic magic, I guess— makers, blacksmiths, warriors. This magic felt like it was in Katie's camp, and by the look on her face, she was bothered.

No one else seemed to notice, however. Mimi bowed off the

stage and made way for two guys who were flipping through the catalog. There was a distinct break in the flow. I doubt they wanted to start so soon after this Mimi had left the stage. Tough act to follow.

I got up, kissing Jai Li on the top of the head, and stood with my hand on Katie's shoulder. Mimi was working her way around a couple of tables and making a beeline to the Hamsters. They crowded her, cheering and making a real hullabaloo.

Mimi caught my eye as Sprocket was hugging her and she winked at me. I had to really consider for a moment. She was dressed like a woman and appeared to be in her sixties, but I was pretty sure she was a guy. Drag Queen for sure. But everyone called her 'she' and honestly the pronoun seemed to fit in my brain, so who was I to judge.

After a few minutes with the Hamsters, Mimi excused herself and walked over to us. "Do I know you folks from somewhere?" she asked.

I shook my head. "No, don't think so."

"You sing really well," Katie offered.

Mimi laughed. "Best karaoke singer in Bellingham, I suspect. Sprocket says you folks are alumni of Western. Maybe I've seen you around campus."

"Not that I'm aware," I said. She felt harmless. I've been in the presence of some badass magical stuff. Mimi just felt like any other person. No special vibe there. Must just be the singing, and maybe I'm paranoid.

Mimi and Katie talked about music and I took Jai Li out onto the dance floor during a fairly decent rendition of "YMCA" by four college girls. Jai Li laughed and laughed, mainly at my expense, but it was totally worth it. The tears from earlier in the day were put away for a while.

By the time we were ready to go, everyone was besties. Katie was getting along well with Mimi, and Jai Li was coloring like a fiend with Anastasia. I was deep into conversation with Sprocket and Dante over the finer points of the local beers, and a sense of tranquility settled over the joint. There was a camaraderie here. These people were a family as much as folks of Black Briar were. It was a comfortable feeling.

Still, something about Mimi tangled in my brain. I suddenly had a memory of Charlie with the Mordred crew, telling us how one of his cohorts had jumped from Deception Pass, and that the only person with him was a woman with a five o'clock shadow. Why did Mimi bring forth that memory? I watched her as she laughed with the others. She looked over at me, making eye contact, and the runes on my scalp tingled. Who was this individual? And I wondered how she felt about avocados.

CHAPTER FIVE

W e started shooting *Cheerleaders of the Apocalypse* again in early August. Skella brought a few of the Hamsters—Sprocket, Dante, and Bianca—with her to work as extras on the movie. Dante was the only one with a car, so they came as a package deal. Carl was a little overwhelmed at first, but I assured him I could keep them all busy. You could never have too many mutants.

After the first few nights, I started bringing both Katie and Jai Li with me up to Everett to do movie work. Jai Li wasn't going to school and kept some strange hours. If she got tired, she'd go back to my props cage and crawl in amongst the used goblin heads and the elephant ears from our old movies and go to sleep.

Katie would read or just play her guitar as long as we weren't actually shooting a scene. It was nice to have them around. Reminded me of the days when Katie came out to Julie's place to watch me smith. Seemed like a lifetime ago.

We ate from the food truck and made an adventure out of it. The crew loved Jai Li, letting her run errands and such if it wasn't too late. Jennifer especially loved having them around. I caught her watching Jai Li wistfully and then casting glances back to Carl. Girl had baby fever pretty bad. I'd have to get her up to see Rolph, Juanita, and little Jacob before too long. Maybe make a field trip out of it and sell my on-location plan at the same time. It could work. The way she was looking and the way Jacob smelled, I could probably even ask for a raise. I just wasn't sure Carl was ready to be a daddy.

On Friday, during the dinner break, Katie started playing this song she made up on the spot—something solemn and mournful. The lyrics, however, caught everyone's attention. She was singing about the movie, about how the hero had seen the cheerleaders of his dream but had been unable to get to them through the sea of mutants.

The world ran sideways the day the poison fell from the sky
And the monsters crawled out of our skins
But among the blight and the hellish wastes
I find a vision of heaven in your bouncing ponytails
And your creamy thighs, devoid of cankers and sores.

It was a love song—you know, with monsters. Okay, a parody of a love song, with monsters. Whatever, she was hella cute singing it.

When she was done, the crowd that had built around her erupted in applause.

"You know," Jennifer said to Carl, "she could do the sound-track. She's got the chops."

Katie was excited by this proposition and said she knew a group she could get that had professional experience. They could totally lay down all the tracks needed for the movie.

Carl and Jennifer went off arguing about his personally created musical stylings on his mom's electric organ, and they shut the office door a little too hard.

We watched through the window as they continued to argue, and with Carl's hangdog expression, at one point, we knew who had won the day.

As we were packing up, I overheard Sprocket and Dante talking about Mimi. Seems she ran the boarding house they lived in. We chatted for a bit before we got around to the fact that Ginny had lived in the house when she first came to Bellingham. Seemed an odd coincidence. When I asked them if anyone else from the house had committed suicide, they changed the subject, crying exhaustion, and headed out for home. That was totally weird.

We cut out around two in the morning with Jai Li asleep in the truck leaning against Katie who talked the whole way back to Circle Q. We'd been staying out at Mary Campbell's farm along with my blacksmith master, Julie Hendrickson, and my old neighbor Edith Sorenson. We were a motley crew of women, and I couldn't think of a better place to be.

Katie had been away from teaching for a while and that was a hole in her. Music, normal music, may be just the tonic she needed to start finding her footing again.

It was a good feeling, listening to the excitement in her voice. I honestly didn't care what she was talking about, I just loved hearing her talk. I'd missed it for far too long.

Unfortunately, I couldn't get the look Dante shot me out of my mind. It wasn't anger or anything, more like shock and anxiety. Had I struck a nerve there? Was there something more to look into? I didn't like the way things were starting to gel together. I needed to check in with Qindra, if she would ever return my calls.

CHAPTER SIX

I left two more messages on Qindra's service. If I didn't hear from the witch soon, I was going to drive out to Nidhogg's and see what was going on. I didn't like the way things up north were starting to find connections, and I wanted some professional advice. Maybe it was time to visit Mimi's boarding house as well.

We waited until the next afternoon to call the Harpers. Even though they had probably been up at three in the morning when we got home—they had likely been out partying at some club or other.

The Harpers were a band right up Katie's alley—part Led Zeppelin, part Jethro Tull, and part The Chieftains. The band leader—Cassidy Aloysius Stone—had heard Katie sing, heard her play guitar, and said she had talent. He'd also said to call anytime she wanted to jam. I had my suspicions about Mr. Stone. My gut told me he had dragon ties, but that wasn't something you discussed in polite company.

With the prospect of creating the soundtrack for *Cheerleaders of the Apocalypse*, Katie and I both agreed it would be a great opportunity to investigate them further. I never wanted to be surprised again.

Katie paced the kitchen, fretting that it may be too early to call, by band standards. I assured her that it was nearly one in the afternoon, and that we could buy them drinks to apologize if we woke them. This seemed to mollify her. We put the phone on speaker and sat at the counter, drinking coffee and listening to the phone ring.

Cassidy answered on the seventh ring.

"Well, if it isn't young Katie," he purred into the phone. "Hey, Maggie," he called to someone with him. "It's Katie Cornett. What can we do for you this fine day?"

Katie explained about the movie and asked if they wanted to be part of the soundtrack. "It's a labor of love," she said. "But they'll provide the studio time and if the soundtrack takes off, we can make some real money."

"Meaning we don't get paid?" he asked, dubiously.

"No, they'll pay us standard studio wages with royalties on sales. Just nothing spectacular."

There was a brief pause. We could hear whispered conversation in the background. "Let me ask the rest of the crew and get back to you," he finally said. "But I think that sounds interesting enough. How ya been, lass?"

"It's been a rough year," she said. "Would take too long to go into details. We lost my brother, but we've got our health."

I looked at her discreetly. Did she have her health? I was dubious.

"I'm sorry," Cassidy said, his voice suddenly solemn. "That's gotta be hard."

"Sucks like you'd expect," she said. "We do what we can."

"Aye," he said growing quiet. "We followed a bit about your troubles on the news," he admitted. "Bad business there before the holidays."

"Yeah," she sighed. "Dark times. But we survived." She sounded suddenly cold and hollow. "We do seem to draw the crazies."

"Crazies indeed," he said. "And how is your young Sarah these days?"

Katie smiled.

"Sarah's fine," I said into the phone. "Still juggling as fast as I can. But that's nothing new."

"Ah, Sarah Beauhall. Prettiest smith this side o' Dublin. You do burn brighter than most I've met."

That was an understatement. If I burned any hotter, I'd explode.

"I've been meaning to ask you something," Katie jumped in, a gleam in her eye.

"Fire away."

She looked at me, grinning. "I couldn't help but notice that armband you wore when we saw you perform up in Vancouver."

"Oh? Now why would that be of interest to ya?"

I wasn't sure if he was being defensive or coy.

"Reminds me of something I saw in a book once," Katie said. "Something about a lost dwarf treasure. Curious if you thought it had any specific meaning, or was it just a pretty?"

"Vanity, I must admit," he said, with a lilt in his voice. "It snared your pretty eye, after all."

"Oh," Katie said with a sigh. "It was worth asking about."

He chuckled. "You disappointed, love?"

"Thought it may be part of the act, you know. Go with the *mighty warrior* translation for your middle name."

"We're in New Mexico at the moment, but we can be in Seattle in a few days. Why don't we revisit this when we're in town?" he asked. "Every story has more than one side. Mayhap you'll care for a different take on it all."

Was that an opening? I could swear the armband was part of a dragon treasure. I just knew Cassidy had to have ties to dragons somehow. Especially with that drawing Jai Li had done, I was positive there was a connection.

Katie winked at me. "Sounds excellent. Call me when you decide on the soundtrack gig."

"Aye, darling. We'll be in touch."

We listened to the line go dead. Was he teasing? I didn't get a bad feeling from him or any of the other Harpers.

Whether or not they knew about the dragons, they were good people.

And sometimes, that had to be enough.

CHAPTER SEVEN

The thing that sucked most, I figured, was that even with all the death and dying, we still had to be adults. It truly sucked. Case in point, Black Briar secret business. We went over there to have a board meeting of sorts. Since we'd lost Jimmy, his wife, Deidre, had taken the running of the clan very seriously. The fact she was wheelchair-bound didn't slow her down. She ruled the roost.

When Katie and I walked in, Gunther and Stuart were already there. I loved those guys. They've treated me as an equal since the first day Katie brought me out to Black Briar.

Gunther was tall and Nordic, with a full blond beard and hair down past his broad shoulders; Stuart was shorter and broad, with a kind face and a muscular frame that always reminded me of Tolkien's dwarves. I mean, he was like five-eleven or something, but next to Gunther he always came off as short.

The five of us constituted a quorum.

The first item on the agenda was an eye-roller. With Jimmy gone, we had a long discussion about who would meet with the Bestellen von Mordred crew. I thought Katie should take Jimmy's place as the last surviving blood member of the Cornett clan.

Katie just shook her head, saying she would rather stay at Black Briar and let me take her place.

"You're a dragon slayer," she argued. "Besides, I trust you with my life."

Deidre laughed at us when we looked her way. "Leave me out of all the intrigue," she said, shaking her head. "I have no desire to enter that particular rat's nest."

So, after a brief discussion, and a bit of general shrugging, we defaulted to me, Stuart, and Gunther to meet the Mordred crew.

"Besides, that kid, what's his name?" Gunther asked, looking at me.

"Charlie Hague."

"Yes, him. He is already comfortable with you."

I raised my eyebrows in his general direction, and he grinned.

"Fair, perhaps he's not particularly comfortable, but at least he's smart enough to be afraid of you."

This brought a laugh from Stuart.

"I think the word you are looking for is respect," I said, straightening my shoulders and glaring at the two of them.

They both laughed then, and I rolled my eyes. Charlie was decent enough, though the rest of Madame Gottschalk's hangers-on left a lot to be desired. They were secretive and seriously better at the Machiavellian stuff than we were. They claimed to be watchers, but I was beginning to have my suspicions about their more ambitious leanings.

They dealt with things I'd never known to exist before I discovered the dragons—you know, magic rings, swords, trolls, giants—those sorts of things. Katie's parents had been part of a similar group when they disappeared more than a decade ago. The Mordred crew was the only real connection to Paul and Olivia Cornett, and Black Briar wanted to learn anything they could about the couple's disappearance.

Charlie was harmless. I didn't trust the rest of them.

Clandestine meetings are so much easier with texting and cell phones. I contacted Charlie, as our point man, and we agreed on the details of a double-secret meeting. We'd met with Gottschalk and some of her people before Jimmy was killed. This time, we settled on just Charlie. That actually made me a little less tense. I figured he wasn't as cloak-and-dagger loyal to the Mordred crew as they assumed he was. It would be good to explore that a bit.

Later that afternoon, we rolled up to a massive park just outside Woodinville where there was a huge soccer tournament going on, if you can imagine it. Three hundred pre-teens and their anxious parents apparently were a good enough cover when you needed to have a clandestine meeting.

Charlie was a mixed bag. On one hand, he could do real magic, like casting spells and such. That was pretty cool. And he'd helped me when the blood cult killed one of the horses out at Circle Q last year. He earned points for that. The real problem with young Mr. Hague was that he'd withheld information about Katie's parents for far too long. None of us were ready to forgive him for that, even after he returned their wedding bands.

"How's it hanging, Charlie?" Stuart said, by way of greeting.

Gunther rolled his eyes, but Charlie grinned.

"To the left," he said. Then he glanced at me. The smug demeanor faded quickly, and he nodded. "Beauhall."

I shook his hand, reminding him exactly how strong I was, which was a dick move. I guess I needed to work on my "not-holding-a-grudge" thing.

"What can we do for one another?" Gunther asked.

Cutting right to the: one of the things I liked about our own Viking warrior.

"Officially, I'm here to offer you sanctuary if Black Briar want to come into the fold."

None of us bothered to respond. After a moment, Charlie cleared his throat and shrugged. "I had to offer."

"You knew we'd decline," I said. "So, why'd you drag us out to this gods-forsaken place?"

Gunther nudged me and I vowed to reduce the amount of growl in my voice.

"To be exact," Charlie began, "just so she can see I'm not lying." He cleared his throat and took a step back. "Her exact words." He was stalling. "Please don't punch me."

I glared at him and he cringed back. Gunther put a hand on my shoulder, and Stuart put one on Charlie's. I settled back, and Charlie accepted the support with a nod. He raised both his hands and made air quotes as he began to recite.

"You are invited to join Bestellen von Mordred, by personal invitation from Madame Gottschalk. If you join, we will happily share any and all information we have about the Black Briar clan, their original members, and everything we know about the region. This offer allows Jimmy and Deidre Cornett to take the places that Paul and Olivia once held."

"Jimmy's dead," Stuart said, and the temperature in our little huddle dropped a few degrees.

Charlie held up his hands. "That was her official offer. I had nothing to do with it."

"Gottschalk is a bitch," I said, letting my pure dislike of the woman imbue each word. "She has to know Jimmy's dead."

Charlie shrugged. "Look," he said sheepishly, "I've held stuff back on occasion." He cast me a furtive glance, then held Stuart's and then Gunther's gaze for a moment, but I've never lied to any of you."

They both looked at me and I nodded. Charlie sighed and went on.

"There's something wrong with her," he said in a rush. "I don't think she knows Jimmy is dead."

I raised an eyebrow at him, and he raised both hands, patting the air between us.

"No, I'm serious. There's something odd going on. I don't return to the home base often, but there's a strange vibe there." He lowered his voice. "I'm afraid. There is something very wrong going on there. Madame is becoming more and more erratic."

We fell silent, letting the sound of screaming parents and children wash over us. After a moment, while children ran around chasing balls on all sides of us, we discussed the changes at Gottschalk's place, the new people coming and going, and the way her cat had been missing for weeks.

"I've done a bit of divining," Charlie said, almost embarrassed. "There are power fluxes I'm unfamiliar with. Things that scare me, if I'm honest."

Gunther prodded for more details. He didn't have much to go on, some hunches, and a few bad readings.

"If I had specifics, I'd tell you." Charlie looked at me directly. "Gottschalk talks in her sleep. Sometimes, when she falls asleep in her chair, we have to watch her, keep her safe. Twice I've heard her crying, begging to be spared."

Gunther patted him on the shoulder. "I can see how that would be unsettling."

Charlie gave a wan smile. "She's not been overly kind her whole life, and I know she's terrified of her sister. But I almost feel like she's being tormented by someone in the inner circle."

"Why?" Stuart asked. "What do they have to gain?"

Charlie shook his head. "Power, maybe. All of us can do some bit of magic. I'm not the most advanced of her people, by any means."

"Who do you think would mean her harm?"

He just shook his head. "Look, every day I feel like some sort of hammer is going to fall. I just want to make sure I'm not between it and the anvil."

I smiled, knowing he used the metaphor to appeal to me, and it worked. Like I said, there is something I like about Charlie, even when he pisses me off—beyond our mutual love of animals. He had a kindness, an innocence, that kept him from being tainted by the powers around him. The necromancer we'd killed was a key example of someone who could let the power of magic corrupt him.

Charlie swung his satchel around on his shoulders and

opened the clasps. He brought out a folder stuffed full with documents—had to be three or four hundred pages.

"This is all the information I could gather on Katie's parents," he said, handing me the folder. "Not much there you don't already know or guess. They were researchers mainly, collectors of esoteric knowledge and the occasional emissary to other groups. They'd worked with us a few times, long before I showed up. There was one time when a group of refugees escaped from the Vancouver area, fleeing that dragon you killed." Again, he nodded at me. "Paul and Olivia helped that group escape to friendlier climes, masking their passage so the dragon never found them."

Both Stuart and Gunther nodded. They knew that story from Jimmy's childhood.

"They also tracked the gods who were reborn. Seems they thought that at least one had snuck past the dragons in the last decade before they disappeared. One of the top three."

"Ranked by whom?" Gunther asked.

"Olivia," Charlie said. "She said it was either Odin, Thor, or Loki. Gottschalk thought she was barking and ignored the signs. But that's how they met Jeremiah Fletcher."

Jeremiah was the oldster who'd come out for Jimmy's funeral; someone who had dealings with the Cornetts in years past.

"Mr. Fletcher is reported to be an operative out of London. Knows where a lot of bodies are buried. He and the Cornetts joined forces to thwart one of the Reaver dragons. Something about a dead prince's hoard, and a book of spells, key to the British Crown."

The three of us exchanged glances. We had *not* heard that story. Katie was gonna love it. Maybe it would get us a chance to meet the royal family.

Stuart jumped in. "Fletcher helped Jimmy, Deidre, Gunther, and me pick up the pieces after Paul and Olivia disappeared. There were some pretty heavy individuals looking to move into their territory, take over their connections, slide in behind them and claim their mission."

Gunther picked up the story from there. "Jeremiah invoked some powerful magic in that first winter, allowed us to cut the needed threads to shield Black Briar from the big bad world. Gave Jimmy and Deidre time to put down some roots, build up a magical barrier, fall off everyone's radar."

I'd always wondered how they'd gone so far underground in so short a time.

Charlie was keeping true to his word. He gave us information we needed, regardless of what he was told to tell us, and in turn we fed him tidbits of news to dribble back to Gottschalk. We wanted him to remain in her good books. Otherwise, he was just as likely to disappear one day.

We all shook hands, and made to leave, when Charlie grabbed my arm, holding me back. Gunther and Stuart stopped a few strides further on, watching, but giving us space.

"I know I said Gottschalk's talking cat has been gone for weeks. Madame is in a state over him." He hesitated, debating on his next words. "He came to me in confidence last night, testing the waters, to see if I would be an ally if things went south."

"So, the cat thinks Gottschalk is in danger?"

"He claims Madame Gottschalk has talked quite loudly of killing him to read his entrails. That doesn't sit well, even for a cat with lives left in his register."

"He must be scared. Didn't you tell me he didn't like you?"

"Yeah, not a fan," he said. "Which is why I'm concerned. If he's reaching out to me, things must be horrible." He shrugged. "Not sure he totally trusts me."

"Give the cat some tuna," I suggested. "I think you can gain some points that way."

"Har, har," Charlie said, but I could see he was a bit less worried.

I turned to go again, and he grabbed my hand once more.

"One final thing," he said, looking like I may punch him. "I've heard rumors from some of the others that they knew about the necromancer and what was going down with them."

I stiffened, ready to punch him as he feared. "Did you know beforehand?"

"No," he said, shaking his head. "I swear, Sarah. I'd have warned you, but I think there are factions within Gottschalk's domain. Watch your back."

He turned to go. He made it half a dozen steps when I thought of something else.

"Hey."

He turned, his face pale with worry.

"You know anything hinky around Bellingham?"

He looked at me like I'd asked him to fly to the moon. "More than a liberal college with kids who smoke a lot of pot?" he asked, going for funny.

My glare sobered him right up.

"I got nothing," he said. "Why?"

I shrugged. "Just a hunch. Keep an ear out for anything, will you?"

"Sure thing." He waved and disappeared into a crowd of cheering nine-year-olds. I watched for him, trying to follow his progress, but lost him in the general scrum of soccer moms.

When we got back to my truck, I told Gunther and Stuart what Charlie had told me about the hints around the blood cult activity out in Chumstick before Christmas.

"That royally pisses me off," Stuart said, all growly and stern. "I definitely want to discuss it with Qindra."

I didn't say anything, but inside I was amazed how our lives were constantly evolving.

CHAPTER EIGHT

I watched Goldbar roll by the windshield, my mind a whirl of the things Charlie had told us. I didn't like the implications of danger and violence. Charlie wasn't exactly a super spy, but he had his act together in most ways. I didn't have enough clues to see the picture of what we were facing, but I had a lot of unrelated pieces. I wanted to talk with Katie about the things I was seeing: the stuff in Bellingham, the suicides, and that singer, Mimi, and the way Gletts was convinced there was a portal there somewhere. Add in the uncertainty of Bestellen von Mordred and the way Madame Gottschalk was not dealing with a full deck, and it all added up to danger for us.

Pulling up the long drive to Black Briar, I felt my ears pop when we crossed the protective wards. The main yard held several cars I recognized. Trish and her crew were hanging in the barracks. Each platoon took turns staying in the barracks, keeping Black Briar defended.

We piled out of the truck, Gunther and Stuart arguing about the merits of going dark, doing what they did back when Paul and Olivia died. I doubted that taking Black Briar off the grid would accomplish much. Nidhogg knew they existed this time around. Not like me killing a dragon would fade from people's memories anytime soon.

We piled in through the kitchen door, the boys arguing for the joy of it. I was fairly convinced they were agreeing, just at a rather loud volume. Katie and Deidre looked up from the kitchen table, where they had been poring over books that they covered up when we came in. They both stared at me, as if daring me to ask them what they were doing. I smiled at them sweetly, walked to the fridge, pulled out a beer, and settled in the chair next to Katie.

She leaned over and kissed me. "How's Charlie?"

She was distracting me while Deidre pulled the books into her lap and wheeled out of the kitchen. She had a hard time concealing the grin on her face, so I figured it was something that would embarrass me. I liked that grin. Her color was better, which helped alleviate some of my anxiety. Deidre, on the other hand, was looking wan. I'd ask our doctor friend Melanie to pop over and check on her.

I'd thought about suggesting some counseling, but Deidre had made it clear that she'd grieve Jimmy in her own way, her own time. Just went against my nature to see people I loved in pain and just sit idly by. Death sucked in all forms. I smiled at Katie, taking her hand.

"Charlie's a pill," I said, and she laughed.

The sound of anthropomorphized animals singing about brushing your teeth erupted from the living room, and I glanced over to see Jai Li and Bub huddled together on the couch. They whispered to each other, casting sideways glances our way. I thought about shooing them outside so we could talk in private, but they had turned the television up as if to block out the adult chatter. As I watched them, Jai Li threw me a kiss. Bub cocked his head to the side, and I got the strangest feeling he wanted to talk with me. Bub was my kobold familiar from the plane of fire, who was tied to the amulet I wore.

I was just deciding to go in there and sit with them a minute, when Deidre returned.

"Okay," she said, taking her position at the head of the kitchen table. No one sat in the seat to her left. That was always Jimmy's seat. The talk around the table came to an abrupt halt and we all turned to face her piercing stare.

"Tell me."

Gunther began, giving her the details of the meeting, the place and circumstance. Stuart jumped in after a minute and began talking about Charlie and the agitated state he was in. They traded turns, going back and forth with an ease of many years of working together.

I admired the ease with which these two communicated. Katie had referred to them once as "Fafhrd and the Gray Mouser" after a long night of revelry, which led to me reading a bunch of older fantasy that I never knew existed. Stuart didn't have the litheness of the Mouser, but he did have a similar disposition.

I didn't speak up. While Jimmy had accepted me as part of the clan, I didn't have the history the others did, so I practiced my active listening. It's something Bub suggested, actually. He's a smart little biter. Part of my *taming the berserker,* as he calls it.

I watched Deidre throughout. I was learning to pick up her tells. She had a way of flipping her hair back on the right side when she was growing impatient and tended to chew her lip when worried.

"What kind of games are they playing?" she finally blurted out.

We all exchanged glances. The twins had covered the meeting in full. There was nothing I thought to add. So, we were all a little flummoxed at her question.

"Which part?" Stuart asked.

"The part where they knew about the bastard who got Jim killed and didn't warn us."

Jimmy had been killed by one of the spirits the necromancer had captured, nourished, and freed upon the world.

"If Gottschalk or any of her people knew about the blood cult, I want to know," she said, her voice low and tremulous. She turned to me, making eye contact for the first time since we'd sat down. "Sarah." She reached past Katie and took my hand. "They need to pay."

I nodded at her. The pain pulsed through her, making the runes on my forehead ache with her grief.

She held my gaze for another moment, then turned her wheelchair away from the table and rolled into the living room. I didn't hear what went on, but Jai Li crawled into Deidre's lap and Bub skulked into the kitchen.

Katie got up to wash the dishes, hiding her tears from me. I got up and hugged her from behind but left her to her nesting. It was something she did as a default mode when her mind was spinning. I found my peace at a forge, she chose dishes or her guitar. My da did the same thing, come to think of it. Doing dishes calmed him. Ma said it had something to do with making things better, even in a small, little way. She also thought the hot water had a calming effect. Funny how people respond to stress.

The rest of us began the awkward goodbyes that accompanied such moments. Gunther left to go meet Anezka, and Stuart wanted to find Qindra. Gunther ribbed Stuart about his sudden fondness for the witch and how much time they were spending together. Stuart didn't deny it. He'd given Gunther crap for Anezka at first, so it was only fair.

Boys ...

Before he left, I made Stuart promise to have Qindra return my calls. He hugged me and said he'd do what he could.

"Sarah?"

I looked down to see Bub, waiting patiently for me to return from my thoughts.

"Can we go for a walk?"

Katie half turned and gave me a smile. "Go on," she said,

grabbing a dish towel and drying her hands. She paused and kissed me before heading into the living room and sitting on the couch.

Bub opened the back door and escorted me out into the afternoon sun.

When we were far enough away from the house, Bub informed me that he thought Katie and Deidre had been planning to trap me in a human ritual referred to as a wedding. He looked so terrified and earnest that I almost laughed.

Once we got out to the memorial for the Black Briar fallen that the dwarves had erected for us, we sat on one of the benches and I explained to him all about weddings. He had been taken from his mother's nest at such a young age, he had no real understanding of his own people's rituals. And as a bound servant, he wasn't privy to such things with his previous masters. It wasn't until Anezka that he began to understand the human world beyond smithing.

It was easy to speak of a wedding in the abstract, sharing with him the generic details, but the whole time my stomach was doing flip-flops. In the end, I told him that the ritual was a thing of power that helped connect two people together in ways that were stronger than the average relationship. This led to a chat about people who love each other, and folks who don't want to get married. He was especially confused about how marriage is a social construct and had nothing at all, really, to do with how much you could love someone.

"Humans are overly complicated," he said.

I couldn't deny it.

Mere months ago, Katie had been wounded by a powerful magical tome, and her spirit had fled to one of the Sideways realms. Her body had been in a coma for a long time, deteriorating near to the point of death.

We'd freed her spirit and battled a fiend known only as the Bowler Hat Man. That's who had killed Jimmy. Only, even with her spirit reunited with her body, Katie had not woken. It wasn't until Charlie had stolen Paul and Olivia's wedding rings from Gottschalk's private collection and I'd placed them in Katie's unconscious hands, that she woke. I could see how and why she chose to interpret that as a wedding proposal. My original intention had been to jar her psyche into waking up.

It's not that I didn't want to marry her. I had no doubt in my mind I wanted to spend the rest of my life with this woman. I just didn't think either of us stood a very good chance of living long enough to make it worth all the trouble. Dealing with dragons had wrecked my already glass-is-half-empty disposition.

On the other hand, as Bub pointed out, there could be no doubt how much I loved Katie.

"Based on what you have told me," he began, taking my hand as we walked back toward the smithy, "you should marry Katie."

I laughed. "I'm glad you approve."

He beamed at that, and I debated the sarcasm in my reply, which he had either missed, or actively chosen to ignore.

Still, the thought of a wedding scared the daylights out of me.

I needed to figure out what I wanted in all this before things got too far out of control. Marriage wasn't something I figured to be in my future once I started knowing boys, and with my social and cultural background I didn't figure it would be allowed. Hurray for progress. Mostly.

I paced, letting my mind get twisted into knots.

"About Gottschalk," he said, shocking me, "you must protect the family from her people."

I stared at him, open-mouthed.

"The news of these Mordred people is disturbing." He began to wring his hands, which was a sign of his nervousness. He thought he was in trouble.

"You heard us?" I asked, stunned that he had heard us over the blaring television.

He shook his head. "It was Jai Li. She reads lips very well."

He dithered for a moment, then blurted out, "Do not punish her, please."

That shocked me more than the other. I'm not sure we'd ever punished her.

"Eavesdropping is rude," I said, "but I won't punish her."

He nodded as if I'd made a sacred vow.

He took a deep sigh. "You must kill them if needs be," he said. "Gottschalk's people. They cannot be allowed to harm our family."

I knelt and hugged the little kobold. He was such a child, in so many ways, that I forget how very old he truly is and his origins on the Plane of Fire.

He grew happy once more. With all the dangers and issues clouding my brain and careening around with the wedding march ringing in my head, I decided it was time to pound metal. Bub heartily agreed, of course.

CHAPTER NINE

Bub suggested that I call Julie to see if she wanted to stop by. That was a first for him, but it was a good idea. My initial thought for creating armor was Anezka, but she was off with Gunther. And besides, she was batshit crazy. Julie was out working one of the new farms she'd picked up since she'd gone back full-time.

I asked if she'd like to stop by Black Briar and do some work with me. I told her I wanted to practice some armor skills, which I knew wasn't her strong suit, but she knew more about smithing than I did. Besides, I just enjoyed her company. She agreed to stop by on her way back from Marysville.

I took a solid ten minutes to stretch and then jogged around the outbuildings to work up a little cardio. I take all this very seriously. I didn't want to let any failings of my body make for a dangerous situation. Smithing was not for the faint of heart, nor the sore of limb.

Julie rolled in thirty minutes later to the dulcet tones of my two-pound hammer striking steel. I was working a short sword—a little something to remind the body and mind how we were going to play together this afternoon. It was glorious.

We didn't have a coal forge at Black Briar, but the propane

forge was pretty slick. Compact and very focused—it allowed for a wide range of temperatures without consuming a lot of propane. I was getting to like it, though for the real important work, I wanted to go back to coal. But propane is what we had, and I needed to learn to adapt. I set aside the partially finished sword and turned to the real reason we'd come out this afternoon: armor. Real, honest to goodness plate armor. I was so excited I could hardly stand it. Even Bub grew giddy at my eagerness.

Nothing like difficult and complex work to nip that in the bud. Julie spent the majority of the afternoon trying and failing to help me understand the intricacies of forging armor. We didn't really have the capacity to make a full set of plate mail with the propane forge, but we could create smaller pieces like pauldrons and vambraces. Everything about this form of creation was new to me. Bub knew armor better than both Julie and I combined, which kept us from killing each other. Of course, if I'd been working with Anezka, who had experience with armor, at one point or another one of us would have stormed out of the forge, swearing at the top of our lungs and accusing the other of questionable parentage.

Julie and I did not work that way.

When you're a maker, you see the world in a very specific way. When you run up against something beyond your current skill set, it goes beyond frustrating. I had the ability and the skill to reforge a broken blade so well that it was once more imbued with the magical powers of its initial creation. That had to stand for something. Not like the metal I was working gave a crap about that, or my ego. I wanted to blame the whole disheartening experience on low blood sugar.

I knew better. Around two in the afternoon I lashed out in a towering rage and flung a ruined spaulder across the room.

Bub and Julie exchanged a knowing glance. I hate it when I can see that I'm acting like a petulant child but have no ability to stop myself from acting out. My brain goes on autopilot and things roll out of my mouth which would not please my mother. Julie got up, walked to the door, and announced that she was going to take a walk before she took a page out of Anezka's book and decided to kick my ass.

That's when I knew I'd crossed a line. Julie Hendrickson was my blacksmith master, and she *did not brook any of my shenanigans*. I've heard her say it so many times it echoed in my head.

Bub sniggered, and I winced. I deserved that.

I dunked my sweaty head in the water barrel. When I emerged, I accepted a towel from Bub, which I dashed over my head and traded him that sodden mass for a broom. He knew me so well. Time for me to sweep the forge. That always helped calm me down. The little guy did have my best interest at heart. I gave him a wan smile and tried not to pout.

Julie has a way of redirecting my passions into more constructive areas when I don't have my head so firmly lodged up my ass. Usually she can make it where I learn a valuable lesson and come out on the other side of a predicament calmer and wiser for the mess. Unfortunately, I'd crossed a line even her normal well of patience could not manage. Instead, Katie came out to the smithy to see what all the swearing had been about. I think she had a good enough idea.

The way she fell into my arms told me she was out-of-sorts.

"What's up, babe?"

She shrugged against me and kissed the side of my mouth. "Why are you dripping?" She took a step back, saw the broom, glanced around the smithy, taking in Bub's sheepish smile, and the twisted hulk of metal that should have been something beautiful. "I see."

I tried to smile at her, but I could feel the blush of embarrassment creeping over my chest, up my neck, along the sides of my face, and into my hairline. She had this look, that kindergarten teacher look that made you ashamed of whatever it was you'd done wrong. I hated when she gave me that look.

It was also a very confusing look, since she was so damned

sexy. I had to squeeze my eyes shut and breathe slowly. Anger is fire, passion is fire. My runes tickled with the reverberations of those passions.

"Tell you what," Katie suggested, taking the towel from Bub and wiping the side of my neck. "Why don't you and Bub see what you can do on your own. You have a good rapport. I'll go back in the house and keep Julie distracted for a while."

I started to tell her how wise she was, when I noticed she'd put on her most innocent face, which alerted me right away. She was up to something.

I shrugged and said okay. Let her have her secrets. Better than me making a bigger ass out of myself with Julie. As Katie sauntered back to the house, I caught a glance from Bub that made me think maybe he was in on the plot. I have no idea what she and Katie could possibly have to talk about. Definitely nothing about a wedding.

Did I mention a wedding? I wasn't nervous. Not one little iota.

For the next hour, I went back to basics, going over the shaping techniques Anezka had shown me previously. Bub had a way of highlighting things that didn't raise my hackles. Anezka always exuded a level of chaos that kept me on edge. She was crazy talented, and I knew I could learn things from her. Just thinking of her and her teaching methods had me on edge. So, I abandoned them.

That took a monumental effort, let me tell you. Bub helped. I was always surprised how much he'd changed when I took possession of the amulet that tied him to this plane. With Anezka he was erratic and violent. With me, he had become thoughtful and kind. Not docile, by any means. I wondered how much of that had to do with Jai Li's influence.

Without my erratic energy bouncing off the walls of the smithy, things went much smoother Bub was enjoying himself and before we were done, I'd made a small vambrace that wouldn't make your average warrior weep.

While Bub and I were celebrating with tall glasses of water—he ate his—Julie came back out of the house. She examined the vambrace and declared it a fine bit of craftsmanship. I beamed. Her praise was hard won and always heartfelt. I was feeling pretty good about myself. Then she launched right in with her patented lecture on personal responsibility and playing well with others. It chafed, but she was right. Then she walked around and inspected the shop, giving me some suggestions on improvements and showing me how I could shuffle things around enough to put in a coal burning forge.

"That way you can really work some armor," she said with a smile. "I know you're frustrated, but this is how you always are. Remember how you were with that first set of andirons I had you make?"

I winced. They were a disaster, and I was sure Julie was going to fire me at the time.

"You had me spend a week making shoes and sweeping floors."

She laughed. "Is that how you remember it?"

I shrugged, feeling churlish. "There were some other things in there, I guess." I smiled at her. "You lectured me a lot."

She clapped me on the shoulders and laughed louder. "Damn it, Beauhall. You have the most convenient memory. I spent half a dozen sessions after work hours helping you with your technique. You don't remember all those late nights with bad Chinese takeout and how sore your arms were?"

I was sore a lot that first year. And bad Chinese takeout wasn't exactly a rarity in my life. "What did we talk about?"

She patted me on my cheek and stepped back, crossing her arms. "Your da and how you'd never find anybody to love."

I grew hot all of a sudden. I think I remembered this. Oh, dear lord. "Was there music?" Please say no.

She laughed again, great bellyfuls. "Oh, Sarah. You played some mix tape you'd come up with in college. All sappy love songs."

My eyes widened. I remembered. "Oh, dear lord, all the Journey?" And then I laughed. That had been a hard time for me. It was right before I met Katie, as a matter of fact. "Man, I was so bound up with fear then."

"Fear and shame." She looked at me square, not judging, not laughing then. Just my old boss and mentor. "I'm proud of how far you've come."

I stepped forward and hugged her, letting the truth of it wash over me. I had no reason to hold back, no reason to worry about judgment or scorn. I was safe here and making mistakes was part of learning. I'd just forgotten that with all the dragons and necromancers lately. Those were places where mistakes got you or your friends killed. I had to learn to separate the two.

After Julie left for home, Bub and I cleaned up, putting the tools away and generally making the place shipshape. It was always more work to clean up and get ready for a day's work when you came into a cluttered space. Better to leave the place ready for next time. Besides, this wasn't really my smithy. Others had the opportunity to use it. It was just good manners.

Just as I was cutting out the lights, Skella called and asked if she could come over. I told her Bub and I were at Black Briar and she popped over through the mirror we had custom built for the smithy. She was looking pretty haggard, like she'd been crying.

She said she had to get away. Another kid up at Western had killed himself the night before—wasn't even on the news yet. Sprocket had told her that these things went in waves: once one kid broke the taboo, sometimes others followed.

She said this young man named Ian had been well-liked, that Sprocket and Dante were pretty upset. She thought maybe I could talk to them, give them one of my pep talks. She was afraid they may quit the movie.

I didn't even realize I could give a pep talk. Usually I figured I just ended up pissing people off. But I promised her I'd do what I could. She said she'd set something up for the next day. They'd need a chance to get everyone gathered up.

Not really sure what I'd just signed up for, but I liked that Skella thought I could help.

Jai Li's laughing screech greeted us as we left the smithy. She and the troll twins, Frick and Frack, scampered across the yard and grabbed Bub—a gale of youthful exuberance and mirth echoing across the yard. Bub cast me a sheepish grin, waiting for my approval.

I smiled and waved him on. He scampered after the others and I watched them, delighted in their joy. I couldn't tell if they played tag, hide-and-seek, or some game Bub had created called tickle tag, which Jai Li loved. It was bizarre to see Bub acting like such a little kid after the conversation we'd all had earlier about killing our enemies to protect hearth and home.

CHAPTER TEN

We rolled into Circle Q around ten. We'd decided to stop at a pizza joint and get dinner. Julie had gotten here hours ahead of us, opting for dinner with Mary and Edith. They'd all been in bed for an hour at least, and the house was quiet. Katie declared that Jai Li could take a bath in the morning, which thrilled her. I, on the other hand, had to take a shower if I thought I was sleeping in the same bed as her. Working the forge was sweat-inducing.

When I walked into the bedroom after my shower, I discovered that Katie had let Jai Li move her pallet to the foot of our bed, so I had to make sure not to step on her as I came through. In the time I'd taken to bathe, they'd both fallen sound asleep. Sleep was healing, I reminded myself. I knew this from experience.

Katie snuggled up to me when I slid in beside her. I loved it when she put her hand on my hip—made me feel safe. She had to be gaining ground. I needed her to be gaining ground.

The last clear moments of conscious thought were filled with worry about the dreams I would have. This was not uncommon these days. I'd spent so much time in the Sideways, Skella worried I may have somehow connected my psyche to that place. If I didn't get the dreams under control soon, I was seriously considering seeing a shrink. Last resort. Instead of seeking professional assistance like a rational grown-up, I'd been practicing willful dreaming, making myself wake up when things got too strange. That usually worked.

As sleep overtook me, I immediately slipped into a vivid dream. Tonight I wandered the dead places again. In the distance the sounds of battle set my teeth on edge. The monster men were closing in on us again. Even though I knew I was in bed, safe with Katie and Jai Li, secure in Circle Q, terror ran through me as I was torn between finding a good place to hide and trying to wake myself up.

Luckily, Julie shouting my name brought me to full wakefulness. Edith yelled something in Russian—some warning I couldn't understand, but the tone was accurate. Then the house went black.

I rolled to my feet, grabbed Gram's case from under the bed and slammed it onto the bed, popping the latches as I called out.

"Katie, wake up, hon," I growled, jostling the mattress for all I was worth. I pulled Gram from the case, and the world shifted a little, all the ambient light blossoming into something just short of dusk. I could see well enough.

Katie was struggling awake, but Jai Li was sitting up, her eyes wide.

"Get Katie under the bed," I said as shots slammed into the front of the house. Someone screamed, I think it was Mary, and two shotgun blasts answered.

Jai Li crawled over the bed and grabbed Katie's hand, pulling her toward the floor. Katie rolled as if by instinct and pulled the blankets off the bed with them. I stood, pushed the mattress over them and knelt by the foot of the bed.

"Stay down," I said. "Let's see what's going on before you come out."

Neither of them answered, but Jai Li nodded from beneath the blankets.

I ran at a squat, pulled the bedroom door open, and thought about all the glass in the house. I took the time to stomp my feet into my Docs, shoving the laces inside instead of tying them. Luckily, I had on sweats and a T-shirt. If Jai Li hadn't been here, I'd have been naked.

Another shotgun shot blasted from the front of the house, and automatic weapon fire stitched across the side of the house, blasting through the kitchen windows and smashing a cabinet full of dishes.

"Where?" I called, seeing Julie in the living room, crouched to the side of the picture window. Or where it used to be.

"Barn," Julie said, reloading the shotgun. "Mary's in the kitchen with her aught-six. We're pinned down."

Damn. What to do? I could find them, if I could get out of the house.

I grabbed my amulet that connected me to my favorite kobold and concentrated as hard as I could. *Bub, I need you.*

I concentrated on that for a good thirty seconds when I felt a tug. It was down in my belly, but I knew he heard me. I frog-walked to the kitchen, trying to avoid as much glass as possible. Mary had the kitchen table up against the window and was hunkered down, watching out toward the barn.

"They can't shoot for shit," she said, "but they have a lot more firepower than we do."

"On it," I said. "Need some food first."

"What ...?" she asked as a loud pop echoed in the room and Bub appeared in the hallway. He swooned, catching himself on the doorway to the kitchen.

"Sarah?" he asked, his voice thready.

"Here," I called, sliding a box of frozen waffles across the floor.

He grabbed them and ate the whole box, cardboard and all. Next, I slid across two boxes of cereal and a five-pound bag of sugar—basically anything I could reach from where I crouched. He ate all of it as fast as I could get it to him. Twice more someone fired into the house, but they hadn't made a physical assault yet.

I turned at the sound of a small hunting rifle from the back of the house, followed by another string of swear words in Russian. It was Edith Sorenson. I didn't speak Russian, but I know she wasn't inquiring about their health.

Flanking move.

"Bub," I said as he let out a huge belch and turned to look at me.

"Yes, ma'am?" he asked, his voice stronger than when he first arrived.

"I need you to port me out behind the barn. Can you do that?"

He looked at me and nodded. "You and the sword. Can't promise the clothes will follow."

Great. Naked fighting. "Okay, good enough. Julie," I said, leaning into the living room. "Can you give me some cover fire as soon as we disappear?"

"Sure," she said, jacking in a new shell. "Stab the fuckers for me."

I saluted her, grabbed Bub's hand, and nodded. He smiled at me and the world went black.

It was like getting punched in the diaphragm. For a second, I couldn't breathe, then the cool of the evening greeted me in all my nakedness.

Bub looked around, pointing to my left and holding up three claws. I nodded to the right, and he held up one hand, crept forward, and looked around the edge of the barn. Four more.

I pointed at him, then to the left toward the *three* bad guys. He shook his head and ran right.

Jerk.

I followed suit as soon as the shotgun erupted from the front of the house. Automatic weapon fire followed as I dashed around the barn. One shooter was squatted down at the edge of the barn, firing into the house, while the other two stood behind him, laughing and pointing.

"House full of women," one was shouting to the other when I swung Gram two-handed into the shooter's neck. His head bounced to the feet of the other guys as blood sprayed across them. They were so cocky, they hadn't even brought their guns up to fire. I swung around, hearing a scream erupt from the other side of the barn.

I swept the legs out from under the next guy, slamming my elbow down on his throat just as I stabbed Gram forward, catching the third guy in the knee. He went down screaming and the guy underneath me didn't move. By the time I could stand up, I'd brought Gram across the third guy's throat and my group was down.

The look on his face was priceless. No one ever expected the naked Amazon with a sword.

I crept through the barn, finding two bodies, and heard fighting outside. There were two gunshots which slammed into the wall to my left and another voice screamed its last.

Bub came around the barn door, one arm cradled against his abdomen and his head bowed. A guy decked out like Seal Team Six, with a fully automatic rifle and night-vision goggles, stepped into the barn, grinning.

"You're dead," he said, raising his gun.

Before he could fire, bright yellow flames erupted all over Bub's body, showing the world just how much he liked getting shot. The mercenary stumbled back, yanked off his goggles, and fired wildly.

I took his arm off at the elbow, sending the rifle spinning at his side, the shoulder strap keeping it from hitting the ground. He screamed, waving his stump around as Bub clawed his way through the guy's Kevlar to get to the soft chewy parts underneath.

Suddenly there was no noise beyond a raspy gurgling sound

from the dying merc. Bub didn't even try to eat the guy. Instead he dropped the flames and stumbled over to sit at my feet.

"You okay?" I asked him, dropping my hand to the top of his head.

He leaned his head against my calves. "Bullets hurt," he mewled. "You failed to mention that."

"Yeah, sorry."

I knelt to the last guy, pulled the night-vision goggles off his head, and put them on. The world settled into a nice monochromatic green. Twice I saw flashes from the back of the house, reflections of shots.

"Stay here," I said. "I'll get that last one."

Whoever was around the house was there to keep us pinned down, not let us escape. They didn't expect we had a way of flanking them.

I crept around the house, praying that Mary or Julie didn't shoot me.

Just as I rounded the north side of the house three shots struck the siding, driving me to my belly. I cocked my head to the side, trying to get a bead on whomever was shooting at the house, while trying to keep as low a profile as I could. It was right then I decided I needed to talk to a guy I knew on the con circuit, Clay. He taught writers how to work against an ambush or how to clear a building. I didn't have much experience going up against people armed with guns.

A bright light flashed from the house. I squeezed my eyes shut as the echoes of that light pulsed in my brain. You'd think I'd have learned from the guy who wore these just minutes ago. Luckily, if the remaining shooter had been looking directly at the house, they were probably dazed as well. Or, so I hoped.

When I opened my eyes again, I could make out the large objects, like buildings, so I shuffled forward in the direction of one of the sheds, expecting to feel bullets smash into me, but they never came. The shooter, a woman, had pulled back, bracing her back against the shed, fumbling with her goggles and holding a pistol in her hands.

"Boo," I said, stepping up to her, but before I could do anything else, she put the pistol in her mouth and pulled the trigger.

What the hell was it with people killing themselves? Sure, I was probably gonna stab her, but great googly-moogly.

CHAPTER ELEVEN

I looked around with the night-vision goggles and decided there were no more bad guys. I called out to Julie, expecting another attacker to join the fray. Luckily for us all, no one stepped up. With a grin, I walked around to the front door of the house. We'd totally kicked their asses.

"Julie," I called. "I think we're ..." That's when the night exploded. Of course, there was another attacker. That was totally fair.

Dumb luck saved me in that moment. I guess my senses were heightened by the runes on my body, the sword in my hand, or the connection I had with Nidhogg, the mother of all dragons. Enough of a push, anyway, to turn my head at the very last second and avoid painting the side of the house with my brains.

The shot exploded by my right ear, rocking my head to the side and into the wall, dazing me. The bastard had been playing dead.

I hit the ground hard with my ears ringing and the side of my head on fire. As I lay there, trying to blink away the pain, a crash came from the back of the house. The shooter didn't even look around. He just straddled my body and aimed the pistol at my face. I started to say something sarcastic, but my biting wit was superseded by Julie unloading both barrels of her shotgun into him.

He flew a good six feet before hitting the ground. Double barrel shotgun packs quite a punch. I bet a giant would feel that.

I crawled toward the kitchen door. Before I could reach up and grab the knob, Katie flung the door open and grabbed me by the shoulders. She was strong, and the adrenaline didn't hurt the situation. She rolled me into the house and kicked the door shut.

At least she was dressed. My nakedness seemed far more awkward now that I was in the house again.

"Jai Li is in the bathroom," she said, kneeling by me with a pair of flashlights. "It was her idea to hit the shooter with these." She held two high beam LED lights. I could tell from experience that they put out a lot of candles.

"Thanks," I said. "My head hurts."

"Someone broke into the house," Edith called from the back.

I tried to sit up, but Katie held me down. "Jai Li," she whispered, and moved to peer around the kitchen doorway and down the hall.

"They did not stay for long," Edith answered.

"Do we call the police?" Mary called from the kitchen."

"No," Edith said, coming through the house with a squirrel rifle and a hatchet. "No police." She pointed at me. "Call your witch friend. This is her problem to fix."

She went past the kitchen to the front door and yanked it open. It took her two tries because the bullets had smashed the frame.

"Where are you going?" I called after the old woman. Katie took that moment to scurry down the hall and pull Jai Li out of the bathroom. The girl clung to Katie like she was drowning. I turned back to Edith and saw she was watching the two of them.

"One of those who attacked us is a witch," she said, and stalked out of the house. Julie glanced at me and followed her.

"I'll get the med kit," Mary said, hurrying down the hall.

"Can I get some clothes?" I asked. "Or a blanket?"

"You were grazed," Katie said, returning with Jai Li in her arms. She kissed me quickly. "There's too much glass back here, let me bring you some things."

She sat Jai Li on the couch, covering her with one of Edith's quilts, and hurried out of the living room and down the hall.

"Underwear would be nice," I called after her. She'd deliberately forget it if I let her.

Jai Li peeked over the arm of the couch and signed, "You're naked," and giggled. Children amaze me.

"Someone ransacked our room," Katie said, handing me a pair of sweats and a T-shirt. "Window gone. Not broken, just gone."

Of course, Katie didn't bring me a bra, hussy. I got dressed and she went to sit with Jai Li. Mary cleaned the burn across my scalp and wrapped a bandage around my head. I looked like that kid out of *The Red Badge of Courage*.

Mary got the generator going, and the floodlights around the farm showed us the horror of the night.

The worst part was Edith. She was out with the young woman who'd shot herself before I'd had a chance to stab her. Edith stood over her, the hand axe down to one side, reminding me of that spirit who killed Jimmy. It was a fleeting image, broken when she turned to look at me coming across the yard.

"Stay here," she said with a shudder. "Do not let her leave."

I glanced down at the dead young woman. Blood and brains painted the side of the shed. Unless there was another necromancer nearby, this girl wasn't going anywhere.

I called Qindra while I waited and, amazingly enough, she answered.

"Yes, I know," she started. "Stuart said—"

"We've been attacked out at Circle Q. There are dead mercenaries and a witch who committed suicide here."

The phone went quiet for half a second.

"I'll get a cleaning crew out there as soon as possible," she said, obviously tired. "I'll report some kids out firing off fire-works to the local police. In case anyone calls it in."

Julie and Mary investigated the barn. Everyone in there was dead. Bub hadn't been messing around—we'd need a shovel to collect all the parts. I'd need to cleanse the place with sage and lavender again. The horses were going to be spooked.

Turns out my group was only mostly dead—the guy with the smashed throat managed to survive. Apparently, I'm not as good as I thought I was. He had a pulse, but he was unconscious. Julie made sure to remove all of his weapons. He was a fairly large guy. I guess he had a thicker neck than I'd imagined.

Katie came to where I was watching the very dead suicide girl and plopped a stool down next to the body, insisting I sit down. Seems I may have been swaying on my feet a little. Only a little.

The seven jacked-up dudes were obviously standard ex-military types: trim physique, hair high and tight, and tattoos that reminded me of things my father sported, though he didn't know I ever saw them. These guys were definitely mercenaries. None of them had any identification of any sort.

The young woman Edith called *witch* was a totally different story. She seemed soft in comparison, used to a life of leisure and lattes. She was armed, that much I'd witnessed, but really, she was dressed like a civilian. How did she fit into this puzzle and why had she killed herself?

The mercs were a distraction. Before they even started firing, Witchie-poo had done some mumbo-jumbo that had alerted Edith. But what or why, I wasn't clear on yet. She'd held back when they thought they had the house under control, waited until Bub and I dropped like a buzz saw in the midst of her hired guns before she'd vanished our window and ransacked our room. And it had been quick. She had to be looking for something particular, and I could only think of two things a witch may be interested in: Gram or Olivia Cornett's diary.

How close had Katie and Jai Li come to being murdered

while I was running around naked? Not a trail I needed to run down. I was just glad the book was not here.

Edith reappeared with a small knapsack. She had me help her lay the young woman's body flat on the ground a distance away from the shed and began to draw a circle around it with a bag of salt, setting up and lighting candles, reminding me of the ritual circle the asshole necromancer had used to kill Mary's prized high-stepper, Blue Thunder.

Edith then muttered a few phrases in Russian over the body and rocked back on her heels as three small items began to glow —a bracelet, a brooch, and a fat turquoise nose ring. That's when I recognized her. The nose ring gave her away.

She was one of Madame Gottschalk's—had served me water when I was at the old witch's house in Kirkland, back before Jimmy died.

I reached down and lightly touched the nose ring before Edith could stop me. Like a flash I saw her on the battlefield where we had fought the blood cult last fall. She had been with the necromancer Justin out in Chumstick. She'd been one of those who used magic to raise the dead.

Son of a bitch.

While I watched, Edith stripped the three magic items from the dead girl and handed each of them to Mary, swearing under her breath as she did so. Then she pulled out a small, very sharp knife with a pearl handle and a serrated back. It was a fish boning knife and it had been sharpened so many times it was barely a sliver in the halogen lights.

"She's already dead, right?" I asked, not wanting to watch her debone this young woman. "She killed herself."

Edith glanced at me and shook her head. "Watch," she said, and cut a long, shallow gash in the woman's left arm. She pressed the bloody flesh open wider with her thumb and pulled out a long thin wire from just inside the elbow.

"Witch," Edith says. "Old school. They drink certain draughts to give themselves power. The longer they've been at it, the more of this they have in their bodies. Essentially it turns their veins to silver or gold, depending on the school of magic. This is why they burned witches in the old days, to find the witch bane. Amulets and such can be made from this stuff which will protect the wearer from magic."

"Yuck?" I asked.

"We will have to burn her," she said, standing and wiping her hands in the dirt. "If we don't, she will heal from her wounds."

I looked over to the brains that splattered the shed and shuddered.

That would be a good trick.

While we waited for Qindra to show up, I called Gunther and Stuart. They both agreed to come out to Circle Q. They arrived ahead of Qindra, which surprised me. I figured Stuart may have been with Qindra. When I said something to him, he blushed and said she'd been at his apartment when I called.

"She had to go home and get a few things," he said, chagrined. "I was already on my way here when you called. I'd given Gunther a heads-up as well."

"Good enough," I said. Mary and Julie were in the house, sweeping up. "Maybe we should get them to a hotel or something?"

Gunther shook his head. "No, they are better off here. At least there will be reinforcements here soon. Besides, if you asked Mary to leave this farm, I think you'd be surprised by the answer."

I got where he was coming from, but this was not her battle.

"Not just no, but hell no," was her answer. She delivered it with that derision one reserved for drunks and fools.

She kept sweeping and Julie just shrugged at me.

As I came back out of the house, Gunther nudged Stuart and smiled. "Told you," he said.

"We have to protect them," I said. "Like the fence out at Black Briar. What do you think?"

"Black Briar has new fences," Stuart said, "but the magic

there is waning. None of the Cornetts live there now. There's nothing to anchor the magic."

Why the hell hadn't I thought of that?

"What about Katie or Deidre?" I asked.

"Next solstice," Gunther said. "I'll take Deidre out, see if we can make it work. Not the same, though. Not sure if the farm will recognize Deidre as family enough."

That was a dreary thought. The farm knew the Cornetts? Magic was strange. Would she have to leave? Or live there with the proverbial shields down?

Gunther went into the house to help when the white trucks of the cleanup crew began to arrive. Qindra was at the tail end of the caravan, her Miata glowing neon with all the magic jewelry she was wearing. She was ready for battle and didn't care who knew it.

Stuart walked over to the car, leaning in to whisper something for her ears only. She kissed him quickly and hurried after the cleaning crew, barking orders.

"We'll need the power company out here," I said to Qindra as she approached the house. "They cut the lines."

"We'll take care of it," she said, taking off her gloves, exposing freshly painted nails. She'd got those runes on pretty quickly. I bet they were press-on. Breaking one would give her a sudden and powerful burst of energy. I'd seen her blow up an attack copter by breaking a similar rune. Too bad I didn't know details on how she'd done it.

Edith stood over the fallen witch, her fist a bloody mass of wires. I didn't even look down at the girl. I had no idea how she'd come back from that.

"Witch," Edith said, acknowledging Qindra with a look of wary respect.

Qindra nodded.

"This is another one," Edith said, pointing at the girl with her knife. "You need to burn her."

"Not here," Qindra said. "It would taint the farm."

Edith nodded and walked away. "She's on your hands now."

When she'd walked around the side of the house, Qindra looked at me.

"Who is that?"

"Long story," I said, glancing down at the girl. The cuts on her arms were already healing and her head was remarkably head-shaped once again. Not healed by any means but getting better.

"And this one?"

"She's one of Gottschalk's," I said. "Also worked with the necromancer."

"Oh, one of the fish that got away?"

"Ran or somehow healed after we thought we'd killed her."

Qindra walked around the circle, drew a few runes in the air with her wand. "Powerful one," she said, looking back at me. "Not Gottschalk's though."

"Oh, I saw her there, back when we visited with Jimmy."

Qindra drew a few more squiggles and shook her head. "She belongs to someone much more powerful than this Gottschalk woman."

I thought back to the events of that day. This young woman was in no way cowed by Madame Gottschalk. In fact, she seemed to treat her with some level of contempt.

"Could she belong to Baba Yaga?" I asked.

Qindra's head snapped around. "What did you say?"

I remembered Charlie's freak-out when I said the name out loud.

"You know, that old Russian folk tale about the witch in the hut with the chicken legs."

Qindra staggered, nearly fell. I caught her elbow, steadying her.

"I need to call Nidhogg," she said, nodding at me.

I pulled back, and she walked back around the house, calling out to her people. Soon three burly men arrived with a large Shop-Vac type container, a body bag, and a stretcher. Two of them put the witch girl in the bag and trundled off, while the third guy began to assemble something that looked a lot like a flamethrower.

Which was exactly what it was. Holy shit!

He didn't even ask what was in the shed, just turned the hose on, fired the starter and sprayed jellied gasoline over the side of the shed and across the ground where the witch's blood had fallen. It reminded me of dragon fire more than napalm, and it was damned effective. The shed was burned to the ground in a matter of minutes, and the surrounding area was melted glass.

That was some powerful heat.

"We'll be back to dig that out," he said, bobbing his head at me. "Needs to cool first."

"And the shed?"

"Send Qindra a list; we'll replace whatever was inside." And he was off around the house again, leaving me to stare at the ground.

Finally, I turned to see the white trucks driving away.

"We'll have a crew out tomorrow to fix the house," Qindra said, handing Mary a business card. "This is the gentleman who will be calling on you. I promise you he does good and discreet work."

"Thanks," Mary said.

Qindra stopped and hugged Stuart before climbing in her car and following the white trucks.

"She gonna be okay?" I asked him.

He shrugged. "Asked me to stay out here with you until she can check on something." He glanced at me, his eyes red and tired, but his face was stern. "She's worried about something, and that should scare the hell out of all of us."

"Amen to that."

He went into the house and I followed him. Most of the furniture was back in its normal places. All the glass was cleaned up and Julie had made coffee.

"No milk," she said, handing Stuart and Gunther steaming mugs. "They shot up the fridge."

Jai Li was asleep on the couch with Bub, who'd had his arm bandaged. Katie sat on the floor in front of the couch and Edith sat in her rocker with her hand on Jai Li's back.

"I know her," Edith said, not looking at me. "That witch friend of yours."

"Qindra?"

"Yes. I knew her mother."

This night just kept getting weirder.

CHAPTER TWELVE

Julie and I started the next morning making noise like we were going to stay home, just in case. Katie and Mary were indignant, like we didn't think they could take care of themselves. It's not like we'd had a heated argument or anything, but they shut down that line of thinking before either of us could truly muster a good offense. Katie said we'd be more of a pain in the ass if we stayed home, fussing around, bored and cranky. It was hard to argue against that. Besides, we both really wanted to work.

And how right they were. The work proved a balm to our frayed nerves. We worked two small farms with a mix of mules and horses. The work was hard, the way I liked it, and satisfying for the effort. Julie handled the clients, who looked at me askance. Once they saw me with their animals, they went from frosty to friendly. We plowed through the work with efficiency and good humor. By the time we broke for lunch, I was feeling a ton better.

It was so damned strange that just the night before we'd been attacked by mercenaries. Frankly, I'm surprised that I wasn't giving off some death funk/psychic residue from killing half of the bastards. The horses and mules didn't seem to notice anything, so who was I to argue?

Still, if these normal folks knew what my life was really like, they probably wouldn't let me anywhere near their animals. I'm honestly surprised how well we both handled the day despite the recent chaos. A year ago, I'd have been jumpy all throughout the day.

Reminded me to call Charlie, though. See what he knew, if he was involved in any way. Went to voicemail, and I told him to call me. No idea if the line was secure on his end.

I may be getting jaded but taking out the mercenaries didn't really throw me off my game. I'd done enough fighting to almost shrug it off. Not totally, but close enough for government work.

The thing that kept cropping up in my mind all day was how Edith Sorenson had behaved. Oh, I must've known on some level that she was deeper in to this weirdness than one would expect for an elderly widow. The stuff with that witch last night came out of left field. My brain was having a difficult time jiving the fact that sweet Mrs. Sorenson, who looked after Jai Li when Katie and I were out of pocket, was also an efficient and knowledgeable witch killer.

That needed some unpacking.

We stopped at the County Line to "knock the dust out of our throats," as Julie would say, and scarf down a couple of burgers. Working horses built an appetite. We had one more farm before we could knock off for the day. They had a dozen horses, but not all of them needed shoeing. Mainly this was a scouting mission. We'd see how they treated their animals, and they'd eyeball us to see if we could work together. They were a referral, so that eased things a bit. Once we got a good handle on the place and their needs, we may work a couple of horses, but most likely we'd be scheduling a follow up. Farm that size would be a full day's work. Would make for a relatively early afternoon, which was nice.

Of course, Katie had taken Jai Li out to Black Briar for the afternoon.

My visits to the County Line were a mixed bag. I'd been in fights here, gotten drunk, and done some very stupid things. Honestly, I'm surprised they let me back in after that first incident with those two cowboys, but the owners were a forgiving sort. Being with Julie helped. That woman exuded calm and professionalism that spoke to these folks. With her around we were not likely to get drunk and start a fight or anything. We liked the County Line. It was our kind of kick-back-and-relax joint. I liked the clientele. They were real working stiffs who just wanted to wind down after a hard day's work.

Of course, my cell phone rang halfway through my beer. Julie was on high alert as I fished it out of my pocket. The song was "Problem Child" by AC/DC.

"Skella," I said to Julie, who smiled in relief.

I grabbed my beer and walked toward the bathrooms. That hallway was fairly soundproof from the open bar, being two turns past the kitchen. There used to be pay phones down there, back when you could find such things.

"Sarah?" Skella asked. "I was talking to Gletts this morning. Can we talk?"

"Sure, I'm at County Line with Julie. Want to pop over?"

"I'll be right there," she said. "Is the bathroom clear?"

I walked into the women's room and looked around. "Empty."

"On my way."

I stood in the hall, blocking the door, just in case anyone showed up. But I didn't need to worry. The door opened behind me and Skella stepped out.

"Cool, let's go." She was bouncing.

I led her back to our table, and Julie looked up.

"What an interesting surprise," she said, giving me the side-eye. "Something important going on?"

Skella shrugged. "Just needed to talk to Sarah about some things. About the Hamsters and such."

Julie looked at us strange, so we explained about the kids Skella had been hanging out with, why she called them Hamsters, and how they were working on the movie shoot.

"Sarah promised she'd talk to them," Skella said, her voice solemn. "They've been hit pretty hard by all the suicides in Bellingham." She turned to look at me, her eyes glistening with tears. "The latest suicide was a tenant in the boarding house Sprocket and Dante live in."

I hadn't heard that. I looked at her, surprised, and she grimaced.

"Two nights ago. They just found his body this morning at one of the motels near the airport. Dante and Sprocket are taking it pretty hard."

"I'm sorry. Did you know him?"

She shrugged. "No, met him once when I was visiting. He kept to himself a lot. Nice enough guy, very shy."

"Lot of suicides up that way," Julie said, poking me under the table. "Anything we should be worried about?"

I didn't want to be involved. Just because I was there when Ginny went over the balcony didn't make them my responsibility.

"I think Sprocket has a theory," Skella said, leaning forward. "You should definitely talk to him." She sat back and drank the glass of water that had sat in front of me. "That Mimi who runs the boarding house knew all those kids," she continued. "Even Ginny. Mimi teaches over at the University. Something in the theater department. Helps run plays or something."

Was it wrong of me to wonder if she could help out on the *Cheerleaders* shoot instead of worrying she was somehow involved? Maybe so. Still, it was interesting news all the same. Mimi had seemed harmless when we'd met her after Ginny's funeral. Just a drag queen with a killer voice.

"You think she's involved with the suicides?" I had to ask. If she was involved in any way, I wanted to know who I was exposing my friends and family to.

"I really don't think so," she said, "but there's something about Mimi's boarding house. The place is amazing. I've been there dozens of time. It's safe, homey. But there is a power there. Something I can't define."

"What did you talk to Gletts about?"

She looked exasperated and picked at Julie's fries. "He thinks there's a portal there. You remember back when he was running around the Sideways?"

I remembered all too well. His spirit had been knocked out of his body, similar to how Katie's spirit had been hiding there in the body of a pregnant rabbit. Long story. But Gletts had been sure he could find a portal back to Alfheim, the elves' true home.

"Could it be the portal he's been on about?"

She shook her head. "Not that I've been able to figure out. I've checked all the mirrors, snuck into all the rooms. Really the only thing odd about the place is Mimi, and that's only in the some-people-are-strange vibe she gives off. You remember how she was at karaoke after Ginny's funeral?"

Totally. Her singing had tripped a few chords with me. Not—*danger*—as much as—*wow, holy crap, she's amazing*—that type of thing. It sure felt like there was magic there, similar to the magic Katie used when she sang.

"Yeah, I remember."

Julie watched us with mild interest. I knew she'd be grilling me to fill in the gaps later.

"Mimi loves running the boarding house. There's something about the way she mothers everyone, looks out for them, you know?"

I shrugged. I didn't really know, but I could imagine.

"All the Hamsters hang out over there. It's a cool place. But I haven't found anything out of the ordinary. I'm not sure it's the place Gletts is looking for, but I think it's close."

"Maybe we should go check it out."

She smiled big at that, changing her face from sullen and pinched to open and pretty. I bet without all the makeup she'd be cute. Not that I was into changing people's appearances. God knows I'd had enough of that as a kid.

"There's a concert next Friday," she said. "You remember Scarlett and Brian? He's in a band."

I remembered. "Yeah, cute blond with the two kids: Thing One and Thing Two."

She laughed. "Better not let Scarlett hear you call them that. Sprocket barely gets away with it."

"Cool, what kind of music?"

She grinned at me, really pleased. "Punk show with some band out of New York. Brian's band is opening for them."

"Sounds like a plan," I said. "I'll talk with Katie and we'll probably make it. Can you get us tickets?"

"Brian has some comped tickets. We'll hold back a couple for you and Katie."

Julie asked Skella a question about the movie shoot, just to be polite, I'm guessing, and I let my mind wander.

I didn't like the news about another suicide. Skella was gesticulating madly about some hilarious event at the shoot when my phone rang again. This time it was "Dragula" by Rob Zombie. They both turned to me and stared. Julie had a pinched look on her face. Definitely not her style of music. Skella's face went neutral, a mask to cover the fear I saw in her eyes. She knew the significance of the ringtone, apparently.

I stared at my phone for a couple seconds, dread crawling up my back. "Qindra," I said and answered it while I slid out of the booth.

"Beauhall."

"Sarah?" Qindra's voice was annoyed, maybe even a little afraid. "I need you."

Shit. "When and where?"

"I'll text you an address. I'd appreciate if you could engage with that lovely elf friend of yours and get a ride. This is urgent."

I sighed, letting my tense shoulders drop. What were the odds? "She's here as we speak."

"Good. We'll pick up her fees," she said. "Extra for the rush job, but I need you here ASAP. Bring the sword. I'll text you the address. We have a mirror set up already. Don't dawdle."

She hung up before I could say more. Julie gave me one of her mentor looks that was part concern and part frustration. "You are allowed to rest, you know."

I almost laughed. "I need to go meet her." I held up my phone as the text chimed and saw it was an address in Bellingham. "This just keeps getting stranger and stranger."

I tossed a tenner on the table. "Come on, Skella. I need a ride."

She nodded and scrambled after me. We walked to the truck and rifled through my gear, pulling Gram's case out from under my coveralls and lunch box. Julie was walking out of the door when we walked back in to hit the mirror in the ladies' room.

"I'll grab my stuff when I get back to Circle Q," I said, smiling at her. There may have been a couple of empty coffee cups and two or three empty water bottles in the back of her truck that were mine as well. "Promise."

She grunted, holding the door for us. "You could wash it too."

She was smiling, but I knew she was only half-joking.

I punched in Skella's number as Julie drove away. Some days are weirder than others.

As it worked out, Skella knew the address. It was the no-tell motel where Sprocket's friend had committed suicide. Wasn't that all kinds of special?

CHAPTER THIRTEEN

Skella didn't hang around after we stepped out into the empty lobby of the motel. Qindra's ubiquitous white vans blocked one of the entrances to the parking lot, and a sheriff's cruiser blocked the other.

"For your services," Qindra said, walking toward us and handing Skella an envelope. Skella nodded and Qindra turned away. "This way, Sarah. Please take out your sword."

Skella scrunched up her face and shrugged. "I'll see ya?"

I nodded, and she stepped into the mirror. How long before she told the Hamsters? Qindra didn't swear her to secrecy or anything. It was a gray area.

I sat my case on the lobby counter, flipped the latches, and opened the lid. Gram lay in her crushed velvet lining, throbbing with power. I grabbed her by the pommel and lifted her from the case. As soon as I made contact, the world shifted ever so slightly and my runes, scalp and calf, flared just as those along the blade began to glow a deep red.

"That's what I suspected," Qindra said. I glanced at her and saw that she looked exhausted.

"You okay?"

She gave me a tentative smile. "Long couple of days."

She motioned and I followed her out of the lobby and down the west wing of the motel. All the doors faced the main road, but Qindra was not bothering to hide when she pulled out her wand, wove a few intricate sigils in the air, and pointed to the second door from the lobby.

There is a lot wrong with the world. I've seen some pretty heavy magic of various kinds, but necromancy stands out for me in a big way. Gram pulsed with a mixture of rage and fear, which was a tad unsettling.

The doorway glowed with the color of black blood and yellowing bruises. Pain and death. As I glanced around the area, I saw where someone had thrown up. As I kept looking, I'd say several someones threw up.

Qindra followed my gaze. "Suicides are never pretty," she said, "but this goes far beyond that."

I stepped over a puddle of sick and approached the door. The runes along Gram flared into flames. "Murder?" I asked.

Qindra remained back, her face impassive. "I want your assessment before we talk."

I nodded and pushed the door open with my boot.

The body was still in the room. That was odd. Skella knew about the suicide. The Hamsters knew. But who told them?

All the furniture in the room had been shoved and piled against one wall. The carpet had been pulled up, exposing the raw concrete underneath. In the middle of the room a summoning circle had been drawn in blood and salt. The pentagram in the middle had burned-out candle stubs where the points intersected with the circle. At one corner a foot had scuffed the circle, breaking it, freeing whatever had been trapped inside. Blood spattered the walls in a few spots, but the blood in the circle had been artfully used as both a binding and a summoning.

Gram sang in my head. The runes along my scalp raged at the vileness of the black magic used here. My head began to ache with the cognitive dissonance.

I squatted at the edge, looking for additional clues. I'd seen something like this before, the first time I'd visited Circle Q. The day I met Charlie Hague. The necromancer, Justin, had sacrificed Mary Campbell's best horse, a high-stepper named Blue Thunder. Justin had used the animal's blood and spirit to fuel his magic. He'd been looking for me, funny enough. Wanted revenge for me killing his dragon patron, Jean-Paul.

I froze. He'd also set a few nasty traps for those who came along behind.

I gripped Gram and let my vision relax. Some bits of magic are best found by not looking at them directly. As my eyes unfocused and I let my mind go blank, I spotted a blurry shape to my left. When I tried to focus on it, it disappeared, but the second I looked away, I could just catch it out of my peripheral vision.

I spent nearly ten minutes hunched down, scanning the room and finding two more such spots. Two were loaded for bear, the magic in them throbbing. The one closest to the door only had a bit of residual magic left, like it had been triggered.

"Qindra?" I asked, without moving.

"Here," she answered me from just outside the room.

I explained about what I'd found, and where each of the nearly hidden sigils were.

"Close your eyes."

I didn't have to be told twice.

Qindra had been dressed for war. Each of her fingernails had a sigil painted on them, but now that I thought about it, two on her left hand had been scratched. Funny how that image came to me as I heard her voice mutter behind me.

Gram throbbed as power swept across the room and I squeezed my eyes even tighter. She disabled the first sigil with a *woompf*, like a small fire erupting and then failing for lack of fuel. That was to my left. The second expired with a scream like someone had been tortured. The third, which I had thought to be expended, pulsed three times before expiring with a whimper like a kicked dog.

"You can open your eyes."

The room looked no different, but I could feel the negative energy had been dissipated. I stood and Qindra beckoned me out of the room.

"My people can handle it from here. Let's talk."

"Where is everyone?" I asked when we sat in the lobby. The couch looked iffy, so we opted for two of the wooden chairs that sat at the one sad little breakfast table near an ancient coffee maker and a rack of very stale bagels.

"Someone cast a sort of *look-away* spell on the whole place. It's been empty for the last three nights."

"And the suicide?" There hadn't been a body in the room Not until this morning.

"That was a puzzle it took us a bit to work out. Turns out two sheriffs and a coroner went missing two nights ago. All we learned was someone called in screaming from this address. The police called in the coroner, saying it was an obvious suicide, then they all disappeared. Found them this morning out on Highway 2, near Monroe. All three of them dumped in a ditch with their throats cut."

"Jesus."

"But no body 'til now."

I waited. She'd tell this at her own pace.

"It was definitely a suicide. We've taken the body for further examination. We've been able to determine that he was dead before the ritual in that room occurred."

"Then why?"

Qindra twisted her wand in her hands. I noticed that actually four of the runes were gone on one hand, and all of them on the other.

"I came out here the morning after your attack at Circle Q," she said, her voice low and dangerous. "Twice the next day, and again this morning. Each of the other times I found myself somewhere else, unable to remember where I'd been for the last hour or more." She looked at me, her gaze scared and angry. "I don't like that kind of magic used against me, Sarah." She sat back with a huff. "I like it less that you could enter that room and not wander off. Though you could be more immune to this particular branch of magic due to your previous encounters."

"Necromancy." The answer was obvious. "I killed a whole bunch of those bastards back at the winter solstice."

"It's my belief that by fighting them with Gram, the sword has absorbed some of the power, giving it both a feel for the nuances and an immunity to the obfuscation." I lay the sword across my knees and stroked the pommel. More reason to love this blade. "This place still creeps me out."

She smiled. "I've expended four of my runes just to keep focus enough to remain within a hundred yards of this place. You finding those sigils has helped immensely."

"I think the kid was already dead when the necromancer showed up."

She looked up. "Singular?"

It felt right. "Based on how the magic felt, yeah. A single practitioner. I think they were trying to speak to the dead kid's ghost." I wasn't sure how I knew that; other than the way the room had felt. "What could be so important to go to all this trouble?"

She stood up and left the room. I made to follow, but she paused. "I want to check something. If you see me wander off, stop me." Then she went out to one of the trucks and spoke with her crew.

I watched as four people in moon suits carried several pieces of equipment into the room. I leaned against the doorway watching Qindra pace back and forth in front of the room where her people worked. Twice, I saw her break one of the runes on her fingernails as her crew tried to wander away. She was pretty pissed off.

It took them so long to get their readings, or whatever they were doing, that the sun began to fall toward the horizon. This time of year the days grew longer. It was getting late, and I was ready to prop my feet up after some dinner.

When another hour passed, I decided to call Katie, but I made sure to watch Qindra while the phone rang. She cast her glance back at me a few times but waved to assure me she was okay. She was down to a final rune. I had no idea what would happen when that was expended.

Katie answered, a bit pissy, but she knew what was going on, mostly, because Julie had filled her in.

I filled Katie in on what was going on, which didn't really take too long. Once she was up to speed, we chatted about the punk show next Friday. She was still out at Black Briar, which was good. I agreed to get a ride out that way when I was done here and we'd crash there overnight. I filled her in about meeting with Skella, which intrigued her and brought us back around to what was going on here at the motel. It's a bad sign that we could brush this kind of crazy off and talk about the bands we were going to see. At least she got pretty excited about the bands.

"Besides," she said. "The last concert we went to was filking, it's only fair we hit a punk show for you."

I didn't have the heart to mention how Ari had been kidnapped by dwarves after that last concert. Hopefully Brian wasn't *that* good a singer. I didn't want to see him get snatched by the next batch of crazies to come down the pike. Maybe we should just stop making friends altogether. Safer for everyone else.

Hell, at this pace, we'd be living in a cabin in Montana just to keep those we knew and loved out of harm's way.

That was no way to live.

CHAPTER FOURTEEN

Qindra dropped me off at Black Briar just after nine. Along the way we discussed what her team had found, and it aligned with my hunch. Someone had captured and questioned the ghost of that poor dead kid. She had no way of knowing what they were looking for, but found it quite possible that it was somehow tied to the attack out at Circle Q. Nothing surprises me anymore. Katie was going to love that news. She promised to let me know if they found anything else, but wasn't hopeful. Basically, she wanted me to keep my ear to the ground and let her know if I found anything on my end.

When she drove away, I saw that the last of her runes had been scratched off, and she wasn't happy at all. I knew it had to be frustrating for her to be this powerful, and work for the mother of all dragons, only to be thwarted by a cult in her own territory.

I waved at a group of fighters training out by the new barn as I hustled into the house.

I walked in to find Jai Li whupping Bub at gin rummy—that would be Edith Sorenson's influence. Katie was watching them so intently I didn't think she'd even noticed I'd arrived.

When Jai Li called gin, Frick and Frack fell off the couch and rolled around on the floor, laughing. Bub took about a second to go from sullen to joyful. He stood, bowed to Jai Li, and placed his cards on the table. Then he laughed and launched himself onto the twins, starting a rollicking, joyful wrestling scrum. Jai Li took her time gathering the cards into a neat pile, shaking her head at the other kids.

I sat down next to Katie at the kitchen table. She leaned back against me with a sigh.

"Don't you just miss those carefree times when we could play games all day with no worries?"

I kissed the top of her head. "Good times."

We'd had drastically different childhoods.

Deidre wheeled into the kitchen and set a basket of towels on the counter. "Hey Sarah, how was your day?"

We made a few minutes of small talk before the conversation died on its own as she turned her full attention to her laptop. The house grew quiet, peaceful. The kids were chatting quietly as Jai Li began to deal the cards once more. Frick and Frack didn't play yet. They were still trying to understand the overall concept of the game, well, that and they tended to eat the cards. At least Bub hadn't done that since the first time Jai Li beat him.

It took me far too long to realize the tenseness in Katie. Her shoulders were like steel bars. I began to rub them, and she half melted.

"There's been this buzzing in my head all day," she said quietly. She glanced over at the kids before swinging around in her chair to face me, scissoring her left leg between mine and taking both of my hands. "The attack on the house last night," she began, her hands trembling.

I leaned in and kissed her. Not to stop her from talking, but to reassure her.

She reached up and touched the side of my head, brushing her fingertips across the stubble above my left ear. "Nothing feels right today."

PTSD. I was very familiar with the aftermath of battle, but

then again, so was she. This was the first dust-up we'd had since she'd almost died ... since we lost Jimmy.

"I keep thinking back to my mother's diary; going over the day I collapsed at school. I'm sure the book had written something back to me, but I can't remember what it said for the life of me, and honestly, it's really pissing me off."

I blinked at the sudden subject shift. I could connect the dots in her thinking fairly easily, though.

"That book almost killed you."

Her face hardened and she grew very still. "You traipsed around the Sideways for weeks with that book, and you were fine."

There was so much resentment in her. I knew she'd been feeling helpless, but reminding her of all the amazing things she'd done and survived didn't seem to appease that anger. I held her hands loosely, not wanting her to think I was trying to restrain her in any way. I just wanted her to know I was there for her. I couldn't solve this problem, short of giving her the book back, and, after last time, there was no way I was bringing that out of hiding again. Not until she got a lot stronger. Especially with the news from Qindra.

And I absolutely knew how controlling that was. I struggled with keeping the book from her. Was it really my place? There are demons and decisions we all live with.

"I just want to find out what it knows about my mother." She sat back, slipping her hands from mine. "It's so damn unfair."

"That book almost killed you," I started.

Katie slid her chair back suddenly and pivoted, leaned her elbows on the table, and pressed her fists to the sides of her head.

"I just want the buzzing to stop."

Sounds of yelling came from the living room and Katie whipped around, as if she'd only realized there were others in the house. I started to get up, to say something, but Katie put her hand on my knee.

"Watch."

Frick was crying, holding his face, and Frack was shouting. Trolls have thick hide, so we knew the child wasn't actually hurt. Apparently one of them had bitten Bub, who in turn had swatted the biter. The three boys looked ready to start punching and kicking. I needed to intervene.

Katie squeezed my knee hard and whispered, "Just watch."

Jai Li looked at them, a mixture of concern and exasperation on her face. In a blink, a calm resolve washed over her, and she stood up. With one fluid movement, she placed her hand on Bub's shoulder and stepped past him, squatted down and wiped the side of Frick's face while at the same time taking Frack's hand.

It was over in an instant. The crying and yelling stopped. Each of the three boys grew quiet, still. Bub sat down beside Jai Li and apologized to Frick, who patted him on his scaly knee.

Frack sat down quickly and the three of them held hands, letting quiet settle over them like a blanket. There were no more tears. Instead they sat in one another's company like they were meditating.

I was amazed. Jai Li had quieted them, pulled away the anger, let the hurt and pain ebb away. That was awesome and a little scary.

Katie stood up then, her chair scraping along the kitchen floor, and the children all looked around. She walked into the living room and knelt down with them. Katie laughed out loud as the kids began to roll around on the floor and wrestle once more.

Children were strange sometimes.

Deidre looked up from her computer screen, glanced at the kids and shook her head.

"Rambunctious bunch. Glad to have Jai Li out here today. The twins were getting anxious, snippy."

"Have you seen that before?" I asked, leaning across the kitchen table and keeping my voice low.

"What, kids wrestling?" Deidre asked.

"No, before that, one of the twins had done something to Bub. He hauled off and clobbered the kid or something. Frick was crying, Frack was ready to fight, and Bub was outraged. In one move Jai Li moved among them, touching each, and quieting the fight in them."

Deidre thought for a moment. "Now that you mention it, they do behave a helluva lot better when she's here than when she's not. I always chalked it up to her being a girl and having a calming influence over them."

Maybe more than we knew. I wondered if this was why she and her twin had been gifted to Nidhogg. It was a little creepy. "It was like she stilled them, just flipped a switch and turned off the anger and pain."

Deidre looked from the kids and back to Katie. "Not a bad skill to have. World could use more peacemakers."

Katie's sudden squeal of laughter rang through the house as all the kids pig-piled on top of her, laughing and howling.

"Never know what gifts a child has," Deidre said, patting me on the arm. "You just have to watch 'em grow and guide them the best you can."

"You did a fair enough job with Katie, I guess."

Deidre laughed. "She was always a willful child. Spiteful at times. Her teenage years were a trial. That's for sure."

I looked out at the kids in the other room. Bub was hundreds of years old but acted like a preschooler most days. Jai Li was only six and the troll twins were close enough to two but acted at least four. And my beloved Katie. Barely twenty-five and carrying more than her fair share of pain.

All of them were orphaned. Did they wonder about their parents?

Family was such a tenuous thing. Easily snuffed out by any number of tragedies. Tears stung my eyes.

"Can you watch them a bit?" I asked Deidre,. "so I can take Katie out for a walk?"

"Sure, hon, take your time." Deidre closed her laptop and rolled into the living room.

Deidre was only in her early thirties. She and Jimmy had just gotten married when his and Katie's parents had disappeared. Katie and Deidre shared a lot of loss. It all made me feel old beyond my years. Was that because of the trauma and the pain? Or was it because I couldn't do a damned thing about it?

Katie came stumbling out of the living room, her face red from laughing. The pain was still there in her eyes, but damn, it was good to see her happy, even for a moment.

I gave her my best smile. "Let's take a walk."

She took my hand and we went out the back door. The wind felt good on my face as we strode across the deck. I just needed to breathe, to have the open sky over my head. It was time that I pulled my head out of my ass and stopped trying to control her life.

"Let's talk about the diary."

She reached up and grabbed my arm, pulling in close to me as we walked.

We walked in silence until we were out beyond the war memorial.

"Qindra called," I said, breaking the reverie. "That mercenary that survived the farm attack led to a network of black ops groups, but she couldn't find any direct connections to witches or dragons. Just a bunch of folks willing to kill people for money."

Katie sighed. "What a fucked-up world we live in."

We walked for a good fifteen minutes, just sharing each other's space. The early evening was beautiful. I always loved it out here. We ended up near the creek that flowed down out of the national forest and onto Black Briar property. Once upon a time, Katie and I had followed a troll up that stream, into the mountains where we killed her. The horror of finding the twins in that cave still made me queasy at times.

Just before the fence that ran along the edge of the property, there was a scattering of boulders that had been laid down by glaciers a billion years ago. It was a pretty place, looking up into the mountains. It would be a nice place to bring the kids for a picnic. When they were older.

We settled on the boulders, and Katie drew a deep breath.

"I still don't understand why they attacked the farm."

She turned and draped her legs over my right thigh and held both my hands in hers. "I mean, maybe they were trying to kill you, but the whole thing seemed like a real clusterfuck, you know?"

Now it was my turn to sigh.

"They were after the diary," I said.

Katie stiffened. "It's in the house?"

I shook my head. "Not anymore." She grew silent, her face blank. "The mercenary did say they were to create a diversion while that witch, Anika, stole something from the house. Qindra said it was something very valuable, something very powerful."

Katie didn't look up, but she pursed her mouth.

"They were misinformed. I moved the book after you recovered. Didn't want it near you."

She looked up then. "It's mine."

If she said the word *precious*, I was going to come unglued.

"When this Anika tried to scry for where the book was, she alerted Edith to her presence. I guess they didn't expect Bub or Edith."

Katie barked a laugh. "Honestly, did you have any idea Edith was a witch herself?"

I smiled. "No chance. She totally caught me by surprise."

"Where's the book?"

"Safe."

"I'm a grown-ass woman, Sarah. I know you love me and all, but it's not your job to control me. You can't protect me from everything in the world, you know?"

I didn't say anything, just nodded and let her continue to talk. There was a blockage in our communication and apparently this was the time to smash through that. She just opened her mouth and all her fears and pain surrounding the events of the last year came tumbling out in a mishmash of anxiety. Hell, she was just as worried she'd lose me, as I was that I'd lose her. What did it say about me that I thought myself more capable of protecting her, than she of protecting me?

I'd done exactly what my dad had done when I was twelve and we'd run. Imagine how utterly shitty I felt for keeping the diary from her against her wishes. Who was I to control her? I was being selfish, and even though it was because I loved her, and was afraid for her, it gave me absolutely no right to make such a dick move. Of course, she agreed wholeheartedly.

It was a painful and cathartic three hours. We hadn't resolved much of anything, but it was all out on the table. The look of relief on her face when we were done made me ashamed.

Learn, Sarah. Learn.

When we tucked Jai Li into bed, we watched as she explained how the day had gone. Katie and I sat together while our daughter laughed and signed all the antics of the boys, and the games, and how absolutely wonderful life was. Made for a pretty great ending to the day.

CHAPTER FIFTEEN

Katie met me at Monkey Shines after work on Wednesday. I'd had a great day out with Julie, and my muscles ached in that way that assured me I was getting back into shape. It was a good feeling. I was sitting in the back, sipping my mocha, when Katie sauntered in with a glow and a smirk that told me she had news. She ordered a coffee and rushed back to where I waited.

"Guess who I heard from today?" she said, nearly bouncing.

"Not Charlie Hague," I said, irritably. He was either dead or avoiding me. I didn't like either option. "I called him after the attack on Circle Q and he's been radio silent."

"Hmmm ... that's not good."

I sat fuming another minute, but Katie started bouncing again. "Guess."

"Um ... Melanie?"

"No, that was Monday. Guess again."

I hated this game. "Gandhi?"

"He's dead, guess again."

I rolled my eyes at her. "You know it's a good thing I love you, right?"

She laughed and bent down to kiss me on the top of my head. "One more guess."

I thought hard. Who would she be excited to hear from? We had the same friends. Her old college professor in Bellingham, McCries-A-Lot, maybe? Rolph? "I don't know. Skella?"

"Nope," she said, flopping down in the overstuffed chair beside me and taking my coffee out of my hands. She took a long shuddering sip and passed it back to me. "Do you even put coffee in that?"

I grinned at her and shrugged. "I like it sweet. That's why I like you."

She pantomimed puking and jumped up when her name was called. The coffee she came back with was smaller than mine and a lot blacker. Real coffee, she called it.

She settled down on the couch beside me with her jacket and shoes off, her back against the arm of the loveseat and her feet tucked underneath my right thigh. The first sip of coffee caused her to close her eyes and wiggle her toes. "Heaven," she said.

"So, who called you?" I asked, trying not to be impatient.

"Cassidy Aloysius Stone," she said, beaming. "They just got back into town and wanted to know if we could meet them, get a beer, hang out."

Interesting. I thought back to the picture that Jai Li had drawn that reminded me so much of him. Apparently, the Harpers were interested in making a movie soundtrack after all. Very nice.

"Did he say when?"

"Saturday night," she said, then blew on her coffee. "I figured we'd be back in town around two. That would give us enough time to get cleaned up, have some quality time with the girl in the afternoon and maybe catch a nap." She wiggled her toes again and winked at me.

"I know all about your naps," I said, running my hand up her exposed calf and under her skirt to squeeze her knee.

She grinned and parted her legs a bit. "Don't stop on my account."

I looked around, suddenly beet red. She was way more brazen than I was, and she knew it. I pulled my hand off her knee and picked up my coffee.

"I thought we should talk to them, feel them out on the whole dragon connection."

A look of concern flashed across her face and she set her coffee on the table beside her. "I really like them," she said, almost pouting. "I don't want them to be crazy, evil people."

I totally got where she was coming from. "Qindra isn't evil."

"True," she said, nodding her head, "and Rolph is pretty okay."

"And Skella?"

"Oh, definitely," Katie agreed. "Skella is one of my favorites."

She studied me, the play going out of her face. "But that Gottschalk woman is bad news. And don't forget Justin."

I put my hand back on her knee and squeezed. Bad feelings, bad blood.

"I wonder if Cassidy will bring that torque?" I asked. He'd been wearing it the last time we saw him perform. I had a good idea it was old, Odin-in-his-prime old. I had a lot of questions for Mr. Stone.

"I may have mentioned it again," she said, slyly.

I ran my hand up her thigh again, causing her to catch her breath. "That's my girl."

She grinned at me as I leaned forward and kissed her. "No more hanky-panky," I said. "I need to get some knitting done. I'm making a present for Jai Li."

"Oh," she said, clapping. "Show me."

I set my empty coffee mug down on the table and picked up my knitting basket. And by basket, I meant the open-topped toolbox I'd picked up at the hardware store. It fit my style a lot better than the woven basket Edith used. I was knitting Jai Li a Mohawk. More of a modified earflap hat with an added fringe of multicolored yarn in a wide stripe running the length of the head from the forehead to the back of the neck.

"She's gonna love it," Katie said. I used all her favorite colors —that is, every brilliant color of yarn I could get. Right now, I was up to seven different ones. "I hope so."

Katie lay her head to the side against the back of the couch and just watched me knit for a long time. It was peaceful. She sipped her coffee and chattered about her day and I tried desperately not to drop any stitches. My hand was feeling pretty good these days. I hated to admit it, but the knitting really was good physical therapy. And my knitting had vastly improved. Not sure I was ready for anything as elaborate as socks yet.

After thirty minutes, she ran out of steam and I put my knitting aside. I rubbed her calves and brought up the harder subject. "We need to move out of Circle Q, consolidate into a place of our own," I said, looking into her suddenly stoic face. "I think we should move ahead on getting a new place. Someplace we can have a little room for Jai Li, maybe have a couple of bedrooms, you know?"

She didn't look totally happy. This wasn't a new subject. "I can teach again next year," she said. "I talked to Principal Nutter today. They're all on board with it."

That was new. She'd missed the end of last year, being in a coma and all.

"They're totally relieved I'm fine and not insane or wacked out on crack."

I raised my eyebrows at her, and she shrugged. "No one believes in magic, and the book is well hidden. Is there any reason I can't teach again next year?"

"Depends on where we live, I guess."

We'd discussed this on several occasions, but I understood her need for consistency; the way she loved her students. I could see giving up the movie shoot someday, but I wouldn't want to give up smithing or farrier work.

"Let's see what we can find and go from there," I offered.

"There's no reason we have to go anywhere extreme. Kent is not that far south."

"We'll see." That meant this conversation was over for now. She didn't want to start getting into an argument at this time. Later, perhaps.

"No worries," I agreed.

We sat in silence for a very long minute, each of us studying our mugs.

"So, guess why they called. The Harpers."

I looked up, confused. "I thought you said that they wanted to get together, to hang with us."

She shrugged. "That too, but listen." She leaned toward me and lowered her voice to conspiracy level tones. "Cassidy asked if it was safe to come back to Washington. If anyone had been asking after them or anything. I asked why, of course." She rolled her eyes. "Seriously. How narcissistic is that? Anyway, I explained that things were pretty quiet here. I didn't tell him about the attack on Circle Q. Didn't feel like something I should be sharing, you know?"

I nodded to her, just happy she'd taken a breath. I was beginning to wonder if she was on speed or something.

"I told him we could come watch you do your movie shoot, etcetera."

"I wonder what he was worried about."

"Who knows. Probably he and/or Maggie slept with someone's wife or something."

"Or maybe he's in tune with what's been going on around here lately." I sat up straight, "Or ..." I looked at her. "Maybe he's somehow mixed up with whatever Gottschalk's doing."

Her eyes went wide. "Or that necromancer bullshit?"

I had to think. There had been a lot of odd things going on since we saw them last in Vancouver. I fervently hoped they weren't involved with the damned blood cult.

But the dragons, maybe. That thought caused the runes on

my forehead to tingle. Not exactly spidey sense or anything, but I was probably on to something.

If he was involved with dragons somehow, was he worried about Qindra and Nidhogg? That would be easy enough to smooth over. Or ... There was that call I'd gotten from Mr. Philips. Could it be as simple as rumors of Frederick Sawyer's baby dragon girl? "Where have they been touring?"

"New Mexico, Colorado, and Arizona. But we're not even sure they're dragon people, are we?"

"Well, there is that picture Jai Li drew."

Katie thought about it for a minute. "We should definitely ask him about the torque," she said finally. "That's what you're most curious about."

I nodded. "Enough to ask a bunch of questions at least."

"First, we gotta survive this Bellingham punk show." She was grinning at me again. "I cleared it with Trisha. Jai Li can stay with her and the twins. Can we get a hotel room?"

It had been a while since we'd been alone together and healthy enough to mess around. It would be nice.

"Of course we can get a hotel."

"Exxxxxcellent," she said, tapping her fingers together like that old dude on *The Simpsons*.

Maybe I should be afraid.

CHAPTER SIXTEEN

I had a full day of solo farrier work on Thursday, which was a nice change. Not that I minded working with Julie, but the money was way nicer when I was solo. Jude Brown over at the Broken Axle had referred me to a new client. Guy from India named Mr. Rajashi Kateel, who had retired during the height of the tech bubble. He was nice enough and loved his animals, which was always a plus. I wouldn't be doing as much shoeing as normal this visit. Mainly trimming hooves and doctoring little things, basically seeing to each of the horses to get them used to me, used to being handled. And of course, give him a chance to see me, check me out, and make sure I was good enough to have around his animals. I respected that.

His horses were never used for work and rarely ridden. Mr. Kateel rode a couple of them, rotating out every few days. He just loved horses, wanted to watch them run from his living room window. The whole place was set up to watch those horses frolic. Overall, they were kept well and let to graze as much as anything.

We had a talk about his horses being barefoot or shod. I explained about the industry controversy over the two choices and explained my reasoning for preferring shod. We discussed the pros and cons of wet weather like we have up here, versus the drier climes like Texas.

It also came down to where he'd be riding the horses. They have better traction and footing in bare feet. So, for sand, snow, soft soil, wooded trails and such, bare feet work. Even concrete, if you keep the horse to a walk.

Also depended on the breed. Thoroughbreds and thoroughbred crosses such as Appendix Quarter Horses had notoriously soft feet and would go lame without being properly shod.

If the horses spent time in warm, dry climes, their hooves would get as tough as iron. Unfortunately, the Pacific Northwest was just too wet.

He said he'd think about it and appreciated my expertise. Good day, solid work, and a nice check at the end of it. I liked Mr. Kateel. He was a straight shooter and treated his animals like family.

Before I left, he asked me if I did anything besides farrier work. I ran through a list of things I'd done besides working with horses and he perked right up. He asked about some custom ironwork and wondered if I was interested.

We walked around his place for about an hour. He wanted to put in a garden: walkways, trellises, maybe some sculpture. He asked if I could give him a quote on a trellis. Something to start the project with. If that came out okay, we'd talk about doing some additional work.

He was great. I can't tell you how excited I was. I told him I worked with a couple other blacksmiths and that one of them had a lot of experience with sculpture. We agreed that I'd put some sketches together based on his ideas. He wanted lots of roses and horses worked into the motif. I promised him some sketches for the next time I visited in six weeks. Maybe things were starting to turn a corner. Was nice to get a new client for a change instead of losing one.

He watched me drive away, waving from his porch. I'd have to thank Mr. Brown for the recommendation.

CHAPTER SEVENTEEN

I got a good look at the new paint job as I pulled into Circle Q. The repairs were finally done. I say finally because it had been an inconvenience. If we'd been a normal customer, we'd still be waiting on bids. Hell, Mary had even gotten new appliances for the kitchen. Good to know people with connections.

I was climbing out of the truck, grabbing Gram and my saddlebags from behind the seat, when Katie grabbed me from behind. I turned to wrap my arms around her, getting a strong whiff of tiger balm and sweat.

"You been working out?" I asked, smiling down at her.

"Hell, yes," she said, stepping back. She was in sweats and a T-shirt. One of mine, no less. I could make out Angus Young's ugly mug just above her breasts. He never looked better.

"We're going to the concert tomorrow tonight," she said, turning to kiss the palm of my hand. "I'll get cleaned up and we'll have a quiet evening at home with Jai Li. Try and reach for some normal. What say?"

It was almost like she was reading my mind. The trip to Bellingham would be fun, especially with the concert and all, but ... "If you're wiped out, we can stay home," I said. "You're more important."

"I'm feeling stronger every day," she said, grinning at me. "I aim to misbehave."

I gave her a look and she laughed.

"We have an opportunity to get away for a night and enjoy ourselves," she said, shaking her head. "No way I'm letting that go. Never know when things are going to get jacked up again, you know?"

I nodded. I did know. She just described the last eighteen months.

That night we had one of the best nights in a long time. The place looked like futuristic robot Martha Stewart had exploded inside. Everything was immaculate. The couch had been replaced with one in a very nice burgundy leather. Two matching recliners flanked the couch, and the focal point of the living room proved to be a brand new sixty-inch flat screen television.

"Holy balls," I said, turning around in circles and looking at the place. "Where the hell did all this come from?"

Mary stepped out of the kitchen. "Thought if we were redoing things, we needed to bring us up to the twenty-first century."

I poked my head in the kitchen. Edith was stirring something on the stove. Smelled like cabbage. At least some things stayed the same. Julie sat at the new kitchen table drinking a cup of coffee and reading the paper.

"Good day?" she asked, folding the paper closed.

"Oh, yeah," I said. I'd only been gone ten hours. Qindra's people moved fast.

I told them all about Mr. Kateel and the ironwork he wanted. I pulled out a sketch pad and showed her a few things he and I had worked out. Pretty soon the whole household was crowded around the kitchen table, adding their two cents to my ideas. Jai Li even started a few sketches of her own, giving me some great ideas.

"Like the gate I made for Qindra," I said, pointing to one particular drawing. "Only you used horses instead of dragons."

Jai Li beamed.

I grabbed a shower and we all sat down to a hearty dinner of cabbage, pork roast, and fresh bread. All during the meal we commented about how great the place looked without all the bullet holes and construction. Mary laughed and said it looked better than the day she'd moved in. I could tell she was thrilled to have her house back. It may not really be our home, but it would do in the meantime.

After dinner, we let Jai Li pick the music and we played games. Mary and I knitted while Julie played rummy with Edith. I had a scarf to work on while I was around Jai Li. Didn't want to ruin her Mohawk surprise. Jai Li and Katie played Candy Land for a while, but eventually they ended up with rummy as well. It was brutal. After a bit, I put aside the knitting and got settled into a wicked game of three-way War with Jai Li and Katie. That child loved to slap the cards down. The delight in her eyes every time she did was priceless.

We had popcorn and cider, told stories, and generally enjoyed the peace of being surrounded by family and friends.

The night was so amazing that after everyone went to bed, I sat up in the living room with Gram on the couch beside me, watching the night through the big picture window and keeping an eye on the mirror over the couch. A night this peaceful had to be a precursor to something nasty. I kept expecting to see Skella or Gletts tumbling out of that mirror, chased by biters and eaters. Maybe I wasn't totally over my exploration of the Sideways after all.

At one A.M., Katie came and dragged me to bed. She even made me tuck Gram away. The house was still. Katie snuggled up against me and slipped off her PJs. She was all naked and warm. I pulled her against me, hugging her back to me, one hand over her breasts, and fell asleep. That night, for the first time in a very long time, I had no dreams at all.

The next day we packed an overnight bag, drove out to Black Briar and left Jai Li with Trish and the troll twins. Frick and

Frack were thrilled they were going to have a sleepover. They wanted Jai Li to play school with them and they'd already gotten every stuffed animal they could find and lined them up. We kissed Jai Li goodbye and hit the road.

We were meeting Carl and Jennifer in Bellingham at this great little pizza place on Railroad Avenue for an early lunch. I hoped it was still as good as it was when I'd gone to college. I'd convinced them to come scout Bellingham before the concert. I had a good feeling about doing some external shots up there for *Cheerleaders*. It would be awesome.

I'd called ahead and got a reservation at the hotel there by the airport on the north end of town. We got there a little early, so we checked into the hotel at 9:30 and messed around for an hour. To get in that early, we had to pay for an extra day, but it was totally worth it. We didn't get up to anything too serious; Katie didn't want to mess up her hair.

Railroad Avenue ended in a cul-de-sac with the pizza joint on the south side. When I'd been at Western, there'd been a used bookstore and a thrift clothing store. Now there was a Starbucks and an adult entertainment store. I grinned at Katie when we drove by it but parked on the opposite side of the parking lot from the adult store. Didn't want her getting any ideas. Places like that terrified me and thrilled me, not that I'd admit to either publicly.

Apparently, Carl had had the same idea, as he and Jennifer were just parking their car as well. We grabbed some awesome pie, chatted about the movie, Bellingham, punk rock, and raising kids. That last one was crazy, the blind leading the blind. Jennifer was definitely in the baby mood. Carl seemed on board, but I don't think either of them really knew what they were getting into.

As for the movie, they'd scouted the locations we'd discussed, confirming what I'd suggested the last time I was up this way.

"I've already contacted the city," Carl told me as we stood at the register to pay. Jennifer was out on the sidewalk chatting with Katie. I was happy to see them getting along so well. I liked socializing with them.

"We'll be able to start shooting here as soon as the permits come through," he said. "Think about props and such for the cheerleader-mutant rumble from the first act."

I'd already put a ton of time into that scene. "We're agreed, hand weapons only, right? No firearms."

Carl nodded as he handed the young guy behind the register his credit card. "Let us get this one," he glanced at me. "Flight Test can pick this up."

I shrugged, "Sure, thanks."

We left the shop well fed and happy. I was thinking about blocking and choreography for the fight scene. Maybe we should bring in some of the Black Briar folks as consultants. They'd be inexpensive and know their stuff.

The sky was a brilliant blue and the temperature was hovering around seventy. It was a gorgeous day and I was feeling fine.

Then Jennifer spoke up, and my stomach fell to my toes.

"Hey," she said, pointing. "Can we go check out that dildo store?"

Carl and I exchanged a look that spoke volumes. He was more terrified than I was.

Katie, of course, saw how I was reacting and got this huge grin on her face. "Absolutely. Always good to get some new ideas, shake things up a bit." She grabbed Jennifer by the elbow and started guiding her down the sidewalk. Jennifer looked back once, smiling, and Carl grew even paler.

"I'll wait by the car," he said. Coward.

"Me, too," I squeaked. Give me a dragon any day. Katie in a sex shop was mortifying.

We stood there, not really looking at each other, lost in our own thoughts. I'm pretty sure Carl liked sex nearly as much as I did, but I'd met his parents. I'm confident his upbringing highlighted the more private aspects of sex. Heck, my parents never even gave me *the talk*.

After five minutes I was getting worried. "You think it's safe to leave them in there too long?"

Carl's head snapped around. "You think they're talking?"

I just looked at him. "Seriously? Katie's in there. Jennifer is probably already talking about your favorite position."

We both blushed again.

"Oh, God," he said. "Maybe we should go in there, assess the situation."

I nodded. "Good idea."

He straightened up and got very serious. "This will be like Vegas, right, Beauhall? What happens here is never spoken of again."

I had to grin at him. Even I wasn't quite that uptight.

"Sure, boss. It's in the vault."

He nodded and turned, striding toward the shop like a man going to his execution.

Imagine my surprise when we walked in and Sprocket was behind the counter. I knew he had a job, but I had no idea it was here.

His face lit up when he saw me. "Hey, Sarah."

Jennifer and Katie were in the back looking at something that needed batteries. They turned as one, grinning. Jennifer handed Katie the fat, purple vibrator and walked over to Carl, kissing him on the cheek and dragging him back to the video section. He looked back once, panicked. I just gave him a little wave and turned to look at Katie.

She put the vibrator down and walked over to me.

"I'm going to look at the lingerie, you should at least say hello to Sprocket. He's anxious to talk to you."

She patted me on the ass and turned, sashaying over to the section of crotchless panties. That girl had no shame.

I went to the counter and tried to avoid looking at the flavored lubricant display. "Hey, Sprocket. How's it going?"

He shrugged. "Katie said you were scared to come in here." He was grinning. "Glad to see you overcome that fear."

"Every day's a growth experience."

"You got that right." He looked around the shop; we were the only ones in the place. He leaned against the counter and his face got serious. "Skella says I can trust you. Says you have good insight into weird behavior."

"How weird?" I asked. "You work in a sex shop."

"Nothing like that." He looked sad all of a sudden, concerned. "Two more kids on campus have committed suicide."

Ouch, that sucked. "Friends of yours?"

"First guy was just an acquaintance, not close."

"And the second?"

"Yeah, I knew him." His shoulders slumped. "He lived in the boarding house with us."

"Oh, right. Skella told me. That's hard."

He began straightening up the bottles of lube, keeping his hands busy. "Guy was quiet, didn't get out much socially. We just thought he was a good student, always studying."

"Well, it's a college. Seems reasonable."

"Yeah," he said, glancing up at me. "He was gay but didn't seem like he was taking shit for it or anything. Western is pretty tolerant about that. He dated a bit and seemed happy."

I wasn't sure why he was telling me this. Tragic, but I wasn't a counselor. "Why did Skella say you should talk to me about this?"

He glanced at me again, then away. Furtive. "You'll think I'm crazy."

"I don't know," I said, honestly. "My life has had some pretty strange moments. I doubt you'd even move the needle."

He smiled at that, gaining some courage. "I think the suicides are linked. I think they all have something in common."

I thought about it a minute. "After Ginny killed herself, there was an opening, a period of time that the suicide taboo had been broken and others could see it as a viable solution to their problems. Pretty quickly, public sentiment shuts that line of thinking down. But once that window is opened, it's not uncommon for several more to take that way out."

I was proud of myself. I'd read that in college. Psych 101.

He looked thoughtful. "Makes sense, I guess. I just think there's something more there. I think they are all tied in another way."

"Like a suicide pact or something?"

"Maybe." He shrugged and pursed his mouth like he'd tasted something sour. "More than that, I think."

"I don't know—" I began.

"Never mind," he said, waving his hands. "I'm just upset. It's probably nothing."

I reached over and patted him on the arm. "Suicide is hard on everyone."

"Yeah."

"Sarah?" I looked over. Katie was calling me, holding a baby-doll nightie set up to herself. "What do you think?"

Sprocket chuckled. "Any chance we can talk about this more later?"

"Sure. We're going to the concert tonight. Maybe we can all get drinks after."

"Oh, right. Hey, you could all come back to our place. Mimi would love to see you again."

"Sounds good." I started to turn, but a thought struck me. "You folks want to grab dinner around five? I've been dying for a decent burger."

"Sure," Sprocket said. "Dinner before, drinks after."

We agreed to meet at Tamatio, a really awesome organic joint a block away from the concert venue. They had fast service. We'd have enough time to eat before heading to the show.

Katie had taken a thong off a rack and was holding it up, pointing to me. Oh, hell no. "I'd better go stop her from committing a fatal lapse of judgment," I said, mortified. What the hell was she thinking? Me in a thong?

"Tonight, then," he said, waving me away.

"Definitely." I turned and walked to Katie. Jennifer and Carl were still going through movies in the back, but I saw that Jennifer had a few in her hand, had already made her selection. I was afraid to know what.

Katie tortured me for another fifteen minutes before sending me off to pick out a movie. She said either I chose one I was comfortable with, or she'd choose one and I may not survive the first viewing. I didn't have much exposure to porn, but I knew a threat when I heard one.

Carl and Jennifer were over looking at things that appeared suspiciously like handcuffs when I walked by, but at least he was looking happy, if a little glazed over. I think they had a hotel room in town as well. I hoped they still made the concert later.

I avoided anything that involved nurses. We'd spent way too much time in hospitals. Instead I opted for something all-girl with a plot. The cover promised real orgasms. Seemed like a good choice.

Katie took the video and told me to meet her at the car. She wanted to surprise me with something. God only knows what she was up to. I'm sure it would be terrifying and amazing.

As I walked out, Sprocket watched me, his face intent. There was something about the way he looked at me, something familiar. It was a feral look, part desperation and part determination. I'd seen it a few times on the faces of those who went into battle, fearful that they'd be killed, but determined to do their best.

I smiled at him and waved. He nodded back but didn't wave. Definitely a sense of finality there. It was strange how deadly serious that look was, how anxious it made me. And damned odd with him standing amid the corsets and dildos.

CHAPTER EIGHTEEN

We met at Tamatio just before five and grabbed some excellent food—all organic—killer shakes, plenty of ambiance. The Hamsters showed up as a herd; six of them moved across the place like a blessing. They seemed to know everyone and moved from table to table shaking hands or hugging every person. It was surreal. I wouldn't have thought they'd be that popular—considered them more of the outcast crew like I'd been. Funny how public perceptions shifted over time.

I didn't think Bianca had ever spoken in her life, at least not that I'd heard so far. She hovered in the back and smiled and nodded. Lilith was the tallest and shepherded the others, keeping an eye on them like a kindergarten teacher herding her wards. Dante was a riot, short and broad like a football player; he had a biting wit and a keen eye for irony. I think the biggest issue he had was in the self-esteem department.

Sprocket was the class all-star. Fearless and daring, not afraid to moon the room as quickly as give out hugs. Total ham. That left the married couple—Scarlett and Brian. Brian was in the band we were going to see. His wife, Scarlett, had set aside the killer mom routine for the evening and had slipped into total smoking hottie. They were so damn cute together.

During dinner, Sprocket talked about the suicides and Dante got quieter and quieter. At one point, when Lilith was trying to steer the conversation to the concert later that night and who was watching Scarlett's and Brian's kids, Dante left the group, excusing himself to go to the bathroom.

Sprocket motioned to me with his head, toward the soft drink dispenser. I got up and followed him to the soda fountain. Like a fourteen-year-old, he took a little of each of the non-diet drinks. We used to call those a "suicide." I didn't miss the irony.

"I'm worried about Dante," he said finally, taking a long pull on his straw. "Can you check on him?"

I looked toward the bathroom. "Sure. You know, as soon as he gets done with his business."

Sprocket just shrugged and ambled back to the table. I stood there, pretending to decide on what soda to drink. I'd had a chocolate shake, and the only thing that went with chocolate was root beer, so there you go. Instant chocolate cow.

Dante came out shortly after. I asked him how he'd been, what was new in his life, made chit-chat. Basically, I got nothing. He was obviously worried about something. I asked him how the crew was taking the multiple suicides and he just shrugged. Said that people were free to do what they thought best. It was a free country.

"I don't think it was free if it hurt other people."

He studied me a minute and shrugged again. "Whatever," he said and meandered back to the crowd.

Sprocket was watching us. Dante was looking more at his feet than the table ahead of him, so he likely didn't notice the worried look Sprocket gave me. When had I become den mother to this crew?

CHAPTER NINETEEN

After dinner we headed over to the concert venue, a fairly large campus bar, with an honest to goodness mosh pit. I was excited.

Brian's band, Pawnbroker, opened. They did some covers—Beatles, Jimi Hendrix, Led Zeppelin—intermingled with some originals. Katie dug them, though it wasn't really moshing music. I wasn't sure why a band like this would open for a punk band, and some of the other attendees agreed.

There was this one guy, head and shoulders bigger than me, who was bitching between songs. Pawnbroker had just finished "Trampled Underfoot" by Zeppelin when the guy started spouting off. Sprocket, who's only about five-two, got into this guy's space, telling him to shut the fuck up. At first the guy laughed and pushed Sprocket away, but the rest of the Hamsters moved in. They were like a hunting pack. My alarms started going off. I didn't really know these kids, but I had the feeling they were no strangers to trouble.

Sure enough, the second the big guy took a swing at Sprocket, Lilith darted in, kicked the guy in the back of the knee, and, as he crumpled, Dante clocked him with a haymaker.

Katie rolled her eyes at me as the big guy's buddies jumped

in. The Hamsters were going to get murderlated, but they were asking for no quarter.

I waded in, pulling Bianca off the guy she had straddled, knees on either side of his neck, punching him in the face.

The big guy had gotten up, knocked Lilith to the ground, and kicked her. I grabbed his arm just before he could punch Dante, and I was in full swing.

The band stopped at one point, but Brian called another song and they launched into a raucous number called "Wednesday's Child."

The fight only lasted a few more minutes. Soon everyone was lying around on chairs, nursing bleeding noses and scrapes and bruises. No one had drawn weapons, and no one had called the cops.

By the time the Rats of New York City came on stage, everyone had become friends. It was the strangest thing. I think they all just needed to get into a fight. People are weird.

The mosh pit lived up to my expectations once the Rats started raging. We had a blast.

Afterwards Katie told me it was like dealing with little kids. They'd be fighting one minute and best friends the next. Too bad we couldn't resolve all our battles with beers after. Of course, I never offered the giants or trolls a pint before we went to weapons. Maybe that would be a better way to start.

Once the house lights were up and folks got down to hard drinking, I excused myself to the bathroom. I was driving, so I didn't want to drink anymore. Besides, we were heading over to the boarding house at some point and I'd drink a little more there.

As I was passing the pay phones—hey, they still had pay phones—I saw a young poser leaning against the wall, his face in shadows. He was dressed like a thug, ball cap, hoodie, jeans halfway down his ass. I was about to write him off as a loser when he turned and the light hit his face just right. It was Charlie Hague from the Order of Mordred folks.

"Hey," I said, crossing my arms over my chest and leaning back against the wall, out of his personal space. "You doing okay?"

He straightened up quickly and leaned forward. "Sarah?"

"Yeah, Sarah. I've been trying to get ahold of you. Glad to see you're alive." I said. "Was hoping you'd have returned one of my calls." I was pissed at Gottschalk and wanted to know what Charlie knew. He hadn't warned us, so maybe he didn't know. Or maybe he wasn't as reliable as I'd hoped. Seeing him here was an odd coincidence, though. I didn't like to think he was sneaking around, following us, reporting our activities. It was creepy.

"I wasn't allowed ..." He shrugged. "Things are hinky at the moment."

I bet. What could he say really? Gottschalk was using him like a Muppet. "You following us now?"

"I haven't been following you," he said, straightening up. "I'm up here for the concert."

I wasn't sure I believed him, but what did I know? "You know what went down last week? Any major operations?"

He looked at me, confused. "Operations? Hell, I can barely get them to give me the time of day. Been busy at work, though." He was petulant and a little drunk. "Things with Mordred are all fucked up right now. No one knows which way is up." He threw up his hands. "It's complicated, they keep telling me. Shit, I know it's complicated. I'm not a moron." He was getting louder, angry.

I'd never seen him like this. But I wasn't around him all that much.

"You know I was never supposed to talk to you. Only Katie or Jimmy."

That was interesting news. Did I frighten this Madame Gottschalk? Was I a liability for some reason? I started to ask when a shadow blocked the light and a deep voice spoke from behind me.

"Is this guy hassling you?"

I glanced around and saw the hunky surfer dude from the Doc Marten's store. "No, just chatting," I said, showing him my pearly whites. "I know Charlie here from horse circles."

"My condolences," the dude said. "By the way, I'm Mark." He held his hand out to me. "I sold you those Docs, right?"

I turned to face him and shook his hand. "Sarah," I said. "You know this guy?"

Mark nodded. "Charlie's my roommate."

I glanced back at Charlie. Secret society stuff on a budget? Interesting. How private could his secret life be from a roommate?

I turned back to Mark. "So. How you been doing since your girlfriend, you know ..." I trailed off. The last time I'd been in the Doc Marten store, he told me she'd dumped him.

"She hooked up with some guy from up in Everett. He's got a steady job, making real money. You know the type."

"Yeah, real upstanding citizen," Charlie said. "She's a loser, man. You gotta let that go."

Mark just sighed. He was clenching and unclenching his fists. Charlie was currently undergoing a near-death experience and he was totally clueless.

"Hey," Sprocket called from the hallway back to the main club. "We're going back to our place for drinks. Bring your friends."

Charlie looked over at the crowd, then glanced back at me. "Do you think you could hook me up with that hot girl?"

I followed his gaze and saw he was looking at Bianca. I laughed. "It's a free country. Give it your best shot."

"Fine," Mark said, "but if you get drunk and throw up on that girl, you can find your own way back to Seattle."

Charlie looked hurt but excited.

And away we went. I had to remember Charlie was younger than Katie. Fresh out of school and eager. Order of Mordred aside, he seemed pretty naïve just now, too young and too green for the horseshit he was embroiled in. A fish out of water.

I got back in line for the restroom and Mark leaned in. "You'll have to forgive Charlie. He's usually not such a douchebag. He's having trouble at work, and he's a little drunk."

I shrugged. "It happens. As long as he doesn't make a pass at me or Katie, I'm fine with him making a fool out of himself."

Mark smiled, but I could tell he wasn't fine with it. Mark would be protecting Charlie. He was a good roommate.

By the time I got out of the little girl's room, Katie was chatting up Mark and Sprocket. Charlie hung back on the periphery of the conversation. I did catch that he made sure to be out of punching distance from Katie. Smart boy. I slid up, snaked my arm around Katie's waist, and pulled her close to me.

"We ready?" I asked, smiling all around.

"Follow us," Sprocket said, heading to the door of the club. "It's in the southwest part of town. Not that far, really."

We followed him out. All the rest of the Hamsters were standing around Dante's car, chatting up the guys they'd fought with earlier in the night. Apparently, the guys had to head back to campus, but they were planning a party some other time.

It was after ten by the time we followed Dante's car to the older part of town. The further we drove, the larger the houses got. Some of them were being refurbished—gentrified. Looked like a respectable neighborhood.

Katie didn't say much on the drive—I had a Godsmack CD in the player, and she was singing along. Definitely not her music, but she was sexy as hell singing it.

CHAPTER TWENTY

We all ended up back at the boarding house where both Dante and Sprocket lived. The place was an old Victorian mansion with a huge wraparound porch and a tower on one corner. It was awesome. The kitchen was huge and we all sat around the table drinking beer, tea, soda, whatever, and just talking. I really liked these kids. They had some amazing ideas about how the world worked.

Mark and Charlie got along well with the others. Blended right in. I think it was something about Bianca, frankly. Charlie tried to hold her attention, but she moved around the conversation, sometimes literally following the thread and nodding a lot, really giving the speaker her undivided attention. It seemed to bolster the room. No one was afraid to speak their mind to her. I found myself relaxing and really getting into the swing of things.

As the evening progressed, Mimi, the house owner and real den mother of this crew, came down to join us. I was confused by Mimi. The Hamsters all referred to her as a *her*, but I was pretty sure she was a guy. The whole cross-dressing aspect was not something I had experience with, and I didn't really know the protocol. Basically, I thought about how my father would react in the situation and figured that was the wrong approach.

We sang songs, relived the battles of the night and swapped stories about college. It was like hanging out with the Black Briar crew, but with more piercings. Mimi had a great singing voice—we learned that at karaoke. She was a gracious host and had a bit of a beard ... at least some fairly obvious stubble. Then there was the Adam's apple.

Around midnight, Mimi excused herself and left us to our devices. We were thinking about heading out on our own—hotel room calling and all that. But I was confused about something, and I knew this crew would be open to my ignorance.

Maybe I'd ask Dante quietly. He was a stoic guy.

"At the risk of being a total dumbass," I began, looking toward Katie for support. "Is, um ..."

Every head in the room turned to me like they had been waiting for me to slip up all night. I was suddenly skittish. There were some things you didn't discuss. Lines you didn't cross in good company. Would they react with kindness and understanding, or would they ridicule me? "... well, I was curious. Is Mimi a guy?"

Sprocket raised one bright green and pierced eyebrow in my direction. He had a half smile on his face but didn't say anything. The room grew quiet. Even Charlie Hague, who'd been hitting on Bianca with absolutely no success, looked over.

"You know, like a transvestite or something?" I wasn't being a smart-ass.

Bianca pulled a wincing face and Lilith tutted at me, but no one laughed or swore.

"Well," Dante said, the first to break the silence. "A transvestite, or transgendered as we prefer to use these days, is someone who self-identifies as a gender other than what they were born with."

He pointed at me. "Cisgendered. You identify as a girl," he pointed to Sprocket. "He identifies as male."

But wasn't Sprocket a guy? I was really confused.

We spent the next hour discussing the difference between

gender and sexuality. Lilith spoke up, explaining her take on being queer. The more I heard, the more I realized that none of it mattered and all of it mattered. The whole gamut of LGBTQIAPK (there were more letters there than I was used to) was about accepting people for who they were regardless of how they were born, who they loved, or what society thought about them. Wasn't that exactly how I'd been feeling my whole life? How was this any different?

Made me think of the dragons. They could change their form, be different when they chose. Us mere mortals had to live with the hand we were dealt—surgery and hormones notwithstanding. It was all complicated and vitally important all at the same time.

Mimi was a woman as far as they were all concerned. There was no real need to question how she may have been born. She was a lovely person who kept a nice, safe place for the queer kids in town. Part dormitory, part frat house.

I took some shit for being a lesbian and being so out of touch with the other letters under the LGBTQIAPK umbrella. It was gentle and loving. We didn't spend a whole lot of time on the subject. They answered my questions and we moved on. It was far less traumatic than I'd expected. Sprocket moved on to graphic novels and we were lost in the next great controversy.

Mark got into the swing of the conversation. The Hamsters took to him like a brother. He knew some esoteric manga shit that Bianca and Lilith thought was fabulous. Charlie, on the other hand, had struck out with Bianca, drank a couple more beers, and fell asleep with his head on the kitchen table.

Around one in the morning, Sprocket put down his tea and jiggled the thread of conversation. "You ever hear about that study they did with Olympic athletes back in the eighties? This group of researchers asked more than one hundred high-end athletes if they could each be given a shot that would guarantee they won gold in their events, but it took ten years off their lives, would they do it."

And once again we were off, arguing and speculating on the absurdity of the survey. Who would give up ten years of their life? "The funny thing was," Sprocket said, "every single one of the athletes said they'd take the shot."

I couldn't imagine wanting something that badly. Was there anything in my life I'd be willing to sacrifice for some short-term glory? I thought of Megan again, of Ma and Da. Had I sacrificed them to have the life I needed or wanted?

Dante, funny enough, got really angry. He shoved back his chair, told Sprocket it was a stupid fucking point and stormed out of the room.

We were all stunned. Well. Almost all of us. Sprocket had a satisfied smirk on his face. What the hell was that about? Old argument, maybe?

Bianca got up and paced for a few minutes, wringing her hands and rolling her shoulders as she walked. I watched her for a bit, making sure she didn't do something crazy. Lilith watched her out of the corner of her eye, but they let her have her space. Eventually she went to the back door, wrenched it open, and strode out into the back yard.

I got up and went to the door. The house was the last one on the drive and backed up to the bluff overlooking the Bellingham Bay. Ginny had jumped off a similar bluff just a short while ago, dying on the rocks below. Not the best thing to remember at a time like this.

The back yard ran back about sixty feet, ending with a short fence to stop anyone from going over the cliff and into the bay. I bet this place was worth a pretty penny with that kind of view. Bianca was out near the edge of the property, pacing beside a small wooden structure that barely came up to her waist. She didn't touch it, just paced its length; over and over, pace, turn, pace.

I crossed the porch and took the stairs down two at a time, "Hey, you okay?"

She didn't look up, just kept pacing along that little structure.

It made me anxious. I thought maybe I should go back in the house and let one of the others look after her. As I turned to go back up the stairs the runes on the back of my left calf flared into sharp burning pain, warning me of pending action. I dropped to my knees, grasping my calf and swearing. Unfortunately, the runes along my scalp remained quiet, not giving me a clue as to the problem. Typical and cryptic.

Behind me I heard Bianca mumbling something. At least I think it was her. I'd never heard her actually talk.

Lilith came out onto the porch. "Sarah? You okay?"

And just like that the pain vanished. I looked up and she was coming down the stairs, looking past me. "Come inside, Bianca," she said passing me like a breeze. "Sprocket is sorry he upset Dante. You need to come in so we can get some sleep."

Neither Lilith nor Bianca drove, so I supposed they were staying over. When I stood up, Lilith had her arms around Bianca's shoulders and was guiding her toward the stairs.

She smiled at me as she passed, her face half in shadows. It wasn't creepy but it was strange. They weren't lovers, Lilith had told me that earlier in the evening. She had a regular boyfriend. Bianca was like a sister. I followed them into the house, the memory of the pain in my calf fading. Just before I went through the door, I thought I saw a flash behind me from near the small outbuilding in the shadows. Out over the bay a light blinked and I realized it was an airplane. That had to be what had caught my attention. I walked into the kitchen and closed the door. Bianca and Sprocket were hugging and Dante stood in the hallway watching us, his arms crossed over his chest. Mark was helping Charlie to his feet, making sure his cap was on his head.

As I watched them the runes on my scalp tickled briefly, nothing like the sudden volume of pain that had shot through my calf just moments ago. More of a low-level buzzing like putting your tongue on a nine-volt battery. Katie slid her hand over my ass and into one of the jeans pockets. I liked her hands on me.

This was a good crew—strange, but who was I to judge. Look at the lunatics I hung out with on a regular basis.

By the time we said our goodbyes everyone was fine. Mark got Charlie poured into his car and they drove off. Lilith made them promise to come back and Mark assured them they would. I was really surprised how mundane and pathetic Charlie had been all night. Maybe the secret society schtick wasn't everything they made it out to be in movies. Seemed like belonging to a really boring but stressful club.

By two in the morning Katie and I said our goodbyes and headed to the truck. As I was backing down the long drive I noticed a gift-wrapped package behind the seat.

"What's this?" I asked, stopping the truck on the street and pulling the package out. Katie took it out of my hand.

"For later," she said, grinning. She placed it in the seat by the door and scooted over to sit right up against me.

I put the truck in first and my hand brushed the inside of her knee.

"Go through town," she said, breathing in my ear. "I like it when you shift."

CHAPTER TWENTY-ONE

B y the time I put the truck into park at the hotel, Katie was bouncing in her seat. She kissed me while the engine pinged and cooled. After a minute, I managed to come up for air long enough to suggest we move inside.

She scooted across the bench seat, grabbed the wrapped package, and went dancing her way across the parking lot. I strode after her, anticipation building inside me. I slid my key card into the door and stepped into the back hallway of the hotel, aware of all the doors lining the hall. I'd lost my buzz hours ago, but my legs were feeling a little rubbery. My jeans were chafing a bit, and I needed to get out of them as soon as possible. Katie was already out of sight.

By the time I got into the room and threw the locks, Katie was standing in the middle of the room dressed only in her blouse. Her jeans, shoes, socks, panties and bra were scattered around the room.

"Open it," she said, her voice husky. Her breasts were rising and falling as she breathed, doing very interesting things to that shirt. It barely covered her more interesting assets.

I tore the paper off the package and opened a thin box you'd expect to find shirts in. There were no shirts in there. Instead I found a long silk robe. I took it out by the collar and let it drop open in front of me. It was red with a dragon running the length of the back. It wasn't like Jean-Paul, Frederick, or Nidhogg. This dragon was more eastern; Chinese characters ran down each short sleeve.

It was beautiful.

I'd been expecting something crazy and sexual, but this was erotic in a way I wasn't used to. Definitely not something I'd have purchased for myself.

"Do you like it?" she asked.

I looked up at her. "I love it."

She clapped her hands. "Awesome. Go try it on. I'll wait here."

She fell back on the bed, leaning back on both elbows. The shirt she was wearing no longer provided any cover. God, she was hot. And it had been way too long since we'd had any quality alone time.

"Hurry up," she said, winking.

I set the box on the desk by the door and carried the robe into the bathroom. I undressed as quick as I could. It seemed to take forever to get my boot untied, but quick enough I was standing in front of the mirror wearing nothing but the silk robe. It came just below my hips, giving me a modicum of cover, if I didn't do anything like move or breathe. Then you got the best view in the house.

I turned around, glancing over my shoulder to see the dragon in the mirror. For a second, I wondered if Gletts was watching us again, but put that thought aside. Boy was barely recovering. Hell, it would be good news if he was up and being his typical stalker self.

I opened the bathroom door and stood with one hand on the doorframe and the other on my hip. I know it was a pose, but I was feeling damned sexy.

"Don't move," Katie said, sitting up. She put her feet on the floor, scooting to the edge of the bed with her hands hanging down between her knees. She watched me, her eyes big and round.

"Sarah Jane Beauhall. You are the most beautiful woman I've ever known."

I blushed, feeling the heat rise up my chest and neck.

"Can I move now?" I asked, overwhelmed with the need to touch her.

"Oh, yeah," she said, standing and walking toward me. "I've got a few ideas how you should move."

She crossed to me and pulled the tie free on the robe, letting it fall open. She stepped back, taking my hands in hers, and looking me up and down, a feral look on her face. "I want to do very bad things to you right now," she said, growling.

I grinned and she kissed me. I had my arms around her and we stepped around, almost dancing. Finally, she jumped up, wrapping her legs around my waist, and I cupped her ass in my hands, holding her against me.

I'd needed to be kissing her like this for far too long.

We fell back onto the bed and I let her set the pace. She was urgent and needful, wanting to touch every inch of me, kissing me, biting, licking.

For a moment I marveled at the way the silk felt on my skin, then I let the fire consume me.

CHAPTER TWENTY-TWO

We checked out of the hotel by eleven and made our way south to Black Briar to pick up Jai Li. The evening had been the best in a long time. Katie had more stamina than I thought she would, but we burned through it at a frenetic pace. She'd recovered enough in the morning to mess around in the shower. She really loved that. I've had several very memorable showers with her.

On the way, Katie got a call from Edith. Turned out that Jai Li had woken in the early hours of the morning with a very disconcerting nightmare, and was so upset, that Deidre had gotten ahold of Skella to transport the girl to Circle Q.

When we pulled into the yard, Edith came out onto the porch, her hands covered in flour. She told us that Jai Li was out in the barns with Mary.

Edith stood, watching Katie until she grabbed all our gear and carried it into the house.

"Be cautious with the child," Edith said to me, nodding sagely. "She has visions, some true, some like those of a normal child."

"Should I be worried?" I asked.

Edith shrugged. "She didn't ask for either of you, if that tells you anything. She said she needed to help Mary work with the horses." She let a smile grace her face for a moment. "She is a sweet girl. We are all lucky to have her in our lives."

Then she turned and went back into the house.

"Borscht and pirozhki for lunch," she called over her shoulder and let the screen door slam behind her.

I shuddered. How much beet soup could I stomach to not hurt her feelings? Sometimes I think she cooked things just to punish me. I thrust my hands in my pockets and made my way to the barn, hang-dog and sullen.

Jai Li rushed out to see me, bounding around the barn door so unexpectedly that she nearly bowled me over. I managed to get my hands out of my pockets and caught her, going to one knee and hugging her all in one motion. She giggled against my neck and the world brightened once again. Then, she pulled away, signed for me to wait and rushed back into the barn. I strode through the door, remembering I needed to burn some sage and lavender in here to keep the horses from being spooked by the violent death we'd had recently, but the place felt just fine.

Mary appeared in the doorway of one of the stalls, a long broom in her hand, and smiled.

"She's been as jumpy as a toad since two this morning," she said, wiping her forehead with the back of her hand. "She's all fired up to show you something."

She turned and we both watched as Jai Li rushed out of the last stall, digging through her pack as she scampered. She always carried paper, pencils, crayons, and needlepoint supplies wherever she went. She ran back, launched herself against my legs and hugged me, a piece of paper crumpled in her tiny fist.

I squatted down and hugged her. Her hair was silky against my cheek as she wrapped her arms around my neck and squeezed with all her might. She was a strong one for her size. You always knew when she hugged you, once you could breathe again.

After a heartbeat, she pulled back and tapped me on the

forehead, then tapped the paper she held in her hand. I took it and straightened it out.

It was a slick flyer on heavy paper with a guy's face on the front. He was handsome, about my age, with dark hair and eyes. Da would say he looked like a shyster.

The caption read:

Are you and your better half fighting over what kind of house to buy? We understand. You'll love our low-key approach to solving the age-old problem of combining households.

We guarantee to find something to fit everyone in your family. We take the stress out of finding that perfect home. Give us a call.

We are Low Key Realty.

I looked at her and groaned. "Low Key Realty, really?"

She signed *yes* twice and tapped the page, then my head again.

"We can call him," I said, smiling.

She looked relieved and hugged me again before craning her neck to look back at Mary.

I followed her gaze. "You trying to get rid of us?" I asked.

"Of course not," Mary said, "but your little gal there says you and Katie have been fighting about a new place, right?"

I just nodded, feeling Jai Li squeezing me tighter.

Mary leaned her broom against the door of the stall and walked toward us, wiping her hands on a bandana. "Someone out at Black Briar had picked that up when they did a grocery run. Your girl there saw it and about had a conniption. She insisted this was exactly what you both needed." She patted me on the shoulder. "Just go with it. What do you have to lose?"

"Your sparkling company and Edith's dazzling cooking," I said, poking Jai Li in the ribs. She giggled and squirmed away.

Mary rolled her eyes. "Borscht isn't that bad once you get used to it. It's good for you."

Jai Li nodded and rubbed her belly, making nummy noises.

"Traitor," I said, grinning. I picked up Jai Li and carried her into the house. "You sure you want to move away from here?" I asked her.

She nodded, grinning like a cat. She signed *home*.

"Yes, of course," I said, tickling her. "You are always right."

She was giggling as we went into the house. Katie stood at the end of the hallway, watching us with her arms crossed over her chest, her head tilted against the doorframe. She had a warm smile on her face which made me feel good all over.

"What's so funny?" she asked as we walked up to her.

I handed her Jai Li, who went to her right away, hugging her and kissing her on the cheek. Then she reached back, took the paper from my hand and held it in front of Katie's face.

Katie lowered Jai Li to the ground, laughing, and took the paper.

"Low Key Realty?" She looked at me, her eyebrows lost in her hairline.

I grinned at her and shrugged.

Jai Li tugged on her shirt and signed *home*.

Katie knelt down and cupped Jai Li's cheeks in her hands and kissed her on the nose.

"You are brilliant," she said. "Any special requests before we talk to these people?"

Jai Li nodded vigorously and ran back toward the kitchen. Mary was walking through the door with the girl's satchel. Jai Li grabbed it, hugged Mary around the waist, and ran back down the hall toward us. She squatted down in the hallway, rifled through the papers, pulling out several drawings and thrusting them into Katie's hands.

"Very wicked," Katie said, passing me the first picture.

There was a large house with a barn and several other outbuildings. The house was purple with yellow trim and a green door. There were horses in the back and the entire front had a long fence covered in roses.

No way I'd ever be able to afford a place like that, but it was good to know the girl had a dream.

"Well," I said, sitting in the middle of the hallway and pulling Jai Li into my lap. "These are beautiful. I hope we can find something like this someday."

She shook her head and tapped the paper, signing, *this one. Only this one.*

"We'll start looking tomorrow," Katie said, patting Jai Li on the head and kneeling with us. "It may take a while. Some things can't be rushed."

Okay, she signed. She climbed out of my lap at the sound of the door, snatched the papers away, and ran down the hallway to Julie, who'd just come in carrying several bags of groceries.

"Hey, you two lovebirds wanna help carry in supplies?"

Katie looked at me, slipped her hand in mine, and kissed me on the cheek. "Sure," she said, pulling me up off the floor.

I watched them as we exited the house; there were six of us here, all women, and the world was not a very scary place at the moment. I thought back to Odin haunting Charlie Hague, witches, secret societies, and suicides.

We are a restless species, always desperate to understand something we likely won't and never satisfied with what we have.

I just wished I could bottle this moment, keep it on a shelf to be treasured forever. But that was selfish and silly. We had our lives, Jai Li had to grow up, and we had to find a way to live in the world the way it was.

But for this moment, I was content to be unpacking a pickup full of groceries and stacking canned goods in a pantry while laughter and warmth flowed around me.

I needed to drive out to Crescent Ridge, see Megan again. Maybe even risk seeing Ma. She'd love it here. This was the home she'd tried to make. She just couldn't contend with my anger and Da's fear.

By the time we had the groceries put away and had shared a lovely lunch, we had laundry running and set about doing chores. I went back out to the barn to help Mary finish cleaning out the stalls while Katie sat with Jai Li to work on her reading.

After the stalls were clean, I went out into the dirt yard between the barn and the house and went through my Tae Kwon Do forms. It had been a while and I was feeling the need to knock the rust off. By the time I was done I was winded and sweating, which was a damn fine feeling. Maybe we needed to start Jai Li in some martial arts. She was old enough. I'd have to discuss it with Katie.

We had a couple of hours to kill before we had to go meet the Harpers over in Seattle. This weekend was getting better and better. I'd go catch a shower and a nap. Didn't get enough sleep last night, but it was totally worth it.

CHAPTER TWENTY-THREE

We arrived at the Thistle and Pipe just after six. We had to push our way through a throng of smokers and were inundated with the stench of weed. Walking through the front doors, you wouldn't realize the size of the place. It was longer than wide and set in among the oddly shaped buildings a couple of blocks from Pike Place. A sign at the front said it used to be a carriage house. The atmosphere smelled of old wood, fresh baked bread, and a lingering tinge of wood smoke. The usual underlying reek of stale beer I had expected was missing—no sawdust on the floors here to soak up spills. This was definitely a more refined establishment than I typically favored.

The bar itself ran the length of the room, a beauty of intricate carvings and dark wood. There was even a brass foot railing running along the length of it just like in the old timey bars. The stage sat in the far back, at least eighty feet from the doors. Music was important, but getting to the alcohol took precedence. A good thirty people were seated at tables and more were streaming in through the doors. We scored a table in the front, far enough from the stage that we could carry on a conversation and out of the draft from the opening front doors.

Cassidy and Maggie showed up soon after. One of the

bartenders, a young man with shaggy black hair and two full sleeves of tattoos, called out to them by name as they entered, and a group of the crowd cheered. I guess they played the joint from time to time. Cassidy just waved at the young man, shaking his head at the call for them to play tonight.

"Just here for a drink and some company, Fergus," the older man said, his voice booming across the room.

A groan rose from the crowd at the news. Several people in the crowd stood from their seats to see who the Harpers were meeting. Katie basked in the attention, but I wanted to crawl under the table.

Cassidy stopped at the table and flung his arms wide. "Katie, my love. Aren't you a sight to behold." He stepped to her and pulled her into a bear hug.

"Leave the girl be," Maggie said, coming around toward me. She stuck out her hand and I rose, giving it a good shake. "How are ya, Sarah?"

And like that we were four old friends, laughing and talking like we'd known each other our whole lives. My initial trepidation about meeting them dissolved at the sound of Katie's laughter. They were both charming and disarming in equal measures. No wonder so many people called out to them as the night went on.

We settled in with four orders of fish and chips, and our first round of drinks. Things were going along merrily until a pipe band walked on stage. Then things went deathly silent. Maggie would not participate in any conversation while the pipes were playing, said it was sacrilegious. So, we got down to drinking and listening. Katie beamed and a few of the patrons got up and began dancing. They played a twenty-minute set and left the stage to a roaring cheer. Only then would Maggie give us any of her attention.

I had to admit, they were very cool people, full of stories about music and being on the road. The whole time Katie was leaning forward, her chin on her fists, drinking in more stories than beer. It was cute to watch. Cassidy had his awesome Scottish accent and Maggie had her Irish. Their voices formed a wonderful harmony that made me feel warm inside. Ma used to love to listen to Sean Connery talk. Made her all giggly. I think I understand why now.

The band played again, and I took that time to slip away, hit the washroom and refresh our frosty beverages. This set included a lot of standards, and the audience sang along. When I got back to the table, all three of them were standing on their chairs with Maggie and Katie to either side of Cassidy. They had linked arms and were belting out the lyrics "I hope you'll understand why Paddy's not at work today." Everyone was on their feet, and the roar at the end, the cheering and the stamping, made me fully appreciate the phrase *bring the house down.*

Our waiter dropped a tray with four beers and four whiskeys on our table not long afterward and we drank to the fair isles, and the pipe, and the beauty of music. I usually had no problem holding my alcohol but keeping up with Maggie and Cassidy was going to prove a challenge.

Maggie ordered another round right away and we settled back, my belly warm from the shot and the last swallow of my beer that went down smooth as silk.

Once the buzz of the crowd settled into a nice undertone, Cassidy took a deep breath and grinned a wicked slash. "Katie, lass. You were asking about a torque," he casually mentioned, motioning to Maggie, who pulled it out of her purse and placed it on the table. "Is this the one you mean?"

Katie looked at the golden armband and nodded slowly. She took up the burnished gold torque and she gasped. She turned to me, her eyes alight, and handed it to me. I nearly dropped it. It was like holding a live wire. Cassidy and Maggie exchanged a look and he leaned back in his chair, a look of satisfaction on his face.

"Looks like we need to exchange a bit o' knowledge."

I placed the torque on the table and took Katie's hand.

"You've some sensitivity to the vibrations," Cassidy said, looking at Katie. "But you, young Sarah—" he turned his piercing gaze to me "—you more so than our young miss here." He inclined his head toward Katie and smiled at her.

"Where'd you get it?" I asked. It felt like dragon. I don't know how I knew exactly what I did, but it reminded me of all of them, Nidhogg, Frederick, and even Jean-Paul. It reverberated with their biorhythms or something.

"What did you feel?" Maggie asked, brushing a strand of hair back behind her left ear. Whether she meant it as a hint, or a clue, I wasn't sure, but her ear had several piercings, each with a gem or loop connected to a golden dragon that reared over the top of her earlobe.

Subtle.

"Dragon," I said, matter-of-factly. Katie squeezed my hand, but I didn't look at her. I was watching Cassidy and Maggie for a reaction.

"So, the rumors are true," he said to us, meaning me. "You've killed one of 'em?"

Maggie laughed. "Surely not, Cassidy."

I didn't smile, didn't say anything, didn't even move.

"Where'd you get that torque?" Katie asked.

Maggie looked between Cassidy and me. "Come on, you're taking the piss, right?"

"No, Mags, I don't think they are." He glanced at her sideways then back at me.

Our waiter arrived with our next round, and we paused while he was within earshot. Maggie winked at him and he nodded. When he was far enough out of earshot, Cassidy turned his gaze on me once more. His eyes were like ice water, pale blue and clear. For a minute I thought to put on a jacket against the chill.

"So, it *was* you." He leaned back in his chair and patted out a rhythm on the table in front of him. "I'll be damned."

Maggie paled and took a long draw on her drink.

"Is there a problem?" Katie asked. She kept her gaze directly on Cassidy.

"Problem?" Maggie said, her voice like tearing paper. "We are so fucked." Only it sounded like "fooked." It was cute—chilling, but cute.

"Let me get this straight," I said, letting Katie's hand go and picking up my beer. "You believe someone has been killed, that we may have had something do with it, and that possibility upsets you?"

Cassidy tossed back his Jameson and knocked the shot glass on the table three times.

"He had a right nasty reputation," he said, "and our patron thought he got what he deserved."

It finally dawned on me. "Christ, are you telling me you work for one of the dragons?"

Maggie took another long drink of her beer and didn't say anything. Cassidy thought for a bit how to say the next thing. "What do you think, Mags, my dear? Might as well be hung for a sheep as a lamb?"

"Hung all the same," she said. Her eyes were quick, darting between the three of us. Nervous, that one.

Cassidy chuckled. "Don't get your knickers in a twist. You've taken more risk than this, I'll wager." He tilted his head to the side. First one way, then the other. I could hear a crackle on each twist. I hated that.

"Let's just say I'm under obligation to keep any associations from the public record," he went on. "We are minstrels, traveling through many a jurisdiction and county. If we were known to be in league with anyone, it would inhibit our ability to perform so widely."

Katie laughed now, laughed like she'd solved the puzzle. "You're spies."

Cassidy shrugged, but didn't deny it.

"And the torque? That isn't Draupnir, is it?" I asked.

He grinned at me like a Cheshire cat.

Draupnir was a dwarven legend. It was rumored to reproduce itself eight times every ninth night. Whoever had that would be wealthy beyond reckoning. Of course, it would also crash the gold market. Tricky magic to deal with.

"If I had Draupnir do you think I'd be busting my arse on the road for drunks and whores?"

"Yes," Maggie said, smacking her empty beer glass on the table. "And loving every second of it, you old hound."

He winked at me. "Nay, lass. She's not Draupnir, but she's one of the copies that my mistress allowed to find its way into the wild."

"Does it really reproduce itself eight times every ninth night?" I asked.

"Tell your boring tale," Maggie said, getting up. "I'm after another round."

I held up my glass and nodded, but Katie covered her half-empty one with her hand, the universal sign language for "I'm driving tonight."

"My mistress," Cassidy continued, once Maggie had gone. "She keeps the original in a special case made by some of the Durin folk. It freezes time, stops it from copying itself. She only takes it out when she needs to make a new one. She uses them to track us."

Katie winced.

This was a big deal. "Why are you telling us all this?" I asked.

He looked confused. "Why, because you asked nice enough."

Was it that simple? "Why'd you think we'd believe you?"

"You reacted when you touched it," he said, smiling. "That's the way of it. If you can sense the little bit o'magic it has, then you're sensitive to other things as well. Besides," he pointed to Katie. "Your gal there has a set of pipes that would make my old Mam weep with joy."

Now Katie blushed.

"They ain't all the same," he said, getting serious. "Some of 'em—especially the drakes in the old countries—want what's best for us."

I thought back to Qindra's motivation for Nidhogg's behavior. They all wanted what was best for those they enslaved. Everything but equality and an open society. So, he was a thrall like Qindra. Bought the story and the culture. I could work with that. No use rocking that particular boat.

Of course, Nidhogg was making some changes to her little slice of the world. I wondered how that news would suit Mr. Stone.

Maggie got back with our drinks and Cassidy raised his glass in a toast. "To new friends and co-conspirators."

Katie looked at me, unsure, but I tilted my glass to his, letting the crystalline collision echo. "Skoal," I said.

Katie and Maggie joined and drank to our new arrangement. We all knew something about the others that we hadn't before. We shared secrets. That was good enough for now.

"Now," Cassidy said. "Let's chat about the goings-on up in Bellingham."

CHAPTER TWENTY-FOUR

We talked all the way back to Circle Q, considering the ramifications of what we'd learned. Before we'd left, they'd asked us to keep their secret, and we agreed. Katie was fine with not telling anyone but groused about how Jimmy had kept things from her when he was alive.

We got back to Circle Q just before eleven. Jai Li was asleep on the couch in the living room. Edith and Julie were playing cards, as was their normal routine, and Mary was reading.

"You girls have a good time?" Mary asked, closing her book and laying it on her lap.

"Yes, ma'am," I said, only a little drunk. "Real nice folks."

Julie put her cards on the table and looked over her shoulder at us. "Your girl there is as content as can be. She kept telling us how you all were gonna buy a nice house up north of here with all the roses and horses and stuff."

Edith dropped her cards on the pile in the middle of the table and got up, grabbing her and Julie's teacups. "She's got her hopes up," she said, not looking at either of us. "I certainly hope you're not toying with her?"

Katie dropped her purse on the chair by the door and sat on the seat. "Why would you think that?" she asked.

Edith stopped in the doorway and took in the entire room. "You're both children in the world, trying to take on the responsibilities of adults."

Mary turned her head toward the window, away from us. She'd been expecting this lecture that was unfolding. I noticed she could see the room fairly well from the reflection in the glass.

Julie lowered her head, but I saw the grin on her face. This was a subject they'd all discussed before.

"We're doing the best we can," I said, trying to keep the anger from my voice. Who the hell was this woman to challenge us? Did she think she loved Jai Li more than I did?

"Hmmmph," Edith grunted, stepping out of the room. "She deserves better."

Katie looked up at me and I took a deep breath.

"Settle down," Julie said, turning in her chair to watch me. "She's just worried, is all. You don't see her while you're gone. The girl's manic, terrified that something's going to happen to you." She got up, picking up cards. "After what happened back last fall, and the attack on the farm ..." she hesitated, collecting herself. "Girl's got a right to be worried, don't you think?"

"Damn," Katie said under her breath. She got up and went over to the couch, sitting next to where Jai Li lay, asleep in her footie pajamas. I watched her for a moment, watched as she carefully moved the hair off Jai Li's face. She was an angel, that one. Took my breath away. You could still see the scar on her neck where the necromancer had almost killed her.

"We'll find our own place," I promised. "You know me, Julie. I do what I say I'll do."

Julie nodded, but glanced at Mary all the same. "I know you always do your best." She shrugged. "You know I trust you. But it's not just your life anymore. That child needs some stability."

"You should stay here," Mary said. "Your gal didn't like the apartment in Kent. Says it made her sad." She looked at us, smiling but melancholy. "The girl needs someplace where she can feel safe."

Katie looked up at that, her face painted with grief. That had been her place, her first apartment after college, the place she lived when we started dating. We had a lot of our relationship wrapped up in those walls. And that's where Odin haunted her for a year, where I fought and killed my first giant and rescued Odin. Lots of history, and not all of it good.

"We've taken advantage of your hospitality too long," I said, crossing my arms. I was mad about this—hurt, honestly. I hated the look in Katie's eyes and I hated that we'd caused Jai Li any grief. The girl had a tough enough life.

Mary started to protest, but Julie waved her hand quickly and shook her head. Mary let out a sigh and sat back, holding the book to her chest.

"I'm okay with staying here until we find something else," I said, watching Katie, "but we need our own place."

Katie nodded, looking from me down to Jai Li.

"But for now, I think we need to get some sleep." The buzz from the evening was totally gone. I walked to the couch, squatted down and slid my arms under Jai Li. "Come on, big girl," I said as she stirred. "Time to go to bed."

She rolled against me, snuggling against my chest. Katie kept her hand on Jai Li until I stood.

We got her settled into the trundle bed in our room and sat on the edge of our own, wiped out. I honestly loved living here. Mary, Julie, and Edith were becoming full-fledged family. I loved how much they cared for us, looked out for us, needed us. I put my head in my hands and Katie slipped round to sit behind me, running her hands across my back.

"We should get some sleep," she whispered, kissing the side of my neck. "We'll talk about it in the morning."

I turned my head to catch her lips, and we lingered there for a moment.

"I'm just wound up," I said, standing and striding to the dresser.

Ever since Julie had moved in with Mary, she'd had the mail from my old apartment forwarded here. I needed to get that straightened out as well. Some of my mail went to Kent now, but most of it came to the old address. I flipped through the day's mail Mary had left piled on the dresser. I'd gotten another letter from Megan. I read it through once and passed it off to Katie. She read the letter while I began to unpack our things.

Things were bad at home from Megan's point of view. No different than when I'd been her age. I could see it for what it was now—chafing against unfair rules, teen drama, wanting to be grown-up, afraid to be. We all went through it. She asked to see me again. Asked if I could come out to her next TKD test, or maybe the tournament at the end of May.

"You gonna go visit her?" Katie asked me, sitting beside me on the edge of the bed and placing her hand on my thigh.

"I'll write her tomorrow. I just don't think I can face Da yet, you know?"

Katie leaned her head on my shoulder and squeezed my leg. "You need to confront him sooner or later. Before it's too late for Megan."

"I know," I said, placing my hand over hers. "Soon."

Megan wasn't gonna put up with my delays much longer. Eventually she was gonna start seeing me as being in league with Ma and Da. Another grown-up who didn't even bother to try and understand her.

Maybe I needed to do more than write.

"I'll drive out Monday," I said, surprising myself. "See if I can catch her at the dojang without Ma or Da being around."

"Want me to come along?" Katie asked, quietly.

"No, this is something I need to do on my own, I think."

She looked at me, her lips pursed, but didn't protest. Was I locking her out? I hated all this. Suddenly I was wishing we were back where we were a year ago, just the two of us, living life as it came. All this responsibility sucked.

And I had promised last fall when I took her out to Chumstick with me. Promised that I'd never leave her behind again.

"How about I set up lunch one day, Megan and Ma, you, me and Jai Li?"

Katie stood up and hugged me. After a bit, she spoke against my shoulder.

"I'd really like that."

The world felt right in that moment. Another good decision. Too many more of those and I would start feeling like a grown-up.

Still, I chafed at the thought that Julie, Edith, and Mary were talking about us and didn't think we were doing the best for Jai Li. I know we were both pretty busy, but weren't most parents? Maybe we needed to do less going out. No more bars and such. I knew things would change with a kid, but maybe I didn't really understand just how much.

We talked together, huddled under the blankets on our borrowed bed. I loved sharing space with her, just breathing her breath as we lay side by side, face to face. This was the most important thing in my life and I didn't know if that was acceptable any longer. Did Jai Li come before my relationship with Katie?

Sleep was long in coming. The whole house was still, peaceful when I padded out to the bathroom around two in the morning. Katie and I had talked past midnight, but she had finally gone to sleep.

I went into the kitchen and got a glass of water. I stood in the window and looked out over the farm. Was this a good place, a safe space for Jai Li? We'd get it protected, defend the borders, but, no matter what, it wasn't our place. We had to have our own space. Jai Li deserved to have her own.

The tile floor was cold on my bare feet, but I stood there,

staring out into the late night. Time for a change. One that didn't involve people dying would be nice.

In the meantime, I'd call Stuart and Gunther to come out to Circle Q and help me set up a perimeter like they had out at Black Briar. Something on the woo-woo side to keep enemies away. I loved these women. I needed to keep them safe.

CHAPTER TWENTY-FIVE

As the next week kicked it into high gear, Katie and I kept going back to our talk with Cassidy and Maggie. She was particular curious about their questions around Bellingham and how Ginny's suicide played into it all. They'd said something subtle was going on there, enough to draw the attention of their patron. Energy spikes, Cassidy had called them. They were minor anomalies—small disturbances that may have been misssed in all the white noise that emanated from Nidhogg's domain if no one was paying particularly close attention. Turns out the death of Jean-Paul had focused their patron's attention on the region. I'd wondered aloud just how many other people had noticed anything amiss. Witches from the Ukraine came to mind. Visions of a hut running on chicken legs invaded my thoughts from time to time. Katie did not find that image as comical as I did.

Maggie had hinted that their delay in answering us had been because they had been waiting on a response from *Her Most Lugubrious*. Cassidy cast her a scathing look and Maggie only shrugged. Frankly, neither of them had been thrilled about returning to the Pacific Northwest. They found it a risk being in Nidhogg's realm.

"Why chance getting outed for who we are?" Maggie had asked.

It was obvious to me that the two of them did not see everything eye-to-eye. Was there a bit of friction amongst the Harpers?

The talk of the suicides just solidified their resolve. Something beyond the normal ken was going on in the region. Something more than coincidence.

I was not a fan of coincidences. Ginny killing herself while I was there was one thing. Meeting the Hamsters and Mimi, getting that vibe about her, and all the crazy from Gletts and his quest to find the portal home to Alfheim. It all pointed to Mimi, in my mind. She seemed like a focal point for whatever was going on.

The others thought I was making something from nothing.

"It's pretty flimsy," Cassidy had said with a laugh and a wave of his long-fingered hand. "Look for something more ominous, like your ley line adventures over the winter."

Meaning all the crap with the necromancer and the blood cult. So, I stopped bringing up Mimi, and the next thing I knew, the conversation had turned to music, whiskey, and women.

"She's an odd one, I'll grant you that," Katie said with a shrug when I brought it up again on Monday. "I'm not sure why you're so obsessed with her."

I wanted to quote Harry Potter about hallows and horcruxes to her, but thought better of it, and the subject just dropped. The runes in my hairline burned constantly now, a low-grade twinge that never quite let me forget their presence. That, and the way my stomach knotted up when everyone else glossed over the mere mention of Mimi. I may have just let it go. As it was, it strengthened my resolve to get Test Flight working up there so I had a ready-made excuse to poke around.

By the next Tuesday Carl and Jennifer called to let me know the permits had been approved and that we would start shooting some of the scenes for *Cheerleader of the Apocalypse* up in Bellingham. We would have to change our normal shooting schedule to get the right lighting for some of the days, meaning we started at one each day instead of six. Katie was going to hate it.

The first week we'd do some wide shots, some mutant scenes, and maybe a cheerleader scene, but nothing with the hero of the story. Carl and Jennifer had started trying out actors to replace JJ, and things were not going well. They'd had a dozen guys try out, but none of them had the juice. Even Dante read, but he was too sullen.

After the last guy left and Carl was hitting his head with a clipboard, I suggested that they should call the guy from the Doc Martens store, Mark something. He could sing well and was easy on the eyes. Dante and Sprocket both agreed loudly and with gusto. I think they both were crushing on the new guy.

And so it went. Every day I headed north before lunch and got back to the Circle Q long after Jai Li was asleep. The first week went okay, but by the second, both Jai Li and Edith were starting to show some wear. Katie and I discussed it, agreeing we needed to do something to get the girl some more quality time with me.

I put the word out with the cast and crew that I was looking for a place to rent in the area and on Thursday afternoon Dante let me know they had an open room at the boarding house, if I was interested. He assured me Mimi really liked me, asked about me from time to time. She'd been the one to suggest it, as a matter of fact. Said I should swing by and chat.

That could be the answer to my current problems and allow me a chance to pursue my hunches about Mimi. I could stay in Bellingham Monday, Tuesday, and Wednesday nights, then head home for a long weekend. It would mean seeing less of Katie and Jai Li, so that was a bad idea. On the other hand, if we all three moved up here, even if only temporarily, it would relieve a lot of my stress all around.

I followed Dante back to the house where he showed me what amounted to a huge suite—basically a two-bedroom, one bath apartment, *sans* kitchen. It was bigger than our place in Kent and gave us more personal space than the room we had at Mary's. Dante assured me Mimi would let me have it for a reasonable rate—two hundred a week—and we could take meals in the kitchen on a fairly regular schedule, but we were free to come and go as we saw fit.

"See," Dante said. "Bring Katie and Jai Li up with you. Problem solved."

He looked so pleased with himself. I couldn't help but smile at his enthusiasm. It was rare to see him so happy.

"Brilliant," I said, withholding my reservations to discuss with Katie later. If there was something odd about this house, or Mimi in general, I wasn't sure I wanted to put Katie and Jai Li at risk.

We had a family meeting the next evening. Carl gave us Friday off, so Katie, Jai Li, and I spent the evening cooking dinner and discussing our housing options. We talked about what type of place to get and whether or not we'd ever be able to afford the dream house that Jai Li insisted on. Katie wanted something more in the city and I wanted a bit of land—someplace I could set up my own smithy. It quickly turned into one of those arguments where you can't win if you love the other person, because you can't fight like you mean it.

So, we dropped it for a bit. I was steaming a little, struggling to filter through my baser emotions to try and see where Katie was coming from. How were we so far apart on this?

Jai Li wanted to be closer to Black Briar. Hell, she'd love it if we either lived at Circle Q forever or even better, out *at* Black Briar. Neither of those seemed to jive with us getting our own place, but she was six. Reality and logic need not always apply.

Being in daily proximity to Bub, Frick, and Frack would be nirvana for that girl, though she quickly assured us that the rest of Black Briar was okay too. Katie nixed that pretty quick. Jai Li had a hard time understanding the concept of not wanting to live in your dead brother's shadow. She had a good idea about death and danger. To her, family and friends trumped everything. She gave in pretty quickly, assuming she didn't have much of a vote. All those years living with Nidhogg had taught her to live with what she was given. We hated to be that way about it, so we discussed compromise and how that worked. There was just no way either of us wanted to live under Jimmy's shade.

In the end Katie agreed the temporary solution in Bellingham was a good idea. "It'll be an adventure," she assured me. "We can survive a couple of months. But we'll stay here. This is a better environment for Jai Li."

"Damned right," Edith said, walking into the room to get a glass of water. While we weren't being secretive about our discussion, the others had stayed out of the kitchen and let us hash things out. Still, the way Edith looked at me, I got the impression I'd committed some massive blunder.

"You stay up there on nights you have to work on the shoot, then come back here on other nights," Katie said, not looking up from the pot of bolognaise she was stirring. "We'll visit sometimes, but we'll call this home base."

It could be like going back to college. The Hamsters were cool to hang with and Mimi seemed nice enough. I wasn't totally keen on the idea of being away from them several nights a week, though it would mean that Katie and I had a place of our own to visit from time to time, away from the others, and maybe away from Jai Li. I know it was selfish, but we needed more couple time.

Mary, Julie, and Edith were mostly mollified by the time we served dinner, but everyone knew it was only a reprieve. Eventually we'd be moving on and none of them wanted that.

Jai Li was very proud of the Jell-O salad she'd made. Edith gushed over it, exclaiming how great it was so loudly and so often that even Jai Li rolled her eyes at the end there. I think Edith would be the one hurt the most when we left. However safer I'd feel if we lived away from town, Bellingham was not my normal stomping ground.

We had to find our own place before the summer was over. That was the deal. I promised we'd look in earnest and Jai Li got excited again. I figured I could just call Qindra. She knew everything that went on in Nidhogg's territory. Surely she'd know of a good place we could rent or buy. That guy from Low Key hadn't called us back. And besides, the name was enough to bug me, just a little. But Jai Li had a good sense about it, and she'd been on the money too many times before.

My call to Qindra was a bust. Seemed that the local real estate market was not high on the agenda for the old dragon. Silly me. Qindra didn't pay much attention to it. It was one of those things that took care of itself. The thralls always managed to get by without interference on this front. I was disappointed, honestly. I'd been thinking it would be a simple solution. Now we really had to find a place on our own.

I hoped this Low Key guy wasn't a total douche.

CHAPTER TWENTY-SIX

Saturday morning, Katie and I were in the kitchen, drinking coffee and planning the coming week, when I got a call on my cell. It was Qindra. She never called me unless it was an emergency. Suddenly I was on high alert.

"Nidhogg has need of her Fist," Qindra said without preamble. She gave me an address in Kirkland, told me to bring the sword, and Edith.

"Why Edith?" I asked, perplexed.

"I'll explain when you get here. Consider the zone hot, no civilians."

And she hung up.

I looked at Katie who had no idea what had just transpired.

"Looks like I'm being called up in my official capacity as Nidhogg's Fist," I told her, taking her hand across the table. "I need to go."

I stood, leaned in and kissed her, then went to the back of the house to change. If I was carrying Gram into a situation, I wanted my chain.

Edith was in the living room playing with Jai Li when I paused, drawing her attention.

"I need you."

She looked at me, confused.

"Official business," I told her. Like that meant anything to her. How much did she know?

"I'm sorry?" she asked, placing her hand of cards on the table.

Jai Li turned around to look at me, scared all of a sudden. I went to her, knelt down and hugged her. "I need to take Edith and go for an errand."

She poked me in the shoulder, making a point of noticing my chain under my jacket. She looked down to the case I carried Gram in and ran out of the room. I turned to watch her run to Katie, climb into her lap and bury her head in her shoulder.

Damn it.

I turned back to Edith. "I've been requested to go to an address in Kirkland to meet Qindra. She asked specifically for you."

Edith stood quickly, glancing over to Julie and then Mary.

"Why me?"

I shrugged. "This is Gottschalk's address."

She frowned. "I'll get my things."

I stood and leaned against the doorframe, waiting.

"You protect her," Julie said, her voice stern. "Why you need an old woman to go along with you on some fool's errand is beyond me."

"Is it about the people who attacked the farm?" Mary asked, setting her knitting down and standing.

"Yes, ma'am. That would be my guess."

She walked past me and patted me on the shoulder. "You get those bastards," Then she went in to sit with Katie and Jai Li. She was stroking Jai Li's hair when Julie spoke.

"Try not to get killed."

I turned to her and she was shaking her head.

If it had just been me, I'd have taken the Ducati, but with Edith, I took the truck. She had a shawl over her shoulder and that same knapsack she'd had the night we fought off the mercenaries.

Edith didn't say anything all the way over to Kirkland, but I could feel her, feel the anger and the indignation. There was way more to this woman than I knew or imagined. I wasn't sure I ever wanted to get the full picture.

The place had been cordoned off a block out. There were cop cars up and down the side streets with lights flashing. Several officers were keeping a group of civilians behind a line half a block down the main road and two fire trucks stood across either end of the street we needed to be on. Odd, but effective.

We were stopped by a uniformed officer who waved us through before I could even say my name. Apparently, I looked unique enough to be known. I wasn't sure how that made me feel. We drove down the street slowly, wending our way around cars with flashing lights and clumps of emergency workers drinking coffee and talking.

Gottschalk's house looked like it had been firebombed.

"Holy mother of God," Edith muttered under her breath.

"That's not good," I agreed, grimacing.

We got out of the truck and met Qindra at the remains of the picket fence.

"What the hell happened here?" I asked. "Do I need Gram for this?"

"You'd better bring it in, but leave it in the case," she said, not smiling. "We need you both inside."

I pulled Gram out from behind the seat of the truck and we followed Qindra into the house. The top floor had been destroyed. Most of the exterior walls were still standing, but everything inside was gone.

Unexpectedly, there was a set of stairs going down near the back of the house. These were rough-hewn stone and went down into darkness. By the pattern of debris, this was a hidden staircase.

"Have you been down there?" I asked, looking from Edith to Qindra.

"Sort of," Qindra said. "We sent down a team of three. They didn't come back up."

This was getting better. "And you want me and Edith ..."

Qindra held up her hand, stopping me. "Mrs. Sorenson is here for another reason." She turned to Edith and held out her hand. "I apologize for not giving you the respect you deserved, *seið-kona*."

Edith waved her hands. "I am a trifle," she said, gravely. "What is it you wish from me?"

Qindra bowed slightly and took Edith by the arm, guiding her over to a spot in the house where half a dozen bodies lay. Madame Gottschalk looked horrible. Half her face was burned, and she was bald. Probably wore a wig when she was alive. She didn't look peaceful, by any means. More pissed off. I recognized one of the others from my visit weeks ago. I didn't recognize any of the rest. It was quite a relief that Charlie was not among the dead.

"You performed a ritual the night your home was attacked."

Edith nodded.

"I'd like you to perform that here, now. We believe there are items of power here that I cannot discover. They are shielded."

Edith looked at me, her face hard. "Why would I do this for you?"

Qindra looked at me. "We need to ensure that they are not reused by those with nefarious intent."

"These were not bad people," Edith said. "They worked for a great, fat spider, spinning her web of deceit and fear, but they were nothing more than watchers, spies, and gatherers of arcane lore."

I looked over at Edith. "You knew them?"

"Knew of them," Edith said. "They were mostly harmless. Those who were doing real evil were infiltrators." She turned to look at Qindra, then down to the bodies on the ground. "You did not need to kill these children. They were not part of the foul one's plan."

Qindra and I shared a look that spoke volumes. What the hell was Edith talking about?

"There is a power older and darker than anything you have encountered, Young Sarah."

Edith said *Young Sarah* like a title, like words she'd used over and over. I wasn't sure I liked the way she meant it.

"Madame Gottschalk has been a fool and a puppet for another power, a great evil from the old country, but they did not deserve this death."

"We didn't kill them," Qindra said, taken aback. "We responded to a disturbance. We didn't get involved until after the house exploded." She looked over at me, the exhaustion and exasperation clear on her face. "This is too public, too messy. People will talk."

"Maybe they want people to talk," I said. "This is probably meant as a warning to others."

Qindra winced and pinched the bridge of her nose—a sure sign of a headache coming on. "We'll discuss it in further detail, after you seek out my team."

I sat my case on the ground and took Gram out, sliding the harness over my shoulder and gripping the sword in my left hand. Qindra handed me a halogen lantern. "I've augmented that a bit," she said, smiling. "Turn it on once you are a few steps down. It will be quite bright."

Edith squatted down and opened her knapsack. I watched her for a moment before turning to the stair. This was not fun.

Qindra was asking Edith questions when I lost sight of them and turned on the lamp. Bright white light shone from the lantern, like a day in the full sun. It worked its way around corners and pushed back any shadow. It was strange and cool all at the same time. I took a deep breath and plunged forward.

I found her people in the room below. The place was a maze of boxes and crates, filing cabinets and, oddly enough, huge urns —like those used to ship wine in the really olden days, large enough to store a body in.

There were no monsters, nothing deadly or hungry I could see. Well, maybe the three investigators were hungry. They were alive at least. Unfortunately, they were trapped in a glowing web of light. I had to shield the lantern a bit to make out the pearlescent bands that held them fast. I'd seen similar last winter when the blood cult had used magic bindings on Frederick Sawyer. Similar, but not the same. Those had required the full attention of mages of some ilk. Luckily for me, I am capable of creating quite a distraction. Well, lucky for Sawyer as well. My interference there saved his life.

The cleaning crew tracked me with their eyes as I crept around the edge of the room. Something felt wrong about this whole setup. There was nothing down here but boxes of crap, like Jimmy kept in the secret room at Black Briar.

I took care to examine the hieroglyphics on one of the urns. They looked Egyptian, but not. There were symbols for three guys holding what looked like vacuum cleaners with lines shooting out of them. The three lines or beams intersected at an amorphous green blob. The streams did not cross, just hit the blob from different angles. Then it struck me—these were Ghostbusters. I rocked back on my heels and sighed. Was nothing sacred?

A low-grade thrum of magic jarred my hand as I touched the urn. One of the tiny painted figures turned to look at me and winked. The runes on my scalp flared.

That wasn't creepy.

I took another deep breath and looked further. No use in rushing to the first magical object I found. I played the light beyond the urns and saw that something had been dragged across the floor here. The dust was fairly thick in this area, except for a trail cut through the worst of it. I followed it over to a small box that had been broken open. Papers were scattered about, but I couldn't see anything worth anything. No artifacts, just shredded paper.

The lid was over in the corner, flung away, but the wood

matched. I scuttled over and picked it up, reading the shipping label affixed to the top. This was headed to Minsk at some point. What had been in that box? Someone had been pilfering. Maybe the same people who'd blown this place up.

That was Qindra's problem.

Satisfied that I didn't see anything else extraordinary in the small room, I walked over to the first urn and kicked it over. Several strands of light winked out while sand poured from the lid of the urn. At least I hoped it was sand and not cremated remains or anything.

It didn't take me long to knock over enough of the other urns to free the three members of Qindra's cleaning crew. This wasn't a deadly trap, just something to hold potential robbers until Gottschalk and her followers could investigate and capture them. By the markings, I assumed it would capture spirits as well. The way my life had been going, I couldn't leave that possibility out. The fact whomever had pilfered this place had avoided the trap, told me it was an inside job.

We all reported back upstairs where they explained how they'd become trapped. Qindra listened attentively as I explained about the markings on the urns and about the looted box that had been ready to ship to Minsk. She promised her team would look into it all and I went to speak to Edith.

Hurray for a quest with no killing. I thought it may be my first since I started on this hero gig. I preferred it when I got everyone out alive. It did sort of bug me that I'd drawn the short straw on exploring the ominous basement, though. Fist did not mean Red Shirt.

Qindra sent a second crew down to investigate once she was sure there was nothing obviously large and bitey down there. I was glad I could be of service. Another satisfied customer, and no stabbing.

In the end, Edith noted several books, two rag dolls, and a set of stacking dolls that Qindra allowed her to keep. I gave Qindra a questioning look, but she had eyes only for Edith.

There was magic there that Qindra didn't know, and she was fascinated. Edith seemed almost embarrassed by the attention. "Kitchen magic," she grumbled when I walked by.

Within an hour we were well on our way back to Circle Q. Edith hadn't said much of anything the whole drive back, just kept stacking and unstacking the dolls. As we pulled into the drive up to the house, she turned to me.

"Madame Gottschalk was my sister," she said. "She and I have not spoken to one another since before you were born."

I stopped the truck halfway to the house and put it in park. "What?" My head was spinning.

Edith looked at me, her hands on her lap over the stacking dolls.

"It is complicated," she said. "I chose a different path than she or my other siblings. One that led me here, to you."

To me? The runes on my scalp began to hum—not burn, not flare up in pain, but hum. Like laying a vibrator against your skin. This was new.

"I'm sorry, what do you mean, 'led you to me'?"

She reached out and touched my hand for the briefest of moments and pulled her hand back to her lap.

"I have been watching for you since before you were born. It wasn't until I'd nearly given up hope that you moved into the same apartment complex as me. I took it as a sign of fate that my long-held *geas* was still required of me. It has been my job to watch out for you."

The world grew fuzzy there for a second as my peripheral vision collapsed and the world tunneled down to a distorted view of Edith Sorenson, the cabbage lady who loved rummy and Jai Li with equal abandon.

I took a deep breath, remembering that it was good for me, and my vision cleared. I think I almost fainted.

"You've been watching me?"

"Watching over you," she said, her face stern and her voice level. "Protecting you as I can. And I am not the only one.

There are others set the task of keeping you safe, keeping you hidden."

She paused, looking down at her hands and laughing quietly. "And yet, you insist on being in the thick of things. When I heard you'd killed the bastard dragon of Vancouver I almost moved away." She looked up at me again, and I sat there, jaw hanging down, stunned. "If it wasn't for Julie's need, I would have fled," she grew very quiet. "I am not proud of that moment of weakness."

"But ... What?" My mind was racing. Watching me? Protecting me? Who were these people and who were they protecting me from?

"I cannot tell you more. Mary knows now, as does Julie. We are concerned that we were the targets of the attack, not you."

The lights out in the yard came on, the big halogen pole lights that turned the area around the house into near daylight. They knew we were out here, had heard us coming up the drive, and were likely watching us.

"You see," Edith said, pointing toward the house. Mary and Julie were on the porch, each with a firearm, looking over to us in the truck. We were too far away, and they couldn't exactly see inside the cab from that distance.

"We should go to them," she said. "We can talk more at a later time. Just know, Sarah Jane Beauhall, that there are those of us out here who are watching over you."

"Who else?" I asked, starting the truck. Didn't want the rest of the crew to panic.

"I do not know," she said, turning back to the front of the truck. "We were never told of the others."

"Who do you report to?" I asked, growing angry and feeling betrayed.

"No one," she said, quietly. "No one at all. We were placed here with one mission and we were to never seek contact with those who set us in place." She turned to me one last time as I pulled up to the house and killed the engine.

"I swear to you," she said. "I never knew who they were, but I have never doubted my task."

She patted me on the arm and got out of the truck. I got out but leaned against the door, staring after her, watched as she hugged first Mary, then Julie. They all three looked back at me before Mary and Edith went into the house. Julie stayed on the porch waiting for me.

Even Julie? Was she being paid to babysit me? Was our friendship nothing more than an assignment? I thought maybe I was going to throw up, but I couldn't stay out here. I needed to go into the house and confront this.

What the fuck was wrong with the world? And who was I that needed this level of scrutiny?

I needed to talk to Gunther. Damn, was he one of them? My head was spinning. How many? Who?

Panic rose in me—urging me to flee, follow Da's instincts. I needed to find someplace remote and isolated. This was crazy.

Before I could totally spin out of control, Julie walked up to me and pulled me into a hug. "Only Edith," she said, reading my panic. "We're just along for the ride."

And the world settled down a bit.

CHAPTER TWENTY-SEVEN

I made it until Monday before I had to ask if anyone else was in on the gag. On my lunch break, I called Stuart, but his phone went to voicemail. He didn't carry his personal cell when he was deep in the bowels of the University of Washington's underbelly. I left a lame message inquiring after his health. I don't think I've got the best phone skills.

Gunther answered his cell on the first ring. Unfortunately, he was at his jazz record store over in Pioneer Square. He always took my calls, but I could hear customers in the background. Bless him, he took the time to assure me he wasn't assigned to watch me and found the idea of any of the other Black Briar folks as Sarah-watchers funny.

"Not Stuart?" I asked over the phone. He had been getting pretty chummy with Qindra.

"Sarah. I promise you."

I paced along the split rail fence I'd been sitting on, ignoring the stunning view of the horses I was working. I let out a long sigh.

"Guess I'm just being paranoid then."

He chuckled. "This is the part that makes you paranoid? Not the giants, dragons, trolls, elves, spirits, hidden worlds, or magic?

The fact your next-door neighbor told you she was set to watch you by no one, with no orders ... that's the final straw?"

He had a point. "You don't think she was making shit up, do you?"

He stopped laughing. "No. Honestly, I think she's being truthful. But I wouldn't worry about it. It will make you nuts. Just be thankful someone out there has your back and go on with your life."

"Yeah, well ... Easy for you to say. I feel like I'm living in the Truman Show now."

"Good movie. Look, I have customers."

We said our goodbyes and hung up.

I stopped pacing and stretched my arms above my head. I needed to loosen up my knotted shoulders. After a bit of stretching, I finished my turkey sandwich and enjoyed the view.

I'd almost cancelled today's work, but I needed the money. More importantly, I needed to be busy. Sitting around doing nothing was a sure-fire way to make me totally nuts.

Julie was out at another farm. Today was a solo day. Small farms with no real sense of the community chatter. This was one of the good farms where they didn't care how I dressed or what the rumors were, as long as I treated their animals well. Seemed like common sense to me.

Mimi called later while I was shoeing a donkey, and I let it go to voicemail. She confirmed the arrangements for me to stay at the boarding house and promised she'd leave keys with Sprocket just in case she wasn't home when I rolled in.

I'd have to go pack an overnight kit before heading north to work on the movie. It would be great to have an earlier sack time, even if it meant sleeping solo. At least I'd have the covers to myself. Katie was a blanket hog.

I put my headphones on and called up a Led Zeppelin playlist. The eerie strains of "In the Light" echoed in my head as I grabbed a shovel to start mucking out the stables. Ever since I'd offered to do that for Mary way back when, I'd offered it to my regulars. Half of them took me up on the offer and I padded my checks a little more while doing something I didn't mind doing.

It gave me time to think.

The house was empty when I got home. I grabbed a shower and packed my kit. There was a note on the fridge, saying that Mary had packed me dinner in an easy-to-eat-while-driving arrangement. Sandwiches, carrot sticks, and wasabi peas. Interesting combination, but at least the sandwiches were cut in half and individually wrapped. Easily held in one hand without falling apart.

There was also a note from Katie, reminding me of brunch with Ma and Megan on Sunday, and two pictures from Jai Li. Another one of the houses she wanted us to live in and one of her riding a big dog. Kids were funny. I'd never thought about getting a dog, but there you have it. This one was the size of a pony. What kind of breeds were that big?

I was blessed. Good friends and plenty of love. I had to keep that in perspective. I'd hoped to see Katie again before I took off for a few days north, but we'd said our goodbyes this morning over coffee. Still, I was gonna miss them.

The drive was uneventful, giving me time to swing by the boarding house before heading to the shoot. Sprocket met me and gave me the grand tour. Of course, I'd been there a few times before, but he was so excited to do it, I just rolled along.

My suite reminded me of a hotel room. Master bedroom, sitting room, and a private bathroom. I'd sprung for something similar once before with Katie and that hotel room had run just under two-fifty a night. The fact Mimi was parting with this for eight hundred a month for the summer was crazy. But I wasn't looking a gift horse in the mouth.

I lay on the bed for a little while, staring at the ceiling and contemplating the twists and turns in our lives over the last couple of years. For some reason, I felt calmer and more together than I had for a long time. I'd even dozed off for just a minute, when Sprocket was back at my door, calling me to head to the movie shoot.

I sat up and looked around. There was a wind-up clock on the bedside table. I'd slept for almost forty minutes. We were pushing it to make the shoot on time.

As I stood and stretched, I felt muscles unkink that I hadn't even noticed were tight before. Best power nap ever.

I wasn't too concerned that Edith had been watching over me. Hell, Katie had a homeless guy who was likely Odin haunting her for a couple of years. Maybe we were all under some level of scrutiny. For some reason, it just didn't bother me at the moment.

I couldn't recall the last time I felt this at peace.

CHAPTER TWENTY-EIGHT

The week went great on my end. I missed my family, but I was riding high—no death threats, no crazies. Just three nights, four days of good work and making progress. Even Carl and Jennifer were thrilled to be shooting on-site. Totally beyond their original scope and they were flourishing. I was looking forward to getting back to the scenes with whoever was replacing JJ. We were running out of cheerleader-only scenes to film.

Saturday, I woke up before dawn with butterflies for the first time in days. Katie, Jai Li, and I were meeting Ma and Megan for brunch in Tacoma. I got dressed and went for a run, taking the time to clear my head and settle my nerves. I only did three miles, then had a quick shower, packing my dirty clothes into the truck and the slog back to Redmond. When I rolled onto the farm, Katie was in the shower and everyone else was busy getting ready. Jai Li insisted on putting her long black hair into an elaborate braid, so Edith was working on that. Julie and Mary were in the kitchen cleaning up from a pancake breakfast so I dove in and started washing dishes.

We were all dressed up in our second-best outfits. Jai Li and

Katie in dresses, me in jeans and a fairly nondescript top. Nothing too frilly, but totally different from my usual metal or punk T-shirts. Jai Li even tried to get me to put on some lipstick when Katie was putting on hers, but I think she was yanking my chain. She was a mischievous little kid when she wanted to be.

We pulled into the restaurant parking lot just before noon-thirty. We had reservations at 12:45, so we were golden.

"Is your mom going to hate me?" Katie asked out of the blue, pulling the rearview mirror around and messing with her hair.

Jai Li rolled her eyes and I poked her, giving her my best mom look. She looked away, but she was grinning. I reached over and took Katie's hand, stopping her from futzing with her hair.

"You're beautiful," I said. "Ma already knows about us, and I've talked about you some to Megan, who has translated it to Ma. The woman raised me and loves me. She's gonna love you as well."

Katie leaned over and kissed me, squishing Jai Li a little. The girl giggled and pushed us apart.

"Right," I said. "Time to face the music."

Katie gave me a nervous smile and I smiled back. We were quite the sight going into the Victory Club Diner. I did sneak a look at my own hair in the reflection of the door going in. I didn't have any product in it, no spikes, Mohawk, or anything crazy. Sides were still shaved, sure, but it lay down pretty nicely. Ma shouldn't freak out too much.

We got seated right on time, but Ma and Megan were late. Brunch was a buffet, so Katie took Jai Li through for some cut fruit to hold her over. She'd skipped the pancake feast earlier, assuring Katie that she'd eat more at the buffet. Now she was getting cranky—low blood sugar. I was strongly debating grabbing something myself if they didn't show up soon.

The place was hopping; without a reservation, the waiting line looked to be a good forty-five minutes deep. I was starting to worry when they were thirty minutes late. At forty-five we went ahead and got our food. I kept checking my phone but no one called. Megan had my number, but neither of them had a cell phone. I debated calling the house, but thought I'd give them more time.

Did they tell Da they were meeting us? I think they'd planned this for when he was off on some project or other with the church. He was always fixing something for someone. He was big on serving the church community. He could fix old cars, do plumbing, run electricity, and just about any other odd job you could think of. I'd always been proud of him for that.

We finished and couldn't really stay any longer after two hours. We'd eaten more than we should've, and the staff really wanted our table. Jai Li was bummed but sated. Katie kept holding my hand and telling me she loved me—her way of reassuring me. What could we really say? They'd stood us up, and that was so absolutely unlike Ma that I was worried.

Finally, after we'd paid and were out in the parking lot, I let the others into the truck, but I stayed out, leaning against the fender and looking at my cell. What if they were in an accident? What if Da had forbidden them to come? What if Ma was just too embarrassed to be seen with me and my family in public?

I punched in the home phone and let it ring. It went to an answering machine on ring five. I didn't leave a message. After three tries with no one answering, I gave up. The brunch was not sitting well on my stomach and I was scared and nervous. Were they screening my calls? I looked around as the truck door opened and Katie came over, leaned her head against my shoulder and hugged me.

"I'm sorry, hon," she said, squeezing me to her. "I'm sure they're fine. Something just came up. We'll reschedule."

I kissed her and forced a smile. "I'm sure something happened at church that needed Ma to step into. She was always busy making food for the elderly or helping out members who suddenly need things like emergency childcare or trips to the doctor. But I wish they'd have called."

We drove back to Redmond with Jai Li sleeping against

Katie and me lost in thought. Short of driving out to Crescent Ridge, I guess I'd have to wait to hear.

And I was oh, so good at waiting.

CHAPTER TWENTY-NINE

Sunday, I went thrift store shopping for the movie while Katie took Jai Li over to Black Briar for a visit. I had a good excursion, finding some interesting things for almost nothing. My favorite part of thrifting. I even managed to pick up a few T-shirts for me. I tended to ruin them almost as fast as I bought them, what with all the working with horses and fire. Some smells just would not come out of cotton.

I returned to the Circle Q and parked the truck beside Mary's. It had been a hectic morning and I just needed a moment of quiet time to get my head together. I still hadn't heard from Ma or Megan, and I'd called the house a dozen times. I thought about calling the Tae Kwon Do school, but they wouldn't be open again until Monday.

Edith Sorenson was in the kitchen making soup when I rolled in. Some sort of vegetable concoction that would be heavenly. She waved at me with a ladle as I walked past lugging three bulging bags of assorted thrift store treasures.

While I admired the strength and tenacity in that old woman, my perception of her had shifted. She hadn't mentioned the whole "watching me" thing after that visit to Gottschalk's place. To her it wasn't an issue. Julie and I had talked about it, but she thought the world of Edith. While she thought I was better off having decent people watching out for me, I was struggling with keeping my cool.

Maybe I was just jealous of how close she'd become with Jai Li. Edith considered their relationship more of a grandmotherly affair—loving the girl heart and soul—and she mostly deferred to our decisions. Jai Li loved her without reservations.

I fretted about this off and on with no clear resolution. I wished we could just pick up all the places—Black Briar, Circle Q, even my parents' place—and group them together in one central location. I think it would make me feel safer in general and would definitely be a focal point for all the love in my life. It would save a lot of driving.

I dropped the thrift store bags on my bed and took a deep breath, trying to clear my head. I needed to focus on things I could actually do and stop stressing about things out of my current control.

I wandered into the kitchen and poured myself a glass of orange juice. Edith watched me out of the corner of her eye when I leaned back and held the cold glass to my forehead.

"You worry too much," she said without turning. "Everyone is safe and accounted for. Jai Li is off with Katie. Mary is out in the barns brushing down a few of the horses. Why don't you go rest before dinner?"

"Yeah, maybe that's a good idea." I downed the juice, rinsed the glass, and left it in the sink.

She hadn't turned to me or anything, but when I walked past her, she reached out and put her hand on my shoulder. That simple touch nearly did me in. I don't know why my emotional state was so jacked up. I covered her hand with mine for a moment and squeezed, then continued on to our room.

I debated just lying back and trying to take a catnap. I imagined if I closed my eyes for more than ten seconds I could probably drop off. Then a thousand things ran through my mind that didn't involve sleeping. Perhaps what I really needed was a run—

pushing my body into exhaustion usually helped set things right. Or at least dulled the overwhelming white noise.

The best thing would be to have Katie here so I could talk to her, tell her about my anxiety over Ma and Megan. I know talking to her would calm me down, but as she wasn't home, a nice long run would have to do.

I changed into my running gear and traded my Doc Martens for my new trainers. Good shoes were critical for a runner. I replaced mine every six months. Expensive, but not nearly as much as replacing my knees when I'm older. I waved at Mrs. Sorenson and took off out the door, a nice mix of metal and psychedelia jamming the ear buds. I was in a "White Rabbit" frame of mind, but by the second or third mile, a little Sabbath or Tull would smooth things out.

I ran down the long driveway and out onto the main road, a two-laner that had light traffic; not a lot of call to come out this way unless you were heading to one of the outlying farms. All the bustle was in the cities and the main traffic corridors. I'd be surprised if I saw more than three trucks and maybe a tractor. That was the record from prior runs out here.

The run really helped clear my head—three miles out, three miles back. I was in and out of the shower by the time Katie and Jai Li pulled up. Jai Li ran in, hugged me as I was walking out of the bedroom, and dashed back out of the house.

"Horses," she signed to me before she banged out the front door and went tearing across the yard to the barns.

Katie came in and hugged me next, burying her head into my shoulder and just breathing.

"You smell good," she said, squeezing me tighter. "Think we can get some alone time soon?"

I kissed her on the ear, and she turned her face, hungry for me. We backed into the bedroom, shut the door, and she tumbled onto the bed, pulling her shirt up over her head as she went. There was no way we were going all out here, but I locked the door just in case Jai Li came back into the house.

"Dinner soon," Edith shouted down the hall. I shrugged at Katie, who grimaced. "I'm going out to the barn for about thirty minutes. Do not let the soup burn."

I opened the door and saw her taking off her apron and laying it on a table by the door. She didn't look back but slammed the door on the way out. I glanced at the clock on the wall. Thirty minutes. I could work with that.

I shut the door and locked it again before turning around and shucking off my jeans. Katie already had her bra off and had her hips in the air, pushing her skirt and panties down past her knees. By the time she'd kicked the whole lot to the floor, I had the rest of my clothes in a pile at my feet.

She lay back watching me with one hand between her thighs and the other held out to me. "Come on," she said, breathless. "We have to hurry."

I leaned back against the door and watched her. "We've got time," I said, feeling my nipples harden. "Let me watch you a minute."

She grinned at me and spread her legs, letting me see her pleasure herself. I loved watching her chest rise and fall, her breasts moving up and down, the nipples firm. She pinched one nipple and moaned as her other hand stroked downward between her folds, glistening and puffy.

I let my own hands trail down my body, over my breasts and down my torso.

"Yes," she hissed, arching her back, but watching me. "Come on, baby," she gasped.

It didn't take long for me to feel that first tingle of excitement flutter through my belly, making my knees a little weak as her breathing grew faster and her hands worked more feverishly. My open passion was building, my nipples aching for her mouth. I let out my own gasp as I slipped two fingers into myself and let my thumb grind down on that amazing bundle of nerves that caused my eyes to roll back and my knees fail me. I slid down the wall, letting my bare ass smack down onto the floor as I began to see stars.

"Do it," Katie growled at me from the bed and I opened my eyes to see her sitting up on the edge of the bed. "I want to watch you make yourself come."

I didn't know when we'd suddenly switched roles, but I was okay with it. I watched her watching me and pressed my head back against the wall as I built toward climax.

Of course, the soup burned. I was lying in the bed, tangled in Katie, both of us gasping and spent, when we first smelled the singed soup. She had been slowly stroking me with her left hand while suckling my right breast at the time, so we were not that chuffed about getting up. She began kissing her way across my stomach and down one thigh, making me contemplate certain acrobatic activities I was fond of, when the smoke alarm went off.

Not good timing, let me tell you.

Katie sat up, laughing. We'd been quite urgent in our love-making, working against the clock. I'd spent a goodly portion of our time bringing her to several orgasms before she'd turned to me.

"Totally not fair," I whined as she got up and grabbed a bathrobe.

"Yeah, well," she grinned at me and unlocked the door. "Edith is going to kill us."

She was out the door and down the hall before I could as much as pull a blanket over me. I sat up, moving to the edge of the bed, contemplating whether or not I should get dressed, when she was back, holding the smoke detector.

"Soup's off the burner, and this," she tossed it on top of my jeans, "needs a new battery."

She closed the door, locked it, and dropped her robe to the floor. "Let's see if I can take care of business." She slid to the floor at my feet, pushing my legs apart and burying her face between my thighs. After a minute I fell backwards and howled.

Later, we ordered pizza. Jai Li was thrilled. Edith, not so much. The others couldn't help but make snide remarks peppered with innuendo and snark. I was feeling pretty good in general, and, with me heading back north on Monday, I was willing to put up with their ribbing. They weren't mean-spirited. Later, as we were lying in bed, Katie told me how proud she was of me. How a year ago I'd have been too mortified to do anything in the house, on the off-chance someone would find out.

Now I was just shrugging off comments about scaring the horses and how Julie thought the farm was under attack again. She was grinning when she said it. Still, I was pretty proud of myself. The times they are a-changin'.

CHAPTER THIRTY

Tuesday night, while Sprocket, Dante, and I were polishing off a really amazing peach cobbler Mimi had left us, Qindra called me. She and Stuart were heading down to Portland again on Thursday for a long weekend, and she wanted me to check in on Nidhogg. They'd managed to cover up the Gottschalk house explosion as a meth lab gone wrong. Didn't take much effort by the cleanup crew to stage some things around. Didn't sit well with me, honestly, but that was Qindra's shtick.

She still hadn't figured out who blew the place up, so she was heading down to talk with Frederick, compare notes, see what he knew. There was something else going on with him that neither Qindra nor Stuart would tell me about. I chalked it up to them just wanting to get some quality alone time, but there were plenty of hotels in Seattle. I just needed to trust her. Not my battle yet. I had enough to deal with.

Thursday morning, coincidentally, Sprocket and Dante were getting up at the butt crack of dawn to drive down to Olympia for some ungodly reason. I decided, like a crazy person, to go with them, at least as far as Redmond. That way I could grab the Ducati, check in on Circle Q, and go in to see Nidhogg. I'm not sure anyone would be awake at Circle Q, but they'd be surprised to see me.

They pounded on my door at 4:30. I thought seriously about stabbing them both but thought it bad form to murder your friends. I showered and got dressed, praying to anyone who was listening that they were smart enough to make coffee. If not, there would be bloodshed after all.

Lucky for them, they had learned enough to save their own skins. Dante handed me not one, but two travel mugs full of chocolate and coffee heaven. My sight was blurry, but my nose worked just fine. I followed them out to Dante's 1984 Crown Vic and fell into the back seat. The coffees went straight into the cup holders.

I thought for a minute I was actually going to get some sleep. Then Sprocket started singing obscure folk songs to help keep Dante awake. I lay in the back with the blanket over my head, debating on a knuckle strike to Sprocket's windpipe as an alternative to the effort of throwing him out of the car. That would take entirely too much energy. So much for sleeping. Instead I put in my headphones and cranked some Rage Against the Machine loud enough to block out my own thoughts.

We hit Mary's driveway just before six. I don't know why I was surprised to find the whole household awake. Edith was in the kitchen making oatmeal. She saw us pull up and waved us in. She didn't know Sprocket and Dante but was willing to refill their coffee mugs for the rest of their trek down to Olympia. Mary was out in the barn with Julie, feeding the horses. I decided to give them a hand before getting the bike out. Would be good to chat with them a bit before going over to see Nidhogg. Julie especially. Always good to let someone know when you are going into a dragon's home. You never know when or if you'll come out again.

Katie and Jai Li had decided at the last minute the night before to stay out at Black Briar. It totally sucked I didn't get to surprise them, but that's what I got for not communicating.

Edith loaded Sprocket and Dante up with a batch of oatmeal raisin cookies and several sandwiches each. The woman just needed to take care of folks.

The guys honked as they drove out of the drive and waved. Sprocket hung out the window and sang to Edith as they drove away. Dante gunned it a little, fishtailing in the gravel, and Sprocket nearly fell out of the window. He was punching Dante by the time they pulled out onto the main road.

I went into the barn, calling ahead in case there were any private conversations going on. More than one had been held in that barn. Especially since Blue Thunder had been murdered late last year.

Mary was feeding the horses, and Julie was brushing down one of her new herd. She had three horses. Two she'd gotten from one of the local riding stables—too old to be teaching anyone else to ride. Julie would give them a good life until the end. The third was a rangy cuss. All legs and withers. He wasn't more than a year old and playful, with a white nose and socks. The rest of him was a nice chocolate brown. His mane was a little darker. Quite a handsome lad. She'd named him Strider after his impressive gait.

"You should've called ahead," Julie said, handing me a brush and pointing to the other side of Strider. "Katie is going to be unhappy she missed you."

"I'll call her later," I said, ashamed. Isn't this what Ma and Megan had done, just flaked and didn't communicate? I hated blatant lessons.

Julie took it easy on me, though. As we talked about horses, she continued trying to educate me. It was like a pop quiz. She'd ask me questions and I'd either snap-to with a quick answer, or hem and haw around until she took pity on me and gave me a clue. It was fun. Mary watched us from time to time, a grin on her face. I glanced her way a couple of times, but she wouldn't make eye contact. Just kept grinning. Julie noticed and shrugged, whispering. "She just likes having us all around."

It was pretty damned cool, let me tell ya. Made my gut squirm a little, though, knowing we were going to get our own place and move out.

But not today. Today I was off to visit the oldest, meanest dragon, who just happened to serve tea and sandwiches with little lace doilies and white-gloved servants. Very old school.

We wrapped up with the horses in quick order and went into the house to get cleaned up. Didn't want to show up for tea with the funk going on.

I waved off Edith's attempt to feed me.

"You are getting too skinny," she said, frowning. "You and your young sassy Katie both. But she eats like a horse. You, you eat like a bird these days."

Julie and Mary both ignored me, taking a sandwich from the tray and grabbing glasses of milk from the counter.

"Fine," I said, letting my shoulders slump in defeat. I'd eat one sandwich. Nidhogg wasn't expecting me until one, in any case.

The chicken salad was heavenly but the three of them were watching me like my hair had caught on fire. It was creeping me out a little.

None of them would cop to anything particular, though, so I just let it roll.

Still, my shoulders were tight when I got on the Ducati and I was feeling like there was a target painted on the back of my skull.

So much for that loving feeling. Was I being paranoid, or were they overly concerned with me going to meet Nidhogg?

I hadn't really discussed my evolving role with the white dragon. But they knew enough, I guess. Enough to worry about me. I tilted my head to either side, relaxing my shoulders as I rode. The Ducati was a fast bike, but not always the most comfortable.

Maybe I should trade it in for something a little more laid back. A Harley Soft Tail or something. I twisted the throttle and edged the bike upwards of ninety for the long stretch back into the city. The vibration of the bike blasted up through my thighs and into my brain, giving me a nice calm buzz.

Or, maybe I'd keep the crotch rocket. It suited my personality pretty damn well.

CHAPTER THIRTY-ONE

I t was a glorious day. I almost regretted the leathers. They were getting pretty warm in the heat of the afternoon but beat losing all that skin if I happened to find myself going down the road on my ass. Not like the Seattle drivers paid that much attention to bikes. I'm just surprised I hadn't been nailed already, even as little as I was on the beast.

The ride to Nidhogg's place was uneventful, just me, the sunshine, and the light-to-moderate traffic. Not even a road rage incident. The jerks were playing nice today. I guess most of them were at their day jobs. I'd promised Qindra I would check in on Nidhogg while she and Stuart were out of town, but they'd only been gone one night. But a promise was a promise. It was like feeding some old lady's cat. Only, this cat had a forty-foot wing-span and could swallow a child whole when pissed off.

I didn't show ID when I got to the gate. I just flipped up the shield on my helmet and the guard waved me through. Just like the cop the other night. How many people knew me by sight now? I was getting increasingly uncomfortable with the level of notoriety I was gaining.

I'd barely stepped off the bike when I was whisked into the house, ensconced into the library with a steaming pot of tea, a small tray of sandwiches—all quartered with the crusts cut off—and two types of sweets. I'd had the quince pastries before, but the others were likely some form of lemon bar. I'm sure it was delicious.

There was a book on the table as well. It was a history of medieval battles that I'd been reading the last time I was here. I distinctly remembered reshelving it, but someone had noticed. There was even a silk ribbon marking where I'd left off.

I looked around the room looking for cameras, but there weren't any I could see. Knowing how screwy technology got with magic around, I didn't really believe I'd see cameras. Likely there were just people hiding behind one of the pictures, watching me to make sure I didn't walk away with the silver.

I was halfway through my first cup of tea when I noticed someone had stuck a blank business card a third of the way through the book. It was so shoved into the spine that I'm surprised I found it. The business card had no markings on it, but the section it was tucked into was about the Jomsvikings.

Someone had mentioned them recently. Who had that been? I read through several pages of history about this fabled elite Viking mercenary troop led by a man named Harald Bluetooth, who was King of Denmark at the time. Sounded like a right bastard, honestly. They had a stronghold on the southern coast of the Baltic Sea somewhere, an island fortress where they raided from England to Norway. Pretty hardcore bunch. They were so ruthless that when outnumbered ten to one, they felt bad for the enemy. Only at a hundred to one would they consider a strategic retreat.

The door to the library opened by the time I'd polished off the last of the tiny sandwiches and was nearing the end of the pot of tea. Honestly, I needed to pee, but in came Nidhogg. I crossed my legs and grimaced.

I watched her make her slow and steady way across the wide floor, toward where I sat near the currently darkened fireplace. It was all very comfortable, except for the having to go pee thing. That was going to get out of control soon.

When Nidhogg finally was within striking distance, I stood and bowed to her.

"Hello," I said, straightening to look her in the eye.

She smiled at me and put one hand on the chair opposite the one I was sitting in.

"I fancy some of those sandwiches you've been enjoying," she said with a gleam in her eye. "Would you be a dear and run off to the kitchen and see about some more?"

I bowed again. "No problem at all."

One of the many bathrooms was between here and the kitchen. My bladder would survive another day.

The kitchen staff outdid themselves once more. They provided twice as many sandwiches, another tray of desserts, this one strawberries and cream, as well as another pot of tea for me. If I lived here, I'd be as big as a horse. Edith would be thrilled to know just how much I'd eaten today.

Nidhogg was quietly sipping her tea when we returned with the new food—I insisted on carrying a tray. These people may be servants of Nidhogg, but I'd be damned if I was going to let them wait on me hand and foot.

Once we were settled back in front of the cold fireplace, Nidhogg set her tea aside and cleared her throat.

"I understand you played your part in the cleanup of the Gottschalk woman's home." She had her hands folded in her lap and smiled a toothy grin.

"Yes, ma'am."

"I appreciate your assistance," she said. "Qindra thinks very highly of you, and I understand Jai Li is thriving with the abundance of support and caring you are helping provide for her."

I watched her, looking for snark or digs. Was she implying I wasn't a good enough mother to Jai Li?

"She's a special child," I said finally, shrugging off the doubt. "Every day with her is a joy."

"I have many fond memories of the girl's presence," she said, her voice quieter. Her grin slowly faded as she spun away into her own thoughts. She stared over my left shoulder just long enough for me to become a little nervous. Finally, I looked over my shoulder to make sure there was no one standing there. My movement must've jarred her from her reverie.

"I deeply regret the death of those children," she said, leaning forward, her hands balled into bony fists. "I swear to you. If I had the power to undo that night, I would do so, even if the price was my own life."

I sat back, shocked. We'd had some blunt and realistic conversations before. Most of the time we spoke of ancient days, other lives and other places. But this time I had the feeling she was looking for absolution.

"I'm sure you regret the loss of your ..." I paused. There was a change with this oldest dragon. How did I say this without offending?

"You can say 'servants,'" Nidhogg said with a sigh. "I know what I am, and I know what I have done to these people. You have shown me a different vision, one that is hard for me to understand, but I am trying."

I nodded at her. What could I really say?

"I meant what I said the last time we spoke," she said, her voice growing steadier, her resolve more firm. "I want to help these people ... my people to have a better life. I just don't know what I can do, what I can tolerate." She buried her face in her hands and moaned quietly. "My life is not what I dreamed it would be back in the early days of this world." She dropped her hands and stared at me. There was fire in her eyes. The fire of her kind: passion and rage, pain and power. "I have done great harm in my day," she said, suddenly standing, her walking stick clattering against the table between us. "The voices rage in my dreams." She started to shake, her entire body quaking. "All is blood and fire!"

Whoa ... I scooted my chair back a few feet, thinking about

Gram out on the bike, and the distance between me and the door. If she started to transform, could I get past her in time?

There was no way I was fighting her here, in her home. If I didn't know she was a fire and scale, tooth and claw killing machine, how would I handle it?

I did probably the stupidest thing a dragon slayer could do. I stepped around the table and folded the old woman into my arms, pulling her to my chest and holding her tight.

"Deep breath," I said, without thinking. "Just take it easy."

We stood there for a very long time. I kept thinking *please don't eat me*, interposed with *please be okay*. It was a bit surreal. She was old and frail in my arms, but radiated heat like a forge. Any second now she would either transform or just spontaneously combust. I was doomed in either case.

Instead of either, thankfully, her breath eased to a slower pace. After a minute, her heart—which pounded so strongly I could feel it in my chest—began to slow to the point she finally stopped shaking.

"Are you going to be okay?" I asked her when she started to go limp in my arms.

She stepped back, falling into her seat. I knelt at her side, holding her hands in mine. Tears rolled down her face. I squeezed her hands and she gave me a shy smile.

"No one has ever held me," she said, her voice catching. She turned her head and coughed into her shoulder but kept a tight grip on my hands. "No one has dared touch me; no one has had the courage or the strength."

I reached up and wiped the tears with one hand. "You have children, I assume you had lovers."

She laughed harshly. "Dragons mate, they do not love. There were those I coupled with in my younger days, but those were savage moments of tooth and claw. Once they had given me what I required they fled, knowing I would destroy them had they stayed."

"I'm sorry," I said. "You must be so lonely."

For a moment she stiffened again and I froze. I'd been lucky so far. Why did I need to keep talking? My mouth was going to get me killed.

"No one has dared talk to me in such a familiar fashion" she said, sighing. "You are a breath of fresh air, young one."

She took one hand from mine and cupped my cheek. "So beautiful and yet so strong," she whispered. "I see why Qindra holds you in such high regard."

I flushed, the heat rising in my neck and face. I struggled with compliments in the best of times, but, coming from the Mother of All Dragons, they proved even more awkward.

She shook her head and pulled her hands away. "Scoot back to your seat," she said. "I am in no danger of ... *losing my shit*, I think is your phrase."

Had I said that out loud? Did she read my mind?

Her eyes twinkled as I stood and crossed back to my seat. I'm sure I'd probably said that phrase before, and probably in Qindra's presence. Still, that was a little creepy.

Nidhogg took up her tea once more and we sipped in silence. How close had I just come to becoming dragon chow?

"I have called a conclave," she said, her voice firm and commanding once more. "It is not something we have done since the earliest days of this current political fiasco you call a country."

Hard to argue with that. "A conclave? Like an Ent Moot?"

Nidhogg looked at me funny and I realized I'd been channeling Katie again. "Big meeting with powerful beings?" I asked.

"Yes, a Dragon Mete. There is much to discuss. I do not like the way the Reavers are starting to explore the boundaries of civilized territories."

I didn't have the heart to tell her that the average individual didn't like being ruled by a dragon overclass much either. Well, if they knew. I'm sure there are some folks out there that would be happy to serve their dragon overlords openly and with sycophantic joy, as long as they got to impose their personal beliefs on the rest of us.

"When?" I asked. "Like soon?"

"It will happen when all those of consequence have been notified," she said. "There are others in the world, other sword bearers who will need to find their way to you before we can proceed."

"There are other sword bearers?" Did that mean dragon slayers like me, or something else? A thousand questions sprang to mind.

She shushed me and foisted strawberries on me as a diversion.

"There is something I need your discretion on," she said, once my mouth was full of berry. She smiled at my wide-eyed look and drove forward, resolve writ large upon her face. "I am a little afraid."

I blinked at her and swallowed.

"This request is for you alone."

I nodded once, trying to keep my eyebrows from rocketing off the top of my head.

"There is a feeling," she leaned forward in her seat, both hands on her walking stick. "A feeling that I cannot be sure is real." She sighed, and making up her mind, apparently, plunged forward.

"When I was young, before we overthrew the capricious and narcissistic Asgardians, I would be visited occasionally by a feeling, almost a premonition of some great power that does not wish to be discovered. Though I searched, I could not discover what this power was. It did not linger, but flashed into existence, then faded, sometimes in a wink.

"There was a time I thought it madness on my part." She shook her head. "I fear I have grown senile, for I have begun to suspect that power has followed me, is closer to home."

I opened my mouth to ask a question, but she held up one hand to forestall me.

"For far too long I averted my gaze from the land north of us, avoided my responsibilities concerning my loathsome offspring, Jean-Paul."

Her hands shook at these words, and she looked up into my eyes. "A responsibility you dealt with, young Sarah. One I do not begrudge you and for which I will ever be in your debt."

I kept my mouth shut at those words. That path was fraught with danger and death.

When the corners of her mouth turned up in a smile, I knew I was safe and I let my shoulders relax.

"The land between here and his home grew dark in my mind's eye as I turned my attention inward over the centuries. While I have compounded my many sins by ignoring his horrific deeds, and refused to even gaze in his direction, I may have unwillingly allowed a portion of my kingdom to grow wild and untamed." She paused, staring at her gnarled hands. "I fear something festers in that blind spot, fair Sarah."

I shrugged. "How far south did he control?"

She shook her head. "He was not permitted to range below the Canadian border."

I thought of the blood cult, the necromancer, and the various stories I'd known of giants raiding, including the incursions fended off by Black Briar in their early years. He may not have been *allowed* to come south of the border, but I had pretty good evidence that he did as he pleased. Not that I'd point that obvious fact out to Nidhogg.

"I understand you have ties to Bellingham. Explore that shadow region, my Fist. Discover what lurks upon my doorstep."

How convenient. I nodded. I wanted to say I was a step ahead of her, but decided it wasn't worth the risk.

For the next hour I listened to her reminisce about the glory days and lament the ills she had begun to understand about our world. She'd really been isolated for a very long time. Coming out to do battle with the blood cult, and rescue Frederick Sawyer in the process, had started a course of change within her. She avoided talking about Jai Li, but I think it was that child, more than Sawyer, who had swayed her to the new path.

So, I was at the forefront of a modern-day revolution. One that, if things went really well, could very well lead to Ragnarök —the end of the world.

Nidhogg could see no other way. The wheel had been shattered long ago, and it was up to us to fix the damn thing so we could break out of the miasma our world has become.

Heady stuff for tea, but I left hopeful, in an *up is down* sort of way.

Hell, I didn't expect to live forever.

CHAPTER THIRTY-TWO

B ack on the road, I thought about how deeply coincidental it was that Nidhogg's suspicions about Bellingham lined up with the things I'd been observing. I thought about the Hamsters and their place in this great unfolding mystery. Were they playing a part in what Nidhogg sensed? Were they somehow more than they let on? I know Sprocket was a crafty one; could he be Loki or something? If that were the case, I'm sure the runes in my hairline would have tingled with the thought. Or maybe they were totally rocking my skull and I couldn't tell over the vibration of the Ducati.

I laughed as I wove out onto the main roads and headed north. Sprocket and Dante were very cool to hang out with, but there was no way they were gods reborn. Of course, I'm sure if I said that to Sprocket, his head would swell to three times its size. I really enjoyed their company and their biting wit. Sure, they had moody stretches, but for the most part they were awesome company. We talked about politics and movies, music and books. They asked me about a million questions about blacksmithing and quite a few about Tae Kwon Do. It was like being at summer camp all of the time.

I didn't forget my last conversation with Gletts either. I know he thought there was a portal or some such at the boarding house that would let his people get home to Alfheim, though I had my doubts. The house was old and Mimi was odd, but overall the place felt fairly normal. No heebie-jeebies.

The ride back to the boarding house was uneventful. I really enjoyed being back on the bike again, though I was still thinking about trading it in for a Harley. When I got to Bellingham I stopped at the store, picked up a few supplies and headed to the boarding house. Later that night I had a quiet dinner all alone in the kitchen after a video call with Katie and Jai Li about our days. I have to say, talking to those two always made me feel more grounded. Anxiety just melted away when I listened to Katie tell me about her day. I could listen to that woman read a phone book and be in heaven. Tonight wasn't the best call we'd had. Katie was miffed I had come into town, but when I pointed out that she hadn't shared with me her plans to stay out at Black Briar, she let it go. The call didn't end stellar. When I told her I loved her and missed her, she teared up. Didn't take away her anger and frustration. Though it did take off the edge.

I had just gotten into bed and turned off the lamp when I got a shudder. Maybe it was the fact Sprocket and Dante were out for the first time since I'd been staying there, or the fact Mimi was nowhere to be found. Whatever the reason, as the night wore on, I got more and more weirded out. Big, empty houses have that effect on me.

I'm not a child, but I pulled the blankets up to my neck and pretended that it was a force field as I fell asleep—made me think of home for good and bad reasons.

I woke up around two in the morning, just sat bolt right up in bed like someone had tossed a bucket of cold water on me. Luckily there was no water, but I couldn't be more awake without coffee. I listened hard but couldn't make out any real noises. The fans running in the back of the house were a quiet drone that I'd gotten used to. This house held heat, and those of us in the upper story got used to the attic fan or smothered. I strained to hear anything of the boys, or Mimi, to no avail. The house was empty besides me and my irrational fears. I thought back to the spate of ultra-violent dreams I'd had recently and decided the energy in the room had a wary vibe.

Regardless of the reason, something had woken me up and I'd learned to trust those sudden shifts of intuition. I slipped into my jeans and pulled a jacket over my T-shirt before stomping into my Docs. Sleeping in my socks helped with hasty exits and kept my toes toasty when I slept alone. Never had that problem when sleeping with Katie, though she was a blanket hog.

I toyed with pulling Gram from under my bed but thought it would be pretty impolite to accidentally stab Mimi. It's possible someone was home, and I'd just heard them go to the bathroom or something. Big empty houses made some awkward noises in the dead of night.

I crept down the stairs, leaving the lights off and navigating by the ambient light. When I stepped into the darkened kitchen, I could see the back door was open. Mimi stood out near that covered cistern that had drawn Bianca the night after the concert. Mimi held her arms in the air and sang to the night. It was a little creepy in a "summoning demons" sort of way. Yet, her voice was sweet and strong, with a languid rhythm that settled my nerves.

I leaned against the counter and strained my ears, listening. When her words drifted to me, they weren't about demons or anything creepy, rather she sang about apples.

The astonishing thing was I'd heard that song before. I leaned against the kitchen counter and racked my brains. Qindra had sung that song last year out in Chumstick. Back before she got trapped in the house. Before Anezka lost her mind and the necromancer's plans began to take place.

In a spot of land, where the rivers run
and the Glori Mundi bloom
I met a girl like the brightest star
A peck of Gallen, like the kiss I craved
were not for such as me

Qindra had said she learned the song from her mother. But her mother had first heard it from an old vaudeville singer from Buffalo back in the waning days of the circuit. The singer had been one of the Ancients. The only other of the Ancients that Qindra had known to still exist—beyond Nidhogg, that is.

Was it possible that Mimi was that same singer? That would be a fucking strange coincidence.

I listened to her sing for a good while, long enough for her to loop back through the song a few times, turning as she went.

I'd done something similar with Gram when I hunted Jean-Paul a year ago. I used the magic to point me to the dragon. Was Mimi looking for apples? What kind of crazy was that? I didn't want to interrupt her, though. It was too bizarre. I crept back upstairs and crawled back into bed.

Apples? Wasn't there some Norse legend about apples keeping the gods, if not exactly immortal, then long-lived?

I was back up at four. I blamed my bladder. Even after a quick pee, however, I couldn't get back to sleep. There was a pressure in the air which reminded me of how it felt before a thunderstorm, back when I was a kid in Kansas. Too many expectations pushing at my chest to allow me to go back to sleep, so I decided it was time for a run.

This time I grabbed some sweats and sneakers. I may regret having too much on by the time I hit the second mile, but it was chilly in the house. The breeze off the bay sometimes brought a cold wind that the rest of the state missed out on. I grabbed my running pack and my cell phone off the desk. I filled my water bottle in the bathroom and crept down the stairs. A run would do me good. I felt tight, wound up. Kicking out a few miles would make me feel much better—less anxious.

Bellingham wasn't like most other cities at 4:30 in the morning. There were a few folks out, delivery guys, and street sweepers, but mostly it was quiet.

I didn't worry too much about where I was going, just wanted to clear my head. I ran down the long lane that the boarding house was on, avoiding side streets, just heading straight into town. I wouldn't get that far in a run, but I knew my goal. There was a park I had in mind. I would hit that, turn around and come home. Should be just under six miles round trip. More than enough to beat my body and brain into a nice torpor. My muscles ached like I'd been fighting. What had I been dreaming before I woke up? My shoulders were especially tight and painful.

By the time the park came into view I'd finally started to loosen up. It helped that I was doing punches as I ran—awkward if you're not careful—can throw off your gait—but I had plenty of practice from my old Tae Kwon Do days. Funny how quickly the muscles remembered. I was pleased that my body was responding like I'd hoped, but my head remained sluggish—not enough sleep, I guess. A malaise lay on the world around me, like a blanket of awkward. That Kansas thunderstorm tension was still in the air, but the sky was clear. Plenty of stars out in the last dregs of night.

I turned at the park, a small little thing with a few trees, two swing sets, and one of those domed monkey bars jobbies. Beneath the monkey bars I could see three dark shapes huddled together. As I cruised past, two large dogs—huskies by the look of them—raised their heads with ears up, intently watching my progress. I couldn't make out the third figure in the shadows, but the gold eyes of those dogs shone in the glare of the streetlights. In this light they looked more like wolves.

I decided to jog around the park, keeping to the opposite side of the street that encircled it. That way I had some distance and could watch the alert animals watching me. I'd run closest to them once I crossed north to the far side of the park. I sped up a bit, irrationally wanting to cross a patch of shadow between streetlights, while the creep factor grew in my belly. Adrenaline began to leak into my blood, accelerating my heart, pumping my muscles to flee danger.

The third figure stirred, reached for one of the dogs, and rolled to his side, facing me. My pace faltered. He sat there disheveled and scraggly, with wild gray hair and beard, and a wicked scar over one side of his face. I knew that face.

"Joe?" I called out. Or was it Woden?

The man rolled to his knees and the wolves moved to flank him, hackles raised. I stopped a dozen strides away, on the edge of a golden halo of light. My breath came harder than I liked.

"Smith?" he called, placing a hand on each of the wolves, for there could be no doubt now. They were huge beasts. "Am I dreaming?"

I stepped onto the grass. The wolves growled, flattening their ears. "Where you been, Joe?" I asked, not really feeling comfortable with the Woden line of thinking.

"Keep back," he said, holding a hand toward me. "My brothers here are not aware of your calling, nor of your deeds."

"Fair enough." I stepped back onto the sidewalk and the wolves settled down onto their haunches, their golden eyes alert for trickery.

Joe sat forward, leaning against the monkey bars. "Dwarves again," he said. "Why is it you truck with dwarves, smith?"

I sat on the sidewalk—legs folded criss-cross applesauce—and rested my hands on my knees. "If by 'truck' you mean visit, then yes. I have a friend among Durin's kin. One who recently had a son."

He chuckled. "Brilliant craftsmen, and fickle friends. Beware, smith. They nearly always have their own agenda."

Yeah, not like you, old man. I waited for more, but he just stared at me, turning his head from side to side.

"How'd you end up here?" I asked.

One of the wolves snorted, as if to say he would like to know as well.

"I follow the storm clouds," he said. "The bones of our mother lie uneasy in this city. I can feel her moans as the thunderheads collect in the aether."

"And this has to do with your children?"

He nodded. "I look for the fallen in the place where they are likely to be."

"So, you believe your kith and kin are in Bellingham?"

He shrugged. "The air north of here is clearing. The wyrm stench fades from this place. I think it will make breathing easier."

Conversation with this individual ... god ... man ... was damned confusing. "Is there someone specific you seek?" I asked. "Someone you know to be lost and not dead?"

"All dead," he moaned. "Each taken from the world by claw and fire. Each shriven from their beds by the blight of wing and scale."

"Dragons, got it." It was like talking in poetry. My college professors would be jazzed.

"I am weary, smith. Fearful."

I knew the feeling.

"Have you found them?" he asked. "Have you word of the mighty Thor, or even the wicked Loki? Has Freya's beauty shone in your eyes, or the mighty horn of Heimdall graced your ears?"

What a puzzle this man was. *If he was Woden, why was he so helpless?*

"I'm afraid not," I told him. "All I know is that the dragons kill each as they are reborn."

The wolves began to growl again, but they didn't raise their heads.

"I am old, smith. I do not know if I will live long enough to gather them to our home again. The way is closed, and the company has been lost. Do you know what it is to be alone?" His voice shook.

I thought of Nidhogg, of her sins and her loneliness; of Katie and Jai Li back in Redmond, and my family failing to show for our arranged dinner. Yes, old man, I know a modicum of loneliness.

He watched me for a breath, then tilted his head back and howled. The wolves lifted their muzzles and added their voices to his. The cries were mournful and full of anguish. If you've never heard wolves howl, you can't imagine the power there. No wonder we humans are scared of them. Fear raced through me for a moment, driving me to flee, but I held my ground and watched them howl.

After a moment, they ceased and Joe fell against the bars, panting. "Time is short. The drakes will find us again.

"Maybe not," I said. "I did kill one of them."

This seemed to perk him up a bit. "Aye," he growled. "You wield the blade with honor and might. I felt his fall, the black-hearted bastard."

I clenched my right fist, feeling the pain of fire for the briefest of moments.

Then I thought of Gunnr and the others. "Why do you not seek the Valkyrie?"

"I have no voice," he growled, sounding as one of the wolves. "I call them and call them, but they do not hear."

I thought of that moment in the glade, before I flew to hunt down the dragon Duchamp. The price to borrow one of the winged horses had been a kiss. When Gunnr kissed me, it was like taking a long, cool drink on a hot day. I bet if I called to Gunnr, she would hear me. "Shall I try?"

He cackled. "To what avail? To mock an old man? To carry me off to Hel with the rest of the dead?"

"Maybe they could help?"

"I need no serving wenches," he barked. "None that fetch and tote. I need warriors. I need my sons with me."

Now he was pissing me off. "Hey!" I shouted, coming to my feet. "You saying a woman can't be a warrior?"

He laughed, slapping his thigh with one hand. "You have the fire, rightly enough," he said. "But you are a maiden, despite your pretenses. Battles need to be fought. Wars considered. What does a milk-fed stripling like yourself understand of man's work?"

"I was good enough to save your sorry ass from a couple of giants," I said, my voice gone cold. I took two long strides toward the jungle gym. "I killed a dragon, didn't I?" My pulse throbbed in my temples as the fire rose in me.

He stood, pulling himself up on the bars. The wolves stood as well, one on either side of him. "Aye," he said once he stood. "You have proven yourself; for that I apologize." He rubbed his forehead. "I have tumbled thoughts, old and new. The images war with one another. And here, in this town, they war as never before."

I stood just out of reach of the bars, my fists at my side, trembling. I could feel the anger hovering at my edges, frustration and desire to prove I was good enough warring with what I knew to be true.

"You are a confounding old man," I said at last, forcing the anger to recede. "If you're angry with your lot, don't push away those who want to help you."

He bowed his head and mumbled something.

"I can't hear you," I said.

He raised his head for a moment and smiled. "Go home, smith. Ask the androgynous one where she has hidden the Gjallarhorn."

"Androgynous one? Do you mean Mimi? What the hell is Gjallarhorn?" I looked at him, willing him to give me a straight answer.

"The way is upon you," he said, climbing out from the bars. The wolves followed him and he pulled his pack and staff from where they lay. "You had better hie back to your bower," he said, striding north. "You are not prepared for the coming storm."

I turned, looking around. The tension in the air was definitely picking up. Off to the south, I heard a low grumble of thunder. When I looked back, Woden and the wolves were gone.

Definitely not interested in getting caught in a summer squall, I started running back to the boarding house. I thought for a moment to go north and follow the old man's trail, but I was fairly sure it would have vanished on the far side of the street.

CHAPTER THIRTY-THREE

The sky glowed with the first rays of sunrise by the time I arrived back from my run. I practically vibrated with frustration over the whole encounter with Joe. Mimi stood at the counter making coffee when I came into the kitchen. I just wanted to slug back a couple glasses of water then hit the showers. I really wasn't inclined to banter. Not with Joe's last words ringing in my head. It was damn hard sometimes to put up with all the psychotic bullshit.

Mimi watched me. Like she was waiting for me to say something. I didn't turn away, but I was in no mood to engage. I finished my water and turned to go. Just before I made it out of the room, Mimi asked, "How was the old man?"

I froze, my heart suddenly racing. She could be meaning anyone.

"He'll use you up," she offered. "You know that, right?"

I didn't say anything, just stood there for a minute, one hand on the doorframe and the other clenched at my side in a tight fist. Blood roared in my ears. I had the sudden urge to break something.

"You're not the first," she said behind me. "And, as sad as it makes me, you won't likely be the last."

I started to say something biting. My mind buzzed, trying to focus on the words.

"He only cares about himself. It's always the same. If he'd cared about his family, he would have done more before his house fell."

I let out the breath I'd been holding and half turned toward her.

"Did he notice the dragon stench?"

I faced her, anger warring with uncertainty. She'd been kind to me, gave me a place to live. But there was something there that rankled me. Some secret she held that impacted me in some way.

"He asked after you," I said with a grim smile.

She flushed, and her face settled into a mask of neutrality. "He's a fool, and so are you if you listen to him."

"I think he searches for you," I said, the idea dawning. "You have something of his and he can't find you. Why is that? What do you have?"

She looked shocked. Her neutrality was coming at a high price. The shadow that flitted across her features spoke of pain and more.

"He's a madman," she said, coolly. There was hatred there that surprised me. I mean, I had no real love for the guy, he was demanding and contrary. But the only thing he'd done to me is mark me with his runes. And that had proven pretty helpful on occasion.

"Is it Jaller's Horn?" I asked, trying to remember the words he'd used.

She choked, attempted to cover it with a cough, and looked at me as if I'd hit her. "Who are you?" she asked me. There was terror there, real to-the-bone fear.

I shrugged. "I'm nobody," I said. "Just someone trying to make it in this world. Same as you."

She watched me for a moment. "Not the same as me," she

said, thoughtfully. "But there is something about you. Something I fear I may live to regret."

"You have nothing to fear from me," I said, meaning it. "You've been kind to me. But you do know about things I thought hidden, things I've only just discovered."

Why the hell had I told her that? There was an innocence to her, an aura of peace and calm. Like a cat, perhaps, languid and waiting, ready to pounce on her prey.

I blinked away the image of her and the moment passed. Mimi reached for the coffee pot and refilled her travel mug. She twisted the cap on it and held it up as if saluting me. "You are a tool of both sides," she said. She picked up her purse from the table. "I don't know about any horn and I'm afraid that you are too young to understand much more than you already know."

She walked toward me, pausing as I stepped aside. She breezed past me, toward the front of her house. At the front door she glanced around. "Take a shower. See if you can get rid of some of their combined taint. There's a nice cinnamon and apple body wash in the hall bath." And she went out the front door, pulling it closed behind her.

I knew I was pretty ripe from my run, but come on. The perfume that trailed in her wake smelled of roses and chemicals. It was overwhelming.

I sighed and trudged down the long cut-stone hallway and rounded the stairs, taking them three at a time. I didn't stop until I'd closed and bolted the door to my room. For a moment I leaned against the door, trying to slow my breathing. The runes on my leg ached and the ones along my scalp tingled. I pushed myself upright and crossed to my bed. Glancing once at the closed door, I squatted down and pulled Gram's case out from under my bed. I had a bit of trouble fumbling with the latches. Once the case was flipped open, I grasped Gram in my left hand and sank onto the bed, pointing her toward the door. I needed to get my jumbled thoughts in order.

Mimi knew. She was one of them. Probably one of the

ancient ones. Someone of power in any case. How had the dragons not come here before? Odin knew about her, for pity's sake.

I heard a car door slam and looked out the window to see Mimi driving off. She went into the college every morning to do volunteer work. I had hours ahead of me with an empty house. It was my chance to take the snooping to a new level. A little breaking and entering, if necessary—maybe violate some personal space. I'd ask for forgiveness if I got caught. Right now, the runes were telling me I needed to find something important.

After a quick shower, I opened the wardrobe and pulled out the gym bag I kept in the back. Inside I had my chain mail and the gambeson that went underneath. I threw on a pair of jeans and a concert T-shirt which proclaimed that things were Slippery When Wet. Then I pulled on the thick cloth shirt and finally the chain hauberk. I slipped on Gram's sheath and slid her home just over my right shoulder.

I felt more comfortable than I had in a good while.

CHAPTER THIRTY-FOUR

When striking iron on an anvil, there's this reverberation that runs through the hammer, up your arm, and ends up in your brain. Once you do it enough, you start to crave that sensation. What was once jarring becomes comfortable, second nature. Just thinking about it gave me a little rush.

I stood in the laundry room downstairs in the partially finished basement and nearly jumped out of my skin. Something nearby triggered a thread of energy which ran over from my scalp, across my shoulders and down my back to fire against the runes on my leg. An answering surge of power raced back across my body and after a minute, my scalp tingled like I had my hands on a Tesla coil. Whatever lay hidden in this house had no intention of giving up its secrets, and yet I could not shake the feeling of lurking malice. Not just malice, that's too black and white. There was anger there, almost hate, but also fear and longing. What in the name of the dead gods was I feeling?

I made two passes through the house, even crossing that social line of searching the other bedrooms. I didn't look under the mattresses or rifle anyone's underwear drawers, but I did rummage through the closets to see if I could find a hidden doorway or something. No such luck. The whole time I was upstairs, I had the strong desire to move back down. The energy drew me almost as strongly as it repelled. It gave me the strangest sensation of battling wills.

The resonance was in my bones by this point, a narrow thrumming that I could isolate and recognize when present. Oddly enough, it grew strongest near the kitchen. It's not like I could pinpoint the source, rather, it felt more like a miasma that permeated that portion of the house.

I was fairly convinced I needed to uncover something inside the house, but I wanted to do my due diligence and explore the surrounding property. I paced the fence line, searching for the same sort of magic that Jimmy had used out at Black Briar, but felt nothing. Not even a shiver of power. I crisscrossed the back yard, thinking maybe there was some external aspect to what I was sensing, but came up empty.

Beyond the back fence was a drop to the bay. I imagined there could be any number of caves below that ran under the property. Maybe like the one that Rowling described in the sixth Harry Potter book. I climbed on top of the cistern to peer over the fence there and could see a good portion of the cliff facing below. Pretty solid stone there. Only real way to see if there was a cave would be to go out into the bay and look back, and I had no access to a boat. Besides, my instincts were telling me this was a fool's errand. Whatever I sensed was inside the house.

The old cistern was locked. Sprocket told me Mimi was always worried some kid was going to fall into it and she'd lose the house in a pending lawsuit. No one bothered it ... well, except for Bianca, who seemed to find it fascinating when she was drunk.

There was something there, nonetheless. The cistern gave off a heat signature similar to the ley line focal point out at Anezka's old place in Chumstick. But the tingling was different, more subdued. Reminded me of cold molasses. I spent twenty minutes examining the cover and the old lock keeping the lid closed before giving up. Whatever was there was not what I was looking for. I drew Gram and did the searchlight shuffle, holding her out in front of me and moving around slowly, concentrating on that thrumming feeling in my bones. After two passes I stopped, Gram pointing firmly at the house. The cistern didn't even give me a hiccup. That cleared things up. My goal was definitely in the house.

I carried Gram in front of me like a divining rod as I reentered the kitchen through the back door. She didn't buck or anything until I started down the hallway. My instincts told me I was looking for some sort of door or portal—an ancient relic—just like the door in our old apartment. A ghost door or the memory of an older threshold steeped with ancient energy.

I thought back to that time I'd been practicing walkabout in the old apartment. How I'd taken the herbs Skella's grandmother had given me to ease myself out-of-body. I'd found the ghost of an old door that had been used before they split the upper floor of the building into two apartments.

Thresholds hold power, and the more often they are crossed, in either direction, the stronger it becomes. I say either way, implying that you can either go through or back across a threshold, like those are the only two options. I learned the hard way about how thresholds can open to the Sideways—the place of nightmares and crystal, broken dreams and eating things.

I shivered at the memories and felt slightly ashamed of the fear that they invoked. And, as is my wont, I doubled down against that emotion. Maybe I needed to take that risk, look at this place in a different way. Maybe I needed to take Gletts's example and explore the house in walkabout.

There'd be no one here for hours yet. I could take a quick spin around the place in astral form and my body should be safe. I'd done it a few times before. Piece of cake.

The runes across my scalp purred. I took that as approval for my decision and settled on a plan. I didn't have any of Unun's tea with me, but I knew the meditations I needed to do to get my mind in the proper state. I'd practiced them enough.

I went back to my room and bolted the door. Then I made a nest of blankets and pillows in the middle of the floor, just in case. Didn't want to somehow flop around and fall off the bed.

I lay in the middle of the nest with Gram in her sheath on my chest. I grasped her in my hands, her business end pointed toward my feet. I imagined I looked like a dead warrior princess.

Don't ask. We all play our head games.

I ran through my breathing exercises and thought of a clear white space. Once I'd cleared my mind as well as I knew how, I tried to picture my spirit-self rising up, leaving my meat-self behind. It was a temporary state as I would remain tethered to my physical form by a silver thread. I never saw my own connection when I went walkabout, but I had seen the phenomenon in others whose spirits had been riven from their bodies.

I hoped to never be in that position. When my time came to die, I wanted a clean break—no ambiguity—just a sharp snapping and a rapid journey onward.

Not that I wanted that any time soon. Hell, I had too many plans, wanted to spend so many more days with Katie and Jai Li. Who knew, maybe I had it in me to reconcile with Ma and Da. I was thinking it would be best for Megan, but deep down, I wanted it for myself.

Eventually those anxieties quieted and I lost count of my breaths. One moment I was feeling the drag of sleep on my mind, and the next I found myself rising without my body. With almost no effort, I willed my spirit into a standing position, oblivious to the body that lay beneath me. It proved to be surprisingly easy, like maybe the house had anticipated the action and had aided me in some way. Previous experiences had been like clawing my way through gelatin. This was like drawing in a fresh breath.

And, as last time, Gram made the transition with me. She was both spirit and steel. I'd learned that already. And I was damn happy to have her with me in this state. I felt less vulnerable.

I glanced around the room, shaken by the riot of colors. I had forgotten how brilliant the world was in this state. I had to concentrate to focus against the overwhelming visual input. With sheer force of will, I propelled myself forward, through the door, and out into the hallway.

Where I recoiled.

Where my room had been a disco ball of input, the house was a spinning kaleidoscope of colors and emotions. It took me a few minutes to overcome the tidal wave of input and center myself once more.

I gingerly crept along the hall. When I passed both Sprocket's and Dante's doors, I could sense the echoes of their intense needs and desires. Dante's room especially glowed with a strong sense of resolve while Sprocket's room glowed with an erratic array of acceptance and love. Underlying them both, however, lurked danger and emotional desperation. I didn't stick around to decipher more. I already felt too voyeuristic. I willed myself down to the main floor.

I didn't relish phasing through more walls than I needed to, so I followed the stairs down. The house pulsed with the dual comforts of safety and home. If anything, I was a little embarrassed for being so negative toward Mimi earlier. There was a comforting aura in every portion of the house, even the bathrooms.

As I willed myself down the hallway toward the kitchen, the echo of the fight I'd had earlier with Mimi rippled out in sharp yet waning waves. There was plenty of anger on both parts, but I could definitely sense a pervasive aura of fear where Mimi had been standing. The emotion was transient and fading. The house itself was pulling the negative energy apart, soothing the spot like someone sopping up spilled wine.

None of my usual alarms were going off, which scared me in and of itself. I glanced around, seeking some threat—the inevitable wicked witch to taint the perfect house. But there was no Hansel and Gretel feel to this place. This was no gingerbread trap for unwary children. It just pulsated with comfort.

I had searched the entirety of the house a dozen times and was about to give up when the healing energy from the kitchen subsided and I was able to see the one flaw I had missed. There was a single blemish against the throbbing, wholesome goodness the house exuded—an old scar that had healed over but never went away. In the hall, where I had paused the first time I searched the house, was an old rotary dial phone Mimi had refused to remove. I found it clever how that bit of ancient technology obfuscated the even older memory.

As I concentrated on the faintest hint of an outline, it resolved into a door. I brushed at the edges, pushing away the layers of hope that had grown thick around the frame.

It took me a bit of effort, but eventually I was able to clear the entire doorway—ancient and ill-placed. It didn't belong here. That much was sure. It was as if it had been superimposed on this wall against its will.

I had to concentrate with everything I could muster to keep it in focus. It kept slipping aside, wanting to be someplace else.

But I knew this was the key. I grasped the edges with my ephemeral fingers and tugged. The cost was enormous. I staggered as a wave of vertigo swept over me. The door was totally bogarting my chi. I floated back, wiping the trailing strands of hope on my jeans. Okay, I was ethereal, but I wasn't exactly naked. You get the point. I pulled Gram from her sheath, grasping her with both hands, and let her infuse me with her power. The door flared brighter. Note to self: always draw the sword in cases like this. The world had crisp, sharp edges.

I wedged Gram into the crack I'd been able to open, and the door flew to the side, sliding into the wall like those doors on *Star Trek*. It even made that *schnuck* sound those television doors made.

On the other side of the threshold a rough-hewn stairway curved away and toward the west. Torches flared to life, casting a wan yellow light. The staircase had wide shallow steps leading down to a small landing before turning out of my range of vision.

I took a proverbial deep breath, not actually needing to breathe here, and stepped through the doorway.

I confess I've done smarter things in my life.

CHAPTER THIRTY-FIVE

The stairs wound downward into bedrock. This was another place. I wasn't in the Sideways, or anything like that, and I was definitely not in one of the other worlds I'd traveled in. I'm pretty sure I could feel that. This place seemed like it was out of phase, a place from another time, or a place pushed out of time like a long-forgotten love letter or something. I could feel energy and the expectancy. The bedrock the house was built on did not like this intrusion, did not appreciate this other place sharing its existence.

At the bottom of the stairs, the room opened out into a cavern. What was it with caverns? Made me think of dwarves.

The floor here was smooth from an unknown number of feet that had trodden the way before me. Partway across the thick darkness of the huge open room the torches along the far wall sprang to life. The lights were poorly spaced, allowing deep shadows to fill the nooks and crannies. I gripped Gram tighter and moved further into the great room.

An ornate throne stood on a dais along the western wall. To the left sat a smaller seat, like where Denethor sat in Gondor. I stopped, shaking my head—chagrined at the thought. My girlfriend may very well have broken my brain.

I glanced back, hoping to catch a glimpse of the pale white glow from the doorway far above me. No such luck, of course. The tunnel had gone a goodly distance into the bedrock. I was counting on that doorway being there when I needed to go back. Call it foolish optimism.

I crept forward another few feet, and the thrones came into clearer view. On the smaller seat reclined a headless body of a woman, slumped against the thick cushions as if sleeping, you know, but without a head. That wasn't freaking ghoulish, not a bit. Her gown didn't appear to be soaked in old blood, so they dressed her after they decapitated her? Definitely did not bode well for whomever called these caverns their own.

On the larger throne sat a desiccated corpse dressed in Viking splendor—full winged helm, scale mail armor, gemstones gleaming on several fingers, a golden torque around the bony neck, and a great spear lying catawampus between the bony knees and up to the left of the gaping skull. Near the head of the spear, one great bony hand gripped the shaft.

Tanned and cracked skin covered the bones, but the underlying muscles appeared to have melted away. I'm not an idiot, usually. Part of my brain urged me to flee from this macabre scene. But that voice was small and held little conviction. The other voice, the voice of experience, called for caution. I continued forward, and the torchlight roared brighter, as if my presence fueled it. Before me I could see that the Viking's face was a ruin—the left eye had been gouged out and was covered with a thin swath of weathered flesh.

This was Odin's broken corpse. I knew it like I knew my own name.

I couldn't take my eyes off him. He had been a big man, powerful chest, broad shoulders and large hands. I imagined he was fearsome in battle. Nothing like Homeless Joe. This was an old incarnation. Maybe the first.

I took another step forward to get a closer look at him, gripping Gram tightly in my left fist. Rings adorned each of his skeletal fingers. One, with a ruby larger than my thumb, glowed with an internal light I could only assume was magic. I reached forward, drawn to the deep red of the gem, mesmerized by the way it seemed to pulse like a heartbeat. Just before I touched it, a flash caught my attention and I glanced up at the spearhead that gleamed in the torchlight. This had to be the legendary Gungnir.

For a moment, the pull of the ring faded, and the overwhelming power of the spear flooded my senses. My hands itched to take it up. The power in that weapon would rival Gram. I placed one foot on the dais and leaned forward, straining to get a look at the spearhead. I was so intent on seeing how the metal was worked that I was surprised when cold hands grabbed me from behind.

First off, I was in spirit form. I should've been immune to grabby stuff. Unless whoever grabbed me was also spirit, or you know, both—like Gram.

I bucked against my attacker. We rocked back, away from the dais, and I saw that the headless corpse was missing from the smaller seat.

I struggled to break the grip as my arms were crushed to my sides. I didn't drop Gram, though. That was lucky. I put one foot against the dais for leverage and was prepared to thrust my weight backwards when the warrior's head turned toward me.

I struggled for a moment as the Odin corpse reached out and grabbed the business end of Gram.

Where the skeletal fingers touched the blade, it crumbled to ash.

Pain rocketed through me, as if my very bones were falling to dust. Gram fell from my grip and I screamed. After a moment of blinding terror, I heard a loud popping sound and was overwhelmed with the strong odor of microwave burritos. Then the world went away.

CHAPTER THIRTY-SIX

K atie sat in the kitchen at Black Briar having a cup of coffee with Trisha and Anezka. Jai Li was in the living room playing cards with Bub while Frick and Frack lay on the couch watching them.

The twins were not really morning creatures. They just wanted to be up with the big kids. They had grown half a foot since Trisha had adopted them; since Katie and Sarah had killed their natural mother. Katie didn't like to think about that too much. One day she knew they'd have to take Frick and Frack up into the mountains to show them the place where they were born and the place their mother was buried. Until then, she was just glad they were happy.

"I should be heading out," Katie said, rising from the table and putting her cup and saucer into the sink.

"I should go out to the smithy and work on something productive," Anezka said, adding her dishes to the sink. "Tell Deidre I'll come back in later and do up the dishes."

Trisha waited a few minutes until Anezka had the door shut, then turned to face Katie. "How's it going with Sarah spending most of her time in Bellingham?"

Katie shrugged. "It sucks like you can't imagine." She smiled at Trisha. "But we'll get our own place soon. I'm thinking about going up for

215

a couple of nights next week. Work on the movie shoot. We've been making good headway on some songs for the soundtrack."

Trisha shuffled her feet a bit, glancing over at the kids in the living room. "I've been thinking," she said, looking back around at Katie. "I've been thinking we need to homeschool the twins. No chance we're putting them in public school."

Katie laughed and all the kids, including Bub, glanced their way. "True, that could prove difficult," she said with a grin.

"Yeah," Trisha said, rubbing her face. "I don't know the first thing about raising trolls, but I think getting them some basic math and reading might be a good start. Definitely arts and crafts. Want to build their creative sides."

"Good thinking," Katie said. "And, you know, if they are going to be anywhere as big as their mother, or god-forbid bigger, you may want to start them on some basic combat training."

Trisha's eyes went wide and she started to shake her head.

"Wait," Katie said. "Talk to Sarah about that. One of the things she's always saying about Tae Kwon Do is that it teaches you how to defend yourself, but also teaches that you should never use the skills out of anger."

Understanding washed over Trisha's face. "Right, good idea," she said, obviously relieved. "Give them the skills so they don't have to use them. Stop them from lashing out in anger or anything?"

"Exactly. Look, we'll talk tonight at dinner. I have got to get on the road. I promised Mary we'd be home by lunch. Laundry day, you know."

At that moment Bub stood up, dropping his cards. He went rigid and a low, reverberating moan leaked out of him. Jai Li rolled onto her knees and reached for him. Frick and Frack began to jabber excitedly, confused.

Katie and Trish both turned at Bub's sudden movement.

"What's up?" Katie asked.

Bub threw his head back and howled.

The grownups scrambled into the living room as Bub gasped and screamed, "Sarah!"

Terror washed over Katie as Bub vanished in an ear-splitting crack.

CHAPTER THIRTY-SEVEN

My eyes snapped open and I realized three things. I was naked, I was in a bed, and someone had recently been in the room. Only I had no idea where I was.

I rolled over, bringing the pillow up to cover my chest, and quickly scanned the twilit room. I didn't see anyone. There were shadows along the edges of the room made deeper by the indirect light from the streetlamp outside on the road.

"Who's there?" I asked, my voice hoarse from disuse. I cleared my throat and tried again, stronger this time. "Come on, damn it. Quit screwing around." I fumbled for the light.

The corners flashed into existence, filled with nothing. I glanced up and down at an all too familiar room. I thought I was gonna vomit. It was my old bedroom—in my parents' house. I started to panic. I looked over the edge of the bed, peeking underneath. Vacant.

How the hell had I ended up in my parents' house? And where the hell were my clothes—and Gram? I sat bolt upright, a solid pain in my chest. Where the hell was Gram?

I climbed from the bed and padded across to the door, listening. I couldn't hear anyone in the place. I started to lock the door, just in case, but remembered that Da had removed all the locks from the interior doors. That had been a result of one of my protests as a kid. He didn't appreciate my attempt to lock him out. Even Ma thought he had overreacted, but at least he didn't take away the doors.

I stepped over to the mostly empty closet and rummaged through the remnants of those items I didn't take with me when I moved out. No clothing.

I was getting cold. The temperature in the house was way below normal, even for Da. I walked to the bed and pulled off the comforter, wrapping it around my naked form. I stood at the window, saw that there were no vehicles in the driveway. Was it possible no one was home? What time was it? There was no clock in the room.

I padded back across the room and put my hand on the doorknob. I had to get out of this house. I felt it in my bones. I just didn't understand what the hell was going on.

I cracked open the bedroom door and looked down the hallway. Across from my room was Ma's and Da's room. That door was closed and I can't remember a time I ever opened it. You did NOT invade their privacy. The thought was horrible. I never ever wanted to risk seeing either of them naked. The thought gave me a shiver.

The room next to mine was Megan's. Maybe she had something I could throw on. Being naked was not the most comfortable thing, let me tell you. Not in this situation, anyway.

There was no one moving in the house. It felt empty. Almost creepy. I definitely did not belong here. The door to Megan's room opened easily enough. Her room hadn't changed too much from before I moved out. The paint was the same, and she still had the old quilt Ma and I made her for her ninth birthday. One wall held shelves full to the gills with books and stuffed animals. Her desk was scattered with papers, pens, books, and three half-empty water bottles.

Made me think how thirsty I was. On the wall above her bed

was a belt rack, holding all her old Tae Kwon Do belts. I had one of those of my own somewhere. I don't think I took it with me when I went to college. I bet Ma had it stashed away.

There was a stuffed rabbit on Megan's bed. I crossed the room in three long strides and sat on the edge of the bed, grabbing that bunny. It had been mine when I was a baby. Once Megan came home with us, after the short bit where Da snatched me and we ran for three days, I'd given her my bunny. The fact she still kept it on her bed made my heart hurt. How had I been such a coward to abandon her? Damn it, I'd be facing Ma and Da soon, if for no other reason than to fulfill the promise of that bunny. I'd told her I'd always be there for her. What a putz I'd been.

I stood, wiping the tears from my face, and turned around once, soaking in all the things that Megan had to express herself. She loved soccer, that was for sure. There were two rows of framed certificates declaring each of her Tae Kwon Do ranks and three for academic achievement. I opened the drawer to her desk and saw the picture of Katie and me in that photo booth.

I looked up in a moment of panic. If Da had seen that picture ... but no. He'd always respected my space. I doubt he'd been in here snooping. That was not his style. He'd grill you over dinner, but he wouldn't go through your sock drawer. I know, I hid enough contraband from him over the years.

I closed the desk, made sure to put the bunny back on the bed correctly and smoothed the rumpled quilt. Didn't want anyone to know I'd been in here. Of course, I had my old comforter wrapped around me. That may be a clue when someone thought to look.

The bathroom door to the right was ajar, but I didn't even bother going in. I could feel the house was deserted. I made my way to the kitchen, lamenting the loss of my cell phone. I didn't have anyone's numbers memorized. I could call for help, if I knew how to get anyone. Maybe I could call information.

I picked up the cordless phone off the cradle in the kitchen and saw it had a memory function. I scrolled through the address book and came across the number for Sa Bum Nim Choi. I guess her personal contact information had always been pretty important to our family. Why was I surprised her personal number was in my family's phone?

I hit the call button and the phone began to ring. After the third ring, Sa Bum Nim Choi's voice echoed into the phone.

"Megan?" There was a hint of anxiety in her voice, not just surprised that a student was calling her.

"I'm sorry, Sa Bum Nim, it's not Megan, it's Sarah, Sarah Beauhall."

I paused at the sharp intake of her breath. Two shocks in one call.

"Can you please come pick me up behind my parents' house on Jones Street, by the Edwards, and can you bring me some clothes?"

"Sarah? Are you in your parents' house?"

"Yeah," I said. "Can you come get me?"

"You shouldn't be there," she said, a hint of panic in her voice. "Turn out the lights," she said, her voice urgent. "Have you touched anything?"

I looked around, shocked. This was weird. "No, what? What's going on?"

"Go now," she said, her voice a whip crack command. "I'll be there soon. Get out of that house now."

Then she was gone. I hung up the phone and hurried back to my old bedroom, replacing the comforter, being sure to smooth out the wrinkles, and turning out the lamp. Why was she worried if I'd touched anything? What was going on?

That's when it finally dawned on me the house had been empty for a while. Where was my family?

I went out the back, careful to close the door as quietly as I could, like maybe I was disturbing the dead otherwise. I hated that that thought crossed my mind. I ran across the back yard and scrambled over the six-foot privacy fence. Luckily, I remembered all the secret footing and handholds. Did not want to risk splinters in my state of dress.

CHAPTER THIRTY-EIGHT

I certainly hoped the neighbors weren't looking. I dashed through the Edwards' yard and hung in the shadows next to their lilac bush, waiting. I'm just lucky they never got a dog. That would have ruined this already stellar evening. I couldn't even begin to understand what the hell had happened to get me here. I'd been in the house in Bellingham, wrestling with a headless corpse. The long-dead god Odin had grabbed Gram, causing her to crumble to dust. Then the world went black.

My mind reeled. Was Gram gone? Was she in the house somewhere and I was abandoning her? I glanced back. Sa Bum Nim Choi had been panicked, even frantic that I get out of the house. I'd never ever seen her flustered, much less harried. That didn't help my sense of dread.

I rubbed my temples, trying to get the runes on my scalp to give me some insight. I thought about cutting myself to let the blood kick things into gear, but I didn't have anything sharp. Like a sword.

I had a visceral urge to vomit.

Within five very chilly minutes a car pulled up and Sa Bum Nim Choi got out, leaving the car running. I looked up and down the street, saw no one, and ran out.

Sa Bum Nim was in the car with the door closed as I slid into the back.

"There are clothes for you there," she said, adjusting the rearview mirror to see me briefly before driving away. "Are you going to tell me how you ended up here, naked?"

"I'd rather not," I said, seeing as I wasn't really sure myself.

I pulled the black gym bag over to me, a sudden shock of realization flooding through me. There were small belt tags on the hook on one end, each representing a rank. It went up to the rank I last tested at. Each one had a design drawn on them in Sharpie.

I unzipped the bag and found a full dobak and belt along with a set of sparring gear and wooden short sword and dagger. I pulled the dagger out of the bag, no longer caring that I was naked. The initials on the handle were SJB. I got a chill.

"Wait, this is my old gear. Where'd you get it?"

Sa Bum Nim glanced back at me through her rearview mirror. "Your parents asked me to keep it at the school, in case you ever decided to come back. They thought it would be more respectful than sitting in a closet at their place."

I pulled out the clothes and saw that there was more than the loose white pants and multi-tied jacket. There was a black T-shirt with the school's logo and a bra and panties. I held up the underthings. "Um ... and these?"

"They were in the bag," Choi said. "I didn't ask."

I slipped into the clothes, dressing quickly. The bra was a bit snug and the panties were on the small side, but overall it was better than being naked. I toyed with the belt tags on the bag and let my thoughts drift to the last time I'd worn this outfit.

"What time is it?"

She looked at me in the mirror and pointed at the clock on her radio, 4:30 in the morning. Christ.

"Are you on drugs?" Sa Bum Nim asked.

I looked up, confused and barked out a laugh. "Drugs? Are you serious?"

The look she gave me in the mirror chilled me.

"Sorry," I swallowed. That glare was devastating. "No ma'am. I'm not under the influence of any drug or alcohol."

"Then what in the name of the seven hells brought you to your parents' house without a stitch of clothing, car, keys, phone, anything?"

"I'm not sure," I said. I had an idea it was related to Odin for sure, but how do you tell your old Tae Kwon Do instructor that without confirming her suspicions of drug use? "Honest," I said. "I was in Bellingham this morning and woke up here in Crescent Ridge tonight in my birthday suit." I glanced out the window. "Where are we going?"

"North," Choi said. "I figured once we got north of Auburn you'd let me know."

I had to think. Katie may be out at Black Briar, but I needed my kit.

"Redmond, I guess." Circle Q. I could regroup there.

We drove in silence. Me lost in thought, trying to figure out what the hell had happened, Choi lost in her own thoughts. We made it up past Kent before she broke the silence.

"Megan has mentioned you several times lately," she said quietly. "She's been talking of getting out, following in your footsteps."

I nodded. Not surprised really. "I can understand, ya know?"

Choi nodded. "I understand her perspective," she said carefully, "but have either of you spoken to your parents about how things are? You especially," she said. "You could talk with them as an adult."

I winced. I was twenty-eight. I'd been on my own for going on six years, longer if you counted college. They didn't have any power over me any longer. Maybe I should confront them, have that talk I'd always dreamed of, vent my spleen, as it were. But to what avail?

"Do you think it would change them?" I asked. "Do you

really think they are going to suddenly start treating either Megan or me like real people?"

There was a long pause, where Choi just looked ahead into the night, not even looking at me in the mirror. "You were always an intuitive fighter," she said finally. "It was as if you could see the attacks coming at you when you sparred. You grasped the intricacies of the forms with an ease and a grace that made me jealous."

I guess it was a day of shocks. I swallowed, unsure of what to say.

"Yet you remain as closed-minded and angry as the day you first walked into my school." Those clipped words were delivered with such abrupt anger that I flinched back. I think I'd have been less surprised to see this stoic woman who taught me so much erupt into tears or break out in song.

"I'm sorry," I said, instinctively. Not the right thing, I know, but my mind was a whirring mess. I wanted to understand this, but the pieces were not falling into place. Not even my runes were a help here. What was I missing?

I took a deep breath and ran my hands through my hair. It was getting long on the sides again, long enough for me to think about shaving. Or, hell. Maybe I'd let it all grow out. Life was out of control in every other way

"I know I have a lot to learn in my life," I said, making sure to keep my gaze away from the mirror. I really needed her to understand I respected her. "What am I missing?"

"Have you asked yourself why your father treats you the way he does? Beyond the religion and the control issues? What is the greater motivation? You knew him for seventeen years, lived with him, watched him."

"Fear," I said automatically. "He's afraid that someone will take us, will hurt us."

"I've suspected as much," she said. "Do you believe your father is running from some organization or individual?"

"Yes."

She nodded. "There were men at the school last fall asking about you." she said. "I told them you'd moved away years before and had not returned. Was that the correct thing?"

I fell back against the car seat. I didn't realize how tense I'd gotten, sitting up, clutching my core, prepared for a blow. I let out a couple of long breaths, relaxing. "That thing before Christmas with the cult."

She nodded again. "I assumed as much. Did you kill those men?"

I breathed in and out slowly before answering. "Yes, ma'am."

There was pain in her eyes, and she tightened her mouth in a way that spoke of bitten words and careful editing.

"They attacked and killed my friends," I said. "They killed a lot of people before we intervened."

The lights of Kent flashed by us. We passed Valley Medical in silence. Once the hospital was past us, she spoke up again.

"I was your mentor for many years," she began slowly. The weight of her words was heavy in the car. "I have always taught you to use violence as a last resort."

I started to speak up, to defend myself, but the runes on my scalp flared a warning and I bit back my words.

"But I have always taught you to defend yourself. By all accounts you have protected those weaker than you, and that is the true way."

I let out a long sigh and relaxed my shoulders. "Thank you." There really was nothing left to say.

"Your sister came into the dojang the other night in a panic," she continued. "Your mother and father had decided to take a sudden trip."

I looked up, trying to catch her eyes in the mirror. "Do you think he's running?"

"That was her fear, but I cannot say. They told her they would only be gone for a few days, but it means Megan couldn't fulfill her teaching obligations."

My mind raced back to the last time he'd taken us and ran.

We'd packed everything we needed to survive and left, not even closing the door to the last place before coming to Washington. I remember watching the house standing open as we pulled away. It was like he didn't have the time to do that one simple act of closing the door. How scared did that make him?

"Did you see them?" I asked. "My parents. Did they come into the school?"

"Actually, yes. Your father came in and apologized for inconveniencing the school and promised they'd be in the following week."

I sat back, contemplating. Scouting mission, then. He wasn't ready to run if he was telling people. "He'll bring them home," I said, relieved. "If he was running, he wouldn't have told you."

She nodded, changing lanes to get onto 405 North.

I gave her directions to Circle Q and sat back with my head against the seat listening to the white noise of the tires on the highway, thinking about Da. He's not running yet, I told myself. But soon. I had to do something.

But what could I do? Just like he had no real power over me any longer, I had no hold on him, no way to keep him here.

But I'd try, for Megan's sake. She'd had a stable life. I wanted that for her more than anything.

CHAPTER THIRTY-NINE

We pulled into Circle Q just after five, with the sun breaking over the mountains to the east. Sa Bum Nim gave me a warm hug and an admonition to call when I figured out what was going on with everyone. I think she may have been crying. It was very hard to tell with her. She always had this fierce look on her face, one that challenged you to step out of line at your peril.

I loved her as much in that moment as I'd ever done growing up. I hugged her back and turned to head into the house. I wasn't even sure who was home. She watched me all the way into the house. I waved at her as she got into her car and drove away.

"Where the bloody hell have you been?"

It was Edith. She was sitting in the kitchen drinking a cup of tea.

"Where's everyone?" I asked, looking around. Katie's car wasn't in the yard. "Is Jai Li here?"

"No," Edith said, getting up and setting a second cup and saucer on the kitchen table. "She went to Black Briar night before last and hasn't come home yet." She motioned for me to sit and asked again, "Where have you been?"

"Is Katie okay? What's going on?"

She looked at me with that old-lady-not-taking-your-crap look she had perfected and motioned for me to sit.

"Seriously," I said, sitting down. "Where is everyone?"

"Your young Katie has run off to Bellingham, looking for you," she said, matter-of-factly. "Yesterday you vanished off the face of the earth, and suddenly you appear here in the wee hours of the morning."

She poured two cups of strong tea and pushed a small plate of thumbprint cookies in front of me. "Your Jai Li made these the day before yesterday. Eat them."

"I should call Katie," I said, picking up a cookie. I nibbled it, then stuffed it in my mouth, chewing quickly. I was famished. I sipped the bitter tea and devoured the plate of cookies while Edith got up and stirred a pot of cabbage on the stove. The world seemed to dim as I sipped the tea. I was so exhausted.

When I could focus again, Edith stood across the room, speaking into the handset on Mary's telephone. It was one of those ancient landlines, even worked when the power was out. It was odd.

"Your Katie is no longer answering her phone," she said firmly. "Black Briar has not responded to our calls and we have had no word otherwise. Mary and Julie left a while ago to drive to Gold Bar and seek answers."

She watched me for a moment, then turned to the phone, dialing quickly.

"Sarah is here," she said into the phone. She nodded once then hung up.

"Mary and Julie are on their way back," she said, sitting down with me and taking up her own tea. "Julie used some words I choose not to repeat at this moment," she said without a trace of irony or humor.

I nodded and added more sugar to my tea. She drank it black and bitter. I think it was the foundation for her sparkling personality.

"I want to ask you something," she said, getting up abruptly.

"Something I have been told is none of my business, but I am an old woman and there is no one here to stop my asking."

As she walked out of the room I glanced up at the clock. It said it was after seven. I seemed to be losing time. She returned shortly with a folder full of pictures, obviously hand drawn and painted.

"Our little darling, Jai Li, has left me many presents over the months you have lived with us," she said, her voice as cold as ice. "Can you explain these to me?"

She laid them out in an array on the table between us. Each one showed a different horrific scene. From Nidhogg raging in her dragon form with bodies scattered through the great house, to a scene of bloody sacrifices and a dome filled with the ravaged dead.

I flipped through them one by one, more horrified as I looked, until I got to the last one—the most heartbreaking picture of the lot. It was a picture of the children's dorm in Nidhogg's house. The small pillows and needlepoint that adorned the empty bed with a pair of worn slippers on the pillow made my eyes tear up. This showed Mei Hau's space. She was Jai Li's twin that Nidhogg had killed in the rage triggered when I reforged Gram.

"I should like you to explain, please," Mrs. Sorenson asked.

I sipped my still bitter tea and considered, wiping my eyes. Both Mary and Mrs. Sorenson were in on the secret of Jai Li's life before us. Why was I holding back? I guess it was just so bizarre. How was I supposed to explain this?

"I'm not a psychologist," I began weakly. "We can discuss it with her counselor ..." I yelped, cutting my lame excuse short when Mrs. Sorenson rapped me on the knuckles with a wooden spoon.

"Do not lie to me, bubala. I survived the gulags and I survived the Red Army. I know from horrors. This child is twice cursed. She is an innocent in a land of monsters. What has happened to her?"

Wait, the Red Army? How old was this woman? I took a deep breath and stared into her eyes. There was pain there and wisdom. And she was a witch, of sorts. Maybe I should tell the whole story. But where was Katie? What had happened in Bellingham?

Both my vehicles were in Bellingham, and Mrs. Sorenson had no car. I wasn't going anywhere until Julie got here to give me a ride.

I took a deep breath. "Where do I start?"

Mrs. Sorenson nodded once and rose. "Yes, it is worse than I thought. Perhaps we should start with vodka."

It was pretty early for happy hour, but she poured two shots nonetheless. She tossed hers back like a pro. I don't think it affected her. She was an experienced drinker. I tossed back the first shot and let the heat course through my body before I started talking. Here I was sitting in a dobak which was not riding too friendly, let me tell you, and the vodka was making me antsy. The runes on my forehead began to throb and the runes on my calf ached like a cramp.

I needed to get away from her, but there was something about her insistence, something in the way her eyes bored into me, that made me talk, and talk, and talk. It wasn't quite the compulsion that Katie had used on Charlie, but it was uncomfortably similar.

I needed to get back to Bellingham. I needed to find Gram. My palm itched from where I'd held the black blade last. Had Odin really destroyed her? Had I hallucinated it?

It was after eight by the time I'd told Mrs. Sorenson every detail I could remember. Hell, I told her things I hadn't remembered.

My head was spinning when I heard the truck in the drive. Mrs. Sorenson handed me a cup of lukewarm tea and forced me to drink it. Almost as soon as the liquid splashed over my tongue my head cleared. No vodka, no exhaustion, and no worry. That was some damn potent tea. I'd have to get some of that from her for the next time Katie and I went partying.

Once Julie and Mary got in, Mrs. Sorenson gave them a very short version of the last couple of hours and Julie only nodded. Mary sighed, said it wasn't how they wanted it to happen, but events got in the way.

I started to ask what took them so long to get back from Goldbar, but Edith interrupted me, saying I should go change.

Julie agreed, "Move your ass and I'll drive you to Bellingham."

I dashed down the hall, stripping off my dobak as I went. To hell with vanity, I needed to change fast and get on the road. Within two minutes I was in a new set of bra and panties, ones that really fit me, plus jeans and a T-shirt. My Docs were in Bellingham where I'd left them, I guessed, so I put on my old trainers. I felt a little underdressed for the occasion, but it would have to do.

I followed Julie out of the house. She pulled the truck in a big U-turn and stopped as Mary came out carrying a shotgun. "Here," she said, sliding the gun in through the window, butt first. She dropped a box of shells into my lap.

"She's not loaded but treat her as if she is." She was all business. "You may be able to get off a few rounds before the thing seizes up."

"Thanks," I said, nodding to her. She stepped back and patted the side of the truck. Julie pulled out at just under the speed of light.

My head was spinning again. Who were these women?

Once we were clear of the farm, Julie agreed we should detour to Black Briar first. I needed to get a handle on what the hell was going on. She had her cell phone so I called them and got Trisha, who said she couldn't really talk, but she'd spread the word that I was on my way. She said the compound was in lockdown and prepared for battle. She wouldn't say anything more over the phone but encouraged me to hurry.

Julie agreed and we sped up. So much for speed limits.

Along the way, Julie told me everything she'd been meaning to tell me over the last few months, only I'd been tied up with all the crap going on with Katie.

Ever since the events of the previous fall, where Justin, the bastard necromancer, had killed Mary's prize high-stepper, Julie had discovered that Mrs. Sorenson was more than a little old widow.

It seemed in Edith's time in the old country, she had been quite a hedge witch. She claimed to have met Baba Yaga once as a small child, shortly after discovering the ability to see things, to compel others to speak the truth, and to cast small protections and wards.

I'd gotten some of that on my own, rather blatantly. Like when the house was attacked, but I let her tell the story the way she needed to tell it.

They'd shared stories and the world made a lot more sense to Mary afterwards. They'd become co-conspirators, agreeing to protect Jai Li and watch out for me and Katie. It seems that the tea leaves, tarot, and even chicken entrails all led Mrs. Sorenson to believe I had a great destiny ahead of me. Great and terrible.

I just listened to Julie talk, letting the sound of her voice wash over me as I nodded off. Great and terrible. That about covered it.

CHAPTER FORTY

Once we pulled up at Black Briar, I knew something was up. Trisha had warned me they'd gone into lockdown mode, but I hadn't expected to find the driveway blocked with concrete construction barriers and metal poles.

When we identified ourselves, one of the guards got into a tractor and used it to drag a huge slab of concrete and rebar out of the way, just wide enough for us to pull through. After that we had to drive a slalom course around three more concrete barriers before getting clear to the back of the house.

Armed guards waved us across the area behind the house and directed Julie to swing the truck around facing back up the drive before letting us out. Two young women escorted us to the back door. They were in full Kevlar and chain with short swords. I recognized them—April and Autumn—two of Stuart's crew. I smiled at them as I got out of the truck, but they didn't stick around for niceties. They were back at their posts before Julie had her door closed.

Trisha came out onto the back deck to see who'd arrived, saw us and darted back into the house, raising a cry. Her crew came out of the house and practically dragged Julie and me inside.

"What the hell's going on?" I asked, as I shrugged off Benny and Gary.

Deidre rolled out of the hallway, Anezka's old shotgun in a holster over the back of her chair. That gun had been worked with runes and magic. It worked just fine in the disrupting presence of magic.

"Where in the bloody hell have you been?" she asked, her voice icy.

Jai Li appeared in the kitchen, cut around Trisha, and launched herself at me. I knelt, catching her and hugging her to me. "I'm okay."

She squeezed me like she was trying to compress me into a smaller space.

"Honest, I'm okay."

"Where have you been?" Deidre asked again, the steel in her voice something I don't think I'd ever heard.

"Long story," I said, standing and pulling Jai Li up with me. I held her against me, spinning to look at everyone who was here. "Where's Gunther?"

Deidre snorted. "He took a dozen of his best north to Bellingham, followed Katie by about an hour. Care to tell us what's going on?"

I leaned against the counter, looked over at Julie who just shrugged. "I'd sure as hell like to know," she growled.

I gave them the short version. Exploring the house, old dead god, Gram being disintegrated, suddenly blacking out and finding myself in my parent's place out in Crescent Ridge.

"That explains Bub, then," Trisha said. "Katie and I were having coffee this morning and he just stood up, called out your name, and vanished like he's done a few times before. Scared the hell out of the twins. It was obvious he was in pain."

I reached for my neck, realizing the amulet was gone. I'd worn it so long, it had become second nature. I didn't even think about it. It's what kept Bub tied to me. Poor guy. Porting to Bellingham and then to Crescent Ridge. That was a little out of his comfort zone. Just porting from Black Briar to Kent before Christmas had nearly killed him.

"Katie tore out of here like she was on fire," Deidre said, angrily. "She's been gone all day, with no word. No call. Gunther lit out after her as soon as he got his crew mustered."

"Any word from Stuart?" I asked.

"He and Qindra were on their way back to Seattle by lunch. Took us a while to get ahold of them.

"So, where are they?"

Deidre looked at me, pondering. "I'd say Qindra was home trying to keep Nidhogg calm. Whatever the hell you did this morning set Nidhogg into a tailspin. She chased all her people out of the house, raging and crying like she'd lost her damned mind." She shrugged. "Apparently she kept it together long enough for them to get out. No casualties as far as we can tell, but she turned. That woman who runs the household said they could hear her smashing things from outside."

Trisha nodded. "Katie tried to call you, but when you didn't answer she just ran out to the barn, put on her gear, grabbed her guitar, and left, telling anyone within shouting range that she was off to rescue you."

"She went up alone?" I asked, handing Jai Li to Trisha and turning to Deidre. "I'll need gear, if you don't mind. I need to get up there and see what the hell's going on."

"Sure, why not?" Deidre said, taking Jai Li from Trisha and turning her chair to the living room. "Run off after the other fools. Should only take you a couple of hours at this rate. Pretty soon everyone will be running into the great unknown and I'll keep these children to raise all by myself."

She was angry and bitter. Jai Li hugged her, but watched me, flashing me the sign to be careful. I nodded at her and turned to Trisha. "Has anyone called Skella?"

"She's not answering either," Nancy, Trisha's second in command, piped up from over by the sink. She was a damned fine fighter and had a level head. "Katie tried to get ahold of her first, make the travel a little more palatable, you know?"

Gary nodded. "Yeah. We've been calling her since yesterday. No answer."

"Damn," I said. "Looks like it's the long way then."

"I'll drive," Julie said. "I can get us there in one piece."

I went out to the barn and started digging through lockers. I needed gear that would fit me. I ended up with one of the old chain shirts we used with the newbies. Not the best quality, but it fit. I also snagged a shield off the wall. Something with the Black Briar insignia—the paint wasn't even marred. Totally new item. I got the chain on over my clothes by the time Trisha came running into the barn.

"Here," she said, handing me a sword and scabbard. It was Jimmy's. Dwarven made and battle tested.

"Fuck, Trish. I can't take that."

"It was Deidre's idea," she said, catching her breath. "She's mad as hell but wants you to bring everyone home. Then she'll just be mad as hell and not scared all at the same time."

I took the sword, drew it halfway and examined the blade. The workmanship was good. He wasn't Gram by any means, but he'd do in a pinch. And yes, the sword was a he. Don't ask me how I knew, I just did.

"Jimmy'd be proud for you to use that," Trisha said, following me out to the truck. "Blade like that's itching to be used, you know?"

"You have no idea," I said, then stopped, turning back to her. "I'm sorry. Of course, you have an idea. Hell, you probably have more idea than the rest of us."

Trisha had been turned into a dragon by Justin, the bastard necromancer. Well, Fafnir's ring had done most of the work, but Justin had channeled the energy needed to make the final transformation and bind her to his will at the same time.

She'd killed him for it, that and his attempt to kill the twins. Just stabbed him from the back, right through his black heart.

I hugged her quick and kissed her on the cheek. "Hold down the fort. I think the farm's safe, but you never know."

She squeezed my arms and nodded. "Go get Katie and let her know how pissed we all are that she's not answering her phone."

I walked to the truck, opened the door and took out the shotgun Mary had given me. "Take this, please," I said, handing her the box of shells as well. "I'm just as likely to shoot myself with that thing." I raised Jimmy's blade. "I'm more comfortable with steel in my hands."

Tricia handed her cell phone through the window of the truck. "It has everyone's numbers in the memory," she said. "Maybe you'll have better luck when you get close."

Benny came running around the barn, two hammers from the smithy in his hands. "I know these aren't the ones you usually fight with," he said, a grim smile on his face, "but I'm pretty sure you know how to swing 'em."

I took the hammers—three-pounders—and slid them onto the floor at my feet. "Take this too," he said, handing me a carpenter's belt. "This has loops you can hang the hammers in, just in case." He stood, watching me, his hands on the door of the truck. "Kick their ass for me, huh?"

"Thanks, Benny," I said, patting his hands. "I'll do my best." Of course, I had no idea what we were heading into. Everyone was sure it was a battle of some ilk. The air was ripe with it.

Trisha pulled him away from the truck, and Julie slipped the truck into first.

The crew got the driveway cleared in short order and we were off. While Julie drove, I tried Katie, Gunther, Rolph, and Skella. We'd be in Bellingham in just under an hour at the rate we were going, but was it fast enough? It was so freaking maddening just riding along with Julie. She drove at the upper ends of sanity, just slow enough to avoid the cops, but definitely on the more aggressive end of the spectrum. I wish I could've gotten ahold of Skella, or maybe Rolph. If there was something wrong with Gram, he'd want to know.

I had a sneaking suspicion that everyone was out of contact due to a sudden explosion of magic. Nidhogg didn't just freak for no reason, and there was that whole, desiccated dead god destroying a major artifact and me being teleported away by a kobold from the Plane of Fire. Who knows what all that did to the space/time continuum.

"Drive faster," I said, and Julie pushed it past ninety. "Don't stop for cops. Let 'em follow us. We may need the backup."

CHAPTER FORTY-ONE

The temperature started dropping as we drove north. Storm clouds were rolling in from the west and lightning flashed all along the western horizon. The sky grew dark as we barreled down Highway 2 and Julie looked at me, surprised. We didn't get a lot of thunder and lightning up this way and the sun didn't set until nearly ten in the evening this time of year. My imagination started working out of control. Odin and lightning were not exactly strangers. And what about Thor? I hadn't seen any sign of him. Why not start now? It wasn't as if I was enjoying the quiet life.

By the time we cleared Everett, the storm was already blowing. Pretty big one, gusting wind, driving rain—way stronger than anything we normally experienced up here in the Pacific Northwest. We had the radio on and got word that tornados had touched down north of Marysville and hail was beating the living hell out of Tulalip. The Pacific Northwest is typically pretty wimpy when it comes to inclement weather. The phrase "snow-pocalypse" came to mind. But this was something totally out of bounds.

It was June. This level of freaky weather made me think of other powers than meteorological. And the fact that the sky had grown so absolutely dark hours and hours before normal sunset had me a little freaked out.

Even before we pulled off the interstate, we began to see effects of the destruction. The highway was littered with downed trees and abandoned vehicles. State Patrol was out directing traffic around a jack-knifed truck, and we slowed to get a bead on the situation.

Julie cut the radio and rolled down her window. "How bad is it?" she asked the young patrolman. He looked to be about my age, and his eyes were wild with near panic.

"Tornado or something just as crazy." His voice trembled as he shuffled from one foot to the other, gripping his Maglite with both hands. He was dressed for a hurricane, and I can't say that I blamed him. "I'd advise getting to someplace secure and waiting this out."

We agreed to be safe. As soon as we pulled away, he darted back inside his patrol car, his face stark white in the momentary glow of the car's interior light. We slowly worked our way around the wreckage and on toward the off-ramp.

The view of the city as we drove down into Bellingham proper made my stomach hurt. Things were actually worse than we first thought. Great swaths of trees were toppled over like matchsticks, and building after building lay in ruin. Nothing was unscathed. We saw a minivan smashed into the upper floor of an apartment complex while others lay tossed around like children's toys. Entire streets were laid waste. The region was dark with no signs of power anywhere.

We worked our way along the south end of town toward Fairhaven, driving around downed trees and making sure to avoid running into any of the abandoned vehicles.

"This is a war zone," Julie breathed.

I couldn't have said it any better myself. The only things missing were bomb craters.

The streets were mostly empty of people, thank goodness, and those we saw only briefly as they ran from one place to another. Just as we started to settle into the numbness you get when overwhelmed by sheer devastation, hail the size of golf balls crashed down on the truck, rattling our teeth. Julie stopped and pulled a blanket out from behind the seat, handing me one end and telling me to hold it up to the top of the windshield in case it shattered. When the hail stopped after a full minute of pounding, there were several fist-sized dents in the glass, the cracks spidering out enough to distort my view of the world. Julie's side was relatively clear, so we managed to drive for a quarter mile in near total darkness and the sudden, eerie silence that echoed with the memory of hail slamming into the steel of the truck.

Then the lightning started up again, shattering the velvety blackness with sharp streaks of fire. The contrast wrecked any chance of maintaining night vision, and Julie slowed the truck to a walking pace. She glanced my way once or twice, but she mainly stared forward, keeping the truck from smashing into any of the downed power poles, trees, or wrecked vehicles. Something had kicked the shit out of Bellingham, and I was worried they weren't done yet.

We drove out old Willow Road toward the boarding house. The quaint little touristy shops and bistros along Fairhaven's main drag were smashed to kindling. It looked like an angry child the size of an aircraft carrier had stomped and smashed this entire part of town. That was some damn powerful wind. Lord, I hoped it was wind. I crossed my fingers and said a quick prayer to a variety of higher beings. Never hurts to cover your bases.

Three minutes later, we rolled to a stop. What I assumed was a school had been dragged off its foundation and strewn across the road ahead of us, obstructing any further progress forward along this route. Julie cut down a side street and attempted to go around, but once more we found the way forward blocked, this time by smashed fire trucks and half a dozen smaller vehicles. I swear to all that is holy that it looked just like some deranged and massive three-year-old had stacked them that way on purpose.

Julie had just thrown the truck into reverse when I saw that one of the vehicles was a van, a white van, a white van with the word "Veterinary" just discernible in her headlights.

"Stop!" I yelled, rolling out of the door before she came to a complete stop. I sprinted to the teetering pile of vehicles and, throwing caution to the wind, jumped up on the top of a blessedly empty pickup truck to get a closer look at the white van. Sure enough, it read "Smythe and Williams Veterinary Medicine."

This was the van Charlie Hague typically drove. What the hell was he doing up this way? All my alarms started going off at once as a moan came from the van, which was unfortunately wedged in sideways between a fire marshal's SUV and a power company truck with its cherry picker extended, balancing the white van. All the glass had been busted out of the windows, so I poked my head up into the interior of the truck. Amid the overturned toolboxes and equipment that had been tossed about, I could see Charlie's crumpled body, still strapped into the driver's seat, only it was shoved halfway back into the cargo area.

"Charlie?" I called.

"Help!"

With Julie's help, I was able to get him out of the van and lowered to the ground without any more damage. Luckily for him, he was only banged up.

"What the hell happened?" I asked, once we had settled him in Julie's truck. I went back for his doctoring kit, and we drove back to the main drag and began looking for a way around the obstacles.

Charlie drank a bottle of water and took three painkillers from his pack before he really had the bandwidth to talk.

"One minute I was racing toward Mimi's place, the next minute I was out cold. All I remember was something huge and blue smashing into me, probably a big rig by the size of it, and waking up to you calling my name."

"I didn't see any rigs in that pile." I looked over at Julie, who hunched her shoulders and turned down a short alley.

"It was big, whatever it was," he said, laying his head back. "Thanks for rescuing me. I probably would've died there."

I patted him on the knee, and he grabbed my hand.

"Oh, God. I nearly forgot. I came up here to warn you. Something bad is going to happen."

"Too late for that, don't ya think?" Julie asked as we broke free to clear road ahead.

"Oh, yeah," Charlie said. "We're so screwed."

CHAPTER FORTY-TWO

A thick wall of white fog rose in front of us as we cleared the blocked roads around the small street of shops and turned onto the bay road. We slowed way down, peering ahead as the headlights diffused across the wall of water droplets.

"I don't like this," Charlie croaked, leaning forward and gripping the dashboard.

"Suck it up," Julie said, as we rolled into the fogbank.

Once we were completely engulfed we rolled forward in an eerily oppressive silence.

Charlie twisted to look out the back window. "This is not good."

I smirked at Julie who gave me one of her patented looks of exasperated patience. Neither of us responded.

In the next instant, a spike of power washed over us—a chilling blast that made my runes ache with the cold. Charlie cried out, clutching the sides of his head as the radio flared to life, blasting the cab with honky-tonk at an earsplitting volume. Julie punched the off switch and the deafening music ceased. My head practically vibrated with the sudden return of silence. I glanced at Julie, who hunched over the wheel as if expecting a blow. This was beyond strange. I glanced down, finding the cell phone totally dead. That was an intense burst of magic.

Julie had the speed down to damn near crawling. We could barely see beyond the end of the hood. After a minute the engine coughed and all the electrical components went haywire. Wipers rocked, lights flashed, the radio squealed with a burst of white noise, then everything failed. The engine died. Julie slammed in the clutch and jammed the gearshift into neutral. We rolled forward, eventually easing to a stop.

I couldn't see the road on my side of the truck, the fog was that thick.

"This can't be good," I said, craning my neck around to look behind us. The entire world was a thick blanket of fog.

"Definitely not good," Julie growled, reaching behind her seat and pulling out a fire axe. "I don't like this one bit."

I grabbed the hammers at my feet and rolled out of the truck. The outside world had vanished. I buckled on the carpenter belt, slipped the hammers in the metallic loops and reached back into the truck to take up Jimmy's sword. The hilt felt wrong in my palm, a little too wide for my taste, but it was a solid weapon. Jimmy had worn it on his hip, but I didn't like that too much.

"Here," I said, holding out the sword to Julie and taking the axe from her. "This will serve you better." The fog swallowed my voice to the point Julie leaned in to hear better.

She took the blade from me, eyes wide. "You sure?"

"I'm finnicky," I said, smiling. "Gram's the only sword for me." I shrugged and reached into the truck bed, pulling out the shield. "Use this as well," I said. "I'm sure you'll get the hang of it."

Julie grinned. "I may have been practicing a little when you weren't around," she said, sliding the shield over her left arm and drawing the sword with her right. "Good balance here," she said, smiling. "But maybe I'll get you to make me one after all this is done, huh?"

I grinned at her. "You got it, boss." I drew the hammers, one in each fist, and spun them, working my wrists and adjusting to the weight. This was more my speed. I felt better than I had earlier. Not as good as Gram but good enough.

"What about me?" Charlie squeaked as he slid out of the truck, clutching his medical bag.

I handed him the fire axe. "Stick with us, and don't get killed," I told him.

The oppressive silence bore down, discouraging further speech. The damp air clung to us, impenetrable and cold, which sucked for summertime, even in this neck of the woods. A rime of ice began to form on the heads of my hammers. I tapped them against my thighs and watched my breath add to the murky fog.

I took the lead as the three of us walked down the center of the road. Charlie came second, and Julie brought up the rear. I strained to hear anything in the damp blanket of freezing wet. We had to be close to the house. This road wasn't all that long.

After another couple minutes, the glow of a fire truck emerged to one side. It had crashed, flipped, and skidded into a streetlamp. We walked around it once, checking. There were no bodies. But the flashers were working, so that was a change from just fifty feet back.

Julie shrugged. "Maybe we went through a barrier of some sort. Fried everything." She looked to me for confirmation.

"Magic must be getting thinner," I said. "Maybe." Definitely not my area of expertise.

"Want me to check?" Charlie offered.

He had a bit of hedge witch in him, but honestly, I didn't think it was that important.

"Nah, no point. Let's just get to the house."

Up ahead we found several abandoned police cruisers parked haphazardly, their bubble-gum lights flashing, but no one was around. This part of town was eerily abandoned.

Julie veered toward me, swerving around an overturned step van, bringing my attention away from the police cruisers.

Ahead something large loomed over us. For a moment, I thought it was a tree, a very large, blue, hairy tree.

Then it moved.

By move, I mean a giant fist smashed down, clobbering the panel van Julie was standing beside, knocking it off the road and into the deeper fog.

I think we found what smashed up Charlie's van.

"Crap," Julie grunted, staggering from the near miss.

"Giant!" I shouted. Giant, but a lot bluer than the last one I'd fought.

Julie ran to the left while I juked right. Charlie stood stock still in the middle of the street and screamed, whether from terror, or what, I wasn't sure, but the giant looked his way. I lunged in and smashed it in the left kneecap with both hammers, a double handed swing that would've punched through an oaken door.

The giant stumbled, roaring in pain, but I hadn't collapsed the leg as I'd hoped. He swung his great shaggy head my way and swatted at me with one of those miniature economy cars that had become so trendy. I rolled to the left and the car smashed where I'd just been standing. I was peppered with shattered glass and plastic, like the stinging of a swarm of bees. Nothing too drastic, though.

Julie darted in and swung Jimmy's sword for all she was worth. The tip bit deeply into the giant's right ankle.

It staggered back a step and roared. The sound was muffled by the fog, but it was loud enough for my ears to ring. I rolled to my feet, ready to fend off the next attack, and we were suddenly surrounded by fighters.

Rolph, my dwarf buddy, screamed a war cry my brain wanted to translate but failed. I think I'd shouted something similar when I fought the dragon Jean-Paul. Suddenly things got a lot more chaotic. He glanced at me and charged past, an axe in one hand and a shield in the other. He had an ecstatic look about him.

"Welcome to the battle, smith," he cried, swinging his axe into the giant's calf. Behind him came three other dwarves, each swinging large bladed weapons.

The giant landed a glancing blow, knocking Julie off her feet, but the dwarves fought with conviction and purpose. It was almost as if they'd fought a giant before.

I ran to Julie, fearing the worst. She wasn't really hurt. Well, nothing more than her pride and a hard landing on her rear end.

I held a hand out to her and she grinned. Grasping my forearm, she pulled herself all the way upright and looked over my shoulder. The giant was falling. It hit the ground with a violent jolt, causing us to stagger several steps to keep our feet. That was one heavy mother.

"This way, smith," Rolph waved at us.

I turned, grabbed Charlie, and the three of us ran after the squad of dwarves. They sprinted toward a huge wolf that was harassing a group of fighters with pole arms: Black Briar folk.

Gunther and two elves came around the house chasing a second wolf the size of an F350. All around the boarding house, I could see knots of warriors and fallen giants. I counted six giants in all, three downed wolves plus the ones currently engaged. What in the name of Odin was going on?

The wolf being chased by Gunther leapt over one of the fallen giants and smashed his front paws into one of the dwarves, knocking him to the ground. Julie ran forward, leaping over the fallen warrior. The wolf howled as two arrows embedded into its left flank. I could see it sported several crossbow bolts and a few slashes along its hindquarters already. It snapped madly, its eyes rolling in pain and fear. Julie lunged forward, sinking half a foot of tempered steel into the beast's neck. It lurched to the side away from her, scrabbling to keep its footing as blood gushed from the neck wound. Julie managed to keep ahold of the sword, wrenching it free in a spray of blood. The wolf stumbled, going down onto its left shoulder. We just stood there, me, Julie, and Charlie, as the dwarves and the others turned away, rushing after another target.

Shock painted Julie as much as the blood. She loved animals of all sorts. Killing this creature may be an act she would never forgive herself for.

"It was mad with pain and fright," I said, placing a hand on her shoulder. "You gave it mercy."

She swallowed hard and nodded. I watched her, squeezing her shoulder, and counted to ten. Then, she drew in a shuddering breath, shook her head, and leaned forward to clean the blood off her blade. She'd survive this. She survived the dragon, after all.

"This is madness," she whispered, sheathing the sword and taking my hand. "Where did these giants and wolves come from? What was up with all this damn fog, and why the hell were all these people here?"

I squeezed her hand and pulled her toward the house in a run. I needed to find Katie before any more of the crazy shit hit the fan.

I glanced back, making sure Charlie was following us, suspicion burning bright in my mind. He knew something about all this, and I meant to find out what.

CHAPTER FORTY-THREE

Someone on one of the balconies blew two sharp blasts on a horn and people came streaming out of the house to tend to the fallen. The dwarf Julie had rescued from the wolf was out cold, but alive. Some of the others weren't as lucky by the way people were reacting.

"Katie's inside," Gunther said, thrusting his thumb over his shoulder. "Damn glad to see you, Beauhall." He looked pissed and relieved at the same time. "Go let her know you're alive, she's out of her mind."

"Watch this one," I said, thrusting Charlie toward my big Nordic friend.

Julie grabbed Charlie. "I got him."

I nodded, turned, and ran across the yard toward the house. Dante's car was in the drive, the left side smashed. He loved that car. I can only imagine how he was feeling. I looked around as Sprocket shouted from the porch.

"It's Sarah," he was shouting. "Holy jumping Jesus fish."

Raucous laughter and cheers echoed all around me. I turned to see the balconies crowded with elves. I raised my hand to wave to them and barely caught the hurtling Katie missile that launched off the porch and into my arms.

I staggered back but caught myself before we spilled over. "I'm okay," I mumbled as Katie covered my face with kisses. I dropped my hammers and wrapped my arms around her, making shushing sounds as she cried. Eventually we just kissed, sharing breath and comfort.

The Hamster crew was out on the porch by the time we came up for air. Dante whistled and Lilith suggested we get a room.

Rolph walked around us, heading into the house. "Nice of you to make it," he said. "The skald was beside herself with grief."

"Where have you been?" Katie asked, pulling her head back and wiping her face. Her tears were bloody.

"Oh, my God, Katie. Are you okay? What the hell is going on?"

She wiped her face, looked at the blood on her fingers and shrugged. "I think I'm dying."

"No, she's not," Mimi called from the doorway. "At least, not yet. Come inside, we need to talk." She raised her arm over to where Julie and Charlie stood. "And bring him. I have questions for that one."

I held Katie by her shoulders, watching her face. There was a sadness there. She wasn't exactly despondent, but she wore a weary expression that bordered on defeat. I brushed her hair behind her ears and kissed her again, gently.

"I'm sorry," I said, not understanding what else to say.

She smiled at me. "You know I love you, right?"

I nodded, trying to stop the tears that threatened to come. I cleared my throat against the ache that was building and drew a shuddering breath.

"What the hell's going on around here?" I asked finally, finding my voice without tears.

Katie took my hand and pulled me up onto the porch and into the house. "That's a long story that I believe involves you disappearing."

That's when I realized that the place was ablaze with lanterns and candles. No electricity, but plenty of light.

"It's all kinds of crazy," I said, looking around at the people in the rooms. There were wounded in the living room being tended by EMTs. Three police officers were among the wounded, but there were also civilians. In the dining room two women and a gaggle of children sat under the heavy oak dining room table, coloring. The children had been crying, but things seemed to be under control.

"Out back," Mimi called from the kitchen. I walked by the place where the hidden door had been and paused, placing my hand on the cold wall.

"What's the matter?" Katie asked, pulling me on. "We need to show you something."

I stopped just inside the doorway to the kitchen, looking at the array of warriors from Black Briar and others streaming out into the yard. Rolph and his dwarf buddies filed past, followed by Bianca and Lilith. Skella sat on the corner of the counter near the stove, and Gletts stood beside her, looking pale and thin. They were arguing in low tones.

Bianca grinned at me, holding up a large meat cleaver. Lilith held a long spear in her hands.

"Welcome to the madhouse," Lilith said to me.

I looked at her, wondering. "This doesn't freak you out?" I asked. Katie shook her head beside me and made a broad sweeping motion toward Lilith, as if to say, *go on, have your say*.

Lilith smiled like a Cheshire cat. "I knew something was up," she said, jerking her head toward Skella. "Birth defect my pale white ass. I know elf ears when I see them."

Bianca nodded vigorously, a manic grin on her pretty face. She had a floppy Jayne hat on her head, the orange and yellow knitted thing from the TV show *Firefly*.

Skella grinned at me and Gletts turned, nodded once, and returned to his intense conversation. I was glad to see him up and about. The way things had gone, I wasn't sure he was going to make it. There was a short blade on the counter next to him. I'd seen him use one of those before. I had no doubt he could hold his own.

Katie tugged at my hand and I followed her out the door. A decent size crowd was standing around, staring out over the cliffs toward the bay, but they were not looking down toward the water. I looked up, following their gaze.

"Holy mother ... is that? Jesus ..." I stammered, dropping Katie's hand and shielding my eyes with both of mine. Cutting through the fog, like a neon sign, glowed a rainbow bridge. It rose from the edge of the yard, near the covered cistern, and climbed into the sky at a steep angle.

I walked out into the yard, passing several sentries, and stopped just shy of the cistern. "Rainbow bridge?" I asked no one in particular, slowly sinking down and landing on my knees. The world sort of faded there for a second as a roaring filled my ears.

"You bet your ass," Katie said, sliding down beside me. She grabbed my arm with both hands and leaned her head on my shoulder. "Isn't it beautiful?"

I took several deep breaths, trying not to pass out. "Seriously?" I breathed, shaking my head to clear it. "I thought that was destroyed."

I couldn't stop looking at it. It was both solid and ethereal. I expected to see winged horses riding across the sky, following the arc of the bridge.

Bianca squatted down in front of us, handed me a flask and winked.

I took a long pull of something oaky and strong, letting it burn the shock away.

"It takes a minute to get used to," Katie said, squeezing my arm. I wasn't sure if she meant the bridge or the whiskey.

I watched it for, like, five breathtaking minutes, thrilled with the way the light danced up into the sky, splitting into the various colors. The light flowed and rippled like water. It was one of the most beautiful things I'd ever seen.

"Is that solid?" I asked.

"Where do you think the giants and wolves came from?" Katie asked, sitting up straight and patting me on the thigh.

I glanced at her and back to the bridge. Okay, if Earth was on this end, what was on the other end? Asgard? I climbed to my feet and looked around at the crowd, suddenly realizing what all this meant.

"What the hell are all these people doing here?" I asked finally.

More people were coming out onto the porch. Cassidy and Maggie from the Harpers, Skella and Gletts, Dante, Sprocket, a cop, two firefighters with axes, and Gunther leaning against the doorframe back to the house.

"How the hell did all these people end up here?" I asked, pulling Katie to her feet and walking back to the house with her close by my side.

Skella raised her hand and waved. "I was at the movie shoot when I got Katie's panicked voice mail," she said, shrugging. "When we heard what happened, I slipped home, grabbed Gletts and as many of our people as I could, and came here." She made a pouty face. "I tried to reach Black Briar after we got here, but we couldn't get the mirrors to open again."

Gletts didn't look too happy. He jerked a thumb over to a smiling Cassidy. "This jerk followed us from the shoot," he said, frowning. "I don't know how," he said defensively. "They didn't travel the ways with us, if that's what you're thinking." He glared at me as if I was challenging him. When I only smirked at him, he harrumphed and went on. "By the time Skella roused Unun and the rest, these two had showed up here. They were poking around the house when we popped into your room," he said.

"Kinda hard to explain thirty people coming out of your wee room," Cassidy said with a grin. "But we'd already assumed something was up." He nudged Maggie with his hip. "Mags here has a bit of the sight."

Maggie scowled at him.

"Just as soon as Skella vanished, she came running to me, telling me we had to get over here." He shrugged. "It's a habit of ours to end up in interesting situations."

The cops and fire guys were responding to the storm. The other civilians were neighbors all cut off from the rest of Bellingham by the fog.

Unun was upstairs with her council, trying to figure out their next move. Several of the fighters were Skella's people, now that I got a good look at them.

"The fog was already closing in by the time Dante and I were on our way back here," Sprocket said. "He's a helluva driver, even in that soup."

Dante looked chagrined instead of happy.

Sprocket laughed. "We sideswiped a delivery truck, flipping it over on its side. The driver's in my room with a broken leg."

I watched them, everyone giving me an account of the storm rolling in, of the wolves coming out of the sky, and finally the giants.

"We've pushed the fallen giants and wolves off the cliff there," Gunther said, pointing to where the fence below the rainbow bridge was smashed down.

I didn't go look. I had no desire to see that.

"We came down on our own," Rolph said. "I was with Juanita and the baby. Called my cousins here. They got across the border just before the storm hit. Tricky business."

The dwarves with him looked hard, mean. Warriors through and through. Each of them nodded to me, but no one gave out any names.

What a motley crew this was. And how many hours until sunrise? The dwarves would be useless to us then.

"How many attacks?" I asked.

"That was the third since dawn," Mimi said, breaking her

long silence. "It won't be the last, unless we can get that bridge closed again."

"How do we do that?" I asked.

Mimi pointed up to the porch, where Charlie was nursing a cup of coffee and letting an EMT patch a cut on his arm.

"Ask him."

That's what I figured.

CHAPTER FORTY-FOUR

That's when Katie succumbed and staggered, nearly falling. I caught her, picked her up, and carried her to one of the three lawn chairs that sat on the porch. One of the EMTs—his uniform said Adam—rushed over to take her blood pressure and generally check her vitals, while a young woman in chain mail appeared to press a cold towel to Katie's face. I held her hand, feeling fairly useless. Adam handed her a sports drink and, after she'd consumed it, she got a bit of color back into her cheeks.

"Insulin crash," he said. "She needs to eat." Then he was back to Charlie, adding a few wound closure strips to the cut on his forehead.

Katie pulled my hand closer, kissed the knuckles, then held it to her cheek. Everyone else flitted away, giving us a bubble of peace. I knelt next to her, placing my head on her shoulder, and stroked her hair with my free hand. Neither of us said anything, but our tears said more than enough.

Eventually she pushed me back and wiped her eyes. "Go check on the others," she chided me. "Folks have been freaked out by your sudden disappearance."

I blinked at her and she gave me a little shrug.

"Go on," she whispered. "Let them see you. I'll be right here."

I sighed and stood. Before she could turn away, I bent and kissed her, the feel of her lips like a drink of cool water on a hot day. Then I left her on the porch and went to see those who had rushed to my aid and those who had been caught up in the crazy that occurred right after.

The sky glowed with the bridge. It was bright enough to cast shadows, even though the world was as black as midnight. I walked across the yard, surprised to see that there were a few campfires burning in the back, closer to the house. I hadn't noticed them before.

The same young woman who had placed the cold rag on Katie's forehead handed me a mug of coffee from a camp stove. Relief washed over me. The warmth felt good on my palms, and the smell was divine.

"I melted a chocolate bar in that," she said, grinning.

I looked down at her. She was small, barely five foot tall, and young—maybe twenty. Just a baby. She grinned at me with that starstruck gaze I'd seen a few times recently. It made me a little uncomfortable. "I'm sorry. I don't know your name," I said with a tight smile.

She shrugged, practically a flounce, looking way too damn perky for the aftermath of battle. "Aliette," she said, giving me a crisp salute.

Gunther stepped up beside her and handed her one of the cups of coffee he carried. "She's our newest recruit," he said, beaming. "Knows her way around a bivouac. Spent the last six years with the Society of Creative Anachronism folks out at the Pennsic wars in Pennsylvania before coming out here to go to college."

Aliette's smile got bigger, if that was possible. "I love it," she said, beaming. She looked back to the house quickly and let the smile drop from her face. "Except for all those people getting hurt, I mean."

I caught her gaze lingering on Charlie, noticed her smile falter.

I gave her a smile when she looked back. "Do you know him?"

"I've seen him around."

Well, that was cryptic. I started to delve deeper, but she turned away and went back to tending her fire, filling travel mugs and thermoses to hand out.

"She's talked about you nonstop," Gunther said, grinning. "Got some hero worship going there."

Maybe I'd imagined the look she gave Charlie. We were all pretty tired.

"She's so young," I said, taking the first sip of my coffee. It was definitely loaded with chocolate.

"Yes, well. You should come around more often," he said. "You could meet all the newbies."

I hugged him. "Any idea where this freaky weather came from?"

"It was the bridge." He shrugged. "We figure when it opened, it brought a butt-ton of atmospheric turbulence with it."

"Any idea where that bridge came from?"

"I was hoping you could tell us," he said. "Bub just called out your name and vanished. We all got up here to find all this mess already rolling."

"Tell me it's at least contained here."

He looked at me, concerned. "You saw Bellingham. We think a minimum of two giants ran north before we got here. At least that's what the cops said when they arrived."

"Fuck! Any working phones?"

He just shook his head. "I sent four of my crew along with four of Rolph's to hunt them. Or at least trail them to where they go to ground. Best we could afford with all the crazy here."

I patted him on the shoulder. "You're a great leader, my friend. Let's figure out what the hell is going on."

"What happened to you, Sarah? It's not like you to just disappear."

I closed my eyes and bowed my head. There was a headache threatening there. "Yeah, well. I've had a pretty fucked-up day before all this." He watched me intently, sipping his coffee. "It's a strange story on my end." I felt the heat rising in my face as I explained about my morning run and about meeting Homeless Joe.

"Odin?" Gunther asked.

I nodded.

"Fook you say," Maggie said from the porch. I glanced over. She was leaning against the railing while Cassidy leaned against one of the support posts.

"Told you, Mags." He looked back at me and smiled. "She doubts her visions, poor thing."

Maggie smacked his arm and he laughed.

"But damn, Beauhall. I had no idea you were bringing down this kind of chaos."

Lilith came down the stairs toward us, Bianca trailing behind. "There's been this old man hanging out around downtown lately. Old guy, beard, one eye. That the one you mean?"

Bianca nodded knowingly and Lilith tapped her own forehead. "Of course, makes total sense."

I just shook my head. What were they teaching kids these days?

I continued on with my story, explaining about the fight with Mimi and my eventual walkabout.

"I need to get Gram," I told Gunther, "before anything else happens. There's a chamber beneath the house. I need to find it again."

"I've been through every nook and cranny of this place," Sprocket said. "There is no basement here."

I walked toward the house, the crowd parting to let Gunther and me pass. Several more people had come out onto the porch, listening to my story. Skella and Gletts watched me from the back. I could see the gleam of hope and obsession in the boy's eyes.

Mimi stepped to the side, allowing me to enter the kitchen, her bony arms crossed over her chest.

"More of a Sideways thing," I said, looking at Skella. She blanched but followed as we walked through the kitchen into the hallway. "More of a trans-dimensional thing." I ran my hand along the wall just past the phone. "Now if I could just find it again."

"I can find it," Katie said, coming in through the door. "But I'm a little afraid at this point." She wiped her nose, bringing her hand away scarlet. "Things are getting a little out of control."

Skella caught her as she swayed a bit.

"Somebody get her a chair," I growled.

One of the civilians got up and slid the chair toward Katie, who sat down with a sigh. "Maybe I should eat something," she said. "Feed the monster."

Whatever disease she had, it seemed to be consuming her when she performed magic. I watched her eat, making sure she didn't keel over. Once she'd polished off three protein bars and drank another energy drink, I told them about my excursion beneath the house, about finding the chamber with the bodies, and how the headless body had grabbed me, holding me until dead Odin's corpse reached out and touched Gram.

Rolph was swearing, damning every god and dragon he could name. I knew exactly how he felt.

I glanced around the room looking for Mimi. This was her house, after all, but she was nowhere to be found.

"Where's Mimi?" I asked.

Sprocket stepped into the hall, glancing around. "She went upstairs. Need me to go get her?"

I gave Gunther a puzzled look and he shook his head once.

"We're good," I said, smiling at Sprocket. He turned to say something to Dante under his breath and Dante just stared at me, his face a mask.

I didn't catch what they said, but Gunther seemed to get the gist.

"Maybe this is a story for a smaller audience," he said, and turned to his crew. It took him about four seconds to clear the hall and roust people back to their assigned stations to watch for further attack or to get back to clearing the dead wolves and giants out into the bay.

Taking his cue, Sprocket and the rest of the Hamsters decided, rather loudly, that the children and those who were watching them should move to Dante's room, which was in the core of the upstairs without windows. "More secure," he said with a wink. "Dante may have some *Star Wars* collectibles as well," he said as he scampered up the stairs ahead of a gaggle of children. Dante stomped up behind him, a rueful grin on his face.

Once most of the folks were away and there were just a few of us left in the hall, I explained about Bub grabbing me and me waking up in my parent's house, naked and alone.

"Then Julie brought me up here," I was saying by the time Katie finished drinking a protein shake. I have no idea how she ate that much, but there was color back in her cheeks and the bleeding had stopped. "We found Charlie buried in a pile of cars, a bit of mayhem perpetrated by one of the giants, I'm sure."

"We'll get to that in a bit," Gunther said, glancing over my shoulder and out onto the porch.

"Get my guitar," Katie said, climbing to her feet. "I can find this door."

Gunther walked briskly back into the living room and returned with a guitar case, setting it on the kitchen table.

"Using a guitar seems to augment the song," she said.

We'd begged her to never use that song again, so of course she'd practiced.

"I sorta thought it was a good idea to understand my limits," she said, shrugging.

Anger flashed and my vision went red. How dare she take

those kinds of risks, especially after all the crap we'd gone through?

Gunther looked over at me as I tried to control my breathing. The door-finding song had nearly killed her once. And her singing had grown more and more powerful, all the while destroying her body in the process.

I must've shown my anger on my face, because she looked at me and scowled. "Don't give me that look," she said, the anger seeping into her tone. "This is what I do. This is my gift. I have to understand the limits."

"And if it kills you?" I asked, trying to keep my voice as neutral as I could.

"I'm not going to die," she said, glancing away.

Neither of us believed that. I stepped forward and touched her on the arm. "You don't have to prove anything," I said.

She laughed bitterly, shaking off my hand. "You're one to talk."

The room stilled. No one seemed to breathe. Or was that just me?

"You don't have to protect me," she said, her voice full of pain. "I'm not a child."

I took a step back, glancing at Gunther who didn't move. He was watching her, calculating. I'd seen that look before, back when he had watched me nearly come unglued, back when he was helping Anezka transition back into the real world.

"I know I don't need to rescue you," I said. "Doesn't mean I want to see you hurt. I love you."

She sagged a little at those words and reached over, taking my hand.

"I know," she said, slumping back into the chair. "I'm just so sick of feeling like a victim."

I knelt down next to her and held her against me. She'd been through some scary shit. Something had to change. I totally understood where she was coming from. I had Gram, I had gods talking to me, dragons depending on me, witches, and other crazy shit, and she'd been a part of all that. Only, most of the time, she'd taken the brunt of the pain and anguish. That was a problem I couldn't fix no matter how good I was with horses and fire, swords and hammers.

So instead I just held her and kept my big, fat mouth shut. My fears and worries didn't matter in this. She had to help, had to feel involved.

"Show me the way," I said, squeezing her knee.

CHAPTER FORTY-FIVE

Katie sang the "Song of the Hidden" so quietly I could barely hear her over the guitar. On the second time through, just as blood began to leak out of her left ear, the door opened a crack. She slumped back into my arms and gave me a bloody smile.

Maggie pulled her from my arms. "Let me take care of her," she said, motioning back to the paramedics.

I kissed Katie and whispered in her right ear. "Do not die, damn it. I need you too much." She smiled and placed her hand on the side of my face for the briefest of moments, then I reluctantly let her go.

Gunther nodded at me once Maggie and Katie were settled in the front room. We each had to do our part. I rolled my head, letting my shoulders drop and the bones in my neck pop. This time felt different, the physical aspect making me more anxious than my ethereal visit had been.

I drew both hammers before I stepped into the doorway. There was definitely old magic here, something that was reluctant to allow me passage, but frail. I pushed through an invisible web with strands that felt as thick as my fingers, but brittle. Gunther came through a few steps behind me, giving me space on the narrow stair. As we neared the first landing, torches sprang to life in soot-encrusted sconces.

I glanced back at Gunther, my eyebrows raised. He shrugged, shaking his head. "I guess magic does what magic does."

"Awful convenient, huh?" I asked.

Cassidy came dancing down three steps, stopping to Gunther's right, armed with a short stabbing spear and a shield. He nodded once, his face stoic. "I'm comin' with ya, lass. Don't argue. No way I'm missing out on this."

Behind him, Rolph stepped up with his axe and shield. "Time to rescue the blade once again," he said grimly. I think he was pissed at me. Not really sure I could blame him. Of course, I didn't lose her on purpose, but I guess from his point of view lost was lost, no matter the blame.

"Okay then," I said, gripping my hammers. "Once more into the breach."

As I took the first step into the darkness, I turned to look back up the stairs. The door above us was a square of white light. Skella stood there.

"I think I'll stay here and keep this open," she offered. "In case it's like traveling the mirrors, you know?"

"Good idea," I said, nodding to her. Glad she was thinking.

On the next landing we found a stack of torches. I sheathed my right hammer and took up a torch, lighting it against one in the sconces along the wall. Further down the torches stopped and the stairs descended into unbroken darkness.

Once we reached the bottom of the stairs, it became apparent that things were different from my last visit. Of course, then I'd come here in spirit form. Who knew the differences between one and the other? Where there had been the roughly dug cavern, instead I saw a long passage.

"There was a cavern," I said. "A rough-hewn room with torches and a dais."

Rolph stepped forward and ran his hands along the passage wall. "Old magic here," he said. "Dwarven work." He studied the joinery and the cut stone that shored up the passage. "It seems this house has been superimposed on top of another place."

"How's that?" Cassidy asked, turning to look at Rolph.

"Two places in the same space," he said, frowning. "This is not a difficult concept."

Cassidy looked chagrined but did not look away. "How is that possible?"

"This place exists someplace else and here at the same time," Gunther said. "Like superimposing one image on top of another. Here we have bleed-through from a more powerful magic into the real world."

"Indeed," Rolph said. "It's possible that Sarah somehow triggered it with her astral excursion. Walkabout, I believe you call it?" He turned to me and I nodded. "Smith, you had the sword the last time you were here, correct?"

"Oh, yeah," I said. "I wasn't walking around here without her."

He nodded and looked back at Gunther. "That could be what triggered the opening of the bridge as well. A significant expression of magic, I think. That would shift the reality in this place."

"I didn't feel anything like that," I said, puzzled. "Maybe it was when he touched the sword?"

Rolph pursed his mouth, biting back some remark, and shrugged.

"We may never know," Cassidy added. "Power of this magnitude feels more deliberate, not happenstance."

Gunther examined the passage, tracing some of the same stonework that Rolph had. "There are runes here." He pointed to one particular stone a few feet further down the passage.

Rolph walked to him and squatted down, tracing the runes with his thick fingers. "Dwarven," he said looking back at me. "They warn us to go back. The way ahead is dangerous."

Great. Like we didn't already know that. "I'm not going back," I said. "You three are free to go if you want, but I need to get Gram back."

"Fair enough," Gunther said with a chuckle. "We go forward on faith."

Rolph nodded and we all turned to Cassidy.

He had his shield slung over one shoulder and held a torch out to the side. "I'm in," he growled, as if we were trying to dissuade him. "This will make one helluva song."

The passage ran west and down at a slight angle. Rolph estimated that for every hundred yards forward, we dropped three. The passage was really long, like out beyond the cliff to the bay. Never argue with magic.

Another sixty yards brought us to a T-intersection. Both sides were dark, but the right passage felt damp, wrong. I'd learned to trust my instincts when I traveled the Sideways. If it felt foul, avoid it. Gandalf would've approved, I'm sure.

They trusted my judgment and we went left. Pretty soon that passage split again, and we took the left again. I know this meant we should be walking back parallel to the long passage we'd followed down, but I had the distinct impression silly concepts like east and west held little meaning in this place. It definitely gave me that Sideways vibe—like maybe if we took the wrong passage, we'd find ourselves out in the crystalline world of jagged edges and hunting feeders. I shivered a little and picked up the pace. The other three followed without saying a word. Part of me wanted to shout to break the oppressive silence, but my crocodile brain thought that just may be a bad idea.

After another twenty minutes the passage opened into the cavern I'd expected to find. If I'd come in from the east last time, this time we approached the passage from the north. Which made no damned sense based on the turns.

Bizarro.

"More twisty and turny than I recalled," I said quietly.

They stepped to either side of me, Rolph and Cassidy on my left, Gunther on my right. We looked into the great room. To our right, against the far west wall, sat the dais.

The dais was just as I remembered it. To my left sat a smaller chair with the headless woman's body clothed in a red shift, slumped as if she'd collapsed, dead to the world. Of course, the whole missing head thing wasn't going to fool me twice. It may have been a trick of the light, but she looked a little singed.

On the right, a larger chair stood, a throne really, and upon it, the desiccated body of Odin, last of the ancient gods. He wore his armor and his great winged helm just as I remembered. Across his body stood Gungnir, his great spear. One hand gripped the spear, great rings glittering on the skeletal knuckles.

His left hand was poised in front of him, in the final position where he'd grabbed the business end of Gram. Unfortunately, Gram lay on the floor at his feet, the first six inches decayed to dust. The rest lay akimbo on the steps up to the throne, like a toy discarded by a willful child. Across the hilt a silver chain lay, the stone at its end cracked and blackened. That had been my connection to Bub.

A pang rose in me. What did that mean? Was he lost to me?

Rolph uttered a quiet sob to my left.

"Yeah," I said, stepping forward. "This is some bad shit."

CHAPTER FORTY-SIX

I'm back," I said, stepping toward the throne, handing
Gunther my torch and sheathing my second hammer. The
others hung back while I took three steps toward the middle of
the room and paused, turning to face the thrones. I studied my
sword lying on the steps, its top third missing. "Well, this sucks,"
I said aloud. "You wrecked my fucking sword, old man."

Someone gasped behind me. Sounded like Rolph. I didn't
have time for his obsequious mamby-pamby shit.

Still, I paused, taking a deep breath, and assessed my next
move. My instincts were to rush forward and grab the sword, but
my better self told me to use my words. "Hey, douche-canoe. I
want my sword back." I crossed my arms across my chest.

Crickets ...

I counted to ten, took another deep breath and started over.

"Yes, I know you're Odin, the great king of the Aesir and the
Vanir, yadda yadda. I've been doing your dirty work for over a
year now and I want my sword back, whole and undamaged."

A dry chuckle echoed from the great corpse and a white light
glowed in the empty sockets.

"You are an insolent whelp," Odin said, his voice like thunder
along the edges of the world.

Rolph fell to his knees halfway between the passageway and where I was standing. I glanced over quickly and saw that he had his shaggy head on the ground, like a collapsed Shih Tzu. Gunther stood two paces back, a cross in his hand, and our torches guttering at his feet.

Only Cassidy stood rigid, unmoving, his torch held out to his left and the spear lowered to the ground in front of him. The look on his face was mingled horror and awe. When he caught me looking his way, he grinned and winked. The scoundrel.

I turned back, making sure neither body had moved, and took another step toward the throne. "Look," I said, holding my hands out in front of me. "I've killed a dragon for you, saved your ass from giants, and generally put everything and everyone I love in danger at your behest."

The skull nodded once.

"So, there are giants coming here to Midgard. Great blue ones."

"Ice giants," Odin intoned, his voice less godlike and more present in this cavern. The headless body stirred but did not sit up.

"I know you're pissed at being dead and all," I went on, eyeing the headless corpse. She'd grabbed me last time. I wasn't giving her a second chance. "But the world's changed a bit since the dragons broke your rule and killed your kin."

"Silence!" Odin roared. The cavern shook with the power of it, small stones scattering down from the darkness above us. "You dare speak to me in that tone? You, a woman no less. How dare you?"

"Fuck you," I said. "I'm the only one helping, you damned fool. How many times do you and I have to have this discussion?"

Of course, when I had this exact argument with Homeless Joe, he was not just Odin. He had his own personality as well.

"Are you one of my shield maidens?" he asked.

"Valkyrie? No. I'm not. But I've met some of them."

Rolph raised upright so fast it caught my attention, and I glanced his way. He wore a look as if he'd been punched in the face with a shovel. Hadn't I told him about Gunnr and her winged horse? Maybe not.

"You have met those who choose among the dead?" Rolph asked, his voice a hiss.

I nodded and he grew even more ashen than normal. He swayed on his knees, threatening to fall forward once more.

Gunther continued to chant something in Latin, holding his cross before him. He knew about the time they came for Maggie and Susan, and then again with Jimmy.

Cassidy shrugged. "I believe ya, lass."

"Thanks," I said with a smile. "Watch my back." I turned toward the god corpse.

"My shield maidens do not come for me," Odin intoned, wearily. "I need to return to my bower, need to take a bite of the golden apple and regain my vigor."

"You're pretty dead, by the looks of things," I said. "I'd like to know how you can be here and inside Joe at the same time."

The corpse's head turned toward the others as Rolph sat back on his haunches. "Be still," Odin said and they froze where they were.

A cold breeze blew across the cavern and the torches flickered. Those on the ground at Gunther's feet sputtered and went out. Only the glow of Odin's eyes and Cassidy's torch lit the chamber.

"Where are my sons?" he demanded of me.

"Dead. All dead. I've told you this over and over."

The skeletal hand tightened on the spear, the bones grinding as they slid across one another. I held out my hands again, palms up, showing I had no weapons. "The dragons killed them all, killed you. Don't you remember?"

The head turned from one side to another, as if he was taking in the chamber. "I remember being wounded," he said finally. "I remember Nidhogg, the great bitch, killing my sons, burning our city with her damnable brood."

"The Valkyrie survived," I said.

He didn't speak for a few beats. Instead the grinding sound of bone on bone echoed across the chamber, setting my nerves on edge.

"They have abandoned me," he said, finally.

"I can call them," I said. "Give me the sword, whole, and I'll call them to you." At least I thought I could. I was sure Gunnr would hear me if I whispered her name.

"It is not enough," he growled. "You are petty. You have failed to serve me."

Heat rose in me, anger like I hadn't felt in a while, a warm embrace from a cherished and scary friend. I was okay with it—acknowledged the berserker. I stepped forward, the full rage breaking across the room in waves. "You are a capricious bastard," I began, working up a good head of steam. "I've bled for you, I've lost friends for you. Hell, I've killed for you. I've served you more than you deserve."

"You mewl in the shadow of the dragon," he echoed. "You wallow in your servitude to the gnawing one. You are beneath the lowest crawling vermin." There was a pause as he tried to stand, but he had no means of moving his bulk; the tendons snapped, and the bones of his legs twisted. "You should beg me to kill you," he growled, settling back against his throne.

I would not be surprised a second time. I jumped back as the headless woman lunged across the dais and grabbed Gram by the hilt. I almost expected power to lash out and punish her for daring to touch the sword. Instead I danced away as she swung my half sword wildly in my direction. I feinted left, then dodged to the right, stepping past her. As she flailed about I spun around and kicked out, sweeping the legs out from under her. Totally not fair, I know. Fair rarely wins a fight. It wasn't my fault she didn't have a head.

When she landed back on one awkwardly crooked leg, I

rolled over, ending up with one knee down on the arm that held the sword, with my other leg across her torso. I had her pinned. I grabbed her wrist with both hands and twisted. The hand flew open as the bones in her arm ground together just a little. I pushed off her, scooping Gram up, and dodged her flailing arms. Fully two-thirds of the blade remained intact. I hated thinking how the old, dead god's touch had turned the rest to ash.

As I stepped to the side to keep both of my adversaries in front of me, I risked a glance back to my friends. Rolph, Gunther, and Cassidy remained frozen, unblinking. So much for bringing reinforcements.

I strode toward the dais and swung Gram, stopping a hair's breadth from the desiccated neck of the old god. "Fix my damn sword," I growled.

His bone-dry chuckle echoed across the room. "You are wrathful, I will grant you that."

I could hear the mad mirth in his voice.

"Perhaps I chose wisely when I allowed this cursed blade to come to you. Is there fire in you still? Does your foolish heart yearn to love another, or do you burn to serve me?"

"You do not want me to choose here, old man. You won't like the final tally."

I heard Rolph gasp again. Not totally frozen then.

"There is one here who fears me," Odin whispered. "One who understands the old ways."

"She serves the blade," Rolph choked out. "She seeks what you seek, mighty one. Can you not see that?"

"He's dead," Gunther said quietly. "I doubt he can see much."

I glanced back at Gunther, giving him a look. He grinned at me and waggled a couple of fingers at me, motioning my attention back to Odin.

Cassidy was shaking his head, like he'd been fighting sleep.

"Welcome back," I said over my shoulder.

"I yearn for the memory of my own land," Odin said. "I know

a way has been opened," his voice faded to a whispered pleading. "Can you not feel it?"

The sorrow in his voice was so strong I felt it would break me. Rolph sobbed behind me and Gunther bowed his head, his eyes downcast. Only Cassidy stared forward avidly, his face alight with a rapturous glow.

Then Odin's voice rose again in anger. "Why have they not come to me? Why have they not taken me to my bier? Does no one serve me?"

Jesus. Drama queen much? I let out a sigh and dropped to one knee. I held Gram out, pommel in my hand, the ruined blade laid back against my arm.

"Yes, I'll help you," I said. "I will be an ally in your cause, but do not push me, old man. You don't have a lot of friends."

His laughter echoed around the chamber. "It has been long since another has dared to speak to me thus." His voice issued from various points around the room—no longer emanating from the corpse. That indeed was a dead husk. The sad remains of a once mighty god. But the spirit was here, the essence that flitted from host to host, desperate to find its people, its home.

"If you lot are all that remains of my thralls and warriors, this world is forsaken."

"It is not so far gone," Gunther said, stepping forward. "There are those who thrive in the shadows of the dragons."

The voice grumbled and moved, circling us, lost and angry. "This woman, this shield maiden slew one of them, I remember. I felt the mighty fall. But she traffics with them, willingly serves the mistress of my demise."

"It's complicated," I said, feeling the anger ebb. "Things were never as black and white as the tales told. Did you not bed a giantess or two in your day? Did you not drink with all manner of folk?"

He grew silent. For the longest time all I could hear was the breathing of my friends, and the pounding of my heart in my ears.

"I have been rash in my life," Odin said, matter-of-factly. "Perhaps I should be wiser in this state. I will grant your boon."

Blue lightning sprang from the corpse and snapped at the end of Gram, sending me backward into the arms of the headless one. For a moment the world swam in a haze of vibrant blue flame as the two of us shook.

And as suddenly as it appeared, the lightning ceased, and I fell to my knees, ears ringing, hair smoking, and apparently with a bloody lip from where I'd bitten it. Everything has a cost. The blue glow faded, and the shining form of Gram came into view. Where before there had been ashen ruin, now there was only shining black metal. I swung Gram in a tight figure eight, feeling for imperfections. Flames erupted along the blade, outlining each of the runes.

And just like that, my black beauty was restored to me. I was surprised it hadn't cost more. Famous last words.

CHAPTER FORTY-SEVEN

I fell to the ground screaming as pain erupted down my left leg. For a moment, I thought someone had slashed my calf open, the pain was so intense. When I drew in a second, ragged breath to renew my scream, the pain diminished a couple hundred degrees and Gram, my mistress in carnage, began to convulse in my fist.

Light erupted from her with an intensity that washed out the room. I brought my right hand to join the left, struggling to control the sword as she bucked. In the distance behind me, I could hear the others' cries of anguish and disbelief, or that's how it sounded to me. I held on to an erupting volcano, a nuclear explosion, the death of a star. For an instant, I nearly lost her as some unseen force pulled her away. No matter how hard I held on, she slid nearly out of my grip until I was barely holding on with my fingertips.

"She's mine," I growled, lunging upright in an attempt to secure my damned sword. The opposing force gave one final mighty tug, yanking me up onto my feet, where I staggered two steps only to be knocked back on my ass as a mighty clap of thunder shook the cavern like a great anvil stroke. As I lay dazed, Gram fell to the stone floor with a heart-wrenching clang as bits of stone and dirt showered down on me.

I flung my arms up over my head, expecting the ceiling to cave in, and in a wink the chaos ended, my vision cleared, and the pain in my leg vanished. My ears rang as I sat up, and I saw that Gunther, Cassidy, and Rolph lay splayed on the cavern floor, lifting their groggy heads to stare around incoherently.

"What in the seven hells?" I asked. Gram lay on the ground beside me, glowing with blue fire for the first time—not the deep red flame of the hearth, but an ice blue from the heart of a flame, hotter than the red, more intense.

As I watched the flames subside, I realized a new rune had appeared. Where one had been obliterated during the mending process back at the beginning of my adventures, now there stood a new one whose meaning baffled me: Perthro—mystery and secret knowledge; feminine mysteries and fertility. Fellowship and joy. I understood the meanings of the runes. I'm not an absolute idiot. From the moment these things erupted from my skin, I'd researched them.

I lay Gram on the ground at my side, and quickly shucked out of my jeans. Sure enough, the runes on my left leg had transformed as well. Just as on Gram, between Dagaz—dawning awareness—and Kenaz—the fire of transformation, the fire of life—stood Perthro.

I looked up and my three companions stared at me dumbfounded.

"That's unexpected," Rolph said.

"Remarkable," Gunther added, climbing to his feet.

Cassidy said nothing. For the first time since I'd met him, he seemed to be at a loss for words.

Gunther offered me his hand, and I stood, shimmied back into my jeans, and picked up my transformed sword.

"This is unprecedented," Rolph said, the awe thick in his speech.

I glanced at him and he stood, his mouth agape, his eyes wide with shock and fear.

When he agreed to fix the blade, I guess Odin wasn't messing around. I turned to face the dais. "I'll call your shield maidens." I knelt at his feet, even though he wasn't really focused in one place.

A breeze swept over me and caressed the runes on my scalp.

"I have marked you?" Odin asked.

"Obviously."

"And," he stammered, "the blade has marked you as well?"

I didn't bother to answer that one.

"I have misjudged." He paused, a whisper flitting around the cavern. "It is hard to control my thoughts. I must seek the unbathed one."

The air pressure in the room dropped suddenly and with the sound of a collapsing void, Odin's spirit vanished. It made me think of Bub teleporting.

Before I could follow that train of thought, the others came around me, oohing and aahing about Gram. Rolph was especially awed by the transformation that had occurred.

"Let me take a spin?" Cassidy asked, holding his hand out for the sword.

I started to say something scathing and probably crass, but Rolph stepped forward and threw his arm across Cassidy's chest. "This is not for you, my friend." He nodded in my direction. "The two are as one. They are not to be separated."

Cassidy took a step back and shrugged. "Just adds to the mystery and the myth," he said with a wicked grin. "She'll make a *lov-er-ly* song."

He placed an arm over Rolph's shoulder, turned the dwarf—who stood a foot taller—and the two of them stepped back, heads together, deep in conversation. Gunther looked from them to me and smiled with a head tilt. Those two together could prove interesting, if nothing else.

I turned to stare at the great god-king, strongly considering the trouble I was volunteering for once again. Calling Gunnr may be more than I bargained for. And the headless woman—I had no idea what she was about, but it creeped me out. She had made her way back to her chair and sat demurely with her hands in her lap. Her utter stillness giving the impression that whatever spirit had animated her had fled with Odin's own.

Don't ask me why, or how. I've given up looking for explanations in all things, but just as I turned away to return to the surface, a face swam into my mind and I was overcome with a wave of emotion that buckled my knees. "Bub?" I croaked.

Gunther looked back. "Sarah? Did you say something?"

The other two stopped and glanced back as well.

I ignored them, returning to the dais. Stooping, I saw under the dead god-king's throne a fine-linked silver chain with a broken amulet, its center stone cracked and pitted. I'd seen it when we first arrived, but somehow, in all the kerfuffle it had gotten tossed into the shadows. I got onto my knees and reached under the throne, being careful not to touch Odin's remains. I snagged the chain and pulled it out, rocking back on my heels. As I held the chain tight in my fist, staring at the shattered stone, the runes along my scalp flared and a memory flashed.

Bub popped into the cavern carrying my limp and naked body. He looked around, confused. Gram lay on the steps to the dais and the headless woman stood over my fallen spirit form. Bub knelt, placing me on the ground with a growl, causing the headless woman to spin in his direction. Howling, he burst into flames and rushed the woman, who fled before his wrath.

With her out of the way, he dragged my body to my spirit form and tried to merge the two together without success.

He looked up and spoke to the dead god, the vision silent as a Charlie Chaplin film. Bub bowed his head and the necklace on my body flew upward, the gem smoking and the chain broken. With the removal of the amulet my body reunited with my spirit and Bub flashed out, carrying me home.

Only, the home he had carried me to was the wrong one.

I shook my head as the vision cleared and the room came back into focus. The headless woman stood near the smaller chair, wringing her hands.

"I have not touched him," I said, standing and dipping my head slightly. "But I see how diligently you have protected him."

She curtsied and stepped back toward the chair, where she slumped back again, lifeless. How very strange.

I glanced at the old god's remains and shook my head. I wanted to get out of here while we still could, before the spirit of the mad god returned. I tucked Bub's amulet in my pocket, patting it once for luck, and strode across to the others.

They were ready and willing to leave. Cassidy paused, looking at Odin. For a moment I thought he was enthralled by the god himself.

"But the spear?" he asked, his eyes glazed. "A power you cannot imagine."

I placed a hand on his arm, and he looked around at me, as if waking from a troubled dream.

"Not worth the trouble," I assured him, pushing him toward Rolph.

He shrugged me off with a laugh and a smile, but I made sure to stay between him and the dais as we walked across the basement toward the east, where I'd first come to the room a day or so ago. Time did not seem to be working in my head at the moment.

Much to our surprise, once we left the cavern the stairs appeared no more than a dozen paces away. I guess going home was always easier than finding your original destination. I'm sure there was a metaphor there somewhere.

Gunther took point, climbing the stairs three at a time. Rolph strode to the foot of the stairs and smiled at me, motioning for Cassidy to go on. He stepped up beside Rolph and leaned in.

"We have much to share, you and I," he said, his voice

pitched for Rolph's ears. I rolled my eyes and shooed them up the stairs, following in their wake.

At the top of the stairs Skella looked at me oddly as she held the door open.

"I'm so glad you're okay," she said. "You were gone for hours."

I just shook my head. Where the Sideways was involved, I wasn't surprised time flowed differently.

"You got Gram back?" she asked, obviously puzzled by the sight of glowing blue runes along the blade.

I nodded. "Piece of cake." We both knew that was a lie, but she let it go.

Gunther stood just inside the hallway, waiting. Cassidy and Rolph walked back to the kitchen, heads together, hatching some plot or other. They would be dangerous together.

As I stepped past him, Gunther leaned in, grasping me by the shoulder. "Be careful whom you call, Sarah."

"Sorry?" I asked, momentarily forgetting my promise to Odin. I mean, it was all a little hard to absorb at once.

"If you call the Valkyrie you may not like the price you must pay."

I nodded at him. "Fair advice. Not my first rodeo." I walked through the kitchen and out into the yard, moved past the others to the very edge of the broad lawn. Mimi and the Hamsters were in a huddle, speaking in quiet tones. A few watched the bridge, but from nearer the house. I was alone at the edge of the world. I faced the water, glanced down to see the broken bodies of giants and wolves being battered against the rocks. That was going to be hard to explain to the Coast Guard.

I held Gram out in front of me, closed my eyes, and concentrated. A deal was a deal.

"Gunnr," I whispered. "Fair Gunnr. I need you."

Gram thrummed in my hand for three quick pulses and the wind brought me the faint aroma of cloves and leather.

CHAPTER FORTY-EIGHT

The rainbow bridge glowed with a pearlescent light—a slash of color in a storm-wracked sky. North of us, lightning played along the horizon and to the west, along the beam of the bridge, the clouds were breaking apart. I wondered what this looked like from a ship. The Aurora Borealis, probably. I'm sure it would be explained away somehow.

Time seemed to linger as I gazed at the horizon, waiting. Gunnr would respond when she could. I had no doubt she would come. She had promised me.

I stood there watching for so long that the cold seeped into me, creeping through my layered clothes and armor, digging deeper into my muscles. Not a good thing if I had to get into a fight soon. The thought triggered Gram, who flared for a moment, sending a trickle of heat through me, pushing the cold back.

I watched the bridge, looking for giants. Ice giants, the old man had said. I didn't like the way the cold was getting worse. Were more enemies on the way? I scanned the length of the bridge, following the trails of colors up from the bluff until they were swallowed in black clouds and lightning. I glanced back toward the house and saw that there were sentries on the balconies, searching the bridge as well. We were getting better at this game. Better at fighting an evolving universe of enemies.

Of course, we'd been pretty fortunate so far. The giants probably had no idea what to expect when they got here, and some of our veterans had experience fighting giants. And there was the additional help of the dwarves and the elves, whose experience rivaled ours. Finally, the civil servants stepped up better than you would expect. I was very impressed how well they were keeping things together.

We'd been lucky the enemy had sent such small scouting parties. Likely they were as surprised at the bridge appearing as we were. With their first few scouting forays not reporting back, it wouldn't be long before they sent a real invading force.

Reaching down to hold Gram's hilt, wondering at the changes wrought in the both of us, holding on to her, I could feel the sky starting to turn. Our connection had grown stronger, but to what end? I didn't draw her. Not yet. She was content just to be with me. Like a child returned to their mother. Made me think of Jai Li. I pulled the cell phone from my pocket and found it was still totally dead. I hoped they weren't freaking out about us. I just wished I had a way of alerting them that we were okay.

We had an hour or two more of full night, then the heavens would start to lighten. I glanced across the horizon. Of course, with those clouds, I wasn't sure how much the day would differ from the night.

Satisfied that nothing was going to come off the bridge in the next moment, I turned to look for Mimi. She was with the other Hamsters up on the porch, huddled around the tables that had been set up there to accommodate the overflow crowd. I walked to them. It was time for more answers.

"I see you have dealt with things in the basement," Mimi said, a resigned, thin-lipped smile on her face. "But you have not emerged unscathed."

I shrugged and she smirked. There was both sympathy and anger in those startling eyes.

After a moment, she turned away and cleared her throat. "I guess that means it's time for a further chat."

I sat on the steps, leaning against one of the support posts, and crossed my arms. A closed affect, I know, making me a poor audience, but I was tired and cranky. Aliette brought over a large pot of coffee and went back to make more. I'm not sure this was what she signed up for, but she was doing it with gusto. I was tired and aching with cold stiffening my joints again.

Sprocket sat on Mimi's right, his arms crossed, with a wide yawn on his face. Dante stood next to him, his hands on the back of Sprocket's chair, eyeing the rest of us as if we were a threat.

Mimi stared at me for a long time. She had intensely blue eyes which swam in tiny worry lines and wrinkles. There was an age there that reminded me of Nidhogg—weary and resigned. I started to say something, but she cleared her throat and put a wide smile on her face.

"How should I begin this tale?" she asked me, leaning forward onto her elbows. "Is there anything that would convince you I am not a horrible person?" she asked. "Any tale that will dissuade you from the judgment I see in your face?"

"The truth is always a good place to start," I said, sipping my camp coffee. This one had less chocolate, but the heat was a blessing.

"Very well," she said, leaning back. "I'll tell you the truth as I see it and leave you to judge for yourself." She patted Sprocket on the head and cleared her throat. "I take in the misfit children," she began, then waved her hand in the air. "That's not fair. They are wonderful, beautiful individuals, each glorious in their own right. But they do not fit into society's expectations."

"Fair enough," Sprocket piped up, leaning his head against Mimi's shoulder.

The look Mimi cast at Sprocket knocked a layer off the ice that had covered my heart.

The funny thing was, her gender wavered in that moment. My mind saw "he" when I knew that she preferred "she." It was difficult when I had to make a conscious effort, especially when my perceptions switched like a metronome. It was very unsettling.

I really wanted to think of him as a "her," to honor his/her wishes, but the physicality of it didn't work in my head all of a sudden. I kept slipping into the wrong pronouns, and it was frustrating.

"The outcasts who have nowhere else," he ... she continued. "I give them shelter, give them space and opportunity to find themselves, to see their own worth."

"Noble," I said, meaning it. "I could've used a place like this when I was on campus."

Mimi smiled. "If you had truly needed me—this place—you would have found us." He/she spread her arms wide, taking in the house, the yard, and the people.

"How long have you been here?" I asked.

Mimi paused, the look on her face long and sad. "A long time," she whispered. "Too long, maybe."

"Were you in Buffalo before here or was there somewhere in between?"

Mimi looked shocked. "Who told you about Buffalo?"

I shrugged. "Pieced it together. A friend taught me this song. Really obscure. Said her mother heard it sung on the vaudeville circuit back in the day."

Sprocket whistled. "If the day was at the turn of the last century."

"A song about apples," I continued, ignoring Sprocket and watching Mimi's face. "I think it has something to do with ancient mythology."

She smiled and shook her head. "Long story," he/she said. "Not one for today, I think."

"Odin spoke of a golden apple," I went on, ignoring her admonition. "And the other Odin, the one that's been following me around for a year, the one who gave me these ..." I brushed my hair back and showed the runes along my scalp. "He spoke of apples."

"The apples are lost to us," Mimi said with a sigh. "That is Iðunn's tale and should wait for her proper time."

I saw that she was resolute in her rebuff, so I let it go. I'd ask again later.

"If we could stay focused here ..." Mimi nodded toward the bridge, and I glanced back, looking for bogies.

"Fair enough." Gunther leaned against one of the posts supporting the porch, smiling. I raised my eyebrows to him, and he nodded.

"We'll stick with you, then," I went on. "I'm guessing here ..." I knew what I wanted to say, but the possibilities it brought up were pretty daunting. I took a deep breath. Nothing for it than to attack head-on. "You're one of the ancient ones." I didn't ask.

"Define ancient," Mimi said with a small titter. "I knew I was having a bad hair day," he/she patted the side of her curls, "but I didn't think I looked that bad."

Dante and Sprocket exchanged a knowing glance. Sprocket was anxious, fretting, but Dante was calm and collected.

Oh, Vanity, where is thy sting? "You know. Ancient, like being around since the old gods fell?"

"Ah, about that," Mimi said, dropping her hands into her lap and sitting up straighter. "I guess it's time I told this. I just hope those of you who matter to me can forgive me."

The Hamsters all made noises of support and concern, but I ignored them. I held Mimi's gaze in mine. She did not turn away, did not give any ground.

"It's really all about the well ..."

CHAPTER FORTY-NINE

My true name is Mímir.

"I came to *be* in the middle of things. I was never a child, did not grow up, as it were. In one moment I did not exist, and in the next, I was a fully realized being with a home and a purpose. I guarded a well. Seems a fairly inadequate existence in hindsight, but in that moment, I knew nothing different.

"It was a time of godlings and valor, a time for great deeds and great despair."

I sat back and sipped my coffee, watching her speak. There was a vibrancy there—an energy that spread from her to those around her. She was protecting them just by sharing her life with them. It was an amazing thing to discover.

"For generations," she continued, "men and gods came to seek my wisdom, and a few came to drink from the well. Those who elected to drink from the well were both brave and fool-hardy, for there was always a price to be paid.

"The cost for a sip was high, but the rewards were immeasurable. The greater the price paid, the greater the boon.

"Few dared drink from my well. Twice, on different occasions, a drinker killed themselves, the knowledge they had garnered much too painful for them to bear.

"Of the others, one became a king of note, and another a great smith." He nodded at me. "Not unlike the fiery young woman we have before us."

I didn't respond. After a moment, his smile faltered and he continued. His, hers ...

"My wisdom was known across the seven worlds. Emissaries came from every race, every realm, seeking guidance or mediation over some grievance.

"Only two of the gods came to me to drink from my well. One left weeping and vowed to never return." Her voice cracked there, and she paused to clear her throat. Her gender kept shifting in my mind, as if she herself had become unstable in the telling of this tale.

"When Odin came to me for a drink from my well, the sacrifice he was willing to make was great. The loss of his eye has been told in tales," Mímir said, "but what they whisper about in smoky taverns and sheep pens is the second price he paid.

"For as surely as he gained the insight and wisdom of all creation, he also took on the mantle of melancholy and despair that is the knowledge of all the pain in the world. It bowed him, broke his mind. That as much as anything is what led to their final fall. The wisest among them had no stomach for war, no stamina for the heartbreaking reality of this pitiless existence."

She drew out a flask, unstoppered it, and took a long swig, wiping her mouth with the back of her hand. She offered the flask to me and I leaned forward, taking it. I took the barest of sips, found it to be a strong mead, and took a second, deeper draw. Katie would love this. It tasted like springtime.

I handed the flask back, noticing it didn't feel any lighter for the missing mead. Mímir replaced the cork and set the flask in her lap.

"Many years passed. Odin ruled with a whimper, and the others grew restless. Some began to whisper that it was my hand —" She put her hands on either side of her head. "—as it were, that had broken their king."

"Jarl," Rolph interrupted from the porch. We all looked around at him. "The word is jarl," he went on. "More like 'chieftain'. Why do none of you get that right?"

I gave him my best "are-you-fucking-kidding-me?" look, and he had the good sense to look away.

"It's true," he mumbled to Gunther, who patted him on the shoulder.

Mímir continued.

"One of them, I never learned who, came to my well one night while I slept and murdered me."

Sprocket swore and Bianca clutched Lilith's arm, pulling the taller woman off balance. They righted themselves and Lilith detached Bianca's hand from her arm with an effort.

"Odin found me beheaded in my glade. He took my head with him back to his golden hall and treated my head with herbs and words of power."

"The Nine Herbs charm?" Maggie asked, coming out onto the porch.

Mímir nodded. "The same. With this charm he was able to preserve my head to serve him. For many years I sat at his right hand, dispensing wisdom and advice.

"Those were bleak days."

He paused, lost in thought. After a moment, he shuddered and returned his gaze to me.

"After the dragons came, when the wolves and giants ravaged the gods before their time—when they broke the great wheel, thereby preventing the death and rebirth of us all—I sat, a head without a body, on the throne of a gravely wounded Odin. While the dragons had destroyed all of the other children, they had taken their booty, corralled the thralls, and abandoned Asgard for Midgard.

"Heimdall had broken the true bridge between the worlds in an attempt to prevent the dragon invasion. The dragons had never known of the second bridge, the bridge to my well. As Odin lay broken on his throne, his body shattered by the hammers of giants and rent by the razor-sharp claws of dragons, no one noticed the bodiless head that had been knocked behind the throne.

"Long after the final battle, after the dragons had flown to Midgard, not hampered by the broken bridge, and after the giants had grown tired of the ruins of Asgard and had returned to their homes and their loved ones once again, I sang the dirge of the fallen."

No one made a sound as she began to sing. It was an eerie tune, full of anguish and woe. For several long minutes she crooned in a language few of us knew, but the dwarves surrounding Rolph hung their heads and wept.

She paused, her eyes shining with tears, and began again, this time in a language we understood:

Where lies the body of my child
broken on the bones of the earth?
Where lies my one true love
ravaged by man and beasts?
Where are the ancient ones
to rectify the wrongs?
Where is the last breath
stolen from me
far too soon?

The air hummed with magic when the final note began to fade. I was filled with an anguish that rose in me like bile, burning any thought of happiness and joy. Then, as the final note slipped away a weight was lifted, pulling away the pain and leaving me empty, wondering.

"Fuck me," Sprocket said, wiping his eyes.

Bianca had her face buried in Dante's shoulder and Lilith hugged them both.

I glanced around. People were turning away, wiping their eyes and clearing their throats.

Mímir paused, letting those around us gather themselves, then went on.

"When the wild animals lost their fear and began to infest the ruins, I sang to them and enthralled those of weak minds and spirits.

"These beasties, rats and crows, carried my head to Mímisbrunnr, along that very bridge." She pointed toward the sky, keeping her eyes on me. "They brought me to my well and dropped me in.

"I could hear a great splash in the back of my mind, felt the cold water on my face.

"I have no clear idea how long I floated on the surface of that magical water. I drew nutrients from the well, and, in turn, I fed my dreams into the deep waters.

"This place that holds Mímisbrunnr exists in no place and all places. It is a conceit as much as a physical location. Only with my will could it remain in one place for long. Hence the ignorance of this second rainbow bridge.

"Without my active will to anchor it in place, the well moved many times after Asgard's fall. I would wake from long periods of dreaming to hear new voices, see new trees or mountains looming above my well. I would cry out, desperate for rescue, but no one ever looked—no one ever heard.

"Finally, I awoke from a long dream to hear coughing and retching nearby. A wounded dwarf had stumbled into the oasis that housed my well at this point, thinking to draw a fresh draught of water to save his life. Imagine his surprise when the first bucket he drew from the well did not contain life-giving water but the severed head of an ancient.

"I found my glade had reappeared deep in an unknown wasteland. This dwarf was a smith and a merchant, returning home from a long trip. He had been accosted by brigands and robbed, beaten, and left to die with the rising sun. Fortunately for us both, his anguish was great enough that the well manifested to his need. He managed to crawl over a final sand dune and roll down into this tiny slice of paradise. I was sure it was the dying wishes of the dwarf combined with my mournful dreams that brought us together. Luckily for us both, the bandits had absconded with this poor man's wealth before my oasis appeared.

"Over many weeks the dwarf regained his strength, hiding in a cave the well created for his needs, allowing him to shelter in deep shadows of the oasis. When he had recovered enough to travel, he promised to repay me for saving his life. He left me back in the well and struck out to recover his fortune.

"Years later, the dwarf returned with a caravan of his people. They set up in the oasis, building a great warren of halls and caverns beneath the earth to hide their work from prying eyes. This dwarf, Ótrson, and his kin used their magic and their smithing to create three bodies. One for the man who'd been saved, one for his wife who had not been left a widow, and one for the child who had not been left fatherless.

"They drew me from the well once again and showed me my reward. I was overwhelmed, I can tell you. I had my pick and chose the body of the child, as I had never had my own childhood. They sat my severed head atop the small body where it melded perfectly and, for the first time in centuries, I had a body.

"The dwarves left a horse and wagon loaded with supplies and two long boxes storing the remaining two bodies. Being built from dwarven magic, they would remain perfectly preserved until such time as I moved my head to the new host. Then the old one would die and the new one would begin to age like any other body.

"The first body was lost in a horrible battle many centuries ago. This is the second body, kept alive with the magic of the well and the deals made with those who drank from its waters."

"And the third?" Sprocket asked.

"I've seen it," I said. "It was in the catacombs with Odin's corpse. It helps guard the old villain."

"Yes," Mímir said. "I have needed to change for longer than you can imagine. I have just been unable to reach either of them. Odin may have been killed by his foes, but that did not change his disposition."

"But, if both Odin and your third body lie underneath your house, why haven't you retrieved them?" I asked, confused.

"It is Odin's spirit," Mímir said sadly. "I was able to recover his body in the last excursion I made to Asgard, back when I had a child's body. All of my compatriots fell that day, but I managed to bring Odin back to my glade before my young body succumbed to my wounds. I just managed to change to this frame before I found myself banished from the dwarven warrens below this land.

"Alas, it is in that moment that I lost him, lost my last host, and, honestly, lost my way. Odin cursed me, blocked me from the very thing I craved most. He blamed me for abandoning him for so long. There was no reasoning with him."

"I'm familiar with that," I said, rubbing Gram's hilt.

"I have been a vagrant since that day, doomed to the winds of fate. I did not understand the need that fueled me while in Buffalo. I fell into melancholy and remorse, unable to pinpoint the source of my pain. It wasn't until the well moved here to this community, did I find my way again. Here, I found a flock, a family of sorts, and a reason to live."

"I'm damn glad you came here," Sprocket said, his voice hoarse and his eyes shiny.

"Hear, hear," Lilith said.

Bianca nodded with enthusiasm, but Dante looked sullen.

"What is this mission, this reason to live?" I asked, sitting on the edge of my seat, interest in the story warring with my angst over Katie's condition, and the very real threat of another attack.

CHAPTER FIFTY

L et me ask you," Mímir began, spreading hands in front of her. "If you could take a sip from my well and be anyone you wanted to be—Olympic runner, scientific genius, world class lover, be taller, smarter, shorter, anything—what would that be worth to you?"

There was grumbling in the crowd around us. Finally, one of the police officers in the back called out. "Anything?" he asked, glancing around the crowd. "I can't imagine a price too high."

Mímir smiled and shrugged at me. "What if it only had one catch?"

"There's always a catch," I said quietly.

"Yes," Mímir said. "There is nothing free. In this case, the catch is you only get five years. Five years to be whatever, whoever you wanted to be. Then, after that, you returned to who you truly are."

"Intriguing," Gunther agreed. "Powerful magic. But is that the original intent of the well?"

"Like the old ones, like this broken and pestilent world, things are not what they used to be." Mímir sounded both bitter and forlorn.

"And what do you get out of it?" Katie asked.

I looked up. She stood in the doorway, leaning against the frame. Maggie stood behind her, one hand on her shoulder, keeping her from falling down, by the looks of it.

I jumped up and went to her, taking her in my arms and guiding her to a chair quickly vacated by one of the others.

"What do you get out of it?" Katie asked again.

"Get?" Mímir asked. "Why is it always the way with your kind? Do you not think the love of my family is enough for me?"

I laughed. "What kind of bullshit answer is that?"

Mímir looked at me, anger flashing over his face. "Do not judge me, you with your taint of him!" She pointed at me, her long bony fingers shaking. Her bitterness was palpable. Dark energy crackled around us, sparking off the metal that surrounded us, nails and hinges, sconces and armor. Like the world was suddenly exploding with dark fairies or something.

I reached to the table in front of Katie and drew Gram without even thinking. Those nearest me stepped back, and the Hamsters came suddenly alert, tense and ready for a fight. Mímir breathed like she'd been running, then lowered her hand. The sparking ceased and the normal night returned. Well, as normal as we could have with the rainbow bridge glowing above us.

Was that jealousy? This wasn't the first time this had come up. He/she knew I was tied to Odin. Knew it and loathed it. Odin had done him/her no favors in the past.

I cleared my throat, trying to look as unthreatening as I could for someone standing there with a thirty-inch blade, one where the runes down the fuller were flickering with bright blue flames.

Katie struggled to her feet and leaned against the table, shaking off the hand I tried to use to steady her. She crossed her arms over her chest and used her best teacher voice. "Tell her," she commanded, a single bloody tear rolling down her cheek.

Mímir only grinned.

"Your tricks do not work on me, skald. I know a thing or two about your situation." She took a deep sigh. "But I will answer the question asked, though it does not get to the heart of the matter. You would be wise to refrain from using your powers." When Katie didn't respond, Mímir went on. "As I explained previously, I am the arbiter of the well and I am its protector. I neither control it, nor gain from it."

Katie started to speak, but Dante stepped forward, imposing his physical presence into the situation. "Ten years," he said, his voice ringing clearly for all to hear. "We give up ten years to gain five. She gains nothing."

Everyone fell silent, turning to face the confident young man.

"Not all can take the regression," he shrugged. "Many would rather end their lives than go back to the way things were."

I looked at Dante and suddenly a lot of things made sense. "Like Ginny? Was that why she killed herself?"

"One presumes," Mímir whispered. "Ginny was once a young man who went by the name of ..."

"Oh, no," Katie breathed, collapsing back into the chair and bringing her hands to her face. "Gil?"

Mímir nodded. "One and the same. You knew him?"

Of course she knew him. They'd been friends before the time he'd vanished. Like so many troubled kids, he just disappeared one day, and she'd been heartbroken.

"It's no big deal," Dante said, his voice rising in anger. "Five years is a long time."

"I knew it," Sprocket said. "I knew you were her."

"I'm who I am," Dante said, stepping back from the group, his fists clenched. "And I'll be who I am in another three years when my time is up." He looked at them from one to another. "It doesn't matter what parts I've got, does it?"

At the end there, his voice cracked. For the briefest of moments, he looked as if he believed they were going to abandon him.

Then, Lilith punched him in the arm, and Bianca dropped her cleaver on the table and hugged Dante, crying silent tears. After a minute, Dante hugged her back, the stony look on his face cracking bit by bit, until he was consoling her with quiet words.

We all looked away, giving them a moment's respite.

I sheathed Gram, placing her on the table in front of me, and drank the last of my coffee. Katie reached over and took my hand, squeezing it, her eyes shiny. I wiped a tear from her face and kissed her on the cheek.

"You sure you should be up?" I asked, looking over to Maggie who shook her head, no.

"I can't lie there and wait to hear what is going on," she said. "My life has been a series of mysterious and hidden secrets. I need to be here."

I glanced back to Maggie, who shrugged and handed me a blanket. I took it and covered Katie with it. Next, I took a protein shake Maggie offered, shook it vigorously, and put it in Katie's hands.

"I'm getting sick of those," she said, pulling a face.

"I'm getting sick of you falling over," I said, opening it for her and putting it back in her hands.

She drank it down in one long pull, gulping it like she was starving. When she was done, she set the can on the table and belched loudly. Everyone around us laughed and much of the tension was dissipated.

Lilith explained how Dante and Bianca had been roommates their freshman year of college, back when Dante had been Daphne, before they had all found Mimi and the boarding house. The story went that Daphne just dropped out of school and Dante started the next quarter, a transfer student from a school out east.

"I forged the documents," Mímir said with a shrug. "It really isn't that hard with the right contacts." She motioned to Sprocket, who blushed. "Sprocket works in the Admissions office and knows all the right forms to fill out."

Dante explained his decision and how he knew one day he'd

transform back to "original factory equipment." This drew a chuckle from Mímir.

But, unlike Ginny, who he knew through Mímir, he had no illusions about what his life was before and after the deal. He'd take his five years, live with his decision, and, when the magic faded, he'd go through with the hormones and the surgery.

"See," he said, a smile blossoming on his face for the first time since I'd known him. "What this experience has taught me is that I was right. I knew who I was all along, and there is nothing anyone can say or do that will change who I truly am. The bits and bobs don't matter. It's who you are on the inside that is your true self."

Mímir rose and hugged him, squeezing him tight and then stepping away.

"I know I made the right decision," Dante said, his voice strong and clear. "I've seen the truth of who I am, after eighteen years of being told I was crazy or confused, and all the second-guessing that engendered." He took a deep breath, holding out his arms in supplication. "I'm free of it. My mind is clear. I know I can do anything, be who I am, even when this," he swept his hands down in front of him, "changes back. I'll be the same person."

Mímir applauded and the Hamsters joined in enthusiastically. Soon the crowd around us joined in and Dante stepped back, his face crimson, but the smile never left his face.

When the noise subsided, Mímir turned to face me again. "Surely this is something you can understand," he said to me. "Have you not struggled with your reality? Have you not suffered by the judgments of a world who would deny your true self?"

I didn't answer her, but Katie squeezed my hand again, harder this time, more urgent. I looked down at her and smiled. Of course I understood. My whole life has been a journey of understanding myself and my identity. This made me understand the whole thing a little better. Gave me an insight about the world from a perspective I'd never considered.

It was all about assumptions and perceptions. I'd seen it with giants and dragons, using magic to be something they weren't— hiding their true nature for something easier. How many of my acquaintances hid their true selves from the world? All just so they could get along. How miserable that made us all. I hated the need. Maybe the Reavers had it right. Maybe we should all come clean to the world, declare who we truly are, and let the chips fall where they may.

CHAPTER FIFTY-ONE

W hat about this fog, the bridge? All of this?" I asked. "We have wounded who would be better off in a hospital. We need to contact our loved ones."

"Don't you understand?" Gunther said from the crowd. "Mímir has no world. She and her well exist in a pocket universe, a place outside the nine worlds. This place only exists when called."

Mímir gave him a grateful look but said nothing. Instead she turned, holding her bony arms out to me beseechingly. "It is as you said earlier. Two worlds superimposed upon one another. I did not call this place," she admitted. "It is not within my power. Someone else has a need greater than they can stand. It is they who brought this into being, and, by doing so, opened the cavern beneath this house." The look on her face was devastating. "I have been cut off from my last body, cut off from my chance to be who I was always meant to be for far too long."

"Why didn't you drink from the well, then?" I asked. "Why didn't you take Dante's gambit and change?"

"She has," Sprocket said, standing. "I understand now. She drinks from the well every day. It just doesn't take. Some days she's more obviously female than others."

Mímir laughed. "He speaks truth. For a time, I am able to have my fondest desire, but I am tied to the way this body was forged, tied to the knowledge of reality that resides in the well. This body can be nothing other than what it is. I am trapped with these bones until such time as I can recover the last body and assume my truest form."

"What of the dragons?" Katie asked. "How is it that something this powerful, this dangerous, exists within Nidhogg's kingdom and she knows nothing about it?"

I looked between them, from Katie's fierce look to Mímir's chagrined face.

And my last conversation with Nidhogg echoed in my mind. She knew of Mímir's existence—knew the well existed. After all, it had been nestled among the roots of the Yggdrasil, the world tree. The same roots that she had gnawed in her earliest days. Was it through willful ignorance, dementia, or pure obfuscation that she did not realize she harbored this immortal in her midst? Each of those options held a different and irrational level of danger. Was Qindra aware of this? Was she part of the charade? I looked at Mímir, wondering how much of my thoughts she guessed.

"I have been free to live my life. Without the interference of gods." Mímir looked around, holding her hand out to Dante and Sprocket. "I have done good with what I have. Is that a crime?"

Sprocket was crying, and Dante held him, two friends—two mighty friends.

"You helped them," I said, the final pieces finally clicking in my head.

Mímir turned to me, beatific, thinking I meant she had helped Sprocket and Dante. Such misunderstanding.

"You helped the dragons." The certainty of it settled on me like a weight. "You knew if Odin drank from the well, that he would be overwhelmed with melancholy. You knew the risks, and you held back. You set him up."

Mímir wept then, great black streaks down her face as the

mascara followed her salty tears. "I was a novelty to him, a toy, a plaything."

"Wait. You loved him?" My head was reeling with the possibilities. Odin had been known as a hound, but for Mímir to love him ...

"No," Mímir said. "Not him. Another."

"The betrayer," Gunther said. "You loved Loki?"

Mímir bowed her head.

"She was helping Loki usurp the throne," Gunther said with a barking laugh. "Loki betrayed Heimdall—taunted Nidhogg, drove her to act against the Vanir."

"Yes," Mímir said, her voice a ghost of a whisper. "But she killed him. Broke him and cast him from the bridge." He looked up, for he was a he now, there was nothing feminine about his countenance at that moment. Rage and fury rose in him, and his illusions, his dreams and wishes were cast upon the ground at our feet. "She promised him to me, and, in the end, she was no better than Odin."

"Then why did you bring his body here?" I asked, confused. "You told us you rescued his remains."

Shrill laughter erupted from him. "Rescued? I took his body so *they* couldn't have him." We turned, following the direction of his outstretched hand.

In the distance, flying over the bay, came three winged riders.

By the old ones, I hoped this was the right move. I looked at Katie and held my breath.

CHAPTER FIFTY-TWO

Gunnr arrived with two other shield maidens at her side. I'd last seen them when they came to claim Jimmy—the older was Róta and the younger Skuld.

They rode through the skies on their winged horses. Meyja was Gunnr's, a beauty as white as snowcapped mountains, as ephemeral as a dream. I didn't know the names of the other two steeds, but, while they were beautiful, Meyja held my heart.

They alighted in the yard and dismounted—three tall blonde warriors with winged helms and great swords on their hips. No one moved except Bianca, who dashed to the edge of the porch and bounced on her toes, clapping.

I stepped around the table, past Bianca, descended the stairs, and walked out onto the lawn, my mind a rush of anticipation and fear.

Gunnr walked across the wide lawn, pulling off her leather riding gloves, and stepped right up to me as if no one else in the world existed.

And kissed me.

Katie's face shimmered in my mind as this languid beauty placed one callused hand behind my head and held me.

The world faded, burned out in that white-hot kiss, leaving nothing but the hammering of my heart.

She broke the kiss and brushed her cheek against mine, whispering in my ear. "I knew you would call me one day," she breathed, and stepped back.

I took a deep breath, steeling myself. For the briefest of moments, I thought my knees may buckle. But I held it together.

"We need to have a talk about consent," I managed to say once I got my brain reconnected to my mouth.

She tossed her long blond hair back with a laugh. "I see the desire in you."

She paused. "Though there is something new." She took a step back, assessing me. "There is something ..." She paused, a thought dawning in her eyes.

"Your master calls you," I said, my voice cracking a bit on the first word. "He has called you for time out of mind and you have not answered."

Róta stepped back as if struck. Skuld gasped. The color and pride in Gunnr's face faded to the palest cream. "What is this nonsense?" she asked. "Our master vanished an eon ago."

Mímir stepped forward, a look of contempt on his face. "Well, if it isn't Woden's whores."

Gunnr lifted her head, breaking eye contact with me and glancing over my shoulder. I took a step back, as if released from magic bonds.

"You?" she said, her hand going to the hilt of her sword.

Róta growled and drew her blade, but Skuld grabbed her arm. "Patience, sister."

"I knew you'd find me one day," Mímir said, her voice a harsh growl. "You and the rest of his harlots."

"Hold your tongue," Róta barked, taking another step toward Mímir.

Mímir turned her gaze to Róta, a smirk on her face. "You were always so anxious for his attention, fair Róta—prancing around him like a pup, always eager to please him, always eager to serve him in whatever way he desired."

Róta blushed crimson, her mouth falling open like a goldfish, opening and closing without a sound.

"I'm surprised to see how tall you are, dear Róta. I only ever saw you on your knees, serving him from one end or the other."

Gunnr held an arm out to her side, catching Róta across the chest as she broke away from Skuld.

"Hold, sister. Do not let this frightened and lovesick fool goad you into action."

Róta slumped, her shoulders sagging. Skuld stepped up behind her, taking her by the shoulders, and pulled her back.

Gunnr took several long strides, closing the distance to the porch by more than half. "I know you, betrayer. I know of your treachery, and I know of your hidden affair with the Jötunn, Loki."

Mímir spat on the stairs in Gunnr's general direction. "You are a lapdog, a harlot, and a fool."

Gunnr laughed. "In some eyes, surely, but your anger and your venom will not touch me." She held her hands up, palms out, and took another step forward. "I do not judge you for whom you love, dear Mímir, only for the crimes you committed against our lord and master."

"He was a bigger fool," Mímir said, her voice almost a mumble. She turned her face away from Gunnr, glanced back at her people and turned back, straightening.

"I regret the loss of so many," Mímir went on, finding her strength once more. "But I do not regret his fall. He who shamed me, who mocked me. He who enslaved me at the end to watch as he allowed his great kingdom to fall into ruin. It should have gone to his true heir." She paused there, taking a great gasping breath. "Not that idiot Thor, but he who had the nine worlds' interest in his mind and actions."

Gunnr bowed her head slightly and lowered her hands. "I know of your grief, dear uncle. I know that you shared from your well with Loki and how it nearly drove him mad with the knowledge he gained."

So, Loki was the second god to drink from the well. It made sense.

"He was such a beautiful man," Mímir said, her voice quiet again. "Such a clever mind." She sat down on the stoop and put her head in her hands. It stayed attached to her body, thank goodness. You never knew.

Gunnr turned and took in the scene around us. Then she glanced back to the bridge. "There has been battle here this day," she said. "But there seems to be no immediate threat of danger." She nodded to her compatriots. "Mayhap it is time for us to recover our lost lord?"

"Yes, please," I said, feeling like I was fifteen again and I'd just kissed Marybeth at the church lock-in. "Gunther can show you."

Skuld and Róta nodded. They jogged into the house, led by a stoic Gunther.

"But none have died in your band?" Gunnr asked, catching my chin in her hand.

I took a step back, afraid that her touch would break me.

"Wounded," I said, my voice husky. I cleared it and took another step back. Katie came limping down the stairs and stumbled into the yard toward me. I stepped to her, catching her before she could fall, and held her up to my side.

"So, this is my rival," Gunnr said with a tight smile. "This broken child has stolen your heart?"

"Fuck you," Katie said, standing straighter, but still leaning on me. "You have no right."

Gunnr looked from Katie to me and shook her head. "So young, so foolish."

Katie tensed, the anger coming off her in waves. For a moment I thought she might attack Gunnr.

Gunnr must have thought so as well because she stepped

back, bowing and waving her hands out to the side. "I cede the ground this day."

There was laughter in her voice, but when she straightened, her face was composed, tranquil. "You are weakened by dark magic," she said, staring into Katie's face. "You are poisoned in both body and spirit. Take care, little butterfly, or you may find yourself consumed in the flames."

She walked past us, toward the house. The crowd parted as Róta and Skuld returned, carrying between them the great corpse of Odin. They strapped him across Meyja's back before returning to the house and bringing back up the headless woman in red, which they settled into one of the deck chairs with reverence and care. Finally, they took the great spear Gungnir, the winged helm and the great shield of Odin, secured them to the other horses, and the three mounted.

Róta and Skuld cantered toward the well and waited. Gunnr turned Meyja back to face Katie and me, her helm held against her hip.

"Be warned, dear Sarah," she called back. "Asgard is overrun with Jötunn and their hounds. Only the area near Valhalla has been kept free of their filth."

I nodded. "Thank you, Gunnr."

She nodded and strapped on her helm. "You have but to whisper my name," she said, her eyes twinkling inside the shadow of her helm. "Day or night, in battle or in bed."

Then she turned toward the west and Meyja unfurled her great white wings.

I looked over at Katie. The hurt on her face was like a knife in my gut. "It's complicated," I said. She turned away, staggered into Maggie's arms and they walked back into the house. Maggie's last look at me was scathing.

That went well.

CHAPTER FIFTY-THREE

I watched the Valkyrie canter across the lawn and take to the air—watched as they flew west across the bay, until they became dots, then specks, then nothing.

"Dawn's approaching," I called. Time for the dwarves to hide. They would hide in the house away from the sun's deadly rays.

Odin was gone from this place. The bridge should've closed by now. But nothing happened. The bridge didn't go away. I waited long after the Valkyrie had gone, and the first rays of the sun began to paint the clouds so that the rainbow was camouflaged to near invisibility. Still the bridge didn't close, the fog didn't clear.

"Maybe we have to close it from the other end," Sprocket offered from the porch. "We don't really know how it opened, do we?"

"I think I know," Charlie Hague called as he pushed through the crowd on the porch.

I looked up, a flash of dread swimming into my belly.

Charlie was hugging his medical bag to his chest as he fought his way through the crowd. He had a few small scrapes on his face and arms, but otherwise looked none the worse for wear.

I raised my hand and the crowd parted, giving him a clear

avenue to where I stood. Gunther motioned and several of his crew stepped back, lowering weapons.

"Charlie, my friend." I rubbed my temple as the runes began to burn. "Tell me I didn't make a mistake pulling you out of that wreckage."

Charlie swallowed hard and held up the bag. There were a lot of weapons drawn in the crowd.

"I didn't do it, but I have a good idea who did."

It took me three deep breaths before I could tamp down the anger enough to look up and smile. "Care to share your thoughts?"

He bobbed his head and dug into his bag.

"When they wiped out Madame Gottschalk's, they were looking for certain artifacts." He looked up as he pulled a sheaf of papers out of the pack. "Here's what they took."

I knelt beside him as he squatted and spread the papers on the ground.

Gunther stood over us, holding a kerosene lantern over us, giving me enough light to read by.

"Manifests?" I asked.

Charlie nodded. "You know I get most of the shit jobs." He cocked his head to the side, trying to get a look at my face. When I didn't agree with him, he shrugged and turned back to the papers. "Here." He pointed to one. "This is for a shipment of items going out to Minsk." He tapped the page. "The crate for this item was found in the basement by Qindra's people, empty."

I had seen that crate. I didn't bother to examine the papers, and apparently Qindra's folks missed some things.

"I found these buried under a pile of sand," he continued.

"How'd you get past Qindra's people?"

He smiled and shrugged. "I've got a few tricks. I'm a quick study, and I pay attention."

Qindra was going to have kittens.

I picked up the first page and read aloud. "One pair of helskór." I looked up at him. "What the hell are helskór?" As soon as I said it, I caught the repeated sound. "Something to do with the goddess Hel?"

"Interesting," Gunther said, kneeling beside me and peering over my shoulder. "Skór means shoes. So, hell shoes?"

I glanced at him, smirking. "Really?"

Charlie took the page away from me and pointed to the shipping address. "These were supposed to go to a group in Minsk that"—he made air quotes—"*takes care* of those types of things."

My runes flared even brighter, making my eyes water. Too many questions warred in my head. Minsk was where Edith came from originally. Minsk was where Baba Yaga was reported to be. My mind reeled with the implications, but those questions would have to wait—we had more immediate problems. "What is the secret power of these hell shoes?"

Cassidy laughed from behind Gunther. "Well, lass. They allow the dead to walk to Valhalla."

I turned, putting one knee on the ground and looking up at him. "Of course they do."

Ibuprofen, that's what I needed. I certainly didn't need more chocolate or caffeine. Not that I'd admit it publicly.

"Do you recognize the name on the shipping label?"

Charlie shook his head. "No. I know of them, but I don't know much more than they are a group like Bestellen von Mordred is ..." He paused and shook his head ruefully. "Was, I guess I should say."

"How many survived the attack?" I asked.

He shrugged, but didn't look up. "No one but me and the cat, I think. No one else has turned up. Of course, someone on the inside did this, so ..." He trailed off again. "I can be pretty sure anyone who was killed is off the hook here."

"Witches have a habit of coming back from the dead."

I turned to see Mimi striding toward us, the Hamsters trailing in her wake. "Let me see if I recognize anything."

I stood, took the paper from Charlie, and stepped toward Mimi, thrusting the page into her hand.

She pulled a pair of reading glasses out of a pocket and took her time situating them on her face. "Clever," she said, glancing down at the page.

I waited, counting to ten in my head.

"This isn't a person precisely. As the boy said," she gestured to Charlie who was scrambling back to his feet, "this is one of those pesky mortal groups that lurk and spy, doing their best to avoid the dragons." She looked at me over her glasses. "And other nastier folk."

She studied the bottom of the page. Her face fell, then she looked up, not at me, but at Charlie. "Is this signature correct? Do you know this woman?"

Charlie took the page and screwed up his face. "Bobbi Visser?" he read aloud. He scratched his chin and handed me the paper. "The date on this is within the last month."

The handwriting was sloppy, but sure enough, this had been signed within the last few weeks. Probably right before Gottschalk had been killed.

Mimi and Charlie shared a glance.

"Bobbi Visser died last year," Charlie said, scrunching up his nose. "Remember when we met for Thai food?" He glanced around, looking for Katie.

That had been the day she'd used her voice to compel him.

I nodded.

"Remember how I told you we'd lost one of our own? How they were last seen on the bridge over Deception Pass, chatting with an ugly chick with a beard?" He paused as a few things fell into place for him.

"Yes, that was me," Mimi said, her voice icy. "Bobbi had made a deal. She traded her life for knowledge." She shook her head. "I never put the two things together. I thought it was a stupid deal to make, honestly. But she said she'd lost a sister and couldn't rest without knowing what happened to her."

"So, she killed herself?"

"Brilliant," Gunther said, straightening. "We've established that given enough time, witches will eventually come back from the dead."

"And the shoes can only be used by one that is dead," Cassidy finished.

"Or has been dead," Mimi countered. "Very, very clever."

Charlie paled again, holding the paper out for someone to take. "Bobbi had a sister, Anika." He gulped and looked at me. "You killed her recently. When she and a group of mercenaries attacked your farm."

Gunther grunted. "Well, she won't be coming back from what they did to her."

"Then, we can just spend all morning discussing how it got opened," Sprocket said. He was getting testy. "Who cares if some born-again zombie asshole opened the bridge? Does it really matter who did it?" He looked to me, raising his hands in supplication.

I shrugged, motioning for him to continue.

"We can't sit around here while another band of giants and such wander by, invade Bellingham, threaten the citizens." He was working up to a good righteous fervor. I'd seen it many times.

"We have women and children here, for god's sake."

I looked over at Lilith, who raised one eyebrow.

"I'll grant you we have children here," I said, giving him a questioning look. "But I think the women have proven themselves capable of battle."

He shrugged a little sheepishly. "Point taken. I got carried away."

Dante leaned in and said something to him. Sprocket shook his head and grinned.

"Are you suggesting we go up the bridge and shut it down from the other end?" Gunther asked.

"Why not?" Sprocket asked, an impish grin on his face. "Take the battle to the enemy."

Cheers rang out from the rest of the Hamsters.

"Only thing is," Gunther continued, "if we get up there and shut down the bridge, how do we get home again?"

That sobered the crowd.

I thought of the innocents hiding in the house, the amount of crazy a rampaging giant horde would do to the world, and realized this is exactly what the Reavers wanted. This was chaos at its most obvious. We had to shut this down.

"We have to try," I said, walking closer to the porch. "I'm going up that bridge. The longer it stays connected, the greater chance we have of a full-scale invasion. How do you think the authorities would take to that?"

Someone in the crowd suggested nukes, but I ignored them.

"Besides, while this is open, we are stuck here in this pocket dimension. We need to get back to civilization and get our people to medical help."

"Into the breach once more?" Cassidy asked from the crowd. "Saving the world again, eh, Sarah?"

I grinned at him. "The minute Superman appears, you let me know. Until then, I'll do what needs doing."

"Better you than me," he replied, coming down the stairs to stand beside me and shake my hand. "Given my druthers, I'd go with ya, lass. But I have my own mistress to attend to."

I nodded and he stepped back, disappointed. I think he'd have agreed to come if I'd asked him. "Stay here and watch Katie for me, keep her safe."

He grinned then. "That I can do."

"We're coming," Lilith bellowed, leading the rest of the Hamsters into the yard armed and grinning.

"Fine, fine," I said, shouting to be heard over the murmuring crowd. "Anyone who wants to go, meet here in fifteen minutes. But we need to take supplies with us, in case we can't come back."

"On it," Dante said, grabbing Bianca and moving toward the house. "We've got emergency supplies stashed."

I looked at him and he grinned.

"You know, in case of the Zombie Apocalypse."

Bianca nodded, her hair falling down over her face. She grabbed Lilith and the lot of them ran into the house, whooping and hollering. It was like we were going to a parade or something.

Several other people turned to follow them.

"Someone get medical supplies," I shouted after them, walking over to Julie.

"You sure about this?" she asked me, wrapping me into a hug.

I let her hold me for a minute, letting the tension and pain fall away for a moment. "Katie was pretty pissed."

"Oh yeah," she said, not letting me go.

"It's complicated," I mumbled into her shoulder.

"Of that, I have no doubt," she said, pushing me back at arm's length and studying my face. "Gunnr is breathtaking, powerful. I can see how she could overwhelm you." She didn't smile or laugh, which I appreciated.

"When she kissed me," I said, the heat rushing into my face and neck again, "all I could see was Katie's face in my mind."

She nodded once. "Good. Why don't you go tell her that?"

I took a deep sigh. "I doubt she wants to talk to me right now."

Julie stepped back and punched me in the arm, hard enough to stagger me. "Don't be an ass," she said. "She loves you and you love her. Besides," she said, motioning to the bridge, "if you think you're going up that damn thing, you'd better let her know exactly how you feel." She shrugged. "You know, just in case."

I glanced up at the bridge. I was going to see Asgard. It was exciting and terrifying. "You're right, of course."

She patted me on the shoulder as I went past her into the house. This was gonna suck.

CHAPTER FIFTY-FOUR

I went through the house to the front room and didn't find Katie. One of the EMTs, obviously aware of the situation, pointed up.

"Thanks," I said, heading to the stairs. I climbed them two at a time and went down the hall to my rooms. Katie had been here a few times, mommies-only time. I grabbed the door handle and paused, listening. I could hear Maggie's voice, low and muddled, but the tone and pitch were unmistakable.

I turned the knob and stepped in. Katie lay on the bed, face down, with a pillow scrunched up in her arms. She was crying. Maggie sat on the side of the bed, stroking Katie's back and saying soothing things in her Irish brogue.

They paused when I stepped in. Maggie shot me a look and stood while Katie rolled over, propping herself up on her elbows.

"Can we talk?" I asked.

Maggie gave me a surly look, but turned to Katie, who nodded, taking Maggie's hand and giving it a squeeze. "Thanks," she said, her voice stuffy. Maggie handed her a tissue and she wiped her face, sitting up.

Maggie walked past me toward the open door. Before she

closed it, she looked back. "Be gentle with her," she said, and closed the door.

I wasn't sure who she was warning. Katie looked like she would blow away in a good stiff breeze, but the anger on her face, mingled with pain and betrayal, was unmistakable. I'd garnered that same look once, back when giants and dragons were myths and the world spun in a different way.

"I'm sorry," I said, sitting on the bed where Maggie had sat. "Gunnr ..."

"Don't," she said, waving a tissue at me. "Don't make excuses. Do you want her?"

"No," I said, truthfully. "Hell, I have no doubt that Gunnr could rock my world in ways I've never imagined, but ..." I reached over and put my hand on her stomach. "I love you, damn it. I've loved you since I met you and not even an immortal Nordic supermegafoxyawesomehawt warrior chick can change that."

She laughed through her tears. "You're such a fifteen-year-old."

I blushed.

"I swear to god, Katie. I didn't want to kiss her. I didn't return it or anything. She's just so damn overwhelming." I looked down, studying my knuckles. "The whole time she kissed me, all I could see in my mind was your face."

She laughed again. "You did look like you'd been hit in the face with a shovel."

We talked for a few more minutes and she scooted over, drawing me into the bed with her.

"I need to tell you something," she said. "Before you run off and save the world again. I can't go with you this time."

I didn't say anything. I know I'd promised to never leave her behind again, but she was too frail.

"Back in Chumstick," she continued. "The night when you were trapped and we fought all those spirits ..." she paused, looking away.

"I can't imagine how it was being alone in that house," I said, pulling her to me. She laid her head on my chest and breathed for a couple of minutes, getting herself together.

"I drank the blood mead," she said finally, her voice barely a whisper.

I sat her up, looked into her face. "You what?"

"Don't be mad at me," she said. There were no tears, but a quiet resolve. "They would've killed me, all those biters and eaters. It gave me the power to fight them, gave me the power I needed to rescue you."

By the time she'd stopped, her voice had raised an octave and she'd grown louder, shriller.

"Shhhh ..." I said, reaching out and cupping her face. "It's okay. Why would I be mad at you? You did what you had to do to survive."

She leaned into my hand. "But I didn't tell you," she said. "And it's been getting worse, not better." She straightened up and took my face in both of her hands. "I think I'm dying," she finished.

I pulled her to me and let her cry against me. After a while, someone started calling for me out in the yard, but I ignored them. This was about her and me now. The rest could wait.

Finally, Maggie slipped back into the room, a pack in her hands.

"Maggie thinks she can help me," Katie said, pushing me off the bed.

"There's a charm. Mímir mentioned it earlier," Maggie said, setting the pack on the bed and crossing her arms. "Woden's Nine Herb charm. It will draw the poison from her." She paused, glancing at Katie, jerking her head toward me a couple of times.

"It's a long process," Katie said, wringing her hands. "There's no guarantee it'll work."

"Sarah?" Sprocket called from the stairs. "We're all ready, let's roll."

I bent to kiss Katie. "We'll talk about the details later," I said. "I'm leading a group up the bridge. We're going to scout the other end, see if we can figure out how to close this to stop the attacks."

Katie nodded, glancing at Maggie again. "Be careful," she said. "Come back to me safe and sound."

I noticed my chain and gear was on the floor at the foot of the bed. That was what I'd been wearing when I went walkabout, back when Bub had ported me home.

Maggie helped me change into my own chain. It fit much better, and I got my own rigging on so I could carry Gram's and my own hammers.

By the time I kissed Katie again and hugged Maggie for good measure, there was a crowd waiting for me out in the hall—Lilith, Bianca, Sprocket, and Dante.

"Let's roll," Dante said, grinning.

I waved the Hamsters in front of me and they barreled down the stairs like fifteen-year-olds. A herd of elephants would've made less noise.

I turned at the last second, looking at the closed door, and blew a kiss to Katie. "I love you," I said, even though she couldn't hear me.

Once this was over, we were finding our own place and healing her up. It was a huge relief now that we knew what was hurting her. And with Maggie saying she could help her, I felt a weight lift from me that had been growing heavier for months. She was going to be fine. A long battle, maybe, but in the end, she'd be healthy and strong. We'd be a family, her, me, and Jai Li. We'd get our own place with a bit of land for horses and we'd grow old together.

It sounded like the best thing ever.

But first, I had a bridge to shut down.

CHAPTER FIFTY-FIVE

We hustled through the house, strangers and friends patting me on the back, giving me words of encouragement. I slid through the crowd in the kitchen where Mímir hugged Sprocket and watched me over his shoulders.

"Protect them," she said to me.

I nodded. "I'll do my best."

Out on the porch, Gunther handed me a backpack filled with food, water, and medical supplies. Also, some flares, a box of matches and one of those folding lightweight NASA blankets that kept you warm and dry and took up as much space as a matchbox.

"Julie took four volunteers to scout the edge of the barrier around Fairhaven—hoping to get a word out to loved ones, and maybe get some allies in case you don't come back."

I loved that woman. "Tell her for me when she gets back, that she's the best teacher and a damned good friend,."

He studied me, taking me by both shoulders and really staring into my eyes.

"Be careful up there," he said, pulling me into a hug. He turned me and I looked out over the backyard. There were thirty people ready to follow me into the unknown. None of the dwarves were there, as they were hiding away from the sun; but all of the elves were there, including Unun, Skella, and Gletts. Two police officers, a firefighter, two EMTs, and three of Gunther's crew, including the new girl, Aliette, and two veterans, Rajesh Ahuja and Jenette Sanchez. Each of Gunther's people carried a forty-five-pound pack and a crossbow with two sleeves of bolts. No idea what else they were carrying in those rucksacks, but they had to be burdened.

"We're ready, sir," Aliette said, saluting me. "Ready to go where no woman has gone before."

Gunther squinted at her, but I grinned. Always good to get in a *Star Trek* reference where you could. I saluted her back and went out to address the troops.

"This is a scouting as much as anything," I told the crowd. "We go up, we look around, try and figure out how to shut the damn bridge down, then we come home."

Unun stepped forward, regal with an air of calm and control. "We will accompany you, Sarah, but we will not be returning if we can help it."

A murmur went through the crowd.

Unun held up her hand, quieting everyone. "We will seek Alfheim in our time."

"We're taking this," Skella said, holding up a mirror about two foot square. "It'll be a tight fit, but it's our emergency exit back home, if things go bad."

Unun looked at her granddaughter—her face a mixture of pride and pain—and shook her head. "If we determine how to shut down the bridge, we'll manage it while you bring your people home."

She had always been a puzzle to me, this matriarch of the Vancouver elves. Here was someone so much older than me, who had such world experiences that I couldn't even begin to imagine how she saw the world. After being stuck on this mudball, what would you do to go home again? That is, if you didn't consider this home.

I turned a smile on Skella. "Good enough. Everyone who is going with me has to understand that there are more bad guys up there. We have no idea what we are walking into."

"Beats hanging around here waiting for the next group to show up," said the firefighter. He raised his hand. "Name's Joshua Cooper. Let's get this over with."

The crowd voiced their consent.

"Can I come?"

I turned to see Charlie Hague standing there, weighted down with a pack like Gunther's crew, plus his medical bag. He didn't have a weapon.

I studied him. He had some skills, though he was green as green can be. Still, he'd risked life and limb to get here in hopes of stopping whatever this was.

"You can come, but I'm putting Aliette in charge of you. You stick with her and follow her orders."

Aliette looked around, shocked. Then a grin spread over her face as she slowly nodded at me. I winked at her and she turned to Charlie, leaning in to start telling him what to do. I caught Gunther's glance and saw that he was hiding a chuckle.

We did a quick head count and exchanged names. The two police officers were Bill Perkins and Scott Bohner—like *Bawner*. Someone in the crowd called out "boner" and Scott laughed.

The two EMTs were Linda Blevins and Keven Crowder. The elves didn't bother to introduce themselves, but I knew a few of them. Not like I'd be giving them any orders. After a few minutes of glad-handing and backslapping we were ready to finally move.

This is what Odin had been begging of me for more than a year. Here is where I would get to see Asgard for the first time. I wished Joe were here, the crotchety old bastard. I didn't know if he'd weep or dance a jig, but he'd be happy to see this bridge. If my phone worked, I'd have taken a picture.

Mímir waved from the porch, and Katie called out from one of the upstairs windows. Everyone was in a rather festive mood for what could turn out to be a suicide run. I felt bad for this crew. You can only understand the horror of battle when you've tasted defeat. How many of these good people would never see their homes again? Hell, for that matter, how many of them would live beyond today?

Going up that bridge was going to take a lot of faith. I stepped to the edge of the bluff and looked down through the rainbow-striped path in front of me. That first step was a bitch. Those who'd seen the giants and wolves coming down it seemed calmer about the whole thing, but, to me, it looked like I was about to step out into a long fall onto jagged rocks.

The troop that waited for me to take that first step practically vibrated with nervous energy. The anticipation of an adventure unlike anything they'd ever experienced was writ large on all their faces. Most shone with anticipation, but a few of the older ones were more stoic. The elves showed no joy in their countenance. They had lived through more horrors than all the rest of us combined.

I knelt down to feel the bridge in front of me, half expecting someone to make a crack about my ass, when Sprocket called over to Dante.

"We should have a name."

I glanced back.

"How about the Rainbow Brigade?" Dante asked, glancing around to the other Hamsters.

Bianca nodded.

"When we get back, we'll make a banner," Lilith said. "I just wish we had time to carry it now."

Sheesh, kids.

I stood, taking a deep breath, and stepped out onto the rainbow. I didn't fall. It was freaky, looking down between my feet to see a broken frost giant rolling in the surf below.

"It's like Mario Racing," one of the cops said.

I guess that was something I missed growing up.

At first the climb was exciting. We walked for an hour or so, looking back at the island that was the southwest corner of the Bellingham metro area. Everything beyond that was lost in a sea of fog. The first hour was a novelty, an exciting experience we were going to remember for the rest of our lives. But by the time the second hour and the third rolled around, we were all feeling the lack of sleep and the steep climb upward.

I called a break at hour four, insisting that people get some rest. We shared out MREs, those military grade food packets that didn't take any cooking, and took turns doing our business off the side of the bridge. The women in the group had a little harder time than the men, but we managed not to lose anyone over the edge. It was a long way down, I'm just glad it was ocean below us. Some things shouldn't rain down on people.

Really the bridge was pretty damn wide, and there was a two-foot curb running along the edge, making it a little easier to traverse, even if only psychologically. As it was, everyone stayed bunched up near the middle of the thirty-foot wide span. Perception is a killer.

After forty-five minutes of rest, we packed up and resumed our trek. By this point we were through the clouds and into a thick mist that blocked anything above or below. It was the same type of fog that blocked Fairhaven from the outside world. It created a disconcerting trek, as only a short span of the bridge was visible in either direction. Made us all a little twitchy. Dante kept mumbling about ambush. I wanted to smack him.

After six hours we broke through the upper cloud layer onto a gently sloping portion of the bridge. That came as a relief to my ass and calves. No matter how much I worked out, I always managed to feel like I was out of shape. Maybe I should add a stair stepper to my regime. Would mean joining a gym.

I glanced around and shook my head. I may not live to see another gym.

Others made their relief known with groans and exclamations. Bianca and Lilith didn't seem phased in the least and kept going when several of the others flopped down to rest.

"Hey," I called out. "Don't get too far ahead."

Lilith waved at me over her head and kept walking. I followed a few paces and stopped when they did.

Two statues rose ahead of us: one man and one woman with one hand on a sheathed sword, their right arms extended in front, palms out. I'd seen similar statues before, in Peter Jackson's vision of the Gates of Argonath. I wonder if he'd seen these statues somehow. Would make total sense. I knew there was something amazing about his vision. Maybe he was more than he seemed. Either way, Katie would be beside herself if she could see these. I took out my phone on instinct to take a picture and was surprised to see I could.

There was no signal, which didn't surprise me, but I could snap a few photos to show her if we made it back. It also told me that we were beyond the magic distortion of Mímir's pocket world. Maybe things like guns and such would work if we got attacked. I glanced around to see that the police officers on our excursion had brought theirs with them. That was a relief, of sorts. Not something we could rely on if my experiences held.

I stepped up to Bianca and Lilith, who stood staring at the statues before us. They were huge, bigger than the giants we had fought below. If I had to guess, I'd say they were Odin and Freya. They were not in good shape. The female statue didn't have a head, giving me an echo of Mímir and her present desire. The male statue was intact, though we could see that the bases they stood on had been defaced. I couldn't make out what was written there, but they'd been tagged by somebody.

Still, they were mesmerizing. While we stared at them, the others caught up with us, joining in the general awe of the moment. I gave them a few minutes to gawk, then called them forward. Beyond the statues, I could see a landing and a balustrade. I crested the top of the bridge, passing the statues with the Rainbow Brigade around me. Where they had been boisterous, even festive on our departure, now they'd grown subdued.

We spilled out onto a wide landing, like a grand observation deck, capable of holding a host a hundred times larger than our meager crew. Twilight grew across the sky as we hurried forward. It was as if no one wanted to remain on the bridge after nightfall. Talk about jetlag. It was midday at the other end of the rainbow.

CHAPTER FIFTY-SIX

We stood at the balustrade and looked down upon the ruins of another world. As far as we could see lay wrack and ruin. From this vantage point we could make out the remains of three different villages with withered fields and abandoned orchards. A deep layer of snow covered most of the area below us but tapered off the further we looked beyond the fallow fields and on to the great walled city that dominated the horizon.

The wall that surrounded the city lay broken in many places, but tall and defiant in others. Beyond the gaping rents we could make out building after shattered building marching along a wide thoroughfare that arrowed straight to the top of a great hill. And atop that hill, a mighty golden hall rose like a beacon, unbroken.

"Behold, Glaðsheimr," Unun said, stepping up next to me. "You should have seen this city in its glory," she said. "And upon the great hill, Valhalla where your Valkyrie dwell, awaiting a Ragnarök that will never come."

I glanced at her. "I have mixed feelings about the end of the world."

She nodded.

"Perhaps the wheel has been broken too long," I offered.

"Perhaps things move to a new tipping point." She didn't reply, so I forged ahead. "I mean, besides. If the world were to be renewed, who's to say it would be better?"

She stared at me, a hint of pity in her eyes. "You are a Child of Man, you have no vision."

I didn't respond to that. She'd had a lot of years being that cynical. I smiled at her and turned to examine the area around our current position. Long sweeping stairs led down from our landing on either side, curving into the valley below. Between us and the nearest ruined village a dozen campfires burned and tents dotted the broken ground. Creatures milled below us, six stories or more. The stairs were really long.

I walked to Aliette, who was letting Charlie scan the land below with a pair of field glasses.

"Those wouldn't be allowed at the Pennsic Wars," I said, settling next to her with my elbows on the balustrade.

She snorted. "Gunther and I came to an agreement," she said, taking the glasses from Charlie and scanning the fires below. "When we go to an SCA event, we'll play nice. Any other time, we play by whatever rules we need to survive."

"Fair enough." I liked this girl. "What do you see below?"

She looked at Charlie, handing him the glasses, and motioned for him to report.

"Definitely, uh ... humanoid?" he asked. Aliette nodded. "But they're too small to be giants." He searched the field below once more before turning to hand me the glasses. "They are definitely as blue as the giants y'all killed back home, but too small. No more than four feet tall."

"Goblins," Dante said, coming up behind us. "Ice goblins."

"Oh, like the ones in *Everquest*," Lilith said, joining our little group. "They're weak, easy to kill."

"This isn't a video game," I said to them, barking a little more sternly than maybe I should've.

"Whatever," Dante said, grinning and hefting a double-bladed axe. "We'll see how well they stand up to the Rainbow Brigade."

At least his axe looked sound. Not a cheap knock-off. He'd paid some good money for that one.

"I wonder if there'll be gnolls," Lilith pondered.

Awesomesauce. They were going to get themselves killed before they realized there was no saved game, no reset button.

"No matter what happens, we need to eat and rest," I said, calling to those around me. I divided our people into squads. I set Officer Bohner and the other civil servants into a squad of five and had them watch the right staircase. Unun sent three of her people with them. They had bows, which seemed like a good choice to defend a staircase that rose six stories. The Hamsters and another handful of elves loped off to watch the left stair.

I took Aliette and her crew with me to explore the landing. There were three short, squat towers, one centered along the balustrade and one on either side by the stairs down.

Before we entered the central tower, Charlie held up his hand, stopping the crew from moving into the building. He pulled a twig out of his medicine pouch and waved it in the air in front of him. For a brief moment, a web of fire appeared in the doorway.

"Tell everyone to stay out of the buildings," he said, very calmly, "if they don't want to die a horrible, fiery death."

We all took several steps backward. Jenette Sanchez took off at a nod from Aliette, heading to warn the others. Gunther had a good crew.

Charlie looked over at me. "Give me ten minutes, and I can break this warding."

"What can we do?" Aliette asked, seeming a little more impressed with Charlie than she had been earlier.

"Maybe see if the elf matriarch ..."

"Unun," I offered.

"Yes, her. Ask her to have a look around, see if she sees anything else unusual."

Aliette sent Rajesh Ahuja running and we stepped back to watch.

"No pressure," I said.

Charlie chuckled and squatted, taking several other things out of his kit. I'd seen him use similar things back when we first met.

"This looks similar to what wiped out Madame Gottschalk's place," he said, spreading a variety of items out on the ground in front of him.

I didn't bother to ask him how he knew. He'd just say he had mad skillz or something stupid and I'd want to punch him. No good would come from that.

Twice he threw bits of something into the doorway, causing the web to spark and sputter, but not explode. I'd seen Gottschalk's house. I moved everyone further back.

Charlie noticed, and turned to me, smiling. "You know, I got things here. Why don't you folks go explore the rest of the landing." He handed Aliette and me each a small pouch filled with salt. "If you are suspicious, toss a bit of this into the door- ways of the other building. It will show the magic, but not trigger it."

I nodded, and we turned to find Unun, Skella, Gletts, and a few others coming toward us.

I explained the situation to them and Unun shook her head in that grandmotherly way that let you know she was disap- pointed in something. Still, she split her people into two groups, and we handed over our bags of salt.

"We'll check the other building and do a sweep of the land- ing," Unun promised. "If you want to look around, that would be good, just stay out of the towers." She dropped the bag of salt I'd thrust into her hands next to Charlie and shook her head again. I heard her mutter something about "children" when she led her crew away and I almost laughed.

Skella and Gletts stayed with me, deciding they would "watch my six" as Gletts put it.

Aliette hung back with Charlie. She saluted me as I turned to go and I did laugh then.

Skella, Gletts, and I searched the great landing for any hint on how we could close the Rainbow Bridge. Not that I expected a big red button that said, "push me" or anything. The way my runes were buzzing, I couldn't tell what I was missing. I think just being in Asgard had both sets off-kilter. My money was on whatever was in the central tower, but we wouldn't know until Charlie did his thing.

We walked the perimeter and came up empty-handed. We ended up back near the left stair tower just as Unun and Jara came out, declaring it fit for us to move into. Then, just to be sure, she sent Jara, their clan chief, to take a small group and repeat the search I'd just done.

"We should place archers on top of each tower," Unun suggested, like she was deferring to my judgment. That shocked me a bit.

"Sure," I mumbled, caught off guard. "That's a good idea."

She smiled at me and waved her hand toward her troop. She'd expected me to agree.

The stair towers were two stories, with a single large room on each floor. A narrow stair led up to a second floor, where we found a scattering of broken furniture and a ladder up to the roof. The roofs were barren, but a crenellated wall ran along the top. This would be great for the archers, offering some protection from the wind and enemy arrows, or whatever the enemy had.

I got a third of our overall force to bed down in one of the two towers that were cleared while the rest were split between the two stairs. They'd need to rotate shifts now that the sun had gone down and the air had grown colder.

Charlie had taken more than his ten minutes on the central tower. I made my way over at the twenty-minute mark and he waved me away, muttering something in Welsh, I think.

I wandered back to the balustrade and looked out over the

fields below, trying to puzzle together the pieces of the last thirty-six hours. Below me lay the ruins of motherfucking Asgard. How crazy was that?

As that reality sank in, I realized I was likely in mild shock. This was way beyond crazy. I had learned to go with whatever situation I found myself in—trained from way back by experiencing Da's special brand of paranoia. And that usually worked, but there was an army below us, the promise of death and carnage that looked to me to be preparing to overrun our position and invade our little blue marble. Mostly I just thought how cool Katie would think this was.

On the other hand, I had a sense of calm that was new for me. I wanted to chalk the feeling up to the discovery of Katie's magical poisoning, putting to rest that fucking nightmare. More likely my personality had been altered, just as the runes had been changed, the moment Odin restored Gram to her truest self. Honestly, that prospect scared me way more than standing between our loved ones and a horde of bad guys.

I turned to look back at Charlie. He continued to weave some sort of spell with Aliette watching him like a hawk. He'd gone twenty-five minutes and was working at a feverish pace. I didn't know his business, but I hoped it wasn't out of his league.

I waved Aliette over. "How's he doing?"

She shrugged. "Sweating."

"It's pretty chill out here for him to be sweating."

"Magic is cool," she said, "but dangerous as hell. He had asked me to step away just in case, but I wasn't listening to that."

I think maybe the girl was starting a crush? Maybe I was just thinking about how much I missed Katie.

"I want to talk with the cops," I said, and we trundled off to the right-hand stairs. Unless Charlie found something in that tower, we'd found nothing here to close this damned bridge, which meant we'd need to go down there and search for answers. I wanted to discuss our options with the civil servants; they had training in how to deal with crises, maybe they'd have some ideas.

Or not. Turns out they were not particularly happy with the situation once they learned we hadn't found anything obvious yet, except for the crap Charlie was dealing with. Aliette assured them that he probably wouldn't blow himself up.

"Do we just go home, then?" Officer Bill Perkins asked.

"Yes and no," Unun said. "We will press on for the golden hall. See what there is to see there."

Damn, elves can be sneaky. I hadn't heard her or Jara come up behind me. Their decision didn't surprise me at least. The others looked to me for guidance.

"We rest tonight, no matter what," I said. "I'm not sure what kind of force we face in the valley below us, but some of us have gone more than a day without sleep."

Aliette held out a bottle of pink pills. "Jetson food," she said, shaking one into her open hand.

I looked at her perplexed, and she laughed. "Instant coffee," she said, grinning. "We use these a lot during finals."

"Caffeine pills," Scott said, holding out his hand. "I'll take one and do first watch."

Unun placed her hand over Aliette's, covering the shaker dispenser of caffeine. "My people require less sleep. We will watch while your people sleep," she said, looking at me. "It is the least we can do after all you've done for us."

"Good plan," I said, motioning for Aliette to put the pills away. "We'll need our minds sharp, not buzzed with chemicals."

She put the pink pill back in the shaker and stuffed it back into her jacket. She wasn't upset at all, thankfully. I didn't think I had the temperament to babysit at this point. Jenette and Rajesh took off to tell the people at the other stair what we decided, and Aliette went back to watching Charlie.

People broke out their bedrolls and spread out inside the two cleared buildings. We didn't light any fires since we had no wood, so the night was going to be a long one. Luckily it was hovering on the plus side of freezing. Not that my jeans kept in much heat. I spun around slowly, getting a good feel for the land around me, what our choke points were, trying to determine the best way to defend this landing in case of attack.

It was overwhelming. Three hundred feet between stairs, so a football field. Each stair was fifteen feet wide and lined with pillars and statues all down to the ground. The landing went back toward home about fifty feet, so big enough to be a bitch to hold, open enough to provide little cover other than the buildings and the balustrade. Running back and forth would get exhausting.

I had nothing I could do. Maybe eat, or rest, but I was far too agitated to do either. So, I joined Sprocket and Lilith at the left stair, where they leaned over the balustrade trying to count the bad guys around each campfire and then add up the number of fires that were springing up now that the night had fallen.

"Hundreds of fires, so thousands of goblins," Lilith said.

I laughed. "Not ice goblins then?"

Sprocket eyed me. "How do you figure?"

"Why would ice goblins need camp fires?"

That stopped them. They exchanged looks for a moment, then Lilith turned and shrugged. "It's not a game, Sarah."

Sprocket winked at me and I shook my head.

"We've got decent choke points on these stairs," Dante offered. "And with the archers on the high ground, we should be able to hold off a force a hundred times our size."

"I hope so," I said, leaning out to look at the ground below, "because we're what stands between that horde and our families back on Earth."

"Midgard," Lilith corrected.

I didn't comment.

We each looked to the left, which my mind pegged as south, to see a long winding train of torches marching into the valley out of the mountains.

"More goblins?" Lilith asked.

"More something," Dante answered.

For the briefest of moments, I let myself feel daunted by the sheer numbers. That was a lot of torches. "Things are going to get pretty damn ugly if we can't close the bridge."

Lilith patted me on the arm, giving me that half smile she dealt out when trying to keep someone from freaking out.

Charlie called out with a great whoop and we spun around in time to see a flash of red spread out from the central tower and fade.

"Hot damn," Dante shouted. "Hope that means we can close the bridge."

"I better go see."

I started to head that way when Charlie and Aliette ran into the building.

"Wait," I called, holding out one hand like I could stop them.

Light and wind flashed across the landing, freezing everyone where they stood. The strange thing was there was no noise. For a full three breaths I couldn't hear anything as the sound was sucked out of the world.

Then I heard a line in Elvish whisper in my mind. Unun's words repeated in my head three times like an ice pick, chipping away at the force that held me fast. I couldn't understand what she said, but after the third time, sound and movement returned to the world.

"Sarah," Skella called from the center tower, where she looked inside with a look of horror on her face. "This isn't good."

I ran to her and skidded to a stop in the doorframe. Charlie and Aliette hovered a foot off the floor inside a golden sphere of light. All around the room small crystalline spheres spun in an orbit, occasionally darting in toward them, only to rebound and smash into the interior wall of the tower.

They were both nicked up, and Charlie held a pair of leather shoes in his hands. He glanced at me, motioning for me to stay out of the building, which was not a problem for me.

The landing shook and we stumbled. Charlie looked up, his

determination replaced by terror as the glass spheres all dropped to the floor at once, shattering into a thousand shards. The golden sphere did not dissolve then, and I realized it wasn't a trap, it was Charlie protecting them.

A second jolt ran through the landing and another of Unun's people called out in Elvish.

"Sarah," Skella shouted, pulling on my arm. "The bridge." She turned, pointing, and I took off at a run.

Another of the elves, quicker and more nimble than me, dashed past and gave a silly smirk as he looked back and flipped me off. To my horror, he didn't stop at the edge of the landing but ran out between the giant statues and onto the bridge itself. The bridge whose colors were fading rapidly.

He should've been paying attention to his surroundings, not me. He had one of those Wile E. Coyote moments as he realized that the bridge was no longer there a split second before he began to fall. He looked so young and innocent in that moment, terrified beyond reckoning.

I dove, belly flopping on the edge of the landing, arms outstretched, reaching for him. His voice ripped at my heart as the fog swallowed him.

For an instant, it was Ginny falling all over again.

Hands grabbed at me, pulling me away from the edge.

"Jesus," I said, rolling to a seated position as the bridge continued to fade.

"Guess that problem's solved." Gletts said, releasing his death grip on my arm and leaning against me. "You gave me quite a scare, Sarah."

"Who fell?" I asked him, watching the blackness that appeared below the fading bridge.

"My uncle," he said. "He didn't like you much."

I turned and punched him. "Didn't mean he had to die."

"No shit," Gletts said, rubbing his chest. "Though, of the two, I'd rather we got to keep you."

A grinding noise sent us scrambling backward as a curb like

those that had run along the sides of the bridge sprang up across the gap, warning us that there was nothing beyond.

"Too bad that couldn't have come up before the bridge stopped being solid," Gletts said, standing and brushing dirt off his hands. He held out a hand, helping me to my feet.

I glared at him. His time in the Sideways had left him a little more glib than I was comfortable with. We jogged back toward the tower. I wanted to know just what the hell Charlie had done.

"Giant," came a great cry from the watchtowers.

"Fire up that damned mirror," I growled as Skella met us half-way. "The bridge is closed, let's get these people out of here."

"That's your lot, sister," Gletts said to Skella, drawing his short sword. "I'll help hold that giant off while you open a way for us to get the noobs home."

He ran back to the balustrade between the left and middle towers, looking down onto the fields below. I glanced at Skella, who ran to the baggage to pull out the two-by-two mirror. It was going to be like crawling through a dog door. But we had to get these people home. I ran after Skella as the others scrambled for combat.

Shouts of surprise and, strangely, joy—from the Hamsters—echoed across the landing. Skella grabbed the mirror, yanked off the quilted cover that kept it safe, and attempted to open the portal. Nothing happened. She tried and tried, swearing as her hands flew around the frame and across the glass. The sound of shouting from below was growing stronger as sweat began to run down her face. I could tell she was putting every ounce of her power into opening the way.

With a cry of anguish from her, the mirror shattered, scouring her arms and face with slivers of silvered glass.

"It fought me," she said, wiping blood from her face. "I've never had that happen before."

"Are you going to be okay?" I asked her, drawing Gram as she stood. I had a fleeting panic of biters flowing out from the Sideways.

She glanced around, shocked as the sounds of battle crashed nearby.

Charlie came running up, carrying his med kit. "Go," he said with a wave. "I'll see to her. You go be a badass."

"What did you do?" I asked him, and he pulled his shoulders back. I saw that he had several cuts on his arms and face to go along with the ones from his first encounter with a giant. "Later," he growled, stepping to Skella.

Aliette ran toward the Hamsters, snatched up her crossbow, and joined the archers along the balustrade.

Skella rolled her eyes but allowed Charlie to start examining the dozens of cuts that crisscrossed her face, neck, and arms.

"Be careful." I turned and hurried after Gletts. Two huge mobs of goblins were surging up the twin stairs, each group being spurred on by a twenty-foot giant wielding a great whip, driving the goblins upward in a frenzy of screaming and cursing.

Archers started firing at will, the distinct twang of longbows punctuated by the meaty thunks of the Black Briar crossbows. Two lines formed up, one across each stairwell, preparing for a rush of blue bodies. I looked from one to the other, debating on the best place for me.

No escape route. Gram throbbed in my fist as I sprinted toward the south stair, toward the young hoodlums from Bellingham and the oncoming goblin horde.

CHAPTER FIFTY-SEVEN

The first battle went our way. As we'd figured, having the high ground served us well. But we had a very limited supply of arrows and food. The archers had smashed the first attack before it got started, but, as soon as we realized that the arrows were running out, we'd taken the battle to the ground. Best to keep some arrows in reserve in case something new and unusual attacked. This meant the ground fighting had grown fiercer, and, for the first time, we had several wounded and much exhaustion. But at least the goblins were fighting uphill. That was a plus.

We were attacked three times that first night—each one less organized than the last. By the second nightfall, I sent two small, armed groups sneaking down either staircase to retrieve arrows and bolts and to toss the goblin bodies back down the stairs. This way, they would hamper the next wave of attackers.

The Hamsters, answering only to the Rainbow Brigade now, were surprised to find some of the goblins playing dead, but managed to beat them back without much more than scratches. One of the goblins had tackled Bianca, but she was one tough chick—never said a word but bit the goblin's ear off in the struggle. The rest of the Brigade saw this as a sign and began taking goblin ears as trophies.

"Makes it easy to figure out which ones were faking it," Sprocket said, holding up his grisly necklace.

The normals were starting to get a little squicked out, but the elves didn't react. Unun already thought we were all barbarians.

We slept in shifts, not even bothering to wake anyone for anything other than a full assault. Scouting forays by the goblins or small squad incursions were dealt with by the fighters on watch.

The Rainbow Brigade proved to be wicked fighters. Twice they'd pursued the goblins back down the stairs and returned unscathed and victorious. The goblins had begun to fear them, running away as the Rainbow Brigade dashed screaming down the stairs, necklaces of blue goblin ears dancing on their chests. The goblins were fairly cowardly; only when a giant was there to flog them on did they come in any number and with any discipline.

Goblins were raiders, it was obvious by their tactics. They were used to overwhelming their enemies by sheer numbers and relying on sneak attacks and ambushes as their primary means of combat. Full frontal assault against a well-defended position was not their cup of tea.

On the third morning Sprocket hatched a plan for the Rainbow Brigade to raid the closest goblin camp looking for weapons, water, and food.

"Leave the meat," Lilith instructed the others. Aliette and the other two Black Briar folks were now running with the Rainbow Brigade, as were Skella and Gletts.

"I'd usually put anything in my mouth for a bet," Sprocket said, with a grin, winking at Aliette, "but I wouldn't touch any meat the goblins would have. Could be people," he said, making a retching sound.

On the fourth day, Unun stayed at the top of the staircases, protecting the base camp with a dozen fighters, while I took the rest and raided deep into the goblins' territory, taking the closest standing building as a temporary outpost. It stood on a steep hill with forty-foot drops on three sides. The slope faced the stairs, which gave us a very defensible position. Even the giants wouldn't attack from that direction. The goblins were learning to pull back, give up the valley, and avoid me and the Rainbow Brigade.

Twice we uncovered great caches of weapons and armor, one of which had dozens of bundles of arrows. The Brigade outfitted themselves but packed the rest back to the landing to outfit Unun's crew, who had already run out of ammunition.

The Rainbow Brigade took up goblin bows, missing more often than they scored a hit, but it sent the goblins scattering in any case, and they got progressively better. Dante was the worst, really preferring the axe he'd been using, but Lilith proved to be quite the archer. Given a couple of years' training she'd rival the elves for accuracy. If she lived that long. The Black Briar crew abandoned their crossbows once the bolts ran out, following the Brigade's lead and scavenging bows. They had training.

Things were looking up for us, you know, besides that whole "trapped-in-Asgard-with-no-way-home" thing. We made our way back to the base camp, victorious and nearly unbloodied. I knew it was only a matter of time before giants and wolves returned to the battlefield, but, in the meantime, we ruled the playground.

By day five, we decided to abandon the bridge landing. No matter what he or Unun tried, Charlie could not get the rainbow bridge to reappear. Seems the shoes only opened the bridge when it was between where you were and Valhalla. From where we stood, we could see that golden hall off in the distance, so no need for theatrics. It was damned annoying. While the landing was a good position to defend, we weren't holding it to protect home any longer. I called a war council to share my plan and we agreed to move deeper into the valley, going northwest, skirting the thicker part of the city, heading toward the great golden hall.

We marched with very little contact with the enemy all through that morning. Twice we broke up small ambuscades, but seriously, Girl Scouts would've put up more of a fight than the goblins at this point. By the way the sun was racing across the sky, and the distance to the golden hall, I realized that we wouldn't possibly make it before nightfall.

Unun, who walked with a tall staff, had taken a small injury to her hand. Several of us had nicks and bruises, but her nearly constant complaining was getting on my last nerve. Instead of punching the surly old woman, I sent Sprocket and Bianca to look out for a place to camp on their next dash out to scout.

Luckily, we didn't have to go far. Over the peak of the next hill, we discovered a second set of twin staircases rising to a huge landing and a second rainbow bridge. Once it came into view of the troops we began to double-time it, throwing caution to the wind a little and beating feet that way.

Hope is a fickle mistress. This time it nearly got us killed. When we caught up with the scouts, Dante reported that Sprocket and Bianca were halfway up the left staircase, huddled against the inside wall, pinned down by a dozen or so goblins. Unun set a few archers to try and pin down the goblins while we sprinted up the right staircase, but things weren't as lucky for us this time.

Like we had learned so well, a small force with bows can hold a high ground with little problem. The goblins took advantage of their position. Scott Bohner fell with an arrow through his neck, and Raj, one of the newer Black Briar kids, went down with an arrow in his left thigh. He was screaming halfway up the stair, near where the cop was down, bleeding out. Things were definitely getting out of hand.

I was just deciding which way to go, retreat or assault the landing and damn the casualties, when the decision was made for me. Wolves howled in the distance, and I turned to see a dozen or more, backed up by a flood of goblins and three huge giants. They were surging down the long road toward us from the direction of the ruined city.

"Fuck this," I called. I took one of my hammers and launched it upward, smashing into a goblin that had been sneaking down the stairs intent on killing Raj, then I sprinted up the right staircase, Aliette and Jenette, the last of the Black Briar crew, following closely behind me. Arrows bounced off my chain as I screamed a bloody war cry in a language that this place probably hadn't heard in an eon.

I glanced back and Unun had the elves climbing the left stair, firing at the goblins, trying to draw them away from my frontal assault.

Pain and I are old friends, believe me, but three steps from the top of the landing something sharp bit into the meat of my right arm, just below my chain shirt and above my elbow. I let the pain focus me as I charged into the four goblins frantically swinging long hooked bills at me, trying to snag me.

I dropped the hammer I was carrying, unable to keep it in my hand, but Gram sang before me, a gleaming black arc of death. Two goblins fell with my first stroke, and the third punched me in the chest with the bill, but my chain held. I'd have a helluva bruise later, but it wouldn't matter if we didn't get the high ground. Several people were down on the other staircase when Aliette and I scattered a knot of goblin archers, sending two over the edge of the balustrade, screaming, to the hard ground below.

Then the Rainbow Brigade was there, a chaos storm of swearing and swirling weapons, slashing goblins like a meat grinder. We were the anvil to their hammer. Aliette, Jenette, and I broke the last of them, and I turned to cheer my people forward. Wolves were on the stairs I'd just come up, so we turned, rushing back down to stand over our wounded, protecting them from the ravening beasts.

Pain throbbed through me, every stroke of Gram sending bright motes of agony through my right arm. The arrow would have to come out soon, but I couldn't let the wolves eat our people.

I brought down the lead wolf and Aliette gutted a second. I kicked them back down toward their fellows, and they got fouled up in the rolling entrails and thrashing brethren. We grabbed Raj from the stair and dragged him upward, holding the goblins and wolves at bay. They were afraid to get within range of our blades.

Then the arrows came. Unun and her crew had replaced the goblins' positions and were raining arrows down on the goblins and wolves. Twice more I darted down the stairs—once to recover poor Scott Bohner, who had died long before I reached him, and once to scatter a squad of archers who were moving in position to flank Unun's archers. It was a bloody day.

In the end, three elves were dead, along with Scott Bohner, our fallen officer. Several of us had wounds that would heal as long as we stayed alive long enough. The wolves had retreated near the end, along with a dozen or so goblins and one of the giants. The rest of their dead littered the ground beneath the two great sweeping stairs.

Skella treated me, breaking the arrow off at the end of the shaft and pulling it through, leaving a puckered hole in my bicep which bled like a mother. I dipped my fingers in the blood while she was tearing bandages and wiped it along my scalp, feeding the runes Odin had marked me with. The night became clearer and I saw the immediate weakness in our defensive position.

By the time we had all the wounded dealt with, fires burning, and food being consumed, I'd worked with the Rainbow Brigade and the elves to fix a gap in our defenses and secure the night.

Skella did a fine job bandaging my arm. She tied it good and tight, so the pain was a dull throb instead of a sharp ache. I hated that we'd lost people. In my impotent rage I stormed along the balustrade deep into the night, throwing chunks of rubble down on the few goblins who were sneaking around below us.

Before too long, however, I gave in to exhaustion and let Sprocket set the watch before falling into a black sleep.

CHAPTER FIFTY-EIGHT

Waking was dreadful. Nightmares haunted my short respite, but at least I could see home in them. I'd come to loathe this gods-forsaken place. It was still dark when I finally rolled out of my blanket and stood. Darkness still covered the land around me, which was a relief.

I learned that Sprocket had taken a group out to scout the enemy under cover of the dark. I was too exhausted to question the decision.

I turned at the sound of low talking and saw that Unun and Jara were chatting with those who stood guard over the long stair to the north. I thought to join them, but on a whim decided to walk the fifty feet out onto the second bridge, right up to the part where Heimdall had shattered it back in the memory of time. It was like standing on the edge of a broken circuit, the edges of the lights sparking and strobing, reminding me of an electrical short. Across the wide gap, a quarter mile or more, the other end of the bridge swept downward back toward Earth. This was the true bridge, the link between two worlds. Far below I could make out the white peaks of a mountain range rising from the middle of a sprawling forest that ran west toward the sea.

I didn't recognize the mountain range. Not like I'd spent much time watching the world from this height before. I don't believe I was seeing Mount Rainier or Mount St. Helens. I think I'd be able to recognize those. I'd seen enough footage of the eruption from the eighties to recognize St. Helens, and for Rainier, that image was everywhere. It's possible the bridge came down over the Himalayas or, more than likely, somewhere in the Nordic countries. I couldn't assume anything. Hell, I had a sneaking suspicion time didn't flow linearly between here and home.

Katie would love this view. It looked like Middle Earth or something seeing it from this high. That forest was huge and looked really damned old. I bet she'd have said something about Ents or maybe even Tom Bombadil. I wiped my eyes, the pain in my right arm bright all of a sudden. We were essentially trapped here, and things were looking bleak.

Aliette's call brought me back from the brink, my thoughts of Katie dashed in the harsh reality of another attack.

"What's up?" I asked as I left the bridge and strode toward the towers along the balustrade.

"The others are back," she said, walking briskly to keep up with my long strides. "You'd better hear this from them."

"Everyone make it back okay?"

She smiled. "Yeah."

"How'd Charlie do?"

She blushed. They'd been sharing a sleeping bag for a few days now.

"He did great."

I glanced down at her. The girl had held her own; good at fighting and bandaging and not afraid of doing hard work. It was cute seeing her and Charlie finding each other in all this mess. I hated that we were going to die here, but I didn't let that show on my face. She knew we were in deep kimchi.

Sprocket was being bandaged, a long cut on the side of his head, right on the line where the red and green dyes colored his short hair. He grinned when he saw me and flashed up six fingers, indicating the number of goblins he'd killed. It was a game to them.

Lilith, Dante, Bianca, and Charlie were huddled off to the side, squatting down together, talking quietly. Charlie laughed at something Bianca said, and moved so I could see the bandage on his right forearm. None of the others looked injured.

They'd gotten Charlie some armor to go along with the mish-mash the rest of the Rainbow Brigade had scavenged. All of them had upgraded from their street clothes to bits and bobs from the fallen enemy.

"There are goblins, giants, and wolves flooding over the hills both west and north from the golden hall." Sprocket said, drawing my attention back to him. His smile faded. "We counted two dozen giants; a couple bigger than any we've fought so far. And the goblins are better armored and more disciplined." He winced as one of the elves smeared a paste over his wound and began to wind bandages around his head.

"We ambushed a couple different scouting groups," he said proudly. "They're coming en masse, but I don't think they know what to expect. I doubt they've been challenged in these parts for a very long time."

"How'd Charlie do on his first mission?"

"Guy's got some guts. And magic. He was able to help conceal us on our first ambush. The goblins had no idea what hit them." He cocked his head, squinting up at me. "He got his first kill." There was something in the way he said it that made me squat down next to him.

"Guy's more a healer than a warrior, but he can hold his own." There was more coming, I could see it on his face. "I'm worried that he's trying to prove something ..." He reached out and put his hand on my shoulder. "Prove something to you, Sarah. You should maybe say something to him before he does something completely foolhardy and gets himself killed."

I laughed at that. "Like running with you lunatics?"

His smile was more bittersweet than I expected. "We all know we're never going home again, Sarah. This is an adventure of a lifetime. But Charlie, he's a good guy. He shouldn't go out thinking all this is his fault somehow."

I nodded. "Thanks, Sprocket. I'll talk to him. You not hurt too badly?"

The elf, a tall woman with a pinched face and quick nimble fingers, shook her head no.

"It's only a flesh wound," Sprocket said with a grin. My mind went straight to Monty Python and the Holy Grail, which was probably his intent.

I smiled at him and patted him on the hand, standing. "Get something to eat. How long until they get here?"

He shrugged. "If they push through, in an hour. They could decide to stop at Odin's place, check out the sights, you know." He was grinning. "We can go back out and scout around later, if they haven't shown themselves."

"We'll see," I said. "Thanks."

He smiled broadly, proud and fearless.

"Make sure everyone gets some food and rest, okay?"

"Will do, boss."

I walked up to the rest of the Rainbow Brigade. Aliette had joined them, fussing over Charlie's wound. We were all exhausted and most of us were wounded. This was not going to end well. I just wish I'd gone with them on that last little scouting trip. I'd have loved to see Odin's digs up close.

"Sprocket reports you folks did a bang-up job."

They turned to me as one, smiles all around. Charlie's was a bit sheepish.

"Mind if I have a word?" I asked, holding my hand out to Charlie.

Aliette stiffened, grasping his uninjured arm like she needed to keep him here, away from me.

I gave her a quizzical look and Charlie laughed, patting her on the hand.

He rose and followed me away from the crowd. We walked far enough away that I thought they couldn't overhear us. I ended up against the balustrade overlooking the valley below and leaned against it, not looking at him.

He leaned beside me. "What's up, Sarah?"

I didn't respond right away, needing to find the right words. I'd vacillated a lot around this guy. He'd been both kind and squirrely. In my heart of hearts, I knew he was a good man. Maybe that's how I should start.

"Thank you," I said finally, turning to him.

He gave me a puzzled look. "For what?"

I looked back at the valley. In the distance I could see the new enemy flooding down from the far hills. "Stepping up, doing the right things, not being afraid to take chances, and being willing to put it all on the line for other people."

When he didn't say anything, I turned and looked at him over my shoulder. He had this look like he was chewing on something bitter. I stood straight and put my hand on his shoulder. "You're a good guy, Charlie Hague. It's been an honor to have you here with us."

He didn't blubber or anything, but he did start crying. Quiet tears filling his eyes and rolling down his cheeks.

"I'm so sorry," he whispered, his voice raw. "I didn't know ..."

I pulled him into a hug and he stiffened for only a moment. Then he melted into me, crying with more gusto.

I could see the others of the Rainbow Brigade, standing in a half-circle, watching us. I patted him until he stopped crying and stepped back, rubbing his eyes.

"I thought working with Madame Gottschalk was going to be brilliant. But it ended up being really shitty."

I laughed. "Welcome to the game," I said.

He laughed too, a small chuckle, and looked back at me sheepishly. "You don't hate me?"

All that bravado, all the times he'd walked into danger eyes-open, and he was still just a kid. Younger than Katie and naïve in ways that kept him innocent when so many around him had been corrupted by power.

"You're a right pain in the ass," I said, "but I'm glad you're on our team."

He beamed then. Aliette came over, sensing, I guess, that the worst was over, and the two of them trundled back to the Brigade, arm-in-arm, heads together.

Damn it. We had to make it out of this mess. Maybe I just needed some cranky, nihilistic advice. I went to look for Unun.

I found her near the ruins of the southern tower watching over the horizon. Of the towers here, only one remained whole. The ones near the stairs were battered to rubble. When I called out to her, she looked at me and nodded, fingering the fletching of an arrow held loosely against the string of her bow. There would be no love there, but I think I'd earned her respect. I guess that's the best I could hope for.

"Hello again, young Sarah. How may I help you?"

I went to stand next to her, looking out at the valley below. "I keep trying to imagine this place before the dragons."

She sighed. "It was indeed beautiful, in the ways of the Æsir and the Vanir. You would have found it quaint, I suppose, with your modern sensibilities."

I toyed with Gram's harness, adjusting it for no good reason than I had an immediate urge to fidget. "And what of your Alfheim?"

She did smile then, a deep smile that spoke of beauty and longing. "Now there is a land to behold." Her voice had gone quiet, breathy. "The air is so sweet it would make you weep from joy," she said, turning to face me. "The fruit of the land so vibrant and flavorful that anything you eat after partaking of our bounty would taste of ashes."

Gee, no wonder she was so cranky all the time. I could really use a strong cup of coffee. At least the headaches hadn't started, despite the rationing.

"I'm sorry I'll never see it."

She laughed, a bright sound that drew the attention to those on all sides. Skella looked up, concerned, and Unun waved her away.

"She worries for us, you know. She's a good child. Twisted in the ways of your people, but she has a heart of peace and joy."

"I think she's swell," I agreed. "I wish we could get everyone home again. It's just so damned frustrating."

Unun actually patted me on the head, like a puppy, or a small child. She was tall, granted, but not much taller than me. "Where there is breath, there is hope, warrior. I have seen you turn defeat to victory more times than I care to remember these last few days. Do not despair yet."

I turned to the sound of shouting and saw that the Rainbow Brigade had charged halfway down the right staircase to scatter a small group of goblin archers that had been sneaking up amongst the debris and bodies.

"Watch," Unun said, taking my arm when I started to dash after them.

A dozen goblins and two wolves appeared at the bottom of the stair, rushing up to help their beleaguered friends. I saw Aliette and Charlie take down the last of the archers moments before the first wolf reached them, only to be brought down by Dante and that damned axe of his.

Soon the battle was over, no more than a handful of seconds it seemed, and we had once again emerged victorious. Bianca was bleeding from a slash wound on her right leg which Lilith was trying to bandage, and Dante was looting arrows from a fallen goblin.

"They are warded, don't you see? The witch, Mímir, has protected them in some fashion. And they are fearless, unlike those who would do us harm."

"Not sure about the warding, but they are fearless, I'll grant you that." I sighed heavily, feeling the weight of all these lives on my shoulders.

"You are a capable leader. Go congratulate them, bolster

their spirits. We will survive or we won't. There is nothing for us to do but our best."

She turned that dazzling smile on me a second time and I felt a bit of the melancholy lift. I steeled my resolve, put away the anxiety as best I could, and went to rally the troops.

I spent the next hour visiting each of our troops left alive, putting a brave face on the situation, listening to fears and worries, doing what I could to leave each with a bit of hope. Another day or so, and all this would be over. We were nearly out of supplies, those we'd brought with us gone in the first few days. We'd been relying on raiding for food and water. As tired as I was, a part of me just wanted it to be over, no matter the outcome. I wish I could get home to Katie and Jai Li, but I'd learned in the last year I was doomed to die before I grew old. If my death would protect those I loved, then I was doing okay.

Too bad my heart didn't listen to the bravado.

I think everyone knew this was our final stand. No one said anything, but I could see it in their eyes. Most everyone was resigned to this fate. The EMTs, Linda Blevins and Keven Crowder, along with the lone fire fighter, Joshua Cooper, faced danger every day. The elves, well—they were enigmatic at best, but Unun held their loyalty, and she preferred to die here rather than go back to their home in Vancouver.

The rest, the Hamsters, Aliette, Raj, and Jenette from Black Briar, and Charlie ... They were still kids; far too young. Yeah, they'd seen some of us fall, but to them death was what happened to other people. I wish I still had that illusion.

CHAPTER FIFTY-NINE

I woke after a few fitful hours of sleep to a foreign sky and three moons. Well, this is apparently how the sky in Asgard always looked, but it definitely wasn't Earth.

Despite the fact that Aliette's kit had included twenty pounds of coffee, we were brewing the last of it and I could feel a caffeine headache throbbing in the back of my eyes. It didn't help that I wasn't getting enough sleep. I rubbed my face as I rose. There'd be no more sleeping, maybe ever. Unun still stood on the tower, looking north and west, watching for the approaching horde. I climbed up beside her and watched as the first rays of the sun broke behind me, driving shadows across the valley.

"They're coming," she said, as the valley was suddenly awash in pink light which reflected off the spears of a thousand goblins —two thousand, maybe. The entire valley swarmed with them, and in their midst, great wolves ranged, many with goblins on their backs. And finally, in the far distance, giants. Two or three dozen of the largest bastards I've ever seen, each wearing armor and carrying mighty axes and swords—nothing like the animal skins and clubs crowd we'd fought so far.

"They've been restless for the better part of an hour," Unun said, casting a sideways glance at me. "You slept fitfully."

I grunted and didn't bother to answer.

A horn sounded in the open field below us and the goblin troops shuffled toward the stair. We didn't have enough arrows. We didn't have enough warriors. All we had was the high ground and two choke points to defend.

"You are an honorable woman," Unun said, placing her hand on my arm. "Thank you for your kindness to my kin. And thank you for destroying Jean-Paul."

It all came back to killing that damned dragon.

I nodded. "You're welcome. I'm sorry we couldn't get your people home."

She looked at me appraisingly. "The day is not lost yet. Where you are involved, berserker, the fates cower and the portents are often obscured."

I shrugged. "You're not wrong there."

She laughed, a mellow sound that caused several people to turn toward the tower. Twice in a day. That was a sound not heard much in this world.

"You are different," she conceded, appraising me as if for the first time. "The dealings of gods and monsters have marked you further, changed you in ways I would not have recognized if not for our circumstance."

I blinked. I mean, really. What could I say to that? "Thanks?"

She laughed again, a deep-throated thing that made her appear decades younger. She didn't do that nearly enough.

An arrow chinked off the balustrade below us as the first goblins came into range.

"Shoot true," I said, and turned.

"Lead your people well," she called and turned to loose an arrow.

Once again, I ran toward battle. Man, I was growing tired of killing goblins.

The north stair, guarded by the Rainbow Brigade, saw the first insurgence of the morning, but that was quickly pushed back. Those Hamster kids put up a wicked defense. Once the goblins retreated from there, a second group attacked the southern stair. The archers stayed mainly in the center of the landing area between the two so they could shift as needed, and they moved like a flock of birds, one way or the other, in a synchronized dance of grace and death. I hung back for the moment, letting those who were more rested deal with things. I couldn't spearhead every battle.

For nearly twenty minutes the southern stair took a pounding from goblins, but we held our own with only minor wounds. We swapped out fighters to let those who had been holding back the horde get some rest. Not a long rest, but enough for them to catch their breath. As happened often enough, ten minutes into the last push a horn sounded, and the goblins fled back down the stair from where they'd been trying to rally for another assault.

Our people cheered, happy for the respite. Several of Unun's elves, taking the retreat as a rout, followed the goblins, attacking the rear and attempting to gather fallen arrows. That was our constant struggle.

You know those movies where the good guys just draw out another gun? Well, we'd burned through what ammunition the cops had on day one. The bolts for the crossbows were spent before we left the staircase at the top of Mímir's bridge and made our way to the remains of the original rainbow bridge.

Arrows—well, the goblins had a lot, and we weren't shy about looting them as we could. Still, they tended to break when they hit armor or stone. And the misses were just sad all around. I shook my head at those role-playing games where no one ever runs out of arrows. Maybe I was too exhausted for this. I snapped back to focus in time to see that the elves, in their eagerness, had gone too far down and didn't hear the cries of their friends in time. One of the giants was bowling the goblins aside as he ran for the stair. He wore heavy armor and swung a great ball and chain. The first elf fell, smashed to the stone steps, before the remaining two turned to run.

And our dear state trooper, Bill Perkins, charged down the stair to help them, followed by two other elves. That was not going to end well. I took off after them at a sprint.

Luckily, the enemy below remained fairly disorganized. The goblins, seeing one of the giants entering the battle, turned back and rushed up behind him, firing arrows as they ran. Our archers returned fire, taking out as many goblin archers as they could, but the real danger was that damned thirty-foot blue monstrosity with a shaggy head of flaming red hair and massive beard which clashed horribly with the color of his exposed skin. Honestly, he looked like a lit birthday candle. No, I have no idea why that bothered me so much.

CHAPTER SIXTY

The ball and chain smashed into the staircase, sending cracks along rails to either side as the treads shifted, their tongue and groove mortise failing under the heavy blows.

Bill rushed past the fallen elves and stabbed forward with his spear, embedding it a foot or more into the calf of the giant, who roared and staggered. The stair shuddered as the huge feet slipped and the monster went down to one knee. The elves who had followed Bill grabbed their wounded friends and made their way back up the stair at a limping pace. Our giant friend roared again and smashed his fist down onto the stair, narrowly missing Bill. He didn't flee, the brave fool. Instead he drew a short sword and jumped onto the giant's shoulder, slashing at every inch he could reach.

I ran as hard as I could, leaping over two archers who were sending arrow after arrow into the giant. I snagged a goblin shield from the pile of booty the Rainbow Brigade had been collecting and slung it over my right arm. I seriously considered pulling a Legolas at Jackson's Helm's Deep, but thought maybe I'd just end up breaking my neck. Bill was yelling and slashing for all he was worth when the first arrow took him in the side. I could hear the breath go out of him as a second caught him just below the ribs, but he kept stabbing the giant, who had begun to slow. I wasn't going to get there in time.

Bill reminded me of Boromir from the histories, taking half a dozen goblin arrows before he finally succumbed. I managed to get to him as the giant fell backward. Bill tumbled down the side of the giant, bouncing off a flailing elbow, then a knee, before smashing to the broken stair. I skidded to a stop beside him as goblins began to howl and rage over the top of the fallen giant.

I don't remember much for about ten minutes as I let the berserker come. The world was a blur of blue bodies, screams of the dying, and my epithets as I shouted myself hoarse.

I had definitely drawn the attention of the other giants. While I routed their elite goblins, they began smashing buildings and throwing the great chunks of stone in my general direction. Faced with my insanity, and the sudden rain of broken pillars and other misshapen missiles that began to fall around us, the goblins broke into an ungainly rout. I came to my senses fifty yards beyond the end of the stair, facing half a dozen enraged giants loping across the countryside toward me.

I turned and ran back to the southern stair as the ground shook with the combined might of the falling stones and the thunderous giant footfalls. I glanced up as shouts rained down on me from above. More goblins had attacked the northern stair while I was keeping everyone's attention to the south.

The stair rocked and shifted, making me think my knees were buckling as I wended upward, thankful once again for the time I'd put in jogging. Still, a six-story uphill sprint was more than I could handle. The ground shook underneath me as the cracks in the stair began to lengthen and spread. The entire staircase swayed as I dodged my way back toward the top. One stone smashed a few feet ahead of me, taking a good six feet of stair falling to the ground below. Puffing like a bellows, I sprinted forward and leapt over the break. I landed hard on my side on the jagged stone and I felt several ribs crack. I scrabbled for a hand-hold, dropping the shield, but refusing to let go of

Gram. I'd knocked the wind out of me and my feet dangled in the open air.

The giants cheered and bellowed while arrows began to snap on the stonework around me. I groped for a better hold as the masonry crumbled and I slid backward, unable to call out, unable to draw breath.

Slender hands grabbed my right arm, and I looked up to see Unun's wicked smile. "Don't drop that pretty blade," the old elf said and yanked me out of the hole and onto the solid stairs above. I let her guide me back to our people, ignoring the arrows that were falling faster around us, and tried to breathe.

When we staggered back to the main landing, Unun laughed. "One less point to defend," she said, pulling me down behind the thick stone balustrade.

"You are a madwoman," she said,

Adrenaline and something more coursed through my veins while my heart began to slow. Gram vibrated like a jackhammer in my blood-soaked fist as the berserker ebbed away. I doubted I'd ever be able to put her down again. It was as if the blood of the enemy had melded us into one being.

CHAPTER SIXTY-ONE

Our archers fell silent as they loosed their last arrows. The goblins didn't rush us immediately, likely looking for a trap, but they had a squad of goblins using the rubble on the north stair as a vantage point to snipe at us. Our remaining fighters hunkered down, knowing the end was near.

All of a sudden, Sprocket leapt up and rushed back to where we had stored our surviving gear. "I have a plan," he cried. He rushed to Aliette's pack and rummaged around.

"Hey," she called, running over to him. "Rude."

Sprocket laughed and pulled her close. Dante and Charlie ran over to join them, and he whispered his mad scheme. Together they grabbed several coils of rope, ran to the middle of the balustrade and began rigging the ropes so they could swing out between the staircases. Did I mention it was a six-story fall from the top of the stairs? Without our archers, we couldn't stop the enemy from advancing up the stairs, and with that cluster of goblin archers we couldn't exactly storm down the stair, climb over the rubble that their giant friends had scattered about, and stop them.

I did think for half a second that I should put a stop to what-ever craziness they were cooking up, but if you've ever met

Sprocket and Dante, you'd know there is no stopping them when they've made up their minds. I watched them as Charlie painted Sprocket with three blue hash marks down the left side of his face. Then he kissed him on the forehead before turning and doing the same to Dante, only on the right side of his face. I held my breath. Sprocket jumped, screaming and ululating like Tarzan as he arced back under the landing and then outward again, angled toward the northern stair. Dante jumped a breath behind him and I thought for sure they were going to collide, but they'd tied their lines far enough apart to avoid one another. Still, they came close enough to give me shivers.

They each had to take two swings. I kept expecting the goblins to kill them, but apparently, they don't hit moving targets very well. Aliette and Charlie ran around to the head of the northern stair and jumped about, shouting and throwing stones to distract the goblins. Bianca and Lilith, who were both supposed to be resting after the wounds they'd taken, scrambled up and made their way toward the stair, obviously too damned stubborn to take it easy. Sprocket and Dante shrieked like the damned, and all attention around me and on the ground below was frozen, mesmerized by their antics.

Katie would say these guys had more luck than a bag of magic rings, and she wouldn't be far off. Sprocket landed in the midst of the archers, sword swinging, bowling over several of them. Before they could recover, Dante sailed toward them. Unfortunately, he let go of the rope a bit too soon and instead of crashing into the goblins, ricocheted off the debris and almost fell off the edge of the stair.

He caught a goblin around the neck and held on, breaking his momentum and the goblin's neck at the same time. I let out a gasp as he slipped over the side, only to have Sprocket reach out and grab him at the last minute. Unlucky for Sprocket, he took a dagger in the side for his efforts, but he saved Dante. Sprocket's scream pierced my heart, but he wrenched Dante up onto the railing, pulled the dagger out of his side, and together they routed the remaining archers. Half a dozen had thrown down their weapons and flown down the stairs to escape the wild pair. Aliette and Charlie ran down the stair toward our boys, with Lilith and Bianca in their wake, calling for them to hurry their asses over the debris.

They had other plans.

I stumbled toward the northern stair, holding my right arm across my chest. Definitely broke some ribs. The elf chief, Jara, and three other elves ran to me with drawn long daggers, their arrows long spent.

"Guard the southern stair," I shouted at them as I ran by, and they sprinted away. Sure, the southern stair was damaged, but I wasn't taking any chances. We couldn't afford to get outflanked.

I paused a third of the way down the northern stair to clamber up onto one of the great blocks of masonry. Broken ribs hurt like a motherfucker when you laugh, which I couldn't help but do once I realized that both Sprocket and Dante were passing arrows over the dividing debris to Lilith and Bianca, who were firing down into the oncoming goblins. Dante stood just below the mass of goblin dead, ready for another assault, while Sprocket clambered over the debris, holding a bloody hand to his side. Charlie grabbed him, pulled him over and began working on his wound, while Aliette scrambled over the stones to the goblin bodies and grabbed dropped quivers of arrows, then tossed them over to Bianca as fast as she could. All the while nearly a hundred goblins were massing two stories below, ready to assault the stairs once more. They had guts, I'll give them that. If they lived, I'd have to help them understand the fine line between being brave and being foolhardy.

I called at them all to retreat, and finally Aliette tossed seven quivers of arrows over the stones before climbing over on her own. Dante came next, pausing to help Sprocket to his feet between him and Charlie. They began hustling back up the stair. Lilith shot the first eager goblin over the stones, sending him tumbling back down the stair, and began backing up, firing as she moved.

A wolf and rider leapt over the stones, nearly landing on Bianca, who was laden with several quivers of arrows. Aliette turned back in time to slash the wolf across the throat while Lilith shot it in the eye. Between them, they slew both wolf and rider. Aliette helped Bianca back to her feet. There was a moment where they looked at each other before Bianca leaned forward and kissed Aliette square on the mouth, before picking up the quivers of arrows and shambling on. Aliette stood there, a little shocked, but I saw her smile as she and Lilith slowly made their way up the stairs, allowing the others to retreat with their booty. Just as they reached the top of the stair, Aliette took an arrow to the knee. She fell to the ground screaming, but Bianca dashed back down the stair and kicked one of the new breed of goblins in the face. Three arrows sprouted out of the goblin's chest while she helped Aliette back behind our lines.

Bianca and Charlie exchanged a quick look after they got Aliette settled behind the stone balustrade and ran back down to Lilith, who had begun rocking the largest boulder back and forth. While they worked, protected from oncoming arrows, the goblins below began to march toward the stair. It took a lot of heaving and groaning to get the damn thing to budge. Part of me wanted to help them, but breathing hurt too damned much.

The absurdity of the moment was not lost on me. The fact that a giant had thrown this boulder nearly six stories up the staircase gave me a sudden and uncomfortable reminder of their true strength.

With a loud "whoop" they pushed the stone over, and it slid a couple of feet before going over the next step, and then gravity took over. It picked up speed as it bumped and rolled down the sweeping stair, smashing against the one-meter thick railing before careening around the bend and onto the oncoming goblins. The apocalyptic sound of crashing stone and smashed meat drowned out the cheers of our surviving fighters. The stone smashed through the tightly organized group of goblins and wolf riders with so much momentum that it rolled out into the valley a goodly way, squashing one of the camps the goblins had set up to block our escape.

With that stone cleared, Dante and Bianca scrambled back down the stair to recover even more arrows. One of the giants decided it was time for us to get back where we belonged and came striding toward the stair, bellowing something that my brain wanted to interpret as *get off my lawn*, but I think it was likely something totally different and full of Jötunn swear words.

Dante and Bianca scampered back up the stair while Lilith came behind, guarding the rear. They practically waddled when they returned, carrying a dozen more quivers of black arrows with short, red fletching. With the seven Bianca had carried up, that gave us nineteen quivers with between fifteen to twenty-five arrows each. That would hold us for a while. Apparently, the goblins had thought they could stay in that spot for a long damned time. Dante and Sprocket had saved our bacon for sure.

A squad of four elves jogged up to hold the northern stair while everyone had their wounds tended. They held short swords and shields we'd scavenged from the goblins over the last week. They were grim and bloodied, but scary warriors. I wish we could get a few of them down to Black Briar to help train our folks. What the Hamsters had in sheer chutzpah and crazed enthusiasm, these folks made up for with a century of experience.

There was little difference between us now. Even Unun had taken to calling our band the Rainbow Brigade. Lilith was pleased at that. For the longest time I'd struggled with anything having to do with rainbows, you know. That whole gay movement symbol and all. But now, here, beyond any other symbolism, I was glad to have that as a rallying call. Seemed silly at first when Sprocket shouted it in battle, but after so many deaths, so many days of fighting, it was a point of pride.

As our archers divvied up the arrows, Dante declared that

these goblins were of the Blood Moon clan. He showed me a symbol on one of the quivers of a white orb with blood oozing down it. Blood Moon clan it was. These were elites; more organized and fearless. As tired as we were, as worn down, we didn't need more efficient killers. We could use a few more legions of the Keystone Cop goblins we'd fought those first few days.

The day wore on toward dusk. Twice more the giant who had yelled at me in ancient Jötunn came back and yelled some more. It was almost as if he expected a reply. After the third visit I saw that Unun was watching me with a smirk.

We all managed to snatch a bite to eat and a drink of water between battles, but it was a lost cause. The giants hadn't really entered the fray. They were content to drive the goblins forward, let them wear us down with sheer numbers. I had no doubt, if the giants came at us en masse, we wouldn't be long for this or any other world.

Charlie made me strip down to my bra and bound my ribs. He pulled the bandages so tight I had to suck in my breath. Made me glad I never wore a corset. Once I was dressed again, I made my way over to Unun. I wanted to know what that smirk was about.

"That Jötunn you defied earlier, he was demanding your surrender," she said, smiling grimly. "When you didn't answer, he questioned your heritage and said all our deaths be on your head." She chuckled. "He did say you proved a mighty foe, for a woman."

"Great," I said, letting the misogyny go, and looked out over to the giant encampment. "Should we surrender?"

"No," Unun answered flatly. "They may keep you in hope of ransom, but most of the others would be killed out of hand. Troops have no value to this lot."

"Well, I'm not surrendering," I said. "I'd rather take as many of them with me as I can, rather than sell you all out."

"Noble," Unun said, watching my face, her own shrewd and

calculating. "I knew you were no coward. But I am pleased to see you in control of your rage."

I laughed. I'd been plenty angry, but she was right. Ever since the battle with the blood cult last winter, when I'd refused to kill Frederick Sawyer or attack Nidhogg, I'd learned I was in control. I didn't have to let the rage overwhelm me and turn me into a killing machine, devoid of care and concern for any around me. Unless I wanted to, of course. I hoped that was a good thing. We'd see before the day was through, I was fairly sure.

The first of the goblins came into bow range. Our archers blunted the attack but we were just too few. Giants drove the goblins forward over their mounting dead, clawing their way forward, pushing the elves back up the stairs, back toward the wider landing. If they reached that point, we were fucked. We'd be overwhelmed.

"Zergling rush," Aliette cried as even more goblins hurried up the stairs. I have no idea what she was talking about, but the meaning was pretty damn clear.

"Get the wounded to the tower," I called. The few defenders on the southern stair ran over to help get our people to safety. The southern stair had remained free since the giants had broken the structure.

"They've eschewed their archers," Unun said, never pausing in her shooting. "This is their final push. The Jötunn will come this time."

Most of the elves stood at the top of the central stairs, where they lay down a wicked hail of arrows into the lead goblins as I rallied the Rainbow Brigade back to the tower. The landing was lost. I fought in the doorway of the tower, fending off several goblins, ready to give my life to buy them more time. Through the cacophony of battle, I heard Sprocket's voice calling down from the top of the tower.

"The eagles are coming; the eagles are coming!"

I felled the closest goblin, wincing at the pain in my chest, and glanced around. In the distance the skies over the great walls of Odin's golden hall were filled with riders on winged horses.

Eagles, Valkyrie. Whatever. Behind the goblins, what we had thought were additional enemy troops turned out to be the raging hordes of Einherjar, the valiant dead that resided in Valhalla.

Most of the giants roared, turning from the stairs to face the new threat. The goblins slowed their assault, confused. Some turned back at the giant's call, and I rushed out of the tower with Aliette and Bianca at my side.

As we hit the goblin line, I saw flying mounted riders sweeping across their flank. I recognized Susan and Maggie—two of the Black Briar dead who had fallen to the dragon Jean-Paul. Gods, I missed them.

We moved forward, pushing the goblins away from the tower and back toward the stairs. Dante and the rest dropped the bows and went to hand weapons, rushing out of the tower and helping us clear the way to the northern stair once more. The goblins fell before us, retreating back from the very edge of the world. Aliette and Bianca stood at the top of the stair, shouting and cursing the fleeing foe. They shared another kiss as Charlie joined them and the three of them huddled together.

There were ghostly warriors smashing through the goblins, bringing down the giants. Those of us still standing scrambled down the northern stair, pursuing the fleeing goblins who fell at the axes and swords of the Einherjar—Odin's heroes.

I waved Gram above my head with a roar, exhausted and elated, as Róta and Skuld swept a giant from the base of the stairs. The final monstrosity turned away from my position with a growl like a 747 landing and lurched to face a new foe. It was Jimmy—by all the gods—Jimmy Cornett riding forward on a destrier the size of a Buick, laughing as he drove toward the last giant. A dozen other riders followed close behind in close formation.

The giant swung his head around, looking for an escape.

Seeing no hope, he dropped his huge axe and took two massive strides away from the landing, only to take Jimmy's lance in the back of his knee. As he fell, the other riders split, each going to one side or another, adding their lances. I realized, as the last rider galloped by, that this was the giant who had asked for my surrender. Maybe I should've offered him the same.

The day was not won yet, but the battle had definitely turned in our favor. I tried to keep the Rainbow Brigade from chasing the fleeing goblins, but lumbered after them when I realized they weren't stopping. I quickly fell behind as their war cries cut through the din of battle. I stopped, hands on my knees, trying to breathe while my ribs tried to shred my internal organs. I really needed to rest. I turned around, realizing that I was alone amidst the devastation and the blue bodies. I saw one of the elves had fallen a little way ahead, so I hobbled toward him to see if he yet lived. If the battle swirled back this way, I was screwed.

Then I heard her—singing in the sky above me. I spun, sure I was hallucinating. But no. Meyja—the beautiful white pegasus —plummeted toward me, her great wings going wide to slow her descent. Gunnr raised her shield in a great shout and I stumbled toward them. When they'd come to a halt, she half-turned, and suddenly Katie slid off Meyja's back, guitar over her shoulder, sword and shield at her side.

I fell to my knees, shock and fatigue overwhelming me. She was here. How was that even possible?

CHAPTER SIXTY-TWO

I woke with a start, buried under thick furs. I groped around for Gram as I tried to determine my surroundings. My eyes wouldn't focus, and I had trouble orienting myself as the room seemed to sway. I lay back, taking steadying breaths in hope that the world would settle for a moment. I tried to sit up, but the coverings were heavy and my ribs hurt so much. For a moment I thought I was on the battlefield, but I saw a wall to my left and a few stars shone down through a partially intact roof. So, I was indoors, probably one of the towers. I patted the ground around me, feeling for Gram again, growing frustrated by the entire situation. When I didn't find her immediately, I pushed the heavy blankets aside with a grunt and tried to extend my reach to no avail. I fell back as chill air washed over my sweaty body. I wasn't wearing a whole lot. Gods, how wounded was I? How had I fought like this?

"Lay still," Unun's voice called from the darkness.

I moaned, falling back, letting my eyes close. If I didn't move or breathe, I thought I could stand the discomfort. I tried to move my legs and gasped as the pain spiked into my chest again.

"Your sword is right here on the table, child. Now be quiet, or you'll wake her."

My eyes snapped open again. Her? So, I hadn't dreamed it. I bent my knees and rolled over onto my side, gritting my teeth against the pain.

"Oh, by heather and jade."

I groaned as I got onto my knees. My chest was bound tight, and other than that I was naked. How on Earth had they gotten my armor off?

"Where ... is ... she?" I grunted, my breath coming in shallow gasps. I glanced around, straining to see in the darkness.

A light flared as Unun put match to candle. The light showed me the inside of a small building with three walls intact, and most of the roof. I shivered as I glanced briefly back at the thick furs. Gritting my teeth, I pulled myself up to the table to my left and looked around the room. Katie stirred on a pallet on the other side of the room, sleeping fitfully. Her face was haggard and she looked like she was fighting a fever. Her hair clung to her face, matted with sweat.

"How?" I asked, moving my head slightly to look in Unun's direction.

"You are a damned fool," she said, stepping to me and helping me into the chair she'd been sitting in. "If you are going to be up, which I strongly advise against, you could at least drink this tea."

I looked at her through narrowed eyes, and she rolled her own, picking up the cup and taking a sip.

"It's not poisoned. Seriously, if I wanted you dead, you'd have never woken."

Fair point.

"Okay," I said, reaching for the mug, but letting my arms fall. They were so heavy.

She knelt beside me, holding the cup to my lips, and helped me take a long sip. The liquid was hot—just this side of scalding —but the sweetness of it flushed into me, flooding my body with a small amount of strength.

"Not so much," she said. "It's dangerous if taken too quickly."

I watched Katie as I sipped, torn between wanting to ask questions and my body's need to consume as much of that heavenly concoction as I could take.

I must have faded a bit, because the next thing I remember, the blankets covered my lap and the sun was rising, pushing back the shadows. Unun sat in a different chair, her head lolling to the side in sleep.

Katie stirred once more and this time she cried out.

I slid off the chair, gasping as the pain reminded me I was wounded, but I knelt by her side, taking her hands in mine.

"I'm here," I said, my voice shaky with pain and fear.

"Where are your pants?" she asked, looking over at me.

My laughter broke with the pain and I fell forward onto one arm.

"Oh, God, Sarah," she said, rolling out of her own blankets and helping me to lie down in her place.

She was pale, though she had strength enough to help situate me before lying beside me and snuggling up against my shoulder.

"Honestly," Unun said, dragging my blankets over and gently laying them over us both.

I closed my eyes and took Katie's hand. She squeezed mine and the world faded once more.

CHAPTER SIXTY-THREE

The next time I woke, Gunnr sat on one of the chairs, dressed in a white shift which did not leave much to the imagination. I blinked rapidly, looking away from her too-obvious body, and realized she was knitting. I had to look a second time to make sure I wasn't hallucinating.

"Ég óska þér góðrar heilsu," she said when she saw me staring at her.

"She wishes you good health," Unun said, coming through the doorway and placing a platter on the table near Gunnr. "I wondered if you would sleep away another day."

Gunnr put her knitting into a basket at her feet and rose, showing me far too much of her stunning form. "I'll leave you to your healer, fair one. I am happy you will survive."

She didn't acknowledge Unun, but swept out the door as if they were enemies.

Unun chuckled once Gunnr was gone and settled in the same seat she'd just vacated.

"Between that one mooning over you, and Katie fretting, I'm beginning to wonder what magic spell you have cast over these two women."

I sat up and realized my ribs didn't hurt nearly as much as they had done the last time I was awake.

"Where's Katie?"

"Walking with your friend Charlie Hague," she said. "They are *mending fences*, I believe she said."

I took a bowl she handed me and drank the broth it contained. It was hot and salty, and my body seemed to fill up with its goodness. When I had finished that, she handed me a biscuit, thick and fluffy and filled with butter and honey.

"Eat this, and we'll try to get you up and around. What say you?"

I didn't exactly snatch the biscuit from her hand, but she laughed anyway. Having the old elf help me get dressed was an adventure I'd rather not repeat, especially the part where she helped me put on my panties.

"Katie insisted that you would want to wear these," Unun said with a shrug. "I never wear them if I can help it, but each to her own."

Someone had laundered my clothes so I didn't reek of days of blood and battle. Once I got my jeans on, and my socks and Docs back on my feet, I was feeling nearly human. My ribs were still bound pretty tight, so I just threw on a cloak. The world could deal.

When I stepped out of the house I was met with applause. The survivors of our mad adventure sat around a great table just outside the doorway, each bandaged and laughing at the sight of me.

Sprocket shouted out that the binding on my breasts was not adequate for me to pass, and the crowd chuckled along.

He was the first to hug me, followed in turn by each of those that had survived. None lingered, but each hug helped fill me with strength.

When I pulled away from Aliette, Charlie stepped up, arms wide. Behind him stood Katie, pale and bright at the same time. If

Charlie was put off by my cursory hug, he just laughed it off. I stepped toward Katie, saw the tears in her eyes, and pulled her to me. Our kiss melted the last of the ice in my heart and the sound of cheering faded as the oxygen in the world was consumed in the fire.

On the third call of "get a room" from Dante, we broke apart and I turned to the crowd, pulling Katie close to my side and wrapping her in my arms.

"What the hell, people?" I called out, laughing.

The crowd cheered again, which was answered by another cheer from behind us. We turned to see a crowd of men and women dressed in finery from a score of centuries, each carrying tables and chairs, platters and kegs, as well as a score of musical instruments.

The Einherjar, the host of Valhalla, came roaring into our clearing, chanting and crying in celebration. Katie and I stepped back as six men ran up with a table, and another six brought chairs, setting the whole lot as a head table, while other tables were brought forth. Soon we had a grand hall set under the brightening day. More and more people came, the honored dead, hand-picked by the Valkyries, each seemingly as alive as both Katie and me.

For a moment, I looked around in a panic. If they were dead, but looked this alive to me, was that because we were dead as well?

As if reading my mind, Unun appeared beside me and whispered in my ear, "You are the most high-strung woman I've had the pleasure to know. You are very much alive."

"But," I said, pointing to the tall man who strode down the aisle that had been formed by the tables, "I know he's dead."

Katie laughed and squeezed my arm. "I had to ask him myself," she said in my ear.

Jimmy strode toward me, his face shining with a joy I had not seen on him in his life.

"Sarah Beauhall, Odin's chosen, Nidhogg's Fist, and Elf friend." He laughed, a great roaring call that was picked up by the crowds of men and women, warriors all, who busied themselves setting up a grand feast.

I held out my hand, and he stepped forward, pulling me into a strong but gentle bear hug. When I stepped away, tears ran down my face, blurring the rest of the chaos around us. "Damn it, Jimmy. How are you?"

"Dead," he roared, and the crowd roared with him.

Katie stepped up to me, sliding her arm around my waist and adding her own laughter to the moment.

"Dead and righteous," someone cried from the crowd, and a chant went up, a dozen chants, each centered in a crowd of warriors dressed similarly. Jimmy stepped back and joined what became a call-and-answer by hundreds of voices. I caught a few words like *honor* and *battle*, *sacrifice* and *joy*. But honestly, it was all so overwhelming that I couldn't focus.

Next thing I knew I was seated at the head table, halfway through a mug of ale, and my head swam with it all.

"Congratulations," Charlie called to me with Bianca and Aliette on either side of him at the table closest to us. The Rainbow Brigade filled the first table to my right, and the elves the table to my left. The rest, dozens more, were filled with warriors who began to drink and carouse with gusto.

Unun sat to my right and Katie to my left. Beside Unun was Skella, then Gletts. To Katie's left sat Jimmy, Susan, and Maggie.

Food appeared on great platters, carried by strapping men and women who boasted and jested as they gorged us with a surfeit of food. My ribs no longer hurt, but then again, nothing hurt after my third mug of ale. These warriors of Odin drank a heady brew.

All day and deep into the night we partied. After the sun began to fade, the musicians brought out their instruments and struck up a cacophony of music from more styles and generations than I could keep track of. Dancing broke out, started by Aliette and Bianca, and soon the entire Rainbow Brigade were dancing in between and on the tables. In a heartbeat, they were joined by the warriors of a host of diverse nations and times.

As soon as I was ready to fall over from drink and exhaustion, one of those bringing food would hand me a goblet of the purest water with a hint of apple, and my head would clear. If we could make this and sell it back home, we'd make a mint.

CHAPTER SIXTY-FOUR

Three days the feast raged. People would fall to the ground and sleep under the tables, or sneak off in pairs to do whatever happy people did away from prying eyes. Hell, some of them weren't as shy about nudity and debauchery and put on a show that would not be tolerated in the circles I grew up in.

I know we slept twice, Katie and I, snuggled together under furs, hidden away from the others. Neither of us was well enough for much strenuous activity, but our lovemaking was quiet and sweet.

Eventually we would wake to the calls and chants of the celebrants, and we would stumble out, pulling on clothing, and taking ale and food to continue the revelry.

It was on the fourth day, dizzy with the madness of it all, that I finally stood and held my mug in the air. Immediately the crowd fell silent, all attention focused on me.

"You're all lunatics!" I cried, to cheers. "If only we were all this joyous when we were alive!"

The crowd fell silent for a moment, and I thought perhaps I had insulted them. Then a woman no taller than a child, with tattoos and scarring crisscrossing her lithe frame, climbed to the top of one of the tables and began to sing.

I had no guess for the language, but the intent was obvious, and the strength of the melody brought all I could see to tears. The power of her voice was soon accompanied by others, and eventually several joined in with drums. They had no need for other instruments. The message was clear to all her comrades, even if me and mine were bewildered.

"She laments the loss of her children," Unun whispered at my side, "and calls for vengeance against those who prey on the weak."

By the third chorus, the entire company sang along with her, the mixture of languages a cacophony of anguish and rage. The music swelled, echoing throughout this once-vibrant city until, by twos and threes the other voices fell.

Eventually, only the voice of the first warrior remained. Then, to my surprise, Katie stood and added her voice, taking up the melody with words of her own.

I feel your pain, ancient mother
in the beating of your ageless heart
I smell the dust of your lands
bitter on the back of my tongue
I hear the bones of your children
rattling in the trees of the lost
I see the rage in your soul
as you prepare for the day of reckoning
I taste your desire for peace
in a world fraught with strife
I know of your weariness
And how you yearn for an end
to the anguish and the grief
For the end of days
So you may join your children in the grave

When Katie finished, she wiped crimson from her eyes and

fell into my arms, spent. The scarred warrior, ageless in her after-life, bowed her head and wept.

The host stood silent, Katie's magic having held them so closely in her grief.

Then Jimmy stood, mug in the air, and called out.

"A toast to the oldest of us all," he held his mug toward She Who Came First. "May the wheel shatter or mend in service of the ancient ones, freeing us all from this everlasting sorrow."

The crowd shifted, watching for a response. The First Among Equals nodded once and drank from her mug, releasing the crowd. Noise erupted all around us as cheering and drinking rose in a clatter.

Jimmy drank to the First, yet did not sit, did not lower his arm. Those around him noticed and began to fall quiet, turning their attention back to him. When enough of them had turned to face him, he grinned widely and took a deep breath.

"And to my baby sister, Kathryn Elizabeth Cornett, heart of my heart. I am both astonished and dismayed to find you among our host."

"I'm not dead yet," Katie called out to general laughter.

Jimmy nodded toward Katie and drank from his mug, the crowd following suit.

She squeezed my hand, and I knew she was spent. It may have been the most powerful magic I'd ever seen her use. The blood that she kept wiping away from her face made me nervous. When I leaned in to ask her if she was going to be okay, the crowd hushed once more.

"It is time, I believe," Jimmy called to the host, and another cheer rose.

I looked around, perplexed, as the old warrior woman strode forward carrying a pile of bright cloth. When she got to the table in front of us, she knelt and held her bundle to Katie, who took it, bemused.

As we looked around, seeking an answer, Katie and I were

whisked back as all of the tables were removed, soon to be replaced with rows of chairs and benches. With that many practiced hands, it took only moments to transform the great room from a drinking hall to a cathedral. As quickly as it had started, calm settled over the crowd, who were now seated in neat rows before us.

"Let's have a wedding," Jimmy shouted, and the crowd roared.

Wedding?

What the ever-loving fuck?

CHAPTER SIXTY-FIVE

I wasn't the only one caught by surprise. Katie lost what little color she had in her face, turned to me, and attempted to say something. I handed the chalice to Unun, who took it without a word, and reached for Katie. She pulled away.

"I'm so sorry," she said, and bolted, tossing the colored cloth into my lap and literally running out into the ruins. Jimmy looked around, horrified, and gave me one of those *what-did-I-say* faces.

I looked out over the crowd and saw that they were all stunned. This wasn't how the revelry was supposed to go, apparently. I glanced at Unun, who gave me a grim smile.

"Here," I said, thrusting the cloth into her lap. "I'd better go after her. She shouldn't be alone out there."

Unun nodded. I got up, pushed my chair away, and made a run for the building we claimed as our own. I grabbed Gram from our sleeping pallet and took off after her.

Jimmy and a handful of warriors met me on the path Katie had taken, but I waved them off.

"Let me handle this," I said to him. He looked like he wanted to argue, so I forestalled him. "If we aren't back in an hour, then you can send in the troops."

He didn't like it, but he agreed.

"And what the hell were you thinking? A surprise wedding?"

He had the good grace to look chagrined at that. "She's my baby sister," he said. "I thought you were both ready to get married. You proposed and she accepted."

"How do you know that?" I asked, glancing in the direction she'd fled.

"You'd be surprised what we know here."

I held up my hand, stopping any further revelations. I wanted to pretend we had privacy from the dead, even if that wasn't the case.

"We'll discuss that later. Right now, I need to go."

The others stepped back and I took off at a jog.

I followed my instincts, trying to think like Katie would think. The streets in this part of the ancient city were a maze of alleys and cul-de-sacs that masked the actual distance traveled.

As I drew closer, I could feel her. I know it sounds like woo-woo stuff, but I swear when I was faced with a choice of direction, an alley to traverse, or a building to cut through; my gut led me in the right direction.

I found her sitting at the edge of a dry and crumbling fountain with shadows covering half of the courtyard. I shivered as memories of my time in the Sideways washed over me and I looked around for exits and enemies. It was a dead end, which made me nervous. She didn't look up as I approached and I could see she had been crying. But not now.

"I'm sorry," she said, her voice barely a whisper. "I've broken everything."

I wanted to reach out and touch her, but as I sat on the edge of the fountain she flinched. The debauchery of the last few days faded in my mind, a surreal mélange of excess and wanton release. The reality of our situation settled over me like the coming of the morning fog over Puget Sound, all-encompassing and overwhelming. We sat in silence, each buried in her own thoughts. I looked back up the great hill and saw that we were much further away from Valhalla and Odin's Glaðsheimr than I expected.

"How are you here?" I asked after a long moment. "I should've asked you sooner, but things have been strange, out of control."

She took a deep breath and stood, pacing the length of the fountain twice before stopping to sit down again. She looked at her feet and wrung her hands.

"When Melanie and I made love for the first time," she started, her voice calm and void of emotion, "I was elated, liberated. After a few haphazard high school romances and awkward groping, I finally felt like I was in a truly adult relationship."

I didn't say anything.

"There's this tree out at Squire's Lake, you know, off Nulle Road?" She didn't look at me, just stared at the blank wall in front of her, staring into the past. "That's where we made love for the first time, Melanie and me." She laughed, the noise quiet and bitter. "We even carved our initials in that tree, MD + KC in a crooked heart. I thought I knew about love then."

I was so lost. Exhaustion pushed at me as my body reminded me how close I'd come to dying. And here the love of my life was tormented—hurting and closed off in a way I'd never experienced with her. I wanted to do something, anything, but I tucked my hands under my thighs and watched her, aching.

"Melanie and I grew distant after a while. She was going away to med school, and I was wrapped up in Black Briar and teaching. Luckily for me, the lust which I mistook for love evolved into a friendship I cherish to this day."

She got up again and paced the fountain's width once before returning to sit near me, but not close enough to touch.

"I made a bargain," she said, her voice resolute, matter-of-fact. "I drank from the well."

My mind reeled. My first thought was the well we sat against, but I leapt to Mímir's well. The world shifted and a few pieces of the story fell into place. Oh, my dear heart. "Katie, why?" I ached to touch her, but she pulled back, clutching her arms tightly across her chest.

"The bridge closed; we couldn't get you back." She took a stuttering breath. "I couldn't abandon you. Couldn't lose you." She took a second breath, trying not to cry. "I've loved you from the first moment I saw you, Sarah Jane Beauhall. Melanie knew it the instant I told her about you, warned me I was ruined for anyone else." She paused, turning to stare up the hill to Glaðsheimr. "I thought I loved her the day we carved those initials," she said, reaching out as if stroking the tree. "I was so desperate to be in love, and she was beautiful and willing ..." She trailed off; her hand held in the air. "I knew she'd leave me in the end," she whispered after a long pause. "Medicine has always been her true love." She glanced back at me, a half-smile on her face. "But for a while, she was the whole world to me."

"Katie?"

"Then you came along and I understood that what Melanie and I had was childish, more lust than anything like true love."

I ached to take her in my arms, to take away the pain I saw in her. But she didn't move, so I left my hands where they were, unable to close the distance.

"Then, the world changed in a way none of us could have predicted. You fixed that sword, and the dragons came, and you bargained for me, rescued me, and killed the bastard." She shuddered. "Then, not even a year later, he was back, a spirit that threatened to kill us both, so I drank the potion, consumed that bloody fucking mead so I could save you, like you saved me."

Hot tears splashed against my cheeks. The sun was setting and the stones of the ruins began to suck away what little heat the day had brought.

"Then we killed that troll mother and I asked you if you ever wanted to have children ..." She looked up at me, pleading in her eyes. "Trisha took the twins, but in the end, we found Jai Li. Took her into our home. But still I thought, someday, we'd have our own child. Thought I'd carry a child." She lowered her hands to her belly, the tears suddenly coming fast and free. "But I had no life without you, so I gave that dream away."

"I don't understand," I said, pleading. "Katie, let me ..."

She slashed her hands through the air between us. "No," she said, her voice filled with anger and loss. "Just listen."

I leaned back, stunned. I'd never seen her like this. Not even when she was so angry at Jimmy. Not after his funeral. Not even when I'd nearly lost her to my own stupidity just over a year ago.

"I've been jealous," she began again. "Jealous of who you've become. Jealous and lost in your shadow." Her tears stopped and the coldness returned. "I know Charlie said one of the witches from his coven called the bridge, but it could have easily been me and my desperate need to make Odin and the giants leave, go back to where they'd come from, and let us grow old together with our own children and grandchildren."

"Please," I whispered, but she went on.

"I wanted to marry you," she continued. "But now ..." She collapsed into herself, as brittle as crystal, her head in her hands.

I rushed forward, pulling her into my arms. She fought me at first, but I held on until she finally gave in and sobbed against my shoulder, gasping.

"I'm safe," I said to her, over and over. "We survived; help came in time. You saved me."

"I know," she whispered. "Because I drank from the well."

The sun set on us as we sat down and talked. I leaned against the fountain while she sat between my legs, her back against me, my arms wrapped around her.

"Gunnr agreed to rescue you," she said, calmer than she'd been earlier, "but she made me promise to give her a chance to woo you."

I choked. "What?"

Katie shrugged. "It was her price. And I agreed."

I was speechless.

"How could I do any less?"

"I'm not going to throw you over for Gunnr," I said, anger rising in me. "What makes you think I'd even consider it?"

"I'm broken now," she said, matter-of-factly. "You'll want to be with someone whole."

I scooted around her, twisting so I could see her face in the near darkness. "What are you talking about?"

She took a deep breath but was cried out. "Gunnr would never come to my call," she said. "I didn't have the connection you do." She paused, looking down at her hands. "I had to make a trade. Mímir has Heimdall's horn, Gjallarhorn. The Valkyrie would hear that call."

I thought back to Mímir and the cost of the well.

"What did you trade?" I asked, afraid of the answer.

She took a deep breath. "I gave Mímir my fertility," she said.

I jerked back, astonished. "You did what?"

"Her body is a construct; she could never have children. Now she can."

Something inside me collapsed. This was too much. "But Katie, you wanted to have a daughter."

She smiled, reached out and took my hands. "We had Jai Li for a while. Maybe that's enough."

I blinked at her and she shrugged.

"We don't always get what we want," she said with a whisper.

"You were supposed to go back to her, love her until I returned. Now we've both abandoned her." I didn't mean it to be a rebuke. I was far more guilty in this than Katie.

"About that," she stood, pulling a folded piece of paper from her back pocket. "She gave me this soon after we got her from Nidhogg."

I took the paper. It was creased and re-creased like it had been unfolded dozens of times. Once it was unfolded, I saw it was one of Jai Li's drawings. I recognized the style. It was a picture of me laying bloodied on a battlefield, with Katie landing a winged horse between me and a horde of giants. At the bottom were the words: "Katie saves Sarah."

I looked up at her and she smiled. "She saw that a long time ago. I had no way to interpret it, but she said I'd know when it was time." She shrugged and smiled. "That girl is scary sometimes."

"You never said anything." I was stunned.

"So, when the bridge closed, I remembered that." She tapped the page. "And I knew I had to do anything it took to rescue you."

"Who will take care of her?"

"We have a village, Sarah. Julie ... Mary ... and especially Edith. That child is loved, heart and soul. She'll be fine."

"Until we return home."

Katie shook her head. "The bargain was to get me here to rescue you. There is no return trip."

"What?" The world was spinning. The hope I'd had on the rescue shattered. We were trapped here. I took a steadying breath. At least Katie was here with me.

She stared down at our hands. "Gunnr came at the horn's sounding, but was under no obligation to do my bidding. In the end I had to make another bargain." She shook her head ruefully. "First the blood mead which is killing me, then drinking from the well which took away my ..." She broke off with a sob. "Then a bargain with the immortal who wants you, and I can't possibly compete with that."

"Jesus, Katie. How could—"

She cut me off. "She was thrilled at the thought of rescuing you. She said by having you here she could more readily woo you."

I laughed a bitter laugh. "That's a definite creepy stalker move."

Katie peeked up at me, a ghost of a smile on her face. "Think I can compete?"

I rolled to my knees, holding her hands and looking up into her face.

"Kathryn Elizabeth Cornett. I want to spend the rest of our

lives together. I love you more than anything I've ever known. No magical angel chick can come between us, no matter how hot she is."

Katie chuckled and started crying again.

"You have saved my life over and over," I continued as she pulled one hand away to wipe her eyes. I waited until she put her hand back into mine. "No matter what happens, I want us to be together. We'll find our way home, I'm sure of it. In the meantime, there are a couple of thousand very cranky, hungover, dead warriors who were hoping for a wedding. You want to give them one?"

"Stand up," she said, pulling me to my feet.

She kissed me, her face wet with tears.

"How could you think I'd ever choose anyone over you?" I asked.

She kissed me harder, desperately. Finally, she turned her face against my shoulder and squeezed me tight enough to hurt my ribs. I might have groaned or something because she stepped back and grew very serious once again.

"Sarah Jane Beauhall. I will agree to marry you under two conditions."

I nodded.

"First, if we are married, we share everything, and that means both the adventures and the money."

I looked at her, puzzled. "Okay?"

She smiled. "I have quite a lot of money from mom and dad's insurance payout. I can buy us a place back home." I made a face, and she narrowed her eyes. "It's a deal breaker."

I squinted at her for a moment, then shrugged. "Fair enough. And the second? Though that first one was really two things."

Her eyes flashed for a moment with a mischievous glint.

"We have another wedding when we get back home, where our living friends are."

I started to answer, and she held up her hand.

"And you wear a wedding dress."

I opened and closed my mouth a couple of times, unable to come up with a response.

"We'll both wear one," she said. "You can pick out yours, and whatever you want your attendants to wear. I'll take care of my side of the aisle."

She knew how much I loathed dresses. I pursed my mouth to say something, and she jumped in again.

"Look, I know you hate dresses, but it's what Jai Li wants. Besides, you are totally hot when you femme up."

I raised my eyebrows, but she laughed.

"Okay, you're hot all the time, but this is a one-time event."

I could see how important this was to her.

"Fine. Back home we'll do the big, formal gala, but here, among these folk, we do a warrior's wedding."

She jumped against me, wrapping her arms around my chest, gentle but firm. She covered my face with kisses. "Then yes, yes, yes."

It's all about the compromise. For a while longer, we were winning. I'd take what we could get.

"Let's go," I said, taking her hand and pulling her along.

"You know," she said as she came up beside me. "If you really hate the idea of doing the wedding dresses, we could always do it skyclad."

I didn't even look at her, just harrumphed and walked back toward the waiting crowd.

CHAPTER SIXTY-SIX

S o, we had a wedding. There was singing and drinking, oh gods, so much drinking. The Rainbow Brigade forced us to walk through an aisle of crossed swords, which the Einherjar thought was grand. There were far too many comments about consummating the marriage, which caused me to blush.

Really it was sweet.

Jimmy gave Katie away. Half the survivors from our misadventure stood up as witnesses for me, and the other half for Katie. There was no officiant, so we took suggestions from several different cultures (and warriors) to complete the rites. We exchanged presents given to us by the attendees, and promised our undying love.

It was pretty amazing to see all those brawny and agile warriors openly weeping. Unun told me there were never weddings here. We may have been the first.

Dante asked if goblins or giants married, which brought laughter from the warriors closest to hand. Lilith said it was a pretty culturally specific ritual, but that any who discounted the culture of others was far too narrow-minded to think they had the high ground. Goblins probably got married, she said. Most cultures had some form of ritual to designate a familial unit.

Most of those who were the loudest turned away with muttering and eye-rolls, but a few listened to her words.

"Knowing your enemy, without turning them into mindless targets, is one way to reduce tribal warfare."

Katie and I slipped away at that point. Not a conversation I wanted to engage with at the moment. Thinking of your enemy as having a family added guilt when you killed them, which was Lilith's intent, I'm sure. Not that it had stopped her from killing her fair share of goblins and giants. She never claimed that violence for self-preservation wasn't a thing. It got a little muddled from there.

We snuck into Odin's hall and made out on his empty throne. We weren't struck by lightning, so we took that as approval of our actions.

The rings were back home, so we used a braided rope to bind our wrists. I promised her for the wedding back home, when we got home, we'd have custom rings made. That made her happy.

None of the Valkyrie showed their perfect faces during the wedding, nor for several days after. I half expected to see Gunnr stride through the door at any moment, her arrogance and stunning beauty distracting the crowd. But it was Skuld, the youngest of the Valkyrie, who found us on the third morning after the ceremony. We were in the main hall of Valhalla, breaking our fast by eating our body weight in spicy and exotic dishes, when she strode in through the great doors at the back of the hall carrying a bundle.

When she neared the podium, I could see that she wept.

"Hail the happy couple!" she shouted as she approached.

Those around us cheered briefly and immediately their voices fell to a low buzz. This was a surprise to them as well.

"We are at a loss to the proper customs of your people," Skuld went on, "but it seems appropriate that some action be taken in this manner." She waved her arm again. "Therefore, my sisters and I have brought forth gifts."

I looked up and a dozen more Valkyrie marched into the hall, each carrying a covered item.

"First we honor a band of stalwart ruffians and honorable fools." She pointed to where the Rainbow Brigade sat at one long table. The Black Briar survivors as well as the civil servants who had survived were all huddled together with them, a single band of warriors forged in blood and fire. Even Charlie Hague had found a place among them. That made my heart glad.

Eight of the ancient Norse warrior women presented arms and armor.

"Your hearts are bold, your cunning shrewd, and your bravado beyond measure," Skuld called as each of them unwrapped matching suits of chain mail and assorted swords, axes, and bows to suit each. Dante gave a large howl as he hefted a beautiful double-headed battle-axe above his head. The rest of the Brigade joined him and bedlam erupted. The Einherjar rose like a flood and pulled them into their midst, where they were quickly stripped of their looted goblin armor and shoved back into the open area clad in their new martial finery. When they were assembled, they raised their weapons to the cheers of all around them. The tumult went on for quite a while before Skuld called for quiet.

"Finally, for this motley collection of rogues and scoundrels —" She looked directly at Sprocket, who laughed high and clear. "—I am proud to present to you colors so your enemies will know who it is that they are to face."

She took a long package from one of the Valkyries and turned, going to one knee in front of Lilith. "As the erstwhile leader of this band of miscreants, I present this unto you."

Lilith took the proffered package and unrolled it as the Rainbow Brigade huddled around them. I couldn't see what it was for a moment, and started get up for a better look. The crowd roared when Lilith finally lofted a great banner with a broad rainbow crossed with sword and spear.

The cacophony rose to a crescendo as Sprocket leapt up on

one of the tables, took the banner from Lilith, and began waving it above his head.

Katie and I laughed long and hard, until it became difficult to breathe.

We had all come so close to death, and now look at us. There is a chaotic joy that comes from surviving, more so when the odds were never in your favor.

I reached over and took Katie's hand, dragging her into my lap where I kissed her soundly. Let them have their pretties; I had a woman who loved me.

CHAPTER SIXTY-SEVEN

The chaos turned to toasts and drinking that ran on for a good twenty minutes before Skuld was able to quiet the crowd once more. Her mood had gone from tentative to joyful, which was a definite improvement.

With the Rainbow Brigade finally seated once more, and the general clamor beaten back to a dull roar, Skuld seized the moment and stood forth with both hands raised.

"For those newly wed, we offer tokens such as we would honor our own."

Katie laughed and struggled out of my lap, making sure to touch me in a few inappropriate ways as she did so. Her grin told me she knew exactly what she was doing. Once she was settled in her own chair again, Skuld flourished her free arm in a way that would get her a job on any game show. Six more Valkyrie I had never met came forward one at a time, set a bundle on the table in front of Katie and me, then bowed and moved to the side, clearing the way for the next.

Just as the host of warriors that surrounded us represented many times and nations, so too were the Valkyrie an eclectic mix of races and cultures far beyond the homogeneous portrayals in common legend.

"Me first?" Katie asked, reaching for the closest package to her. It contained a beautifully worked suit of chain mail—the precision and quality far beyond anything either of us had ever seen. Dyed links showed a guitar crossed with a sword on the upper left breast in gold. I marveled at the detail.

I leaned forward for a closer look and saw that the gold was individual links, not something painted over the links themselves. I was impressed.

She let it flow over her hands and sighed. "Do you think this is mithril?" she asked in a whisper.

I smiled and shrugged. It was good to see her astonished. "I think Tolkien made that up, but we can ask Rolph when we see him next."

She smiled and nodded. Her second bundle revealed a short blade and scabbard worked with silver, jade, and amethyst. It was quite striking.

When she pulled it from its sheath, Skuld called out, "From our own armory." And the crowd cheered. "May it serve you as well as she who forsook it."

That was odd. I started to ask what she meant, but Katie held the blade out to me, and I could see that the craftsmanship was flawless. A fine filigree of silver wings adorned the hilt.

She stood and stepped away so she could swing the blade a few times without maiming anyone.

"It's perfectly balanced," she said, her voice filled with awe. "Seriously, Sarah, you need to try this."

I stood, and she handed me the sword. It was a couple of inches shorter than Gram, and while superb, did not suit me. I handed it back and she sheathed it, setting it atop the chain mail.

The third and final bundle proved to be a book of hand sewn leather and thick vellum. Half the book was empty, but there were a dozen or more songs transcribed within. Katie looked up, dumbfounded.

"A few of our favorite songs to share, and ample room for you to capture your own."

"Thank you," she said, bowing to Skuld and the crowd. "I will cherish these."

She sat back down, pulled the book into her lap and began reading.

"My turn?"

She waved me onward without a glance.

I laughed. These truly were gifts that spoke to Katie's nature.

"You have no need for a blade," Skuld said as I unwrapped a suit of chain similar to Katie's.

"Lighter than I'm used to," I said, noticing the runic symbols worked in red links, while across the chest was emblazoned Yggdrasil, the world tree, in fine green links. I traced the runes and felt those on my scalp and leg tingle at each touch. There was power in this armor. Though pristine, it had known millennia. When I placed my palm against the symbol of the tree, a pulse throbbed. Wicked. There was more to this gift than I was being told. I wonder who it belonged to originally.

The second bundle held two stout wooden rods each carved twin to the other. The world tree rose along each, with a stylized Nidhogg at the base, an eagle at the top. One had a squirrel with a tusk—a unicorn squirrel—running toward the eagle, the other toward the dragon. When I held them up to Skuld, she shrugged. Róta called from the back of the crowd, coming forward as the warriors parted. "They are twin branches from the world tree. We can offer you no hammers, but you can use these when you forge your own."

They were strong and fit my palms perfectly. They would definitely make for excellent hammers.

I set them to the side and opened the third bundle. Katie looked up, curious at last, as I unfolded the leather wrapping to find that itself was the gift. The inward side of the leather had been carved and painted with an immense map.

"Holy cats," Katie said, sitting forward and closing her new book. "Is that a map of the nine worlds?"

Unun came over to look as well. "That is a rare gift indeed."

I studied the map, mesmerized, and didn't notice immediately as a disruption rippled through the crowd. As the murmuring grew loud enough to register, I looked up to see Gunnr striding into the hall, her countenance black. For a long minute the only sounds were the crackling of the great fires and the sound of Gunnr's boots as she strode the length of the hall.

"Careful, warrior," Unun said quietly. "This one is full of rage."

Gunnr stopped several paces from the table where we sat and cleared her throat.

"Our bargain was for you to give me a chance to woo this woman," she said, the growl in her voice unmistakable. "By participating in this ridiculous human ritual," she cast a scathing look at Skuld, "you have made it quite clear you have no honor." She drew her sword and pointed it at Katie. "You leave me no choice but to challenge you to a trial of honor."

Astonished chatter ripped through the crowd at this announcement.

I glanced at Katie who sat open-mouthed, then over to Unun, who squinted at Gunnr but held her peace.

Katie half rose, ready to protest, but Gunnr cut her off.

"You are not worthy of this woman." She pointed the blade at me.

Katie stood, her face hard, and drew her new short sword.

Gunnr saw the blade and took a step back, as if struck.

"What is the meaning of this?" She wheeled around, searching the crowd of Valkyrie who stood behind Skuld,

"I suggested this gift," Róta called, and both Gunnr and Skuld turned to face her. "The blade should not be held as an item for you to fawn over in your despair, sister. It should be used by someone worthy to defeat the foes that assail us."

Gunnr's knees gave way and she collapsed, her sword clattering to the ground. Skuld moved to help her but Róta held her back.

"This child of man owes you no debt of honor," Róta said, her voice kindly but firm. "We have recovered the remains of our great master. Perhaps it is beyond time we let the past remain in the past and look to a new tomorrow."

Gunnr looked up as if slapped and the sneer I saw on her face took me aback.

"She abandoned us, dear sister. Left us bereft and alone. And yet, I love her still. Do you deny her betrayal?"

Skuld looked as confused as I felt.

Róta shook her head and held a hand out toward Gunnr. "You seek to replace the love of one with the love of another, neither of which were yours to claim."

The Einherjar had gone deathly silent. We were all missing some very important details here, and now this didn't feel like a safe place.

Gunnr spurned Róta's hand and rose on her own, picking up her sword and returning it to its sheath. She took a single step, half-turning toward Katie, but keeping Róta to her front. She turned her head and spat on our table. "Fie," she growled. "You are beneath my contempt."

I stood, ready to punch this ancient one right in the mouth. Katie stepped in front of me.

"I offered her your bargain, and she rejected it. You did not stipulate a time frame for this wooing, and your advances have been spurned." Her voice shook as she leaned against the table for support. A small bubble of blood frothed out of her right nostril.

When I looked back at Gunnr, she had collapsed in upon herself. Her shoulders slumped and her head was bowed. A quiet sob escaped her as she turned and walked away. At six paces she turned back, her face a mask of pain and loss.

"I would have loved you with an intensity that would have

altered you forever. I could have shaped your spirit in ways you cannot imagine."

I gulped. The power of her was nearly overwhelming. "I'm good, thanks."

Katie reached over and took my hand, staring at Gunnr with daggers in her eyes.

The air had been sucked out of the room. I looked around and saw that most of the crowd looked down at their hands, or huddled with close comrades, avoiding looking in our direction.

When Gunnr went out the door, the room sounded with the released breaths of nearly everyone.

"Buzzkill," Sprocket said, leading the Rainbow Brigade over.

The party was definitely over.

They hugged us each in turn, and left for their own quarters. They chattered about their new equipment and especially their new banner.

"Mímir is going to freak," Dante said as they moved out of earshot.

The Einherjar left in groups as well. Eventually there were only a few of us left in the room. Jimmy, Susan, and Maggie stood near the main doors of the hall, waiting. Róta and Skuld chatted with the other Valkyrie for a few minutes. There was a rift in their ranks. I did not envy them. Those I did not know filed out of the hall while Róta and Skuld walked toward us.

Unun stepped in and hugged us both before the Valkyrie joined us.

"Your Katie is a brave woman," she said in my ear. "Do not lose her."

The rest of the elves followed her out and we were left alone with the two Valkyrie.

I turned Katie and wiped the blood from her face before kissing her.

"One of these days you are going to get killed, or kill me in the attempt."

She laughed and hugged me. I could feel how weak she

suddenly was. How much power had that confrontation cost her?

"I want to go home now, please. Is that a thing we can do?"

She buried her face against my shoulder.

"No easy way I know of."

Great.

CHAPTER SIXTY-EIGHT

I held Katie for as long as we could get away with comfortably. When I released her and turned, both Róta and Skuld were still there, waiting.

"This will pass in time," Róta said.

Katie picked up her sword and buckled it around her waist.

Skuld looked uncomfortable, twisting her hands and shifting her weight between feet. "Gunnr was really upset."

Róta shrugged. "You don't remember what it was like before Eir left us. Back when Gunnr was a whelp greener than you."

Skuld straightened at that, ready to retort, but Róta held up her hand. "Peace, sister. We all start somewhere."

"So this sword belonged to Eir?" Katie asked, putting her palm on the hilt, pushing it forward, causing the blade to rise and poke me in the thigh.

I crossed my arms and let out a deeply held breath.

"Yes. She was a mighty warrior, but more than that, she was a peacemaker. She had the ability to calm nearly any situation and help opposing factions see the wisdom of parlay."

"And Gunnr loved her?" Skuld asked.

Róta nodded. "They had a passionate romance for years. Long after Father Odin and the others were killed, long after we had given up all hope of their return. It was Eir who kept us together, kept up our spirits enough to carry on in our sacred duties."

"What happened to her?" I asked.

"We are few in number, but mighty in battle," Róta said. "Even the mightiest of us fall to despair, or worse, to love."

I gave Katie a look and pulled her to me, wrapping my right arm around her waist. "Which befell Eir?"

"Alas, love."

Skuld turned to Róta, confused. "But you said Gunnr and Eir were in love."

Róta laughed. "We are shield maidens. Our only love is battle." She paused. "Mostly that is true. We are sisters of the sword, sworn to serve the ancient gods long dead, and to follow their last edicts. If that is not done from love, then we are all mad."

The jury was out on that in my book.

"But Gunnr loved Eir, I can see it on her face. Do you mean Eir did not love Gunnr in return?"

Katie laid her head against my arm and squeezed my hand.

"For a time. But Eir was no fool. She knew that their love was fleeting. Gunnr did not believe so."

"What happened?" I asked, afraid to hear the answer.

Róta smiled at me. "She broke our most sacred law. She fell in love with a warrior on Midgard and, by forsaking her oath, saved his life."

"That's not so bad," Katie said, and both Skuld and Róta looked at her, shaking their heads.

"The tale is a tragedy. He died soon after, for his time was at hand. But Eir had lost her place among us, given up her vow and her sword in pursuit of a dream that could never be fulfilled."

"What happened to her?" I asked.

Skuld stepped back, her hands in the air. "I know nothing of this heretical tale." She glanced toward the entrance as if seeking an escape.

"Go," Róta said, and the younger woman fled.

"That tale is beyond this mete," she said when the three of us were alone. "Suffice to say it is a winding tale of which I only know portions. You may discover some of it on your own in due time."

I squinted at her. That was a dubious answer.

"Regardless," she went on. "It would be better for everyone if you were to finalize your plans and prepare to leave here in the next few days."

"What the what?" Katie asked, taking a step back. "Will you help us get home?"

Róta shook her head sadly. "Alas and alack. Gunnr overstepped herself in bringing you here." She grasped each of us by the shoulder. "It has been a joy to do battle again, and to see such a glorious rout of our enemy, but we must return to our vigilance. That and the return of our master has given us much to consider."

"Thank you, Róta," I said, reaching up and grasping her shoulder as well. "Your hospitality has been more than generous."

She nodded.

"We would ask for a few days to gather supplies and make plans for our next course of action. And to say a few goodbyes." I looked at Katie, who nodded in agreement.

"I want to talk to Jimmy again before we leave."

Róta stepped back and struck her fist across her chest in salute. "I will arrange for him to come to you. You may have two days to make your peace."

"That's fair," I said with a sigh. "I'm sure, being mere mortals in Asgard, we won't all get killed and waste your valuable efforts."

Róta grinned and shook her head. "Clever words. Use your time wisely."

And she was gone.

Katie turned and hugged me. "Where will we go?"

"Well," I said, kissing her on the top of her head. "I've got this wicked cool map, and a few ideas." She looked at me curiously and I grinned. "There's a witch here who opened the bridge, and I have a mind to find her."

We picked up our gifts and made our way back to the house we had been living in these past days. The food and drink of Valhalla had proved to be a boon in my healing, and, while I was not completely whole, I knew I could make do.

"Tomorrow we'll get with the Rainbow Brigade. I'm sure they'll be happy to travel with us a bit further."

"And the elves?" she asked as we walked side by side.

"Unun will want to study the map to remind her how to lead her people home. We'll have to wait and see what they'll do."

We put the gifts aside and made our way to the bedrolls. We consummated our nuptials a few more times before the dark of the evening began to fall around us. I had started making plans in my head when Katie spoke into the darkness.

"Mímir said that by removing Odin's body from her basement, it would free her realm to travel once more. I doubt she'll be in Bellingham when we return."

I had to ponder that. "Can you imagine what it is to live an eternal life, always at the whim of others, forced to pick up and start anew each time someone had a need great enough to call the well?"

"I'm sad for her, honestly. Her life has been so fraught with loss and betrayal. She only truly found peace at the boarding house, rescuing those who reminded her of herself."

That was a pretty enlightened insight. I squeezed her to me and sighed.

"The world is changing," she went on after a bit. "More sorrow, more conflict, hatred and bigotry on a global scale." She paused to take a deep breath. "I think there is a reckoning coming."

I told her about Nidhogg and her want for a dragon mete.

"You may be the harbinger," she said, running her hands up my side. "Our world is destined to end in fire, you know that."

Now it was my turn to be introspective. "Fire is cleansing. Fire allows for a fresh start. Perhaps it is less an end, and more a new beginning."

She laughed. "I love when you take the happy side. It gives me hope." She snuggled against me, skin to skin, and settled into sleep.

I lay there, absorbing her warmth, contemplating what we would do when we left the safety of Valhalla.

A song ran through my mind.
In a spot of land, where the rivers run
and the Glori Mundi bloom
I met a girl like the brightest star
A peck of Gallen, like the kiss I craved
Were not for such as me

You see, there's this goddess, or used to be, by the name of Iðunn who had these golden apples.

I bet if we could find her orchard, we could bribe the Valkyrie into helping us get home. More importantly, as these apples are what allowed the old gods to remain forever youthful, I would bet good money that eating one of those could cure Katie. I damn well planned to find out.

REMEMBRANCES OF J.A. PITTS

John Pitts, beloved author from the Pacific Northwest, passed away on October 3, 2019, a great surprise to many of us. John had a loyal following, and WordFire Press was honored to pick up his acclaimed Sarah Beauhall urban fantasy series. We released *Night Terrors* in 2016.

John gave us the manuscript of his last novel, *Rainbow Brigade*, the culmination of his Sarah Beauhall series, in early 2019. The book was in production when John died.

We were pleased that we could send him the finished cover, a gorgeous painting by his friend Jeff Sturgeon, although we were unable to get the book finished in time for him to see it.

With a Heart Big Enough for All of Us....

John Pitts was a huge man, with a smile fit to light up a room, calves the size of tree-trunks, a slight Kentucky twang, and a heart that knew love is about pulling together, about support, and about family. He was many things: writer, tech worker, friend, family man, father, hero.

I'm writing this in January 2020, the same month that many of us gathered for his remembrance. We met at a hall in Bellevue, Washington, where we filled the parking lot, the parking lot of a nearby park, and a number of local streets. People came from other states. They brought the full rich variety of America today: conservative, liberal, transgender, gay, straight, happy, lonely, angry, successful, and disenfranchised. In the hours we spent together we shared stories and grief, and I left feeling a little bigger and more united. I suspect almost everyone else felt the same. Because that's what John left behind. A world made bigger by his presence.

If you've picked up this book or this series, you already know that John's characters fight fiercely for their chosen families, that they slay dragons when they need to, and most importantly, that they love each other.

John took risks with his work. Who would have expected a traditional family man from Kentucky to write a successful, first-person, lesbian blacksmith story? He sent me the first draft of the first Sarah book without telling me he was writing from the viewpoint of an LGBTQ woman. If he had, I would have expected him get it wrong. It wasn't the life he lived, after all. But he got it right, and since it is a life I live, I could judge reasonably enough. I still remember the relief on his face when I told him it was wonderful. He has a manuscript about redneck elves. I'm certain no one else in the world wrote a novel about redneck elves and made it work.

Most of us are not as strong and good as our characters. John was better. One of his best friends passed before him and John practically adopted his daughter. He and his wife Kathy acted as godparents for the child of a single mom. John and Kathy opened their home to the local writing community for summer parties, for wakes, for any form of gathering that we needed. John knew that even though it's out of fashion to talk about love and hope and hard work, they need to be talked about and lived. He did both.

John and I were in the same writing group and read many of each other's early manuscripts. He was great at honest feedback on plot and character, and often came up with ideas for how to make fictional people more real and more interesting. Even though he worked a demanding day job and finished a book or more a year, he found time to encourage others. Many of the stories at his remembrance were simple stories of emails received just when someone needed a bit of inspiration, just the right comment when they needed a push, and hugs when that was all that could help.

After our gathering for John, I walked away feeling that the best way to remember him was to be as big as I could be, as loving, as hard-working, and as brave in my writing. I also felt the need to strive for John's brand of inclusivity. Parts of our culture today are exclusive about inclusivity—people say things that amount to *If you don't believe in freedom X or Y or Z, then I don't even want to talk to you and I shall defriend you or even shun you.* John would never have taken that stance. He was inclusive of all of us. He could love people that he didn't agree with on fundamental issues. He saw the best in people and helped us be bigger.

John Pitts left the world a greater and kinder place than he found it.

—*Brenda Cooper*

J.A./John Pitts

I had heard of the writer J.A. Pitts long before I knew the man. I'd seen his books around the dealer rooms at the various cons. He had a following with his urban fantasy series, the Sarah Jane Beauhall books. The Pacific Northwest is an isolated area compared to the rest of the country, and the science fiction community pros and fans are a tight bunch; it was only a matter of time till we met.

About ten years ago, through mutual friend writer/publisher Patrick Swenson at Norwescon, we were formally introduced, and we realized that we had a lot in common. We struck up a friendship that would only deepen over the following years. Besides both of us being from the Midwest, he from Kentucky and myself from Indiana (though we had lived most of our lives on the West Coast), we were both big men ... which would come in handy when trying to find someone in a crowded dealer's room, and we both had minds that wanted to know more about everything.

In 2015 I launched a dream project, of building a world through a series of paintings and written history that would coalesce into the *Last Cities of Earth* anthology. John became one of the pillars of this project for me, along with Kevin J. Anderson and my wife Leslie Kreher, among others. John knew the world as well as I did. He was instrumental in helping me flesh out the backstory and prepare the "bible" the authors would use for the project. He was a firm believer in LCOE, and at times when I doubted or was dealing with health issues, he was always there for me—as he was for so many others.

When you work with someone on something like this, when you collaborate, especially in writing, you bond. At least we did. My experience working with John gave me so much confidence in my abilities to write, as he did with so many others, as the testimonials show, but more importantly John became a dear friend and it was an honor to do the cover of *Rainbow Brigade* for John.

He was a beloved family man, a friend that never wavered and was always there for you. I will miss him.

—*Jeff Sturgeon*

John Alvin Pitts: An Appreciation

In October 2019, we lost a great light when John Alvin Pitts died unexpectedly of amyloidosis. He had just seen the cover to this book (beautiful work by our mutual friend Jeff Sturgeon) and was looking forward to seeing *Rainbow Brigade* out in the world.

I met John in November 1997 and we were instant brothers. Not only was he my first writing friend but the roots of our friendship went deep down into my life, transforming me as it went. I can't count the number of epiphanies I had because of his love and understanding in my life.

I remember back in 2008, we both threw legendary sword stories at Denise Little for an anthology workshop Kristine Kathryn Rusch and Dean Wesley Smith hosted on the Oregon coast. She passed on mine. But I remember that even as she grabbed up his short story, "Black Blade Blues," she also told John (and Kris and Dean both concurred), "Now go write this novel."

It was the second novel he'd written and the first he sold, to Tor Books, not long after. Tor put out the first three volumes of Sarah Beauhall's adventures. Kevin J. Anderson picked up the last two for WordFire Press. I know that at one point, John planned ten novels, but I don't know what notes were taken. I hope that one day, if there is demand and a writer can channel her well, that Sarah Beauhall will finish out her tale.

Until then, hold this near to your chest for a moment and close your eyes with me. This last novel was fashioned from the heart and soul of a giant Kentucky man named John Alvin Pitts. He told stories well and he loved people well.

He and his words will be missed.

—*Ken Scholes*

ABOUT THE AUTHOR

J.A. Pitts learned to love science fiction at his grandmother's knee, listening to her read authors like Edgar Rice Burroughs and Robert E. Howard during his childhood in rural Kentucky. His life has always been heavily influenced by strong women, his mother first among them:  raising three boys after the death of his father, with grace and wit. There were always women coming and going in the house, friends, family, folks who needed a hand, and folks who had a hand to lend. All of Pitts's life has been steeped in the stories of average people doing extraordinary things—and most of them were women. He says, "That is why I was drawn to the character Sarah in my new novel. She embodies all the strength of the women who have influenced me over the years.

"I can't remember a time I wasn't absorbing and creating story. I read early and became a regular at my local library. There for a while, I thought the coolest thing in the world would be to grow up and be a librarian."

He lives his life surrounded by books and story. The characters and worlds he builds have been given loving care by some pretty spectacular editors. "I've been very lucky. I continue to launch my words into the world for all to read, if they have the mind. I just hope you are entertained in the process."

Rainbow Brigade is the fifth published novel in the Sarah

Beauhall series. The others are *Black Blade Blues*, *Honeyed Words*, *Forged in Fire*, and *Night Terrors*. His collection, *Bravado's House of Blues* is available from Fairwood Press.

IF YOU LIKED ...

If you liked *Rainbow Brigade*, you might also enjoy:

Night Terrors
J.A. Pitts

Prospero Lost
by L. Jagi Lamplighter

Band on the Run
by D.J. Butler

OTHER WORDFIRE PRESS TITLES BY J.A. PITTS

Night Terrors
J.A. Pitts

Our list of other WordFire Press authors and titles is always growing. To find out more and to see our selection of titles, visit us at:
wordfirepress.com

MAR 1 8 2021

9 781680 570410